PRAISE FOR JADE LEE
AND *DEVIL'S BARGAIN*!

"Jade Lee has written a dark and smoldering story...
full of sensuality and heart-pounding sex scenes."
—*Affaire de Coeur*

"[An] exciting erotic romance...."
—*Harriet's Book Reviews*

"A luscious bonbon of a sensual read—the education
of an innocent: hot, sensual, romantic, and fun!"
—Thea Devine, *USA Today* bestselling author of *Satisfaction*

"A spicy new debut...."
—RT BOOKclub

"Highly charged and erotic....
You won't be able to put it down."
—*Roundtable Reviews*

"*Devil's Bargain* is a definite page-turner...
a must read this summer."
—*Romance Reviews Today*

THE FIRST STEP
TOWARD IMMORTALITY

"You have no fiancé," the man snapped. "You are..." He struggled a moment with the English language. "My servant."

"I most certainly am not!" Thankfully, she was still struggling with an upset belly or she would have leapt straight to her feet despite her lack of clothing. Indeed, she wondered if she could slap his face from her position on the bed.

Fortunately for her dignity, he merely dipped his head in a semblance of a bow. "My apologies."

"I should think so!"

"You are my..." Again the pause as he struggled with the language. Abruptly he brightened, his eyes actually lightening to a kind of reddish-brown. "Slave."

Other books by Jade Lee:
DEVIL'S BARGAIN

White Tigress

JADE LEE

LEISURE BOOKS NEW YORK CITY

To Chris Keeslar, editor extraordinaire,
who said, "What about China?"
And to Pattie Steele-Perkins, agent extraordinaire,
who said repeatedly, "Go explore your heritage."
Was this what you meant?

A LEISURE BOOK ®

January 2005

Published by

Dorchester Publishing Co., Inc.
200 Madison Avenue
New York, NY 10016

ISBN 0-8439-5393-4

The name "Leisure Books" and the stylized "L" with design are trademarks of Dorchester Publishing Co., Inc.

Printed in the United States of America.

Visit us on the web at www.dorchesterpub.com.

If God lets Shanghai endure,
he owes an apology to Sodom and Gomorrah.
—Shanghai missionary

Chapter One

Shanghai, China—1897

"Aaaah-ho. Aaaah-ho." The low, dirgelike chorus drifted across the Wangpu River, settling into Lydia Smith's ears until she shivered in excitement. She had heard stories about the sound. It was the mournful beat of the poor Chinese laborers—the coolies—as they built houses in ever-expanding Shanghai. And now, at last, she was hearing it for real.

"Aaaah-ho. Aaaah-ho." It was a slow sound, monotonous and dull, like the low beat of the city's heart, and Lydia strained to hear every pulse. Just as she struggled to hold the smoky air inside her lungs and see the white bungalow houses behind the brick walls of this new and flourishing city.

She couldn't, of course. The forest of masts obscured all but the boats that clogged the port, and yet Lydia still stood, grasping the rail with her smudged white gloves as she tried to absorb it all.

"It's so beautiful," she whispered, though it wasn't. The sky was overcast, and the air caught thick and moist in her throat. And it tasted faintly of ginger. Still, she repeated over and over, like a litany, "Beautiful Shanghai. My new home."

"Yer sure no one's meeting yuh at the docks, Miss Smith? Not even yer fiancé's servant?"

She jumped as the captain's broad shadow darkened the railing. She turned, wariness mixing with the excitement in her blood. She hadn't liked the looks of him from the beginning, but the temptation of a discounted passage from England to China helped her overcome her scruples. Especially as that meant she was now arriving a full two weeks early.

She couldn't wait to see Max's face when she surprised him.

Meanwhile, the captain was shuffling his feet, apparently concerned for her welfare. "It ain't safe in Shanghai. Not fer a lady alone."

Lydia smiled as she clutched her fiancé's last letter to her heart. "I have his directions and Chinese coins. I shall manage just fine."

"But you don't speak the language, miss. Not a word," the captain pressed, and Lydia felt herself relax at his concern. The man had grumbled about her presence nearly the entire trip, but now that they had arrived, he was obviously worried about her. In truth, he reminded her a bit of her father—gruff on the exterior, but with a heart of gold inside.

"Oh, I know a great deal more than a word." She wasn't fluent, but she was getting the hang of Chinese. "The crew has been teaching me some, and I had an instructor before that. A missionary who'd lived here for years."

He grimaced and began to walk away. "Shanghai's a dangerous place," he grumbled. But if he said any more, she didn't hear it; her attention had turned back to the docks.

Normally, the business of docking at a port would interest her. She'd learned quite a bit about sailing during the journey, had even made some friends among the crew, so she would have liked to be interested in their work right now—these last few moments among her own countrymen. But, of course, nothing could compete with the slowly clearing view of Shanghai. She saw now that it was a cramped city—not unlike London in that regard. The rich and the poor moved side by side, neither noticing the other except to grumble. The rich looked just like they did in London, including the latest fashions and equipages. Even the poor coolies seemed familiar, appearing like sailors to her, with their shortened pants and no shirts they squatted on the muddy banks. Behind them, the tenement houses rose inside bamboo scaffolding, imposing and ugly, in the way of all such buildings.

In short, the scene was no more intimidating than any other big, dirty, living city—or so Lydia reminded herself. She had no reason to feel untoward. After all, she had lived in London nearly all her life. Although no Englishman, no matter how poor, would work without a shirt. But strange sights were to be expected among heathens, or so Max always said.

The sounds, she realized, were very different, and she pushed her bonnet back in the hopes of hearing more clearly. Early by the clock—not more than nine in the morning—the city was already alive and cacophonous. The high-pitched nasal tones of the Chinese language bombarded her from all sides, only growing in volume as she was at last allowed to disembark. She heard hawkers' high-pitched squeals as they sold their wares. The more rounded tones of her own countrymen added a kind of trumpet accompaniment, an occasional ornamentation rather than the main melody. And beneath it all came the steady drone of the coolie *aaaah-ho*.

It was all so wonderfully different, and Lydia could barely keep herself from dancing up the dock toward the row of rickshaws awaiting passengers.

A strange sight, indeed, this line of cabbies without cabs. Though she had heard of rickshaws, she had never actually seen one. Now she found them comically bare, with no more than a bench set upon an axle between two large wheels. They had the addition of two long poles extended from the sides for the driver—or runner, really, as a coolie served the function of a horse, pulling the carriage with his every step.

Thinking carefully, she chose a larger conveyance, one that included an umbrella-like covering for shade and a long extended cart for luggage.

"Take me to *this* street," she said in Chinese, holding out the written characters for Max's address. She would have tried to speak the name, but Max had not given her any indication of how to say the strange symbols, so she could only pray that the driver could read.

Apparently he could not, because he barely even glanced at the page. Still, he smiled warmly, showing his crooked teeth, and gestured for her to climb into his carriage. Meanwhile, all around her, the other runners began speaking and gesturing as well, all in a loud jumble of language, none of which she understood.

Fear made her mouth taste bitter. Things were not quite as easy—or as comfortable—as she'd imagined.

"Do you know where this is?" she repeated in her stilted Chinese.

The driver merely grinned stupidly and tried to help her climb into his rickshaw.

Frustrated, Lydia yanked away, turning to the entire row of drivers, raising her voice to be heard above the din. "Does anyone understand me?"

"Yer speaking in the wrong Chinese, miss," came a familiar voice behind her.

Lydia spun around to see the captain standing there, a grin splitting his coarse features. "It's like I feared, miss. You learned the language from Canton. These here speak Shanghai."

She frowned, surprised. "They do not have one language?"

"They's ignorant savages, miss. They ain't got the same of anything anywhere." He sighed, folding his arms in an irritated gesture. "I ain't planned on this, but I got a bit o' time. And my own regular driver over there." He gestured to a covered rickshaw and a driver in a cone-shaped hat who grinned and dipped his head at her. The captain took her letter and quickly scanned the page. "We can take you where ye need to go."

Lydia smiled, suddenly overwhelmed with gratitude for a man she'd barely tolerated for the last month. "That would be a great help, sir," she breathed. "I had not thought there would be different kinds of Chinese."

He didn't answer except to gesture for his driver to take up her luggage. It was not a great lot for her bridal trousseau—only one trunk—but after her father's death, she and her mother had been forced to practice some rather stringent economies.

"Follow me," said the captain as he escorted her down the line to his waiting rickshaw.

It was then she heard another sound, this one from one of the other drivers in a mixture of English and Chinese. "No, no, laiiddeee. Come wid me. Not wid him. No, no."

She turned, trying to understand what the frantic man was saying, but the captain grabbed her arm in a bruising grip. "Stay with me, Miss Smith. They are thieves and ruffians, every last one of them."

She didn't argue. Indeed, she knew that even London cabbies could be devious if one didn't look sharp. She didn't want to contemplate what could happen to her here without even the right Chinese language to assist her. And thank God the captain was her countryman—a familiar rock amid this sea of strangeness.

So she allowed him to guide her as she stepped uneasily into his rickshaw. The bamboo seemed too flimsy to hold herself and her luggage, but to her surprise, it did not even bow beneath her weight or that of the captain as he shoved his massive body in beside her. Then, before she had time to gasp, they tilted backward. The coolie had lifted the poles and begun to run, quickly pulling them along.

She frowned at the Chinese man. Like his countrymen, he had a small frame. But apparently there was great strength in his wiry muscles, because he had no trouble pulling Lydia and the captain, her trunk, and the rickshaw frame behind him. And besides, there was little choice in the matter, as there weren't any horse-drawn carriages available. So she settled into silence, content to watch her surroundings as the coolie ran them up the street.

All too soon, even the golden pagoda-like buildings and long banners done in reds and golds could not hold her attention. She was looking again at the sweating man pulling their rickshaw. Beneath his cone-shaped hat of dried leaves, the man seemed all bone with little muscle and no fat. She had never seen anyone so thin. Indeed, every bump in his spine, every shift of his ribs as he huffed stuck out as clearly as a nose or an elbow. Just looking at him, Lydia felt guilty for every crumpet she had ever eaten, every fattening ounce that he was now hauling up the street. She wanted to stop him, to apologize, to tell him not to bother with her; she would walk. But she knew she could not. This was his livelihood, and he would not thank her for shortening her ride.

So she sat in uncomfortable silence, finding herself aware of the bob of the rickshaw, the huff of his breath, even the slap of his crude sandals against the stone street. She felt herself begin to breathe with him, stupidly wishing she could breathe for him, pull with him, do something to ease his labors.

She felt certain she would tip him generously, even if the captain did not. Except when the moment finally came, the captain left her no time. As soon as the rickshaw stopped, he grabbed her hand and nearly dragged her off in one sweeping movement. She barely had time to gasp a quick *"Xie xie"* in thanks before the captain was pulling her toward a building.

"Please!" she gasped. "Slow down!"

But the man had apparently wasted too much time with her and was anxious to be gone. No more than she wished to be rid of him, despite his aid. And so she allowed him to rush her into a large building among a whole street of beautiful buildings. All were lavishly decorated, with ornate doors. She had the brief impression of beautifully carved black wood painted with red and gold dragons or swans or other such Chinese decorations, of red paper lanterns hung from the front eaves next to red banners with gold characters. She couldn't read any of the words, of course, but they had a festive appearance that lightened her heart.

Then she was inside, looking at an elaborately carved staircase of the same black wood as outdoors. To one side, Lydia saw an elegant sitting room furnished with more carved chairs done in slightly faded red fabrics. She saw tables and linen, wall hangings in silk, and gilding everywhere, though obviously gold paint rather than gold leaf. It was loud and gaudy and tended to overwhelm the senses for all that it was empty of people. Especially as there was a slightly nauseating scent of something much too sweet lingering in the air.

"This is so unlike Maxwell," she murmured to herself. "He is such a restrained person, I cannot think he likes this entryway." But from what she had seen, all of Shanghai was overdone in gaudy colors and loud tones. She was sure his apartment upstairs must be more sedate. So, with that thought in mind, she moved toward the staircase, only belatedly remembering her manners.

Turning back to the captain, she extended her gloved hand. "Thank you, sir, for bringing me here. I am sure I can find Maxwell now." She glanced upstairs. "Indeed, I suppose his rooms are directly above."

The captain did not even acknowledge her gesture; his gaze was trained over her shoulder into the sitting room. Lydia turned to find she'd missed the entrance of a Chinese woman of indeterminate age flanked by a burly man of clearly mixed heritage. It was he who drew her attention first as she studied his features. Though almond-eyed like every Chinese, his skin was less golden, more pale in hue. His nose was more pronounced, but his jaw and brow less so, as if his entire body lagged behind a Romanesque nose. Still, he was muscular and broad-shouldered, especially by Chinese standards, and he was clearly unused to smiling. This attitude was enhanced by his clothing—a stained gray tunic over black pants.

Truly he was the shadow of the woman, who, though shorter, carried herself with a pride that infused every part of her—from her powdered face, through her form-fitting black-and-gold silk gown, down to her black-slippered tiny feet. And if that were not enough, her black hair was coiled high atop her head and held by two ivory combs that glittered in the dusty light. She said nothing and neither did the captain. Instead, the woman pursed her dark red lips and openly inspected Lydia.

It was bizarre and unnerving, so Lydia decided it was time to take control. Smiling with more warmth than she felt, she stepped forward, all the while praying the woman understood English. "I apologize for the intrusion, but I am Maxwell Slade's fiancée. If you could just show me to his rooms, I can wait there for him."

Instead of answering, the Chinese woman simply smiled and turned, waving at her burly companion. "Tea!" she said imperiously, and the man bowed before hurrying away.

"But—"

"Don't bother arguing," interrupted the captain in low tones. "It will only insult her. Just drink the tea, Miss Smith."

"But Max . . ." Her voice trailed away as she suddenly felt the weight of the truth. It would be many more hours, at least, until she would see her beloved fiancé again. He was likely at work and would return home in the evening. She might as well do what she could to charm her new landlady. Mustering a joy she did not feel, she turned to the woman and smiled. "Of course I would love some tea," she lied as she began to untie her bonnet.

The Chinese woman gestured to a small square table—one of many in the room—and Lydia sat down, doing her best to feel at ease. In truth, she wished only to put up her feet in Maxwell's no-doubt pristine quarters. Instead she sat at the table, turning to address a question to the captain.

Except, he had disappeared. Indeed, twisting slightly, she saw his heavy form already thumping back down the walkway.

"Captain?" she said stupidly. Then she recalled her trunk. He was no doubt bringing it inside for her.

"Sit. Rest," said her landlady, effectively distracting her from the captain's abrupt departure. "Drink tea," she continued, her voice deeper than Lydia expected. And significantly more nasal. Indeed, thought Lydia, she would have to work to understand this woman's English.

It was just as well that her first task in Shanghai would be to learn the language as quickly as possible. Meanwhile, her landlady's companion returned carrying a pot of tea in one hand and a small round tray in the other. As he slowly set down the tray, Lydia got her first look at Chinese teacups. Small and round, they did not even possess a handle. And once again, the decorations were done in gold paint. To match the decor, she supposed.

While she was still looking at the elaborate design—a gilded lotus—her landlady leaned over and poured the tea.

"Drink. Drink."

Lydia frowned. The woman was still standing over her, gesturing to the teacups. But there was more than one cup on the tray. "Won't you join me?" she asked. Then, in case the woman didn't understand, Lydia gestured with her hands, inviting the woman to sit at the table with her.

"No, no," answered the woman, with a smile that did not reach her eyes. "You drink."

Unsure what else to do, Lydia lifted her cup. Looking into the brew, she saw the dark swirl of a single escaped tea leaf. She smiled at the sight, feeling an inner tinge of satisfaction that she knew why. This was how the Chinese brewed their tea, with the leaves actually in the water when served, not strained out as in England. Maxwell had spent an entire letter on the evils of Chinese tea.

Yet she supposed if a whole nation of people drank their tea with the leaves in it, the brew would not kill her, so Lydia took an obliging sip, somewhat eager to taste her first real cup of Chinese tea. It was more bitter than she was used to, and also had an undercurrent of sickly sweetness, as if the Chinese woman had tried to make English tea but somehow failed.

Lydia set the cup down, frowning as she tried to analyze the taste. But the moment the cup left her lips, the woman was beside her again, actually lifting Lydia's hands to get her to drink.

"No, no. Drink. Finish tea."

Lydia did. Indeed, how could she not without appearing horribly rude? So she swallowed the stuff down, surprising herself by not spilling it. She wondered briefly if this was some Chinese custom—to drink the tea without stopping—and envisioned sharing this experience with Maxwell as soon as he returned. Would they laugh about her ignorance? Or about the landlady's obsessive need to have people consume her tea?

Oh, she had so much to tell him! When would he get here?

Setting down her cup, Lydia looked at her landlady. "Please, can you tell me where Maxwell works? I should like to meet him there."

But the woman wasn't listening. She was pouring Lydia more tea.

"Oh no, thank you." Lydia extended her hands to stop her, but the lady would have none of it. She finished pouring, then rudely shoved the cup back into Lydia's hands.

"Drink!"

"Please—"

"Drink!"

The woman's tones were strident, and so Lydia did as she was bidden, finishing the cup just as she had the last. But that was all she was going to drink until she had some answers. So, setting down the cup—somewhat harder than she anticipated—she frowned at the woman.

"Maxwell Sade—"

"Yes, yes," said the woman, nodding as she poured more tea.

Lydia frowned. She had not said that right. "Maxwell Slllade. Where does he woke? Work. Where does Max work?" How odd that her tongue felt numb. And she was having difficulty forming certain sounds. Meanwhile, the Chinese woman was saying something in heavily accented English.

"Your man come soon. You drink now." She was leaning over Lydia, pushing the teacup on her once again.

But Lydia had had quite enough for one day. She twisted her head away, pushing to her feet. The man was coming toward her from the other side, but Lydia ignored him. She regretting having to be rude to her new landlady—the first real Chinese person with whom she had ever had a chance to converse—but it was necessary. She absolutely refused to drink any more of the vile stuff.

Except, something was wrong with her feet. As numb as

her tongue, they would not support her as they ought. Indeed, the moment she came to stand, she just as quickly began to collapse. Her head felt three sizes too large, and ungainly on her neck as well.

What is the meaning of this? she demanded of the woman. Or rather she tried. What came out, she was very much afraid, was something more like, "Wha!?"

Then she knew no more.

Cheng Ru Shan curled his lip at the opium stench that pervaded the Garden of Perfumed Flowers. Though not as strong here as in a lower class establishment, he could still detect the nauseatingly sweet scent. He caught other odors as well—perfume from the "flowers" of this particular garden, tobacco smoke from the men content to look at them, sweat and stale yang essence from those who wanted more.

All in all, Ru Shan found this garden as revolting as the "nail shed" shacks in the Shanghai slums, and he spun on his heel intending to leave. But his companion stopped him, her small white hand firm on his sleeve.

"To catch a tiger's cub, one must enter the tiger's den," she intoned softly.

"I have no need for a tiger cub today, Shi Po. And no patience for this . . ." What word to use to characterize the worst of what China had become? "This corruption."

She smiled at him, her beauty still somehow shining through the veil that obscured her features. "Have I not guided you well until now? Trust me a little longer, Ru Shan. All will be made clear."

Before he could reply, the Garden's proprietress came forward, along with a hulking half-breed standing guard behind her. "Greetings, greetings. How may I assist your honorable selves today?" she asked, her bow deep and respectful.

It was on the tip of Ru Shan's tongue to tell her to give up her occupation, free her unfortunate flowers and devote herself to ascetic contemplation, but he knew his sarcasm would be lost on her. Worse yet, it would serve only to inflame his already irritated temper. So he remained silent, knowing Shi Po would have her little game. After all, in this, she was the instructor and he the student. So he remained silent when all in his nature urged him to act.

Shi Po was looking about with the disdainful superiority that came from her husband's wealth. "We wish to view your whitest flower."

Greed flashed, hot and hard in the proprietress's black eyes, but her movements were slow and graceful as she bowed again. "Of course, but she is resting now. Perhaps you could come back later?"

Ru Shan recognized the ploy for what it was—a way to add anticipation to the purchase and a way to cover the real truth that the girl would always be resting: she was no doubt drugged insensible. But appearances had to be maintained, and so the game continued.

"Perhaps we could just glance at her a moment?" Shi Po asked. "We shall remain absolutely silent." They wouldn't, of course, because the girl wouldn't wake until the drugs were washed from her body. And that, sometimes, took days.

"She is very delicate," hedged the mistress.

"Then," Ru Shan snapped, his patience worn thin, "we should just leave her to her rest." He turned for the door, fully intending to escape.

He was stopped, of course, but not by the aged hag who ran this business. Shi Po's voice stopped him, her tone low and hard. "You came to me, Ru Shan. You asked for my help because I am the senior in these teachings, a tigress far ahead of you on the path to immortality. Will you take the instruction I offer?"

Ru Shan stopped. He had to. He was in desperate straits. His mishandling of this situation was simply a further example of how much he needed whatever aid Shi Po could give him. He bit back his sigh and turned around.

He didn't even hear if the proprietress said anything else. He merely followed mutely as he and Shi Po were led up the stairs. The half-breed, of course, brought up the rear, his presence a significant obstacle should Ru Shan try to leave again. He would not. He had already shown himself much too intemperate already. He would not leave the middle path again.

Or so he swore to himself. As he had been swearing perhaps a dozen or more times each week for the last two years.

The mistress led them to the highest floor, and then to a tiny, stifling closet of a room in the back of the house. It was hard for Shi Po to totter on her bound feet even with the help of a cane, but she was determined. And that more than anything else told Ru Shan that the woman was in earnest. Still, he hated this place and this tiny back room where no window lightened the dark interior nor did any breeze lessen the stale air. How did anyone—man or woman—breathe in here, much less do anything else?

He knew the answer, of course. A pig did not care if his sty stank. Only the man forced to wade through it to find . . .

A white woman, round and pale, chained to a bed. The shackles were not obvious but hidden beneath a thin blanket. Still, Ru Shan could see the telltale bulges even in the dim light of a single lantern.

The proprietress was speaking, expounding on the woman's many assets—beauty, health, modesty, and of course absolute purity. He ignored her, stepping closer to search for whatever treasure Shi Po wished him to discern. The white woman's hair appeared dirty gold in the dim light, and her mouth was slack and revealed a dark, moist cave surrounded by full red lips. Her face was a pleasing oval, her ears round with long, solid lobes.

"Well?" asked Shi Po, interrupting his thoughts. "Do you see it?"

He frowned, annoyed that he would have to answer in the negative. "She is a white woman, drugged and chained to a bed. What should I see?"

Shi Po frowned in annoyance, then waved the proprietress away. The woman bowed out, taking her half-breed with her and giving them the illusion of privacy. But it was only an illusion. Every room in this establishment likely had at least two different peepholes. Shi Po obviously understood that as well, for when she spoke, her voice remained barely audible despite its hard note of censure.

"Look again at the girl," she ordered. "See how much water she has in her? See her breasts, how full and round they are? They will give much sustenance to a man with too much yang."

Ru Shan grimaced, knowing she referred to him. Indeed that was the source of his problem, according to her: too much male yang. Too little female yin. And he could not deny the hunger he felt when he'd first viewed the white girl's plump breasts, only half-concealed beneath a gauzy shift. Still . . .

"I need not go to a white slave woman for more yin," he snapped. That was why he'd gone to Shi Po. Still, he thought as his eyes drifted back to the full dusky circles of the girl's nipples, she would indeed give amply of her yin essence. Certainly much more than Shi Po, who was dominated by the wood element and could sometimes be quite stingy with her dew.

And while these thoughts flowed through his mind, Shi Po drew closer to him, raising up as tall as she could so that she spoke directly into his ear. "You must replace what was lost. What you destroyed."

"I cannot," he rasped, the pressure in his mind growing once again. "And if I could, it would not be with her."

Shi Po exhaled in a loud rush of heat that scalded his cheek even through the fabric of her veil. "You are too hasty in your estimate. You see an egg and expect to see it crow—"

"I see a crossbow and expect to see a dove roasting," he finished for her, the old proverb like ashes on his tongue. She was reminding him to be patient, to find the middle way of the Tao. "How can this woman replace what is lost?"

Shi Po moved away from him, twisting so that her back was to the wall most likely to contain peepholes. Then she folded her arms and spoke crossly, her voice nearly a hiss despite her low tones. "You killed a white man, Ru Shan—"

"I killed an animal!" he retorted, his voice equally low.

"If that is so, then why has your sleep been disturbed? Why do you fast one moment only to eat like a starving slave the next? If you killed only an animal, then why have you so clearly abandoned the middle path?

He had no answer for her, because she spoke the truth. He was lost in the wilds and had been from that ill night over two years ago.

"What you have taken must be restored."

"I cannot bring him back to life. I do not even think I would if I could."

She nodded, silently agreeing with his statement. "But you can raise up another white soul. Teach your treasure to another white foreigner, and in so doing find your way back to the middle path."

He felt his jaw go slack in astonishment. She couldn't possibly mean what she was saying. "You cannot expect me to teach her to become immortal?" He twisted, looking at the ghost devil, as whites were often called. "These ghost souls do not have enough substance to become immortal."

Shi Po shrugged. "Perhaps not. But try. And in so trying, find peace on your pillow again."

Ru Shan shook his head, struck dumb by the thought of such a task. He? Teach a white woman what few of his own countrymen understood? It wasn't possible.

"Kui Yu tells me some of them can be quite smart in their own limited way," Shi Po commented, referring to her husband.

"Then let me teach one he knows. A man."

"As if you need more yang, Ru Shan," she sneered. "No, a man would only exacerbate the imbalances in your body. You need a white woman, and a water one at that." She gestured disdainfully at the girl.

"But I cannot teach her the ways of the tigress. Only a woman can reveal those secrets."

"You know enough," she interrupted. "And I can advise you as needed. She will not need to learn the higher rituals. She will not be capable of it, and she is not the point." Shi Po stepped closer, her spicy perfume mixing imperfectly with the scents of the house, pushing Ru Shan's mind into further turmoil. "You are the point, Ru Shan, the arrow that must be directed. She is merely the bow that will launch you into Heaven."

He understood her words, saw the purpose in them. And yet, Ru Shan still could not accept them. "I cannot come here every day. Nor can I be sure that she will remain uncontaminated in this house." He glanced back toward the door, knowing well that the proprietress would happily sell and resell the white girl's "purity" to any man willing to believe the lies. In truth, once the evening opium pipes began, he doubted he could ensure his own safety, much less a helpless white girl's. Even breathing the air would be a risk.

"Very true," Shi Po agreed. There was a hint of regret in her tone. At the mournful sound, Ru Shan began to hope that he had escaped this most unwelcome task. But then she lifted her chin, resolution clear in her stance. "You will have to buy her."

"What?" He exploded, his horror overcoming his restraint. "The cost of it . . . her price . . ." The thought boggled his mind. He had nothing in his store to equal the price of this one white girl. Indeed, she would cost as much as a year's income, if not more. "I cannot afford her. Not since . . ." Not since that night two years ago.

"You must borrow the money."

"No!" The very idea revolted him.

"Then you have abandoned the Tao and all the gains you have made these last nine years. You will never become an Immortal. Even your status as a jade dragon will disappear."

He felt his jaw tighten at the thought, the heat in his belly rising with his temper. Nearly a decade of study, of diligent effort and constant attention, all would disappear? Because he would not sacrifice his family to his goals? Not possible!

But one look at Shi Po, and he could see she would not change her mind. Ru Shan's name would be stricken from the records, his gains of the last nine years wiped away.

And yet, he could not do it. He could not risk his family's future. Not even if it meant forfeiting everything he had worked for since he'd first met Shi Po so long ago.

He bowed his head, accepting his fate. "I cannot get a loan, Shi Po. Any moneylender would expect collateral, and I have only two things to offer—the Cheng store and the Cheng home." He straightened his spine. "I will not risk my family's home or livelihood."

Shi Po sighed as if she had expected such an answer. Then she continued speaking, her voice low and relentless.

"Your life is already at risk, Ru Shan, and your family home is the least of it. Do you discount the torments you suffer now? Do not think they will abate. Having once known the peace of the Tao, you will find eternal torment with the unenlightened. Your mind will never be at peace, your bed will never offer you a single night's rest. You will walk endlessly in the dark, lost and alone, for I cannot help you in this. Our time together will be over."

He shuddered with a violence that frightened him. He knew what was happening. What part of him remained in the Tao was revolted by her words, terrified enough to want to shake the very idea from his body. But he could not. Shi Po's words remained, their horror as pervasive as their truth. And so he spoke, barely even realizing what he was saying.

"I cannot continue as I have been. I shall go mad within the month. Already my body is growing weak." He held out his hands to her, revealing the latest of his shames. His hands trembled like an old man's, the unrest of his spirit fully revealed in his rapidly aging body. "I must find my way back to the Tao."

"Then you must buy the white girl. You must establish her in an apartment close enough to see her every day. You must partake of her essence every moment that you can." Shi Po stepped even closer, pressing her point. "And as her water flows into you, your family's fortunes will recover and your pathway back to the Tao will be revealed." She lowered her voice into a seductive murmur. "Your mind will find peace, your body rest. You will return to the middle path with new energy, and as her yin mixes with your yang, the spiritual embryo will be born. You will become an Immortal. You can, Ru Shan, if only you will do what is necessary."

He nearly wept at the picture she created, the dream for which he yearned during every sleepless night, after every intemperate act. "But how will I find the money?"

She bowed her head, slowly and gracefully lifting the veil that obscured her face. And as she did, he saw on her cheek the tear she shed for his sake. It glistened there, her yin essence glittering even in the dim light. In a rare act of generosity, she lifted that drop from her cheek and carried it to his lips, giving it to him. He drank greedily, silently wishing for more. An ocean more. An entire woman's worth more, to cool the yang fire that constantly burned him.

She pressed her lips to his ear, giving him another gift: the means to accomplish his task.

"My husband will loan you what you need."

From the letters of Mei Lan Cheng

20 May, 1857
Dearest Li Hua—
    What an amazing day! First wife to Cheng Sheng Fu! Did you see him at the wedding? Is he not handsome

and strong? I know his father picked me because of my embroidery designs. Father says they have a small shop in Shanghai. They want me to design the decoration on their clothing. "Sheng Fu" means "rising wealth." Father says my skills will make his name true.

But I do not care why we are wed, only that I am. First wife! I can barely breathe with all the excitement.

I must go now. He is coming. This . . . tonight. I am so scared. But Li Hua, I will endure anything today. Because I am a first wife!

                                                                —Mei Lan

Half an orange tastes as sweet as a whole one.
　　　　　　　　—Traditional Chinese proverb

Chapter Two

Lydia felt absolutely wretched. Her head ached. Her lips felt parched. But mostly she just wanted the entire world—including her aching body—to go away. Unfortunately, she had other matters to attend to first. Like using the necessary. Now.

She never would have made it by herself. She barely managed to put her feet over the edge of her bed when a groan escaped her raw throat. Then a miracle happened. A maid appeared at her side, silently assisting her to just where she wanted to go.

It wasn't until after she was done, sitting back on the bed with a glass of water gently being held to her lips, that Lydia realized the maid was actually a boy. A young man, really. Chinese. With a bland face and a long queue of black hair that fell halfway down his back.

She would have choked on the water if she hadn't already drained the glass. As it was, she simply stared at him, a dull rush of embarrassment flowing through her entire barely clad body. Unfortunately, right behind it came a full wave of dizziness and even a bit of nausea.

Not good. Not good at all.

And while she was struggling with that, other disconnected thoughts whirled through her foggy mind. What was she wearing? A coarse white nightshirt. That wasn't hers, was it? Where were her clothes? Was she on the boat?

There was something else as well. Something different about her body. But what? She couldn't quite focus her mind on the question. On much of anything. Yet she still found the strength to look at the young man directly and to croak out a question.

"Where am I?"

He didn't respond, merely urged her to lie back in bed. Some small part of her brain registered tiny details of her environment. She lay in a simple bed, well padded and rather large. The room was sparse as well. There was one window, very high up, with decorative lattices over the opening, an ornately decorated screen, and behind that the privy. But where was . . .

"Max," she croaked. "Where's Maxwell?"

Again, the Chinese man didn't answer, and before long she discovered she was lying back on the bed, her head gently supported by a silk-covered pillow. Truly, it was quite nice to lie here and simply let her cares float away.

She might have done just that if it hadn't been for a flash of memory. Or of nightmare. Or something. She remembered a sickly sweet taste and a dark room with . . . shackles?

"No!" She struggled upright. She needed to escape. She needed to find Max. She needed . . .

"Safe."

She blinked. She had heard a word in English. From the young man.

Blearily, she focused on him as he pushed her firmly back on the bed.

"You safe," he said clearly. Slowly.

She nodded, understanding his words, her fear beginning to abate. Why she trusted him, she didn't know. But she certainly didn't seem in danger now. And she was so very, very tired.

"Max?"

"Well. You are well."

No, she began, but her mouth would not form the word. She slept.

She woke quickly the next time, the nightmare fading, only to be replaced by a dreamy reality as confusing as the first. The young Chinese man was at her side again, feeding her something she now realized was not water at all, but weak tea with a tangy flavor. She'd thought it quite strange at first, but now she was beginning to like it.

As always, he assisted her to the necessary, waiting politely on the other side of the screen while she accomplished her business. He laid out a change of clothes for her—another plain white nightshirt—and never spoke except to assure her she was safe.

As she stared at the boy, for she guessed him to be about seventeen years old, questions began to form in her mind. Where was she? She was obviously on land, likely Shanghai. She had unfortunately begun to remember the other house—the one that the captain had taken her to, claiming it was Maxwell's. Well, if that was Maxwell's home, then she was a purple toad.

But how had she escaped that terrible place and come

here? Who was paying for this home and the Chinese servant? And who had . . . performed the change in her body?

That was another thing she had figured out. What before had felt a nameless difference, she now saw in the stark light of day. She was completely shaved. Totally hairless. Not the hair on top of her head, for that remained neatly braided in a long queue down her back. It was all her other hair—from her legs, her arms, and her . . . From *everywhere*.

But who had . . . ? And how? Not this boy. He couldn't—

She didn't know what to make of the situation, and she certainly couldn't ask, even if she thought the man understood English. Her only option was to wait and see. It was probably some traditional Chinese medicine or some such nonsense. One never knew what bizarre customs a primitive culture might have. She didn't have to think beyond that.

But where was she? And how had she gotten here? If she had to guess—and that was all she could do—she figured somehow Maxwell had discovered where she was and rescued her. This little apartment was her new home until she was well enough to speak her vows. Maxwell was always one for observing proprieties.

Yet she couldn't understand why he absented himself so much. Likely some business deal had stolen him away. He had written that he'd saved enough money to buy property, that he was merely looking for the right investment. He would come to her soon enough, bringing roses and an engagement ring. Something large and beautiful to replace the one that had been stolen from her.

So Lydia schooled herself to patience as the Chinese man brought her a thick soup. In truth, she felt much better, and so she smiled brilliantly at him.

"Thank you. Good food."

He nodded. "Good food. Yes."

"You may tell Maxwell I am well enough to see him now. He can come any day."

"You are well, yes."

Lydia sighed. You'd think a man as meticulous as her fiancé could have found a servant who spoke some English. But perhaps they were in short supply, she reasoned. She would have to learn the language eventually. She might as well start now.

But when she tried to converse with the boy, he merely smiled his bland smile and bowed himself out of the room. So much for learning a new language today. Instead, she had to content herself with looking at the decor, sparse as it was, and wondering at the other strange sensations in her body.

First off, her belly seemed to be rumbling quite a bit. Embarrassing, often painful sounds kept emanating from her lower region. It felt like a tiny cauldron was burbling and gurgling away down there. That alone would be bad enough, but whatever was happening gave her the most awful flatulence. It was just as well that Maxwell wasn't around, she told herself firmly. He definitely preferred refined women, and such a noisy body would not appeal to him.

Though she doubted he would mind, of course. He loved her. She simply wanted to appear her best before him. And farting loudly was not at all appropriate when seeing one's fiancé for the first time in nearly three years.

If only he'd thought to give her a book to read or something else to do. Some clothes, perhaps, beyond this basic nightshirt. Even the window was designed for ventilation, not viewing. It was much too high to look out of unless she had a chair to stand on, which she did not. Nor did she have a sketchbook or her charcoals. Or a journal. Not even some stitching.

Just a rumbly stomach and a bored mind.

So it remained for another hour at least, until she heard the low murmur of men's voices from the other room where the servant resided. She had been dozing, but came instantly alert as the doorknob jiggled. She was immediately flooded with excitement, along with a good deal of trepidation, as she rapidly patted her hair and adjusted the covers.

Maxwell was here at last!

Except that when the door opened, another Chinese man walked in. Or rather, he strode in, his black eyes piercing as he looked at her.

Disappointment cut through Lydia at the same moment that she released an enormously loud burst of flatulence. She felt her face heat almost to burning as she rapidly pulled the covers up to her shoulders, for she was not suitably attired for strangers.

And all the while the man just stood there, staring at her, his thin eyebrows pulled low over his coal black eyes.

He didn't say anything and neither did she, for she was much too mortified. But though her tongue appeared frozen, her eyes were not. She looked at him in stunned amazement, seeing her very first well-dressed Chinese man up close.

He wore silk, that much was obvious, a gray tunic with dark black pants and the ever-present roundish hat over his long black Manchurian queue. All in all, it was the standard Chinese attire from what she remembered of her quick rickshaw ride through Shanghai. But what stood out, what seemed truly exceptional, was the embroidered design on his tunic. A dark green dragon wove in and around his upper body, its flame tongue coiling into the red Chinese buttons—*frogs,* she thought they were called. On the opposite lapel, an embroidered ball of fire hung just out of reach. A truly exceptional design, she thought, and fabulously executed, for it made the wearer appear both man and dragon. An awesome sight indeed.

"Excuse me," she squeaked. Then she cleared her throat, doing her best to sound strong and not at all intimidated by this dark man towering in her doorway. "Excuse me," she said more firmly. "But why are you in my bedchamber?"

She had meant to sound powerful, for Max had written that the only thing these barbarians understood was strength. He'd meant the strength of cannons blazing from warships, but she figured the notion applied in person as well. Unfortunately, her words did not sound powerful as much as haughty. And in a squeaky, little-girl voice to boot.

The man continued to stare at her in some dark Chinese way. It wasn't like when the servant looked at her. The boy's face often went blank from incomprehension. This newcomer's expression was clearly a mask. Carved wood gave more away than his brooding eyes. She rapidly began to squirm under his scrutiny.

Abruptly, he spoke in rapid-fire Chinese to the boy who waited impassively just outside the bedroom. The boy answered, also in Chinese, while Lydia sat, uncomprehending. It was excruciatingly difficult, and for a moment she had the strongest urge to cry.

Rather than do that, she stiffened her spine and consciously released the blanket from where she'd held it almost up to her chin. It drifted down, thankfully not slipping below her cleavage. "Please, sir," she said as calmly as she could manage. "When will Maxwell be coming?"

"Maxwell?" he asked, his voice strangely melodious.

"Yes. Maxwell Slade. He is my fiancé."

"You have no fiancé," he snapped. "You are . . ." He struggled a moment with the English word. "My servant."

"I most certainly am not!" Thankfully, she was still struggling with an upset belly or she would have leapt straight to her feet despite her lack of clothing. Indeed, she wondered if she could slap his face from her position on the bed.

Fortunately for her dignity, he merely dipped his head in a semblance of a bow. "My apologies—"

"I should think so!"

"You are my . . ." Again the pause as he struggled with the language. Abruptly he brightened, his eyes actually lightening to a kind of reddish brown. "Slave."

At her gasp of shock, he continued, still with that ridiculously pleased expression. "I have extended myself greatly to purchase you. You were most expensive." His tone indicated disapproval, almost anger. "But it is done now, and you will perform such tasks as I require when I require."

"I most certainly will not!" Throwing caution to the wind, Lydia tossed her covers aside. If he'd thought she was a sickly, retiring female, he was about to get a surprise. Ignoring her state of undress, she stood directly in front of him, poking him right in the embroidered dragon's eye. "I am Lydia Smith, fiancée to Maxwell Slade. And you will take me to him immediately!"

She didn't even see him move, neither him nor his servant. But almost before her words were finished, he had grabbed her wrists and pushed her backward onto the bed. From out of nowhere appeared straps—thick leather straps that he and his servant snapped around each of her wrists and ankles, tying her to the iron grid that supported the bed's mattress. And no matter how much she fought, how much she bit or tried to claw her way free, she ended up flat on her back, her arms and legs spread, her nightshirt halfway up her thighs.

She screamed, screeching out her anger and horror and that she was an Englishwoman and they had no right to treat her this way. And yet they did nothing. They simply stood and watched her, no matter how much she said Max's or her own name. No matter what she threatened or babbled or pleaded. In the end, she lay exhausted on the bed, tears of frustration flowing freely down her cheeks.

The dragon man approached her. Looking down, he smiled almost beatifically, and in the oddest gesture of reverence, he reached out to touch her face. She tried to turn away, but there was nowhere to go, and soon his forefinger was wet with her tears. He lifted his finger slowly, closing his eyes as he brought it to his mouth, obviously tasting and enjoying the salt of her tears.

She stared at him in shock and horror, not knowing what to make of his action. And then he looked back at her, his smile more natural.

"Shi Po was right. You are an overfull cup." Abruptly he turned, his long queue snapping behind him like a serpent's tail. "Your lessons will begin tomorrow."

And then he was gone.

Her lessons did not begin the next day. Indeed, nothing began the next day because she would not allow it. She fought, she struggled, she refused to eat. She even fouled her own bed. Only to find out that fighting rubbed her skin raw, giving her painful welts that burned and bled. When she refused to eat, she didn't eat. No one particularly cared. And when she fouled her bed, no one cared either. She lay in her own filth, miserable and abandoned.

And worst of all was knowing Maxwell had abandoned

her. He was nowhere to be found, though she sobbed his name like a litany.

In her more rational moments, she knew Maxwell wasn't at fault. In fact, her fiancé was likely blissfully ignorant of her state, happily believing his future wife safe at home in England. It would be months before enough messages crossed between Shanghai and England for both him and her mother to discover she had disappeared. Months. In the meantime, Lydia would be trapped here, slave to some deviant Chinese monster.

Months. As a slave.

The thought was insupportable. Impossible. And yet she could not deny the reality of her situation. When she was rational, that is. And so she spent as much time as she could irrational.

Or at least she pretended. A couple of days of raving lunacy convinced her that insanity got her nowhere. It did not relieve the agony in her mind, nor did it affect her captors in any appreciable manner. So she tried a different tack, feigning exhaustion—even cooperation—in the hopes that she could overpower the servant boy and escape.

She failed. The boy was stronger than he looked, more than a match for her. And when she was left alone—unbound—in her room, she found that the door was locked and the small, high window barred. That beautiful iron latticework she'd so admired was in truth iron fixtures designed to prevent escape.

Still, she raised herself up as high as she could, screaming herself hoarse in the hopes that someone would hear her and come rushing to her rescue. Maxwell was in the forefront, of course. But though she screeched her throat raw, no one came to her aid.

And all the while, her hatred of the dragon—that was

what she had come to call him in her mind—grew. She who hated to kill a mouse would have easily, happily wrung the dragon's neck and danced upon his dead body.

Indeed, she had elaborate fantasies, each more gruesome than the last, as to how she would kill her captors. God would give her inhuman strength and she would crush them with her two fists. God would give her a voice that could shatter eardrums, and she would scream until their heads exploded. God would give her fantastic powers of the mind, and she would overpower them with a thought.

Maxwell no longer figured in her dreams except to be gloriously amazed by her ingenuity in engineering an escape. Though she still wished he might somehow find her, rush through the door and rescue her, she realized now it would never happen. She would have to find her own way out and to his side.

So it was, around a week later—at least, she thought it was a week; time was difficult to track in this place—when the dragon stepped into her room. Lydia was curled on the floor in a corner, quietly humming to herself. The tune an old nonsense rhyme that her mother had once sang to her, and which she found oddly comforting.

She knew she was a disgusting sight. Matted hair, filthy nightshirt, bruised and swollen body from the more violent encounters with the houseboy. But she did not care what the dragon thought of her. Indeed, she very much hoped she disgusted him and he would toss her out on the street.

But that did not happen. Instead, he came to stand over her, glaring down in fury, his lip curled in disgust.

"Are you done with this now?"

She didn't answer, so eventually he continued.

"Have you accepted your situation? Because I swear to you that my patience is at an end. If you do not stop your fighting, then I shall return you to the whorehouse where I first found you. I will recover whatever monies I can, and I will be done with you forever."

She looked up, hope sparking within her. He crushed it.

"I do not know if you remember what happened at that place, but I can tell you what will happen when I return you. You will be beaten, that much is assured. Then you will be addicted—to opium, no doubt, because it is easy and will make you docile. Then your virginity will be sold as many times as they can manage until you become an old harlot."

Her mind exploded. She screamed. She launched herself at the dragon.

He was prepared, of course. And strong. He had no need of the boy to assist him in slamming her onto the bed. Then he continued speaking, his voice low and implacable.

"But it will not end there, ghost woman. No. If you learn quickly and spread your legs easily, they will keep you on for as long as you bring in customers. All the while your craving for opium will increase. You will do anything for the drug. You will spread your legs, debase your body and others', anything and everything, just for another taste of that vile drug. And then, when you are old and wasted, they will throw you out on the street to die. But you won't die. You will crawl into the Shanghai slums, find a shack and a filthy piece of wood so that you can spread your legs for whoever will give you another taste. In the end, you will die in that black hole of your own filth, and no one, least of all your precious Maxwell, will ever know or care."

The life he painted seemed too real to be a lie. Indeed, Max had once written of the poor fates of men and women who became addicted to the opium the Chinese adored. And if Lydia doubted, she needed only remember the time she had spent in that other awful place. As bad as her treatment here was, her injuries were all a result of her own actions. Her many indignities were nowhere near what she had experienced in her moments of lucidity at the whorehouse.

She could not go back there. She would not! Which meant she had to stay here. With the dragon. Until she could find a way to escape.

She did not want to stay and please this monster. She did not want any of this, but God had long since turned a deaf ear. She would have to make her own plans, her own bargains. And yet, she had no strength to begin. She simply lay on her side and sobbed loud, messy tears of the truly wretched.

In time, the dragon stood up and stared at her, seemingly unmoved by pity or remorse. "I give you one day, ghost woman. One day to present yourself to me in such a way as to prove you are worthy of my attention. Fight Fu De in the least, and I will chain your hands and feet together and toss you back into the cesspool from which you came."

He meant it. Every evil word. He would toss her back and she would die. This she knew.

And yet, long after he left, she could not stir herself to care. She longed for death. Prayed for it. Desperately she needed an end.

But there was nothing in the room with which to harm herself. Even the iron bars that provided the framework for the bed could not be used. She had tried. At the time she had been looking for a weapon against the servant—what was his name? Fu De. The frame was solid and unwieldy for any purpose except as a bed. Even her gown was not long enough to create a noose from which to hang herself. In short, she would have to make a bargain with the dragon, and pray for a time when she could find an escape.

As morning at last lightened the room, she made her

choice. She got up from her bed and presented herself for cleaning. Apparently there was little time, and she was the one who would have to perform most of the tasks.

The first thing Fu De did was to bring her a mop and bucket. While he stripped and changed the linens of her bed, she was to clean every inch of her tiny bedroom. Then, when that was finished, he dragged in a large tub which he filled with tepid water. He handed her a soft, scented soap, then bowed himself out. One English word lingered in the air behind him:

"Hurry."

She stripped quickly, settling into the tub with a sigh of pleasure. Immersed in the water, planning to wash her hair, the thought of drowning came to her. She could do it. She need only hold her breath until she became unconscious. Then she would drown. Quietly. Quickly, even. If she was strong enough.

If Fu De had brought her the water yesterday, she probably would have done it. Or at least she could have tried. But the work—the mopping and the cleaning—had done her good. It had brought life and strength back into her body, and she found herself unwilling to embrace death so easily.

It was a difficult choice. After all, good Englishwomen were taught that death was preferable to dishonor. And she had no doubt that whatever fiendishness the Dragon intended, it would certainly dishonor her.

If she were a proper Englishwoman, she would attempt to kill herself right away. But she didn't want to die—certainly not before she knew exactly what type of dishonor the dragon intended. After all, he was a strange man from a strange country. What if all he wanted was to drink her tears? She could handle that. She could cry buckets for him. And, eventually, some opportunity for escape would present itself.

She would not drown today, she decided. She would clean herself and wait. She would learn what her captor wanted and then reevaluate her choices. After all, she could always drown herself at some later date.

Having decided, she threw herself into the task of bathing, making sure she appeared as clean and respectable as possible. And when Fu De brought her an elegant blue silk robe, she pulled it on, wrapping it around herself in the most modest but pleasing manner. She even took pains with her hair, knotting it loosely atop her head.

When the dragon arrived—a bare ten breaths after she had finished fussing with her hair—she was prepared to face whatever came. With dignity and with good English courage.

From the letters of Mei Lan Cheng

4 August, 1857
Dearest Li Hua—

I hear you are to be married to an honorable gentleman. How fortunate, and my best wishes for double happiness on your house. I know you have long hoped for such a thing, and I know, too, that you are as nervous and scared as I was.

Do not be afraid of what is to come, Li Hua. How strange to think that our old teacher was right: do not fear the man as much as the mother-in-law. Have you met her? Is she kind? She is the one who can make your life miserable. If she is lazy, she will order you to do her work. If she is greedy, she will take all of your things.

Your husband's attention takes only a moment at night. But the mother-in-law is at you from before the sun comes up to long after it goes down. Truthfully, Li Hua, I like my Sheng Fu's attentions. It gives me an excuse to leave his mother. Otherwise she would pick at me all night as well.

But I do not wish to make you sad in this time of joy. Write to me soon and tell me of your new family. I regret that I will not be at your wedding. It seems my father's predictions were true. The Cheng shop has become very prosperous in Shanghai. We see my embroidery everywhere now. Or I would if I were ever out to see it. I spend my dawns with my sketches, my days supervising the dyeing of threads and cloth, and my evenings in chores.

At least we now understand why I am so ugly. My mother-in-law says it is because Heaven does not give such wealth to one woman. All my beauty has gone into my designs, leaving none left over for my face. It was only my father-in-law's great wisdom that brought me to their family where the entire clan could make money from my ugliness.

At first I cried greatly at her words. I thought her very cruel, and no doubt you do, too. But Li Hua, she is right. I am never more content than in those early hours before everyone wakes when I can paint as my mind wills, as my beauty decrees. It is a great gift from Heaven, and the one that fills my heart with fivefold happiness.

If only I could conceive a son. Then, my joy would be complete.

—Mei Lan

Thy breasts are like the seeds in a newly opened lotus.
—Ming Huang compliments Yang Guifei
somewhat naughtily in the Tang Dynasty

Chapter Three

He was wearing something different today, though the effect was still the same. A gray silk tunic over loose black pants. But this time the gray was embroidered with dark blue threads in the shape of clouds. And if one looked closely—which Lydia did—she could see the tail of a dragon here, the curve of a fin there. Wherever she looked, she found the hint of a dragon slipping through the clouds—a four-toed foot just around a button, and there, on his right breast, the circle of a single dragon eye watching her as intently as she watched it.

It was powerful and unsettling. It took everything within her not to shrink away as he stepped into her room.

She was sitting on her bed, her blue silk robe knotted tightly around her. It was the only thing she wore, and so she was excruciatingly aware of her state of undress, of the feel of shimmery smooth silk against her skin, especially whenever she moved. But she wasn't moving now. She was sitting on the bed, her legs tucked beneath her, the fabric of the robe covering every hint of skin. She appeared, to the best of her ability, a proper Englishwoman.

"Your hair is restrained," he said, the harsh growl of his voice making her jump. "Release it."

She did as she was bid, her hands shaking as she unwound the knot. It tumbled down in an unruly mass, but the more she tried to smooth it, the more it became tangled. In the end he stepped forward, his hands surprisingly warm as he stopped her movements. Gently pushing her arms down, he untangled her hair. And, of course, Fu De was on hand to give him a comb. Soon he was straightening out her hair with long, gentle strokes.

She ought to be grateful, she told herself, that he was doing no more than brushing her hair. And yet, his every touch made her more anxious, and every moment he worked, her chest tightened even more as panic threatened to overwhelm her.

"You have metal in you," he said. "A gold that flows from you almost as freely as the water."

"My hair is not gold," she said firmly—almost primly. "That is merely the *color* of my hair. It is not metal."

He stepped back, his eyes narrowing, and she silently cursed her unruly tongue. She should not have corrected him. But really, he was savage indeed if he didn't understand something so basic. Then he was speaking, his voice as perplexed as it was harsh.

"Do you seek to annoy me? Or do your people truly know nothing?"

She looked up at him, startled by his statement. "My hair is not metal."

"Of course it is not metal," he snapped. "But it shimmers

like gold, and your complexion is more ivory than ruddy. That indicates metal in your . . ." His voice trailed away as he struggled for the word.

"Personality," offered Fu De, in a low voice from just outside the room.

The dragon dipped his head in agreement. "Yes, personality."

"But that is ridiculous. My hair and my skin do not dictate my personality."

"Of course they do not dictate," he snapped. "It is a reflection."

"But—"

"Do you wish to challenge me?" he asked, and though his tone was matter-of-fact, she felt anger boiling beneath his surface. So Lydia dipped her head, looking to her hands as he eventually spoke. "I do not know if you can understand such things, but do not try to correct your betters."

Her head would have snapped up then, if she had not exercised rigid control. The thought that this Chinese heathen considered himself her better was flatly preposterous. But, for the moment at least, he was stronger and had the keys to her jail cell. And so she would have to swallow her pride and keep silent, allowing him the illusion of dominance.

"Because I am a generous man," he continued, "I will instruct you as I can. Learn, and you will profit. Ignore me, and remain a stupid animal. It is your choice."

Her tongue got the better of her. Her head shot up and her hands clenched. "I am no animal! I am an Englishwoman, and you have no right to speak to me that way!"

He shook his head, his grimace almost mournful. "No constancy."

Fu De offered something from the background, his voice a quick-running river of Chinese sound, and once again the dragon nodded.

"Yes. It is the fault of all water souls. No constancy." He reached out, lifting her chin so that he could study her face. Despite her best efforts, tears were already flowing down her cheeks. And still he continued. "You are a water soul, prone to washing from one thing to the next. The moment you resolve to be strong, your will washes away and you speak and say things you do not want to. Is this not so?"

She tried to look away but could not. His eyes were too piercing, his words too true.

"Answer me!" he snapped. "Is that not so?"

"Yes," she finally ground out. "But if I am water, then you must be fire, for you snap and growl and burn!"

She had meant to insult him, to strike out in the only way she knew how—with her mind and her words. But instead of the flash of fury she expected, the dragon pulled back, his eyes wide with stunned surprise.

"You understand," he murmured. Then he glanced over at Fu De, who stood equally amazed in his spot in the doorway. She could not follow the Chinese they exchanged, but she understood the meaning. They could not believe she comprehended their primitive concepts.

She didn't know whether to be amused or angry at their reactions, but either way she had momentarily gained the advantage. So she pressed her point, shifting to her feet to stand before the dragon.

"So, now you know I am not a fool. Therefore it is wrong to keep me like an animal. It is wrong to hold me against my will." She hesitated, mortified that she needed to resort to pleading. But she did it anyway. And hoped. "Will you not release me? Please?"

She didn't know what she expected. Certainly she could not expect such an intellectual appeal to hold sway with a barbarian. Still, disappointment cut deeply into her heart when the monster's face hardened, and he roughly shoved her back on the bed.

"You are not completely stupid. But you are still a woman, and nine virtuous Chinese women are not the equal of even one lame boy. You, ghost woman, are worth even less than a Chinese woman. So you will obey me. And you will learn to the best of your ability. And perhaps when this is done, you will have profited more than you can imagine."

Truly angry now, she straightened as much as she could. "I imagine freedom. Will you give me that?"

She hadn't expected him to consider her request. But nothing in China went as she expected. She was stunned when he at last nodded.

"When this is done, I will consider releasing you."

She stared, hating the hope that sparked within her. It had already been extinguished so many times. "You will release me?"

"If you give me what I want."

Her blood chilled, but she forced herself to ask the obvious question. "Wh-what do you want?"

"Yin." And when she did not understand, he tried to explain. "Your water. Your womanly water to balance out my yang. My fire."

She swallowed, terribly afraid of what he meant. "My tears? You wish my tears?"

"I need a great deal more than that." Then he glanced out the window. "And it is time we began. Arrange yourself on the bed. Seated. Facing me."

She knew better than to refuse, but she moved as slowly as possible, terrible images forming in her mind. Did he mean to stab her? To bleed her as a means of getting her water? "If you hurt me, I could bleed. And if I bleed, I will die and you will get no water."

He started, his body jerking slightly as he settled on the bed. "I have no intention of bleeding you!" He sounded insulted. "I am an honorable man."

"Who keeps a female slave!"

He blinked, obviously not understanding. "Yes?"

And at that moment, she saw the truth in his eyes. "This is commonplace, isn't it? Many men keep women here." Her voice was a mere whisper, but he understood anyway.

"Of course. Such is the way with men and women."

She stiffened. "Such is not the way with men and women in England!"

"Then you should have stayed in England."

And right there was the crux of her problem. She had left England, left the safety and security of her home to come to China, a land where one woman was not more than a ninth the value of a single lame boy. And now . . .

She had no more thoughts as a hand reached out to untie her robe.

She scrambled backward, instinct taking control. From the doorway, Fu De sighed in frustration, and she saw fury build within the dragon. His face hardened, and the embroidered eye of his robe seemed to narrow in hatred.

"Return to your position," he said—not in a bellow, but a low hiss of controlled rage.

She swallowed, but could not otherwise make herself move.

"I have told you that my patience is at an end. If you will not present yourself for training, then Fu De shall make arrangements immediately for your return to the Garden of Perfumed Flowers."

The whorehouse. The terrible place where . . .

No, she resolved. No, she would not go back there. So she would have to do as she was ordered.

She moved slowly, but as she did, her thoughts kept returning to one question. How was this any better than that? How was the dragon any easier a taskmaster? After all, perhaps there she would have better opportunity to escape.

But in her heart, she knew that was not true. At least here she wasn't shackled or drugged. And yet that did not make obeying the monster's commands any easier. Nor any less humiliating.

Still, she knew she had pushed her luck too far. She returned to her place, kneeling in front of the dragon on the bed. And when he reached for the tie of her robe, she merely closed her eyes and tried not to breathe. Or sob. Or even to remain conscious.

He loosened the tie and pushed the robe off her shoulders. The silk slipped free to pool around her hips, covering everything from her waist down but leaving her entire upper body exposed.

Unbidden, tears began to flow from beneath her closed eyelids. Then she felt his hand, a brief touch on her left shoulder, and she flinched.

She could get through this, she repeated silently to herself. No matter what happened, she could survive. Eventually, she would find Maxwell again and everything would be all right. She would become his wife, they would have happy children, and everything would be all right. It would be all right.

Finally, she heard the monster sigh. It was such a strange, unexpected sound, that she opened her eyes in confusion, having to blink several times to clear her vision.

He was looking at her, his Chinese face unreadable, but

his sagging shoulders told her that he was disappointed. He even pulled her robe back around her, his movements reluctant and heavy.

Anger flashed within her. Well, what did he expect? That she would rush gleefully into ravishment? She reached up, gripping the fabric closed between her breasts.

"What is your name?" he asked, his voice abrupt but not hard with fury.

"I-I beg your pardon?" she stammered.

"Your name," he snapped. "What is your name?"

"L-Lydia." She swallowed back some of her misery to speak clearly. "My name is Lydia Smith."

"I am Ru Shan. In your language it means 'Like a Mountain,' in that I am steady and constant." He sighed. "Or I would be if all my elements were in balance."

She hesitated a moment, scrambling to fit the pieces together. It took a while, but eventually she thought she understood.

"That's why you need me. My water. You think that I will . . . will quiet your fire." This, at least, was a concept she recognized. She had heard other people—one of her uncles most especially—who became downright surly if he did not have relations with his mistress on a regular basis. Clearly, he was like her uncle, needing relations on a regular basis. "No matter what the country, men are still men," she intoned bitterly.

He nodded. "Yes, I suppose that is so, but I believe you will find a significant difference with me."

She did not respond, though she suspected her opinion was clear upon her face.

"You do not believe me," he said gently. "Fortunately, my nature does not require your approval. What I require is your yin. Your water."

She shook her head, frustration making her surly. "I don't know what that means."

"It means that I require your feminine fluids. But not your virginity."

She blinked, sure she could not have heard him correctly. "You do not intend to ravish me?"

He shuddered—he actually shuddered—at the thought. "I am working to become an Immortal. Ravishment, as you put it, would require a release of my yang power—my manly fluids and energy—into you. That would decrease my ability to attain Immortality."

She frowned, trying to understand. "But you need my female energy, my—"

"Yin."

"My yin to . . ."

"To mix with my yang energy and create the power that will take me to the Immortal Realm."

"You'll die?" she gasped.

She thought perhaps his expression lightened at her dramatic statement, but his tone remained level. "No. I will become an Immortal. Any man or woman can visit Heaven, but only if they have sufficient spirit to take them there."

"Spirit? You mean a mixture of your yang and my yin."

He nodded. "Yes."

"But that is . . ." She stopped herself short of saying ridiculous. She knew better than to insult any person's beliefs, no matter how preposterous they sounded. "It sounds impossible," she finally finished.

"Perhaps it is for one such as you."

She grimaced. "You mean a woman?"

He shook his head. "Many believe the women have an easier time, since their fluids stay within their bodies."

Then he looked sadly down at her. "It is impossible for ghost people."

She frowned. "Because I am English?"

"The ghost people do not have enough substance to attain immortality," he explained.

She stiffened, absurdly insulted. "But you seem to think my yin essence substantial enough for you."

He nodded. "In my particular case, you have exactly what I require. Or so I hope."

She opened her mouth to ask another question, but he stopped her with a single upraised hand.

"Enough questions," he said firmly. "I promise you that I have no interest in your virginity. I also promise that if you provide me with what I require, then I will release you to your Maxwell."

"My . . . I . . ." She swallowed, sure she could not have understood correctly. "You will return me to Maxwell? Still a virgin?" she pressed.

He nodded, one firm slash of his chin. "Yes. But first you must ready yourself to give of your yin." He straightened. "It will not hurt, especially as you have an overabundance. Now present yourself," he ordered. "I have already lost much time on you. I will not tolerate more delays."

She nodded, absurdly pleased with the bargain. After imagining every possible future for herself, this seemed ridiculously benign. "Do you want me to cry?"

"Do not draw away." And then, once again, he opened her robe, pushing it off her shoulders so it pooled about her hips.

She tried not to flinch. Indeed, now that she understood she was not about to be raped, she felt the burn of embarrassment more than fear. But then he pressed the four fingertips of each of his hands on her collarbone in the center of her chest.

She stiffened. She could not help herself.

He frowned. "How can you let your yin flow freely when your body is tight, your breath caught in your chest?"

She had not even realized she was holding her breath, yet even knowing that, she could not release it. She could only remain as she was, kneeling before him, her eyes pulled wide as she stared into his dark eyes.

"I am going to move my hands now. Slowly. Breathe out with my movement."

She couldn't even nod. But then he began to stroke his fingertips down on the hard bone between her breasts, and almost by magic her breath slid from her body.

"Good."

His hands continued, flowing underneath each breast, circling back around to the starting point.

"That is one circle," he said softly. "We will do seven times seven circles, and then seven times seven again in the other direction."

"But why?" The question was out before she could stop it, but he nodded as if pleased.

"We must purify your yin before it can be of any use." He began another circle, and she found herself breathing with his movements despite her curiosity. "This motion pushes the waste from your body and encourages new yin liquids to form. Do you feel a change in your body?"

She did, but she was too mortified to say so. Indeed, she had been doing everything in her power not to think of his hands as they circled her breasts, of the slightly rough texture of his fingers as they stroked her, of the warmth she felt seeping into her body from his hands. And most of all of the tingling he produced inside her. A tingling and a fullness.

"Tell me what you feel!" he ordered, his voice sharp. But his hands continued to move despite his tone. "I cannot tell if the exercises are working otherwise."

She swallowed, unnerved to have to say these things out loud. Certainly not in front of a stranger.

"Li-dee!" he snapped, mispronouncing her name.

"I . . . ," she stammered. "I . . . no one has ever touched me here before."

"Speak with the downstroke," he ordered, though his voice had gentled.

She nodded, adjusting her thoughts to his rhythms. "I do not think this is proper," she said. And then she closed her eyes in horror. Of all the ridiculous things to say! Of course this wasn't proper. None of this was proper. But what she meant was that these feelings he engendered, this tingling awareness, that was not proper.

"Why?" he pressed, as if he could guess her thoughts. "Your breasts are part of your body. Why is it not proper to make them young and healthy?"

She bit her lip. She had no answer.

"Perhaps you believe what you are feeling is wrong? Perhaps you enjoy this feeling and so you feel shame?"

She turned her head away. She knew better than to try and shrink from his touch. Besides, for some reason, she did not want to move away. She found his strokes . . . soothing somehow. And all the more unsettling because of it.

"Look at me!" he ordered, and she had no choice but to obey. "This is a restful stroke. One designed to bring peace to the woman. Is that how you feel?"

She nodded, though not with certainty.

"You feel more than peace?"

She wet her lips. She could tell by the intensity in his expression, by the focused stare of his dark eyes that she would have to answer. And so she tried to explain. "I feel uncertain," she said. And then her eyes dropped in shame. "And it feels . . . nice."

He smiled. It was a small movement, but one that softened every feature in his Chinese face. As if he removed a tiny bit of his mask to reveal a gentleness she had not expected. "Honesty is good. Honesty with me is excellent. Honesty with oneself is absolutely necessary." Then he leaned forward, his voice dropping lower as his breath skated across her cheek. "I am going to reverse the stroke now. Look into my eyes and tell me exactly how it feels. What you feel. Do not think of me or of anything but my hands on your breasts."

She flinched slightly at his bald word, but then chided herself for such stupidity. He had been touching her for a good twenty minutes or more; why would he draw back from simple words? He was touching her breasts, she told herself firmly. And it felt . . .

"Tell me!"

She nodded, the movement unsteady. Then she did as she was told, setting her gaze on the fold of his eyelid, the dark circle of his eyes. This close, she could see the individual colors in his eyes. The iris was actually a circle of very dark brown hues radiating out from the black pupil in the center. It was bizarre to be thinking such things, and yet, the sight of his eyes gave her such an expansive feeling. As if she were slowly flowing outward from him. From the center of his eyes.

Then, she began to breathe with his stroke; exhaling as he began the downstroke, this time on the outside of her breasts, to circle underneath. As he drew his fingertips up

through the center of her chest, she inhaled, simultaneously drawing his hands up and pushing them deeper into
her skin.

"I feel the heat of your hands," she finally said. "They
are so large. I know it is not possible, but I feel as if you are
leaving a part of you behind with each movement. And that
I . . ."

"You what?"

She inhaled deeply. "I am meeting it. I am meeting your
heat, your fingers."

"That is your yin, rising to greet my yang. Tell me
more."

"My br . . ." She could not say the word. "I am so warm.
I feel as if I am growing. Expanding." Was it his eyes, or
his touch that was doing this to her?

And then something changed. There was a build-up of
pressure, a swelling of some kind. Abruptly, her breath became tighter, more erratic. She tried to remain calm, but
she could not. It was as if a fountain had sprung up inside
her, welling up and up until her chest then her head began
to swell. And with her gasp, it exploded. Quietly. But loud
enough that she felt and heard a bang inside her ears.

"Oh!" she said. "I . . . there was . . . a sound." She could
not express it any more clearly than that.

"That was your body throwing off its age," he responded, and she found herself grasping the soothing notes
of his voice, using them to ground herself as yet another
wave began to build.

"I don't understand," she whispered, unable to find enough
breath to speak normally.

"You do not need to understand. Only accept. You are
growing more youthful with every moment."

"But—"

"You are avoiding your feelings. Tell me what you feel."

She flushed, knowing he was right. She would much rather think about his bizarre philosophies than about the way her breath was completely keyed to his movements, her entire body throbbing to his stroke.

"I feel . . . everything." All of it. Focused on her breasts, flowing toward her breasts, aching inside her breasts. "I am so full." She had no idea what she was saying, but he apparently did. She watched his eyes crinkle as he smiled.

"We are almost done. Let everything flow to your breasts. Let them grow full. Let them understand what it means to be breasts."

She barely heard him, so wonderful was the experience of fullness. It was all drawing together, pushing toward some peak that she did not understand. That she wanted desperately.

And then it was over, and he drew his hands away. So startling was the moment that she actually cried out when he withdrew. She looked down at her chest as if such a movement could draw him back to her.

What she saw amazed her even more. Her breasts were pink and peaked, full and yet not nearly as large as she felt. It was as if her spirit had grown outward from her physical body. She even drew her hand up, holding it just beyond her skin. And she could swear she could feel it: the heat of her own hand, the pressure of her body against her hand, though she never touched herself at all.

She looked at her captor, confusion filling her.

"You must do this every morning and every night," he instructed. "To yourself if I cannot be here to assist you." Her hand was still held before her, a bare inch away from her skin. "But whatever you do, do not touch yourself here." He took hold of her hand, tilting it so that it cupped but did not touch her nipple. "This is your peak."

And as he said the words, her hand jerked, pushing forward toward the tip of her breasts. It had not been her intention to do so, and yet she now knew that was what she wanted. That was where she wished to be touched.

"Do not do it!" he ordered. "It will damage the work that we have already done." She looked up at him as his eyes narrowed in annoyance. "Do you have the discipline to do this? To keep yourself from touching there? Or must I chain your hands away?"

She pulled back in horror. "Do not chain me!"

"Then listen to what I say."

She nodded, her breasts feeling full and heavy and aching for the very thing he had just denied her.

"I will return tonight. I do not think you can be trusted."

She straightened, insulted by the implication. "I—"

"Fu De will watch you during the day. Look for me this evening, and we will continue." Then he abruptly drew her robe back around her, careful to prevent the fabric from touching her aching breasts. He couldn't prevent it entirely, but what little did touch made her feel all the worse. She could feel the fabric about her, so close, so cool and silky. And yet she already knew that such a whisper of touch would not be enough. She wished for more.

Evening could not come fast enough. To her shame, she desperately wanted to return to what they had been doing. And that thought horrified her more than anything else.

She was a good English girl, raised to be chaste and modest. What was she thinking, what was she doing to so want a Chinese man to touch her like that? To do to her . . . what?

Her body tingled in excitement, and her mind rebelled at

her own eagerness. She was a captive, she reminded herself. A prisoner. Her only hope was to watch for a moment when she could escape, when she could rush outside and on to find Maxwell.

And yet, as the outer door shut behind the dragon. . . What was his name? Ru Shan. As the door shut behind Ru Shan and Fu De came to stand in her doorway, watching her, Lydia could only think over her strange morning and her bizarre experiences. What was happening to her?

Worse, if she was in such turmoil after one such session with Ru Shan, what would she be like by the time she was finally able to escape?

From the letters of Mei Lan Cheng

3 February, 1862
Dearest Li Hua—
    A son! A son! I have given birth to a son! And such a handsome boy he is that all say he takes after his father. They have even named him Ru Shan for "steadiness as a mountain." This may seem odd to you, but you do not understand my mother-in-law. My husband is a handsome man, full of life and vigor. With my designs, the Chengs have prospered greatly.
    But not so greatly as one might expect.
    My husband loves his friends almost as much as he loves his customers. His father tries to moderate the damage, but Sheng Fu's temper is easily unleashed, and he is a large man with heavy fists. As he is the one who brings in the customers, he rules even over his parents.
    And so, when my son was born with a face so like his father's, my parents-in-law named him Ru Shan

for steadiness. He will be the Chengs' hope for a wealthy old age.

What they do not know is that I have already made offerings for the child before the ancestors and at the monastery. I escaped one day when I was supposed to be buying vegetables. Instead, I rushed to the monastery and gave them all the money I had saved from our food. You know how excellent a bargainer I am, so it was quite a lot of money.

They promised me that the boy will be a great scholar. And truly, his head is very large, his brow most auspicious for study. He will be a great sage, perhaps even an Immortal. I have been assured of this!

I must stop now, Li Hua. My labor has kept me from my work, and so I am very behind. Write me soon and tell me if you have made amends with your mother-in-law. Truly, they are the most terrible of creatures!

—Mei Lan

Where there are humans, you'll find flies and Buddha.

—Issa

Chapter Four

The abacus beads hit with a satisfying *clack,* but the numbers still were too low and Ru Shan sighed. The family was depending upon him to make good on the promise of his name—Steady as a Mountain—or as grandmother phrased it, a Mountain of Wealth. Either way, he was not proving himself capable.

After Ma Ma's death, the customers simply were not as interested in the Cheng cloth as before. With good reason. Without Ma Ma, the embroidered designs were not as inspired.

"Your brow is furrowed, and your face burns. I sense that your yang still dominates."

He looked up, grateful for and surprised by the interruption Shi Po provided, even though he knew she would buy nothing from him. Her husband was his nearest competitor, and so it would be a grave error if she were to be seen purchasing his wares. Indeed, it was a risk for her to even appear in his family store. So he immediately stood, ushering her to the tiny garden behind his shop. At least there she would be safe from most prying eyes.

She nodded graciously, walking with great difficulty upon her bound feet, her tiny hands gripping the carved ivory cane she sometimes used. He wished to support her, to carry her, but he could not. It was not his place. And so he could only watch in excruciating stillness as she passed before him.

Glancing outside, he saw her four men waiting for her, her ornate sedan settled upon the street between them. "Was it necessary to come here in so public a fashion?" he asked as she at last made it out the door.

"Of course," she said with a smile, "as I am personally delivering an invitation for you to share wine with my husband next week." She handed him the thin paper, etched with gold leaf.

"You do me a great honor," he lied. The truth was that her tight-fisted husband wished to check up on the loan he had given to buy Li Dee. Ru Shan still did not know how Shi Po had convinced her husband to offer such a generous sum. Likely, with her tigress skills, she had Kui Yu completely at her mercy. Either way, Ru Shan did not appreciate this invitation.

He would, of course, attend the dinner despite his feelings. Not to do so would be a grave insult, and he could not risk offending either his benefactor or his teacher. Of course, none of that explained the true reason for Shi Po's sudden appearance in his store. But once again, it would be impolite for him to ask. So he waited patiently and they conversed about the early spring, the flowers in his garden, and even the carved stone that sat in the center of his goldfish pond.

At last, Shi Po came to the point. "How does it fare with your new pet?"

He hesitated, unable to settle in his mind exactly how things were going with Li Dee. Finally, he decided on the most obvious. "She is not what I expected."

"And what did you expect?"

He shook his head. "She is both more intelligent than I had thought and more nervous."

"She has settled into her training then? She has accepted her fate?"

He nodded. "By all appearances, yes." Of course, now that he had an idea that she was not as stupid as her other countrymen, he wondered if she could be deceiving him. Was she indeed smart enough to pretend to accept her life? He already knew the answer was yes, and yet he had not thought any ghost person, least of all a woman, could possibly plan that far ahead. Not a one of his English customers could delay their amusements for a moment, much less plan for opportunities ahead of them.

And yet, he was already aware that Li Dee was not like his ghost customers.

"You have begun her training?" asked Shi Po, interrupting his musings.

"Today. And more this evening. But she is like a nervous hare, very difficult to settle." He sighed. "I believe it is the water in her that makes her inconstant." Except, of course, the water would make her flexible, not agitated as she had already demonstrated.

Shi Po's tinkling laughter startled him. He stiffened at her insult, which naturally made her laugh even more. "So much yang, Ru Shan," she said, humor still lacing her tone. "You forget that she is English. You cannot expect her to simply throw open her clothing with lustful abandon. These ghost people are dried up and insubstantial. They cannot understand the finer philosophies, and so they try to control their animal passions the only way they can: by stopping them entirely. Their children are taught from birth not to enjoy anything of their bodies." She reached out, gently touching his hand. "Surely you understand this. So many of our own countrymen make this same mistake. You can hardly blame the ghost people for such ignorance."

He nodded, knowing it was true. And yet, Li Dee did not seem too stupid to understand, merely uneducated. But either way, Shi Po was right. Li Dee was obviously anxious. He had thought she would embrace her experiences as any other Englishman he knew—wholeheartedly, without any thought to the consequences. Apparently, Englishwomen, or perhaps *this* Englishwoman, were very different.

"Now . . . what do I do? Her water runs deep. I have already felt it. How . . ." His voice trailed off as he struggled to phrase his thoughts.

"How can you use her yin to balance your spirit?"

"Yes."

"You must tell her your secrets."

He stiffened, shocked by her suggestion. He had not even told Shi Po his secrets, and she was tigress to his dragon. Few more intimate relationships existed. Here she was suggesting he reveal his soul to a white woman?

Beside him, he heard Shi Po sigh, clearly frustrated. "Do you wish her to give you of her innermost self?"

He nodded, for the purified yin could not flow otherwise.

"Then you must give of yourself as well."

"But—"

"Listen, Ru Shan. I have told you that you are the arrow. She is only the bow that aims you toward the middle path of the Tao. If you do not understand her, and understand the ghost people through her, how will you ever understand why killing a white man has taken you from the middle path?"

"But I have no secrets," he lied.

"Begin tonight. Tell her your thoughts." Then she shook her head. "No, you must tell her your feelings. That is the root of yin. She will not understand your thoughts, but your voice will calm her. Animals can sense when you speak from the heart. And when you do, she will share her feelings—her yin—with you. In the end, you will find your balance."

Ru Shan stood, shaking his head vehemently. "It cannot work as you say."

She looked at him, her gaze steady and hard. "I have seen it, Ru Shan. I know it to be true."

He felt his breath catch in awe. "You have attained immortality?"

She licked her lips, then slowly, sadly, let her gaze slip away. "I have gained a higher level. In the Chamber of a Thousand Swinging Lanterns. Once there, I hear things. I feel things. But no," she sighed. "I am not an Immortal yet."

He softened, coming to sit beside her again. "Soon, Shi Po. Soon we will both walk the heavenly gardens together."

Her hands twisted in her lap. "I have long wished for such a thing, Ru Shan. But you cannot progress—you have not progressed since that night. We will never walk together, Ru Shan, unless you do this." She looked at the garden path, no doubt gauging the time by the lengthening afternoon shadows. "It is late. I must go." Then, abruptly, she reached out and gripped his fingers. "You must go as well. Speak from your heart to the ghost girl. And then we can return to our studies together."

Ru Shan nodded, though the movement was slow and reluctant. "I will try."

"You must *succeed*," she corrected as she allowed him to help her stand. "You must succeed or all your work—all *our* work—these last nine years will be for nothing."

Fu De opened the door quickly, but Ru Shan didn't enter. Instead, he stood and twisted his hands together inside his robe. He knew better than to show anxiety in front of his servant. He knew it was the height of folly to be anxious before visiting his own slave. And yet despite the way it looked to Fu De, despite the silent recriminations he screamed at himself, he couldn't force his feet to cross the threshold. Not until he resolved exactly what he intended to do.

Naturally, Fu De did not question his master's bizarre behavior; he merely stood to one side of the door, his face impassive. And when Ru Shan continued to stand there in silence, Fu De offered a single comment.

"She has been very unsettled all day."

Ru Shan's gaze sharped on him. "Why?"

Fu De bowed deeply. "You have chosen well. I believe her yin is beginning to flow and she does not know how to manage or release it."

"I don't want her to release it. Not yet. Not until I am here to absorb it."

Fu De's expression lightened into an ironic smile. "Then it is most fortunate that you are here now to help her." He shook his head in dismay. "The ghost people truly are closed to their passions. It is no wonder so many of them are insane."

Ru Shan nodded, understanding Shi Po's words completely. Without access to higher understanding of their

energies, the white people had no choice but to either release their passions in wanton displays of recklessness or
stop them up entirely and risk madness. Clearly the white
men chose the path of licentiousness, while their women
were expected to dry themselves up into old prunes. Neither path would bring enlightenment—or even good judg-
ment.

Ru Shan sighed. No matter what his own reservations
were, he had begun the change in Li Dee. Because of his
actions, her yin had begun to flow. It was now his responsibility to aid her in controlling and directing that energy.

With her health in mind, he crossed into the tiny quarters. As he did, he felt a wash of relief flow through him. It
was Li Dee's yin, of course, strong enough to saturate even
the air. And as some of it settled into his soul, he began to
think more clearly, more logically.

If nothing else, this feeling of relief showed that Shi Po
had steered him correctly. His own balance would be restored by the white woman's yin. It was logical, therefore,
to assume she was correct about the next step as well. He
had to talk to Li Dee, opening up not only his body to her
energy, but also his mind and soul. Only then would he return to balance.

It had to be done. He would begin talking to her. But
first, he had to drain off some of her yin and thereby settle
her body.

He crossed firmly into the second room, pushing the
door open. She was there, waiting for him, her robe tied
neatly about her body, her golden hair braided down her
back. She appeared to be in complete control, even if her
hands were knotted tightly in her lap. Then he looked into
her eyes. Those blue eyes were stormy today—the color of
the sea on an evil day. Fu De's assessment was correct: Her

yin had begun to flow, and she hadn't the slightest understanding of what to do about it.

Ru Shan stepped forward, and she flinched. He had not made any threatening movement, and yet she was already more skittish than before.

"You are feeling unsettled," he said in English.

She nodded, once.

"Why?"

She wet her lips, and he felt his body hunger for the moisture she left there. But he did not betray his hunger. Instead, he watched her with an intensity that startled him. They were like polar opposites, yin and yang drawn magnetically toward one another.

"Do you know why you feel unhappy?" he repeated.

Her body sagged slightly in annoyance. "Perhaps because I am a slave? Because my freedom, my future, possibly my life have been taken from me?"

He nodded, knowing those things were all true, but dismissing them. "It is the nature of women to be locked away. They cannot be trusted in the world of men."

"It is in the nature of men to lock us away because they are the ones who cannot be trusted."

He felt himself smile despite his intentions. He had not thought a woman could be so clever with words. Certainly not a white woman. And yet here was Li Dee, bantering with him like the most skilled of courtesans.

"You may be correct," he said, surprised that he was already feeling charitable toward her. "But this is your situation. You have had ample time to accept it."

She sighed, the sound more like the flow of a swift, deep river than the arid sound of a week before. "I do not like it." Then she let her head drop in the way of all submissive females. "But I have accepted it."

He stepped forward, reaching out to lift her chin. She did not resist him when he tilted her head back to make her look at him. "Your yin has begun to flow," he explained to her. "It is time to continue to purify it. I will also try and drain some of the energy off of you." He saw the flash of panic in her eyes and rushed to explain. "It will not hurt. You may even like it."

Far from soothing, his words seemed to spark in her a further panic. Her breath caught as if dammed up, then stuttered out of her in a gasp. She tried to pull away, but he could not release her. He had to make her understand.

"You are afraid because you have been taught this is wrong. You have been told to stop your . . ." He struggled for the right words in English. "Your womanly water. Your energy. They have told you that it is wrong to feel this flow."

She frowned, as if she were trying to sort out his words.

"Did they tell you never to touch yourself? As a child, did you ever try to talk to someone about your bodily fluids, only to have them hush you into silence?"

She nodded. "My aunt told me it was sinful to talk of such things."

Ru Shan exhaled in disgust. "That is ignorance of the highest order. How can a person learn if something is not talked about?"

She didn't answer. She obviously knew he was correct.

"Your fluids, your female energy and power—they are all natural. They are a normal part of your body. How can any of that be sinful?"

She shook her head. "I don't know."

"But that is what you were taught."

She nodded.

"I am teaching you differently." And with that, he shifted

his tunic and settled on the bed before her. "Come. Let us begin."

She must have sensed his impatience, because she did not fight him. Her hands shook as she knelt before him, just as they had this morning, but beyond that she gave no sign of her turmoil. In truth, he felt some pity for her. It was not only the English who taught their daughters these ridiculous things. The Chinese, too, repressed their women with nearly as much zeal. But he could not allow his compassion to show. In the way of all animals, Li Dee would capitalize on his weakness, trying to delay what she feared. She needed this training as much as he needed to give it. And so when her hands fumbled with her robe, he pushed them aside, throwing the garment off her shoulders with a quick flick of his wrists.

And there they were: her breasts. Gloriously pink and white, already peaked in readiness. The evening light was dim, adding a slight touch of shadow to her flesh, but it only made her appear more milky white. In short, her skin was beautiful. She had indeed done well to keep such youthfulness in while her female energies were stopped. How much more would she glow once the yin began to flow freely? He actually smiled in anticipation.

"What—Why are you smiling?" Her high voice betrayed her anxiety.

"I am pleased with your skin. It has excellent tone and texture." For proof, he reached out and stroked the edge of one breast. Her breath stuttered within her as she unconsciously continued to block her energy flow, and he felt the ripple in his fingers as that energy lurched within her body.

He knew he needed to talk more. When he did, she focused on his words, allowing him to work with her body more freely. And so he began to explain. "I am now looking at the shape of your breasts. They tell me much about you."

She frowned. "What can they . . . what can you . . ." She bit her lip, then once again wet her mouth with her pink, darting tongue. "What do you learn from them? About me?"

"Your breasts are what we call bells. See how they are round and full below."

To demonstrate, he opened both his palms, sliding them slowly and gently beneath her breasts, lifting them slightly. He was pleased to note that she did not flinch. Indeed, she was concentrating on his words, watching what his hands were doing as he spoke, and so her breath steadied and her body stilled.

"This tells me that you matured early and have strong passions." She did not disagree with him, so he continued. "But see how your nipples flare outward, their peaks pointing not straight ahead, but to opposite sides. It is as if your yin wants to go in two different directions instead of straight ahead."

To demonstrate, he pushed her breasts straight, then let them ease back into their wider, more natural position.

"This tells me that you will have ample energy for all of your children, when they come, but without children to care for, you are pulled in too many directions without control. You are . . ."

"Impetuous."

He blinked, not knowing the English word.

"It means I rush ahead without thinking things through. My mother always said I go every which way without purpose."

"Your mother is correct. Because your energy is headed in different directions, it is doubly hard for your mind to contain your passions." He smiled at her. "But I will help you find a way to channel them."

She nodded, clearly not reassured. But she knew she had no choice in this matter, and her acquiescence pleased him.

"I will begin just like this morning."

He flattened his hand, pressing three fingertips on the inside of each breast. Her flesh was warm, her skin soft, but that was nothing compared to the fluttering beat of her heart, which seemed to tremble just beneath his hands. He wanted to press his palms deeply against her, feeling her breath as it flowed through her, thrumming with the beating of her heart.

He didn't understand these feelings. Certainly he had never felt like this with Shi Po. But, then, he was not the one who had initiated her into her tigress practice. He only knew that the task before him was simple, the most basic of beginnings. And yet it had never seemed so important. Li Dee watched, her water-colored eyes wide with anticipation, and he felt the weight of her entire soul focused directly upon him.

He moved his fingers, sliding them between her breasts before making a tight circle beneath her nipples, then back up again.

"Your hands are so warm," she whispered.

He nodded, again pleased that she was speaking so easily with him. "That is my yang fire. It has always been so with me."

One circle completed. The second circle begun.

"This is not the same as it was this morning."

His gaze shot to her face, surprised that his attention had been so focused on her breasts. Surprised, too, that she had noticed the change in his stroke.

"You are correct," he answered evenly, though it took a great deal of effort to keep his voice calm and his strokes even. "This morning was a simple introduction. What I am doing now is how we will proceed in the future. Can you explain what is different?"

"Of course I can." She sounded irritated, and so he focused on keeping an even pace to help soothe her. "You are . . . your hands are making smaller circles. Nearer my . . . my . . ."

"Your nipples."

"Yes."

"You may use the words here. It will make it easier if I don't have to guess what you mean."

She nodded, but didn't speak.

"Yes, this is a beginning stroke, designed to smooth over any restrictions in your yin flow. We begin in tight circles around your nipples then slowly widen each circle."

"But you are only touching my . . ." She swallowed, clearly working against a lifetime of silence when it came to her body. "My breasts," she finally said. "What if my yin is restricted in my arm? Or my leg?"

"Yin is centered here." He passed his hands over her nipples without touching them. And as had happened this morning, she gasped at his movement and he felt the heat of her yin straining toward him. "There will be no restriction in your arms and legs unless you have injured yourself."

She shook her head, and her breasts jiggled in his hands, momentarily brushing against the tops of his knuckles. It was such a pleasant experience that he flattened his hands even more, pressing first four then all five of his fingers against her. Until he circled beneath her breasts. Then he lifted his wrists, enjoying the feel of her breasts as they brushed across the sides and backs of his fingers.

At last he completed the outermost circle. It was time to begin again, right next to her flushed, pointed nipple. How wonderful it would be to taste it. His mouth watered at the thought, and his eyes were riveted on her peaks. Was there any moisture there yet? Was she that overflowing?

The answer, of course, was no. She was nowhere near ready, and so he continued his circles, starting in close, then steadily expanding.

Soon, the exercise began to work. Her questions faded. Her breath keyed to his movements, exhaling on the downstroke, inhaling on the up. He too began to breathe rhythmically, to flow with the sensations of her skin sliding beneath his fingertips, her breath heating his face, while his gaze remained transfixed by her growing, blushing breasts.

"Forty-nine." His mouth was dry, his voice rough. He wanted her water so desperately, and yet he knew he had to be patient.

Shifting his hands, he began the next step, circling in the opposite direction, in a wide motion that steadily narrowed toward her nipple. "Now that we have brushed away any blockages, it is time to encourage good flow."

She had closed her eyes, no doubt concentrating on the changes in her body, but now she opened them, gazing at him with a dazed, unfocused look. "Will I begin to produce milk? As if I'd had a baby?"

What a surprise she was, understanding what many took weeks to grasp. "Not unless you wish it. Your body will produce something else. A different kind of water."

She nodded as if she understood. She didn't, of course. She couldn't. Not until her yin milk began to flow. And so he began his circles, touching her with as much of his hands as he dared, always longing for more, always wishing . . .

Once again, both Ru Shan and the woman's attentions focused on her body, her breathing, her very fluids. And for a time, they seemed to become as one. His touch regulated her breath, which flowed into him, so that his own breath could not begin until hers did, his own heart could not beat unless with hers. And with each ever-tightening circle, he felt her heart speed up, her breath whisper across her open lips with increasing speed. Her yin was accelerating, moving. Soon it would flow. Soon . . .

But then he finished just beneath and around her nipples. He had to begin the circle again from down along her sides. Her breath slowed, and her heart, and he returned to the quieter place. Except, of course, he was not as relaxed as she. He knew what was to come. He knew and wanted and waited, his yang fire burning hotter than ever inside him.

If only he could have some of her essence to cool his heat. Then he would be able to sleep again, at least for tonight. He would be able to breathe fully again, without a scorched, cracked throat.

Forty-seven circles.

Forty-eight.

Forty-nine.

He could not stop himself. He had to see if she was ready. He needed to touch her nipples just once. And so even though he knew better, he pulled his fingers tighter, stroking the last of the yin flow, pulling it to her full, erect nipples and squeezing to release it.

She cried out in her alarm, her body shuddering, but he did not release her. He pulsed his fingers—once, twice, even a third time—while she shivered in reaction.

It was too soon. He knew that. Her nipples remained bone dry. Worse, her eyes were wide with confusion. Her jade gate and her womb had not convulsed, of this he was certain. But her body trembled, trying to flow through breasts after only one day in training.

"It feels . . . I feel . . ." She did not have the words, and he could not blame her.

Carefully he withdrew his hands, drawing her robe back around her, covering her completely. She drew her arms together over her breasts, pressing her hands tight against them.

He explained, "The fault is entirely mine. You were not ready." He reached out, gently pulling her fists away from her chest. "I will not rush you again."

"But, what is happening?"

"You feel a fullness in your breasts?"

She nodded.

"That is your yin. The more we work like this, the more ready your nipples will be to open, releasing your yin milk. But your body has not had time to adjust, and so the passageway was blocked even as the yin pressed against it. That creates confusion in your body as it both flows forward and is held back." He lifted her fingers to his mouth where he pressed dry kisses to her knuckles. "Do not judge me by this, Li Dee. I will be more respectful in the future."

She nodded and slowly withdrew her hands from his. The session was over, her training done for this day. She would accept no more from him. And so he bowed deeply to her, trying to express his apology. A woman's yin—even a white slave's yin—was always to be respected. And he had failed in that.

Deeply ashamed, he turned and left.

From the letters of Mei Lan Cheng

10 March, 1869
Dearest Li Hua—

How fortunate you are to live deep inside great China. The barbarians have not only come to Shanghai, but they have overrun it! The village is nothing like I remember only a few years ago. The Chinese city is nearly surrounded by the white apes, and none of them are like Father Dodd.

You remember the white missionary who lived near us? I used to play with his daughter, and she taught me to speak English. Now I wish I had never learned, because the white apes here are not at all like Father Dodd's family. They are noisy and belligerent and smell terrible! But my husband thinks they are the best of people: easily flattered and wealthy beyond measure. He says the white apes are like ghosts who have too little soul to keep anything. Those of them that have the fortune to make much money cannot hold it. They spend and spend and spend, looking for the trappings of substance.

He thinks they are Heaven's means to give us money. I know only that I am afraid of them and wish to run away whenever I am called to translate for a customer. I have prayed and prayed to the ancestors that these ghost people will soon grow tired of Shanghai and leave forever, but they have not given me any sign at all. I do not know if I have fallen into disfavor or if their power is nothing against these barbarians.

But there is one thing, Li Hua. These ghost people sell a powder that my mother-in-law likes very much. It is expensive, but after she smokes it, she is quiet for many hours, leaving me to work in peace. But lately, it has not been enough for her. She wants more and more and gets very angry when she does not have any.

Truly, Li Hua, I do not think these ghost people have brought anything good to China.

—Mei Lan

Twirl the lotus, but do not harm the petals
The Dragon plays in the tigress's cave.
—White tigress manual

Chapter Five

Lydia released her breath in a slow, controlled movement. She focused on the passing of air over her wet lips, the contraction of her mouth muscles and the shift in her shoulders. She did not want to think about the fullness in her breasts, the tingling that seemed to hit her unawares from different spots all over her body, or, most especially, the strange moisture lower down on her body.

What she thought about now was her captor, Ru Shan. He might claim his name meant steady as a mountain, but he'd been everything but steady with her—one moment kind, the next demanding, the next cruel. When he was kind, she was often tempted to soften toward him, to think him human after all. Especially during his so-called training sessions. The feelings he generated in her . . .

But she was not thinking of that now. She was reminding herself that despite his obvious shame a moment ago, despite his clear apology and the tenderness with which he'd kissed her fingers, he was still her captor. And she would do well to remember it.

Fortunately, she had one huge advantage. Ru Shan was a man, and in the way of all men, he thought he understood what she was thinking. He was completely wrong, of course, and therein lay her power.

He believed she had accepted her captivity. Wrong. She was only pretending, waiting for her opportunity to escape.

He believed he was readying her body for some mystical flow of yin. In truth, he was merely preparing her body to accept his lascivious attention. Even she—an innocent in these matters—knew he was simply covering sexual hunger. And yet . . .

She sighed. There were some things he was correct about. She had been taught not to think of her body or these sensations at all. When he touched her, she felt—still continued to feel—a kind of growing. Not just a physical swelling, though she supposed there was a good deal of that. Her breasts felt fuller than ever before. As if they projected another foot more in front of her. Except, looking down, they seemed the same size they always had been. They just *felt* larger.

But it was more than that. Ru Shan thought his last touch, the one on her nipple, had created a confusion in her body. There had been no confusion. Her body had liked it and wanted more of it. The conflict had come from her mind. She had felt on the verge of a change—a mind change, a soul change. As if from that moment on, she could never go back, never return to who and what she had been.

That alone was what frightened her. She felt poised on the precipice of something huge. Soon Ru Shan would push her over the edge, and she might never find her way back. And even worse, part of her longed to make the leap. There was something more here. Something to discover. But shouldn't this be done within the sacred bounds of matrimony? Shouldn't she be learning these things with Maxwell?

Of course she should be. But somehow, she couldn't imagine her beloved Maxwell taking the time to circle her breasts with fingertips so warm they felt like the folds of a heated towel. And with a stroke so tender and mesmerizing as to lull her into a kind of trance. Not just a half-asleep trance, but long moments of such awareness that she seemed to merge with her captor. She felt as if she was both Lydia Smith feeling a Chinaman's touch and the Chinaman too, Ru Shan and his hands moving over her.

It was an amazing experience. Sensual, yes, but more as well. Expansive enough that she would risk a great deal just to continue learning.

So, if she could not learn this with Maxwell—could *never* learn such things from him—then why not take the training from the man who could teach her? No matter the circumstances. Perhaps she could even later teach Maxwell.

She shook her head. No, she realized, she could never mention this to Maxwell, much less teach him. The man was morally upright in all his thoughts and manners. This experience—no matter that it was certainly not her choice—would appall him.

Which, of course, brought her back to her initial dilemma. Should she embrace this training, learn what she could despite the circumstances? Or should she risk everything and anything on escape, now, before she tumbled into the abyss?

In the end, she resolved to do both. She would build upon Ru Shan's false belief that she had accepted her captivity. And if any opportunity came—however remote—to escape, she would seize it. And she would pray that it came before too late.

Her first target was not Ru Shan, but his agent Fu De. She had already begun tracking the young man's movements and tasks. He obviously lived here, for she rarely saw him leave. When he did, he locked both her door and the outside door—she heard the sound of the metal clicking of a very English deadbolt. Whenever he opened her bedroom door, she caught sight of his pallet right next to the cooking supplies in one corner of the outer room.

In short, he was almost as much a prisoner as she. So her best bet was to gain his trust and somehow manufacture an escape. But how?

She didn't have to think long before she came up with an answer. What must plague Fu De almost as much as it plagued her? Boredom. And what was her greatest weakness when trying to find her way in this strange land? Her lack of language skills—she could neither speak nor read Chinese well enough to navigate.

Therefore, she would play on Fu De's boredom and get him to teach her his language.

Smoothing her hair and clothing as best she could, Lydia stood and knocked on her door. As always happened, Fu De was quick to respond. But as she'd learned before, he was also lightning fast and amazingly strong; she could not run past him no matter how hard she tried.

So, this time after he opened her door, she smiled winningly at him—or in a manner she hoped he found appealing.

"Time moves so slowly in China," she sighed.

He did not respond, but she hadn't truly expected him to. Mostly, she was hoping he understood her English.

"Aren't you bored?" she asked, hoping to see some response in his expression.

Nothing.

Obviously subtlety wasn't going to work. It was time to try the direct approach.

"I want to learn to read and write Chinese. Can you help me?"

Again, nothing. Neither his eyes nor his body betrayed his thoughts.

"I will help you speak English. I have taught children before." Well, she'd helped her niece with schoolwork once on the nanny's day off. "Speaking English will help you get a very lucrative job," she offered. Maxwell had once said that the English-speaking Chinese earned a king's ransom here.

Damn. Maybe he didn't speak English at all. But she'd thought he'd shown signs of understanding her before. It was time to try her very, very bad Chinese.

"Wo yao xue zhongguo hua." *I want to speak Chinese.* Or that was what she hoped she'd said.

The boy shook his head. "Shanghai-hua."

Progress! He was talking to her. But what had he said?

"Shanghai-hua? Shanghai talk? Yes! Wo yao xue Shanghai-hua."

He nodded, and she thought his lips curved upward just the tiniest bit. Then he said, equally slowly, "I want Englit speak." Then he moved his hand. "Write."

She nodded vigorously. "Yes!" Then she frowned. "Hao!" *Good.* "Hun hao." *Very good.*

"Mey hao."

She frowned, trying to understand.

It took her a while—days, actually—but eventually she realized the language she had learned from the missionary at home was actually Peking Chinese. What she needed to learn was Shanghai Chinese—an entirely different dialect. Fortunately, Fu De understood both, though he was better at Shanghainese.

She sighed. So much she hadn't realized, hadn't even guessed, before leaving England. Who would have thought a country would have more than one language? That Chinese was, in fact, many different dialects, entirely separate from one another?

Well, she thought with a slight shrug, there was no time like the present to start setting things to rights. She and Fu De began teaching each other right away.

It became clear as well that they both wished to learn how to write. She set him to copying the alphabet. Fu De handed her a bucket of water and a large sponge brush, indicating she should practice her writing on the floor. Dipping her brush in the water, she could form Chinese characters, seeing the strokes clearly on the cement until the hot air evaporated the water.

Fu De bought paper and ink, along with strange Chinese brushes for writing, but apparently paper was very dear. And so, he took another brush and began writing English letters in the same manner as he'd shown to her. Day after day, they stood side by side writing on the floor, the air drying their mistakes and their triumphs. And in this way they began a tentative friendship.

Except that, in all this time, Fu De never relaxed his guard and Ru Shan continued to visit morning and night to continue her other training.

Lydia found herself once again faced with the perplexing question that was Ru Shan. He was extremely respectful, never once expanding the scope of what he did to her. In truth, the part of her that reveled in what he was doing truly wanted more speed, more experience. But he would not hurry. Plus, whenever he arrived for a session, he bowed to her as he approached, and bowed again as he departed. He spoke honestly with her, almost reverently, often complimenting her on her progress—though in truth she did nothing more than experience what he did to her. And he always, always thanked her for her time—as if she had a choice in the matter.

But for all that, she never once forgot that he was the master, she the slave. Especially when one evening, over a week later, she pretended exhaustion to see if he would postpone her evening exercises. She didn't know if he guessed the truth or not, but the fury that darkened his features made her rush to accommodate him. She was on her bed, her robe pooled about her waist before he could do more than glower.

That evening, his breast circles were harsher. Not that he was physically rough, but she had become so attuned to his nearly worshipful attentions that this perfunctory touch rocked her to her core.

And then, as he left, he added a new exercise to her ritual. He pulled out a dragon carved from milky white jade and laid it in her hand. Its weight was solid, though not overly cumbersome. The length from snout to coiled tail was perhaps a handspan at most, and the girth no more than three fingers pressed tightly together.

She stared at it, disconnected thoughts swirling through her mind. The shape seemed somehow naughty to her, but she could not understand why. At least, not until she remembered the pictures of Greek statues she had once seen. She had been young, of course, and highly curious about the male anatomy. It was only when she compared the two images that she realized she held a carved male phallus.

Her face flushed with heat, and she nearly dropped the item, but Ru Shan had obviously been expecting her reaction. He neatly caught her hand, wrapping it firmly around the dragon when she would have let it slip away.

"It is time for you to begin practicing with the dragon," he stated firmly.

Her eyes widened at the thought. Exactly what did he want her to do with it?

"You must insert it into your jade gate. Only to the dragon's eyes and no more. Then you need to squeeze. Squeeze with all your strength for seven seconds. Only then may you release the dragon and expel your breath."

She did not need to ask where her jade gate was. His hand motions clearly indicated that he meant the entrance to her womb. "But I am . . . how could I . . . but I cannot . . ." Words failed her, and she stared stupidly at him. She had already pressed him once this day by pretending exhaustion. To challenge him now was the height of folly. And yet the thought of inserting anything inside her . . .

"If you will not do this, Fu De and I will tie you to this bed, spread your legs, and do it for you."

She recoiled in horror at his blunt statement, and one glance at Fu De—still in position just outside her bedroom door—proved her newfound friend was no friend at all. Fu De would do exactly as his master bade.

Biting back horror, she forced herself to shake her head. "I-I will do it myself."

"I will know if you do not. There is an energy stored in the jade when a woman strengthens herself in this way. An energy I can feel and smell."

She did not doubt him. Nor did she doubt that he would check the dragon every day when he visited.

"Seven times seven squeezes," he repeated. "Morning

and night. You may do them sitting first. Then, later, you must stand with your legs spread." He demonstrated by widening his stance. "And keep the dragon inside."

She nodded, her throat too tight to speak.

"After one week, I will test you. You must demonstrate the ability to hold it in position or I will know that you have not been practicing correctly." He reached out, lifting her chin so that she looked directly into his eyes. "If you cannot do this, then I will be forced to take more strident measures to see that you comply. Do you understand me?"

"Yes," she whispered. How could she not? She believed his every word. "I will do these exercises."

At that, his face softened, though subtly. "We are strengthening your body for what is to come. These things are done for your own benefit."

She nodded, worrying not at his motives, but at her future. What exactly did he have in mind that would require her to be strong . . . there? He did not tell her, of course, but bowed respectfully and prepared to leave.

His last words to her were part order, part threat.

"Begin *immediately*," he said. And then he was gone.

She stared down at the dragon, her hand trembling slightly. Fu De locked the outer door and came to her side, but she quickly scampered backward. She didn't know if he meant to threaten her if she didn't comply or was simply offering to help. Either way, she didn't want him there. She gestured that he should leave. He bowed to her, quietly withdrawing. But she noticed he didn't completely shut her bedroom door either. Likely he sat next to the wood, listening to whatever sounds she made.

It was horrible. She didn't even realize she was crying until she felt a tear plop onto the blanket on her bed. But she was crying—in frustration, in humiliation, even in anger. And yet there was nothing she could do. She had to do this hateful thing. Now.

With shaking hands, she spread her legs and tried to insert the dragon. It was a difficult position from which to see the stone. "No further than the dragon's eyes," Ru Shan had said. But how did one curl around enough to see the damned carved bubble of an eye?

Fortunately, her evening's breast circles had created that now-familiar wetness between her legs. The jade slid into place, though it was an uncomfortable girth.

And then it slipped right out again as she clenched her muscles.

Cursing under her breath, she tried again. With the same results. Indeed, it took many tries before she could manage even one second, much less seven. And by that time, she felt hot and messy and aching in places that should never hurt.

But that was not the worst of it. As she began to get the understanding of which muscles to squeeze, how hard, and in what sequence, her body betrayed her even more. She began to shudder. Not a simple, delicate, ladylike lift of the shoulders. Her entire body shook, building from below, gaining in strength, until her head whipped back and forth like a child's bobble-head toy. The truly violent shudders were accompanied by an explosion of sound in her ears.

None of this was painful, merely disconcerting. And humiliating. And she hated it. Every single moment. And yet she dared not stop.

She'd never been happier to reach the number forty-nine. When she did, she threw the hateful dragon across the room. She watched it fly, both hoping and dreading seeing it shatter into a million pieces.

It didn't. It merely thudded against the wall, then clattered to the floor. And all Lydia could do was curl onto her side and sob.

"How are your exercises with the dragon stone progressing?"

Lydia shifted uncomfortably on the bed, her body aching in places she couldn't even name. "You said I had a week. It has only been four days."

Ru Shan folded his arms across his chest, but Lydia could see a flash of humor in his eyes. "I did not ask you to perform with the stone. I asked you how the exercises were progressing."

She bit her lip. "It hurts."

His eyes narrowed. "What kind of pain? A sharp tearing pain? Or—"

She was already shaking her head. "Aches. In the muscles." Or what she thought must be muscles, though she'd never truly thought of that area of her body as having muscles.

He nodded, his expression softening. "I understand. But that is to be expected."

She abruptly pushed to her feet. "It is *not* to be expected. I don't like it. I don't want to do this anymore." Where the flash of temper came from, she didn't know. She wasn't even sure if this was wise. But her humiliation built every time she tried to work with the stone, every time she curled herself into that ridiculous position just to see the damned dragon eye. And so she let it flow—all the anger and pain and hatred, blazing out of her in a white-hot fury.

To her shock, Ru Shan did not even flinch. He merely stood, all humor sliding from his eyes. His face darkened. But his tone, when he spoke, remained even. Almost pleasant.

"Exercise is not for pleasure, Li Dee. It is for strengthening. I do not enjoy my exercises either, but I perform them daily."

She paused, abruptly thrown by his statement. She couldn't imagine him with a stone dragon. Where would he put it?

He must have read the confusion on her face because he released a quick burst of laughter. "I do not work with the dragon stone as you do. But I have exercises as well. One cannot become a jade dragon without extensive training."

"And you are a jade dragon?"

"Yes," he responded, with a slight dip of his head for modesty.

She glanced over her shoulder at Fu De. "Are you one as well?" she asked.

"No," the young man answered in English.

"Fu De is a green dragon, not yet accomplished enough to become a jade. He asked to assist in your training so as to learn."

She opened her mouth to ask for more details. In fact, she had so many questions, she wasn't exactly sure where to begin. But Ru Shan would not indulge her. Instead, he held up his hand.

"I will ask you only one more time, Li Dee. How are your exercises progressing?"

She wasn't sure exactly how to answer, but she could tell he would brook no more distractions. "I . . . I don't shudder as often now."

"You have less age to throw off."

She nodded, knowing he believed that the shudders were her body's way of releasing the evil energies that aged a woman. Add to that the breast circles and the special foods Fu De was feeding her, and Lydia was supposed to be moving backward in time to her adolescence. And perhaps, she reluctantly admitted, Ru Shan was right. She did feel better. Her skin was softer, more supple, and her body seemed stronger. Of course, that could simply be because she had been locked in a small room for all this time with no exercise, indulgent foods, or anything else that might stress her body.

Ru Shan crossed to the window, reaching up to the sill where she had left the carved dragon. She watched as the rosy dawn light momentarily painted his face. Then he spoke, asking questions she resented. "Can you stand without it falling?"

She looked away, not wishing to see him. "Not completely. Not for seven seconds." But she was getting closer. Indeed, it was becoming quite a challenge to her now.

"Good." He picked up the dragon and brought it to his nose, inhaling deeply. Then he held the stone in his hands and closed his eyes. "Excellent," he said, his eyes still closed. "Your yin is becoming most pure. I can feel it in the stone." Then he opened his eyes and smiled. "I have wonderful news, Li Dee. I believe you are ready to release some of your yin to me."

She stepped back, abruptly realizing her time had run out. Ru Shan was prepared to push her over the edge into whatever abyss these Chinese deviants inhabited. And there was nothing she could do about it.

"Do not be afraid," Ru Shan soothed. "I have promised you that it will not hurt."

She nodded, though her heart still raced. She did not think it would hurt. Indeed, she very much feared it would not hurt. That she would *like* it. That she would want more and more and more, just as her Uncle Jonathan did, unable to go for a day or more without visiting his mistress. His thoughts, his body, his entire being was consumed with finding the next moment to rut. Like a beast in heat was what her aunt said, with no more refinement or culture than a pig.

Was that what she would become?

The very thought terrified her, and yet how could she escape?

Meanwhile, Ru Shan was coming closer, his body large and imposing though he seemed no taller than average. "Why are you afraid?" he asked, obviously perplexed. "Why would I harm that which I have gone to great effort and expense to purify?"

What he said made logical sense, but it did nothing to ease the panic that gnawed at Lydia's chest. She had to leave. Now. No matter what the cost.

"Li Dee," Ru Shan continued. "I will not hurt you. . . ."

She could not wait any longer. It was time to escape. She forced herself to relax, to breathe calmly. It took all her effort, but she was determined. And was rewarded. As she seemed to relax, so too did Ru Shan and Fu De. They smiled at her, and Ru Shan even gestured formally to the bed, indicating that they should start.

But midway through his bow, she bolted. She flew past Ru Shan, skirted Fu De, and tore out of the tiny flat. Or so she imagined. So she wanted and hoped and desperately wished.

In truth, she never made it past Ru Shan. He caught her around the waist, easily lifting her off the ground. So she kicked him. She screamed, she bit, she fought, she did everything she could imagine, but he was stronger. And with the help of Fu De, she had no chance.

Through it all, he was trying to talk to her, trying to speak. "Li Dee, I do not wish to harm you. No pain, Li

Dee. No pain, I promise." He descended into Chinese, curses by the sound of it. Then, to one side, Lydia saw Fu De nod and scurry out, returning quickly with bright red silk cords.

Seeing them sent her into a frenzy. She redoubled her efforts, managing for one brief moment to struggle out of Ru Shan's grasp. But it was only for a moment. He caught her quickly, using his entire body to position her on the bed. Then, the very next moment, he toppled her over, pushing her onto the mattress while he pressed down on top of her.

"I do not want to bind you, Li Dee. Stop! You must stop!"

But she did nothing of the sort. She fought like a demon.

To no avail. All too soon, with Ru Shan's heaviness atop her and Fu De assisting from the side, her hands and feet were bound, and no matter how much she twisted or pulled, she could not escape.

So she screamed. She bellowed and hollered and sobbed, begging for help in English, in Chinese, in any language or way she could imagine.

At last, Ru Shan pulled a silk handkerchief from his pocket and stuffed it into her mouth. All the while he was shaking his head, visibly disturbed by her actions.

"I have left it too long, Li Dee. I am terribly sorry. The yin has made you insane. But it will not be long. I promise. I will help you. I swear."

"No. No," she sobbed through the silk fabric. She was shaking her head, tears flowing freely as she begged him not to continue. And she saw great sympathy in his eyes as he touched her cheek, gently wiping away her tears.

"It is entirely my fault, Li Dee. This yin—just like the yang—too much of it leads to insanity. It must be drained off. It must." Then he reached down, adjusting her attire.

Only now did she realize how exposed she was. In her

struggles, the robe had come completely open and rucked up to just beneath her bottom. Only the silken tie remained across her belly, but beyond that, she was completely open to his gaze. His touch. His evil.

Except he did not touch her in an evil way. In fact, he readjusted her robe so that it covered her lower half, just as if she were sitting up. Just as they had done for nearly two weeks. Indeed, he did not touch her down there in any way except to smooth the fabric.

But even that had her legs twitching in reaction, her body tensing in horror.

"We will begin as always, Li Dee. We must. To get the yin flowing in the right channels. But afterward, I swear, you will have your release."

His words caused her to cry out again, hauling as hard as she could on her bonds, but they did an excellent job of re-straining her. There was nowhere for her to go, no way to escape Ru Shan's interest.

And so it began. With simple breast circles, beginning near her nipples in an ever-expanding spiral. She tried to fight her body's reaction. She tried not to breathe as she had been taught, tried not to feel the slow release of ten-sion. But they had been doing this for so long now that she was unable to prevent it. All too soon she was exhaling with his downstroke, inhaling with the up. He was being especially gentle, she could tell, out of respect for her. But his chivalry did not extend to stopping.

And all too soon, she did not want him to stop. Her ragged sobs ended, and her stuttering breaths evened out. Until he reversed direction.

"We are beginning the flow now, Li Dee. We are build-ing the yin behind your plum flowers—your nipples—and then I will suck out the nectar."

His circling drew tighter and smaller, only this time, instead of stopping with a small tight circle around her nipples, Ru Shan closed his fingers around one. The first time she felt his fingers there, her entire body tensed, and she shifted on the bed with his motions so she would not feel them so much. She had no desire to tingle as his long, warm fingers lifted her plum flowers, as he called them. And when he continued his circling, drawing her breasts around by their peak, she simply closed her eyes and tried not to breathe.

But she could not maintain her resistance for long. As he began his second narrowing spiral, she found herself pushing into his hands rather than away. Then, as he delicately lifted her nipples, she felt as if he tugged on a long cord that began with his fingertips but extended down through her body, down into her very womb. And as he gently lifted and swirled her breasts, that cord began to tingle, then hum.

The sensation grew with each one of his spirals until she felt as if he pulled directly on a spot deep inside her belly. But it was not just her belly, for the energy radiated outward from there until heat and energy suffused her entire body.

"Stop," she whispered, afraid of what was about to happen.

"Do you feel the yin?" Ru Shan asked. "Do you feel it drawing from everywhere in your body?"

She nodded. How could she not? It was true.

"I am drawing it forth, Li Dee. Bringing it from everywhere directly to your plum flower. Do you feel the stem when I pull?"

He tugged gently on her nipples, and even her toes curled with the draw of power.

"Can you feel the yin course through your body? It comes to here." He pressed the flat of his hand over her belly, just above her womb. He moved his hand gently, in rhythmic circles, and inside, the flow of power seemed to increase. Seemed to build. "You must let the energy flow from here. . . ." He shifted on the bed, pressing both of his palms against her belly. "To up here." So saying, he let his hands flow upward, opening around her ribs, but always moving upward, gathering the energy until he lifted her breasts and narrowed his hands. Finally, he once again grasped her nipples, squeezing them in the same pulsing rhythm that beat inside her.

"Let the yin come, Li Dee. Open your plum flower."

She didn't know what was happening. She certainly wasn't opening anything. And yet, she felt everything he said, every idea, every image was echoed in her body. It was as if she had a river inside her, flowing from the furthermost places of her body into her womb, where it concentrated into two tight lines that headed directly for each breast. Each nipple.

And then he began the tightening spiral again.

She hadn't even realized she was breathing rapidly, her body beginning to tremble with what he was doing to her, until he began his circles again. Her breath slowed, but only slightly, fitting itself to his timing. And as the circles tightened, the river flow began again. And when he put his hands on her belly, she felt her stomach cave deep inside, letting him press almost to her spine. Except it wasn't her spine. It was this incredible river of power that flowed upward, following the path of his hands through her breasts and to her nipples.

And his mouth came down over her left breast.

She didn't cry out. Indeed, she barely registered the

change from his hands; it all seemed one and the same. His mouth was wet and warm, just like the river that now flowed through her, peaking at her breast. And he sucked in the same tempo, the same pulse as he had built within her. The river flowed to him, bringing heat and moisture and joy as it passed.

Out of her. Into him.

But only through the left breast. The right was left full and aching and closed.

And yet she barely noticed that, so amazing was the feel of his mouth. His tongue continued the circles just as his fingers had done. His mouth lifted her breast, just as his hand had done. But there was more. So much more, as her breast quivered from the flow. On and on he sucked, and she felt as if he drew her very last breath out of her.

Then he stopped—not suddenly, but slowly, gently narrowing his lips, tighter and tighter against her nipple, drawing the peak seemingly to the sky before releasing it with the gentlest of kisses.

And as he at last released her, so did she release her breath, letting the last of it flow outward from her mouth.

"It was helpful, yes? Releasing that yin?" he asked, his eyes gentle, his expression slightly dazed.

How to answer? she wondered. It had been more than helpful. It was incredible. And yet, it was not enough. "Please," she whimpered, not even knowing what she meant.

"Ah," he said, "your other breast is overflowing." And so, with the gentlest of touches, he began his circle again, but only on the right breast.

She felt the yin gather, just as before. She felt his palms press deep into her belly, just as before. But this time, she gave herself completely over to the experience. She not only experienced the flow of yin, she sought it out. She encouraged it. She wanted it. So that when he at last opened his mouth around her right breast, she thrust her nipple inside, crying out in joy as he began to suck the river from her.

This flow went on even longer than the other. The power, the pulse, the beat of her yin gushed into him, and she trembled with its leaving as she throbbed to the circling of his tongue, the pumping of his suction.

And when he at last released her breast, she stared at him in dazed confusion.

He said, "You must rest now. We will continue tomorrow."

He stood, a serene smile upon his face as he bowed deeply, respectfully to her. And after he left, Fu De came into the chamber, quickly releasing her bonds, before he too bowed himself out, closing the door behind him.

Lydia remained where she was, her body still humming, her mind still swirling in chaos.

What had happened? Had she really just released this Chinese yin? It could not be, and yet she could not deny the experience of the last hour.

Hour?

She looked out the window, seeing the total blackness of the night sky. It had been an hour at least. And at that moment she knew the truth: she had fallen into the abyss. She had tumbled, and now she was lost to the person she once was. It was not because a Chinese man had tied her down and suckled at her breasts. It was not because yin had flowed from her body into his.

She was lost because she had enjoyed it. Not just enjoyed it, but relished it. Wanted it. And she was nearly desperate for it to continue.

Was this his mystical release? Had this been intended to make her feel better? It didn't. She didn't. What she felt was achy and tired, and yet still humming with tension. Because she wanted more. She wanted to do it again. Now. This very second. And she wanted more of that yin flow. Rivers more. Entire oceans more.

Exactly what would she give up to get more of that experience? To do that again and again?

She didn't know. And she was frightened as never before.

From the letters of Mei Lan Cheng

14 June, 1873
Dearest Li Hua—

Another girl? Oh Li Hua, I am so sorry. I am sure, though, that she will grow to be like you, a credit to her family name. Like you, she will be a great beauty, a gentle woman, and a great friend to all those who love her. Treat her kindly, kiss her often, and then I am sure Heaven will reward your diligence with a son worthy of your courage and your husband's great strength.

My daughter, I am afraid, is not so blessed in her heritage. With my looks and her father's temper, she is not so favored by Heaven, only by her grandmother. My mother-in-law dotes on the girl, teaching her a hunger for things she should not have. Both seem to be infected with the ghost people's hunger for things without substance. She has even allowed the child to take breaths of her opium!

Fortunately, my husband was as angry as I at such a thing. He does not care about what the smoke will do to the girl, of course. He was furious that such an expensive thing was wasted on a child. Whatever the reason, little Ying Mei will not smoke again.

Ru Shan is also growing well. He is a strong boy with a good mind. Even his temper is as steady as his name promised, but I think that is because any childish outburst is met with the swiftest punishment. So little Ru Shan has learned to be a quiet boy who studies hard, as every great scholar must. I see him, though, staring outside, his tiny hands wrapped around the wood decorations on our windows. I know his heart longs to be out in the sunshine, and my spirit pities him. But a great scholar must find his freedom in his studies, and so I rarely allow him to escape. All his tutors are pleased with his progress, so I know the monks are fulfilling their promise; Ru Shan will achieve merit in his scholarship.

But Li Hua, there is one thing that I must tell you. One thing has been preying upon my sleep. My husband wishes to ship our clothing to England. Yes, to the barbarians in England! He says if the ghost people here are so easily separated from their money, then how much more would it take to bring in the gold from over there?

But Li Hua, he does not speak English. He does not hear the things they say when they think we cannot understand. All Sheng Fu thinks of is opening his hands and having the ghost gold fall into them.

I have tried refusing. I have tried pretending illness or exhaustion or even helping Ru Shan with his studies, but Sheng Fu will not hear of it. He has refused us money for food until I come speak with a ghost captain. I am to translate between him and Sheng Fu tomorrow. Oh, Li Hua, I am so afraid!

—Mei Lan

Once, an old man kept monkeys. When his grain was running short, he thought to cut down their food, but was afraid of their anger. He said to them, "I'm thinking of feeding you with acorns, three for the morning meal and four for the evening meal. Will that be sufficient?" The monkeys all rose to their feet in anger. Seeing this, the old man said, "Then how about four for the morning and three for the evening? I presume that will be enough." At this, the animals all prostrated themselves before him in joy.
—paraphrased from the writings of Lie Yukou

Chapter Six

Ru Shan walked slowly, trying to be mindful of his soul center, but finding his thoughts constantly wandering. He had expected to feel a great contentment all morning, but peace eluded him. Indeed, he had long awaited the moment he could finally start drawing off Li Dee's purified yin, and so had anticipated this morning's activities with great relish, imagining the joy and contentment that would surround him all day.

But it had not happened. Instead of quietness, he found himself especially disturbed. His mind constantly replayed moments from their morning activities. And not that joyful feeling when her yin flowed into his mouth, but the ugliness beforehand when she had run in terror.

What was wrong with him? Why did he focus on her terror, not his own pleasure?

He could only surmise that Li Dee's panic just before he began the massage had somehow polluted her energies.

And those pollutants had flown into him, giving him the same anxiety that Li Dee experienced.

But why had she been so upset? She had accepted her situation. Fu De said she even seemed happy. And yet she had run screaming in horror from him. Her overabundance of yin explained some of her reaction, but not all of it. And he was at a loss to explain.

Fortunately, it was time for his weekly meeting with Shi Po. Hopefully, she would have some insight to Li Dee's bizarre behavior.

He reached the tea house in good time. The business was owned by a fellow jade dragon, and so was often used for dragon/tigress meetings. It had a secret back entrance and many discreet rooms for conversation or practice. Ru Shan had already sent a note ahead, requesting that tea with special herbs be set out for them. It was tea for conversation, not for study. They both knew they would not be practicing today. At least, not with each other.

Shi Po had made it very clear that they would not touch one another until he resolved his current disharmony. She would be especially distressed now that he had to report an additional failure. But there was no help for it. If he wished her cure, he had to tell her of the ailment.

She had already arrived when he entered, though she had waited to begin her tea. She wore a full dress of fine blue silk. The design was not as great as Ru Shan's mother's work, he noted with a bit of smugness, but nothing could detract from Shi Po's beautiful skin or youthful red lips. Ah, how he missed their sessions together. Though, he abruptly realized, he had not truly thought of them for some time. So perhaps he did not miss her as much as he'd first imagined.

Either way, it was good to see her, especially as she began pouring tea. He settled carefully on the reclining cushions, wishing he had more time to relax with her. As it was, he had less than an hour before he would be needed back at his shop.

As these thoughts bubbled in his mind, they began to speak the usual pleasantries. But all too soon, Shi Po was pressing into his distressing thoughts.

"Your brow is troubled, Ru Shan. Have you not been able to harvest some of the ghost woman's yin yet?"

"I began this morning."

"And yet, it does not seem to have helped. Were you unable to begin the flow?"

He shook his head. "Her yin flowed easily and most heavily. I drank deeply and with much joy."

"That is excellent. But from your tone, am I to guess that it was not as satisfying as you hoped?"

He nodded, his dark mood already slipping past his restraint. "She still fights us. I don't understand it."

Shi Po frowned, leaning forward. "Truly? But how can that be?"

He set down his teacup, wishing he had the skill to read his own tea leaves. "I would not enjoy such a confinement. One room with nothing to do."

"But she is a ghost person, and a female at that. You cannot believe she thinks as we do. Ru Shan, they live in herds like oxen. They have more in common with a pack of dogs than they do with us."

Ru Shan did not look directly at his companion, but instead he let his gaze settle upon a fine ink painting of wild horses running free. "Some horses do not take well to breaking," he said slowly.

She nodded. "Then you must be firmer with her."

He shuddered at her tone. "I do not beat my dog, Shi Po. I will not beat Li Dee."

She sighed, but did not speak. Nevertheless, he felt her displeasure.

"What if we are wrong, Shi Po? What if the foreigners are people, just like us? With minds just as capable as ours, merely less educated." Given what he saw of Li Dee's intelligence, he had begun to believe it might be so. "If that is true, then I am doing her a grave disservice. I have stolen her freedom."

Shi Po's lips pursed in displeasure, but her voice remained calm. "I have a favorite dog. I believe he is happy to see me when I come home, and I think he purposely misbehaves when I am not there. Indeed, I think he is the cleverest of dogs, Ru Shan, but I never forget that he is simply a dog."

"The ghost people have made a great deal of money from China, Shi Po. They buy and sell land with intelligence—"

"With greed, you mean."

He nodded, knowing it was hopeless to speak of business matters with Shi Po—with any woman—but such was his distress that he persevered. "I think we judge the Englishmen by what we wish to see rather than what is."

"The finest men in China have said the ghost people are no more than oxen with hands. Do you doubt their intelligence? They have more experience than we do."

Ru Shan shook his head. "They come to my store. They buy things. I have even seen husband and wife, parents and children."

"They have learned a great deal from us. Like monkeys, they mimic quickly and easily. But to them a family is like a small herd. Have you not seen the men exchange their women like toys?"

He nodded. Of course he had seen it. One could not live in Shanghai without hearing of the Englishmen's debaucheries.

"I think you are searching for the difficulty in the wrong location. How does the shop fare? Have your fortunes turned around?"

"Not significantly," he answered without heat. In truth, his family's fortunes were going from bad to worse. In addition to the loss of his mother's artistic hand, his suppliers of fabric—cotton and silk—were turning away. Many simply did not deliver their goods. Others brought less than what was promised. He had no explanation for the sudden lack, but if it continued, then his family would be in dire straits.

Thankfully, Shi Po took his answer at face value, not questioning any further the matters that did not concern her.

"Very well, then tell me more of your work with your pet. Have you been telling her your secrets?"

"I have no secrets to tell," he argued. He'd said it before.

" 'If you turn your attention inward and observe yourself, the profound mystery is in you,' " she quoted.

Ru Shan nodded. He recognized the words of the Sixth Patriarch Hui Neng, but he was still unsure of Shi Po's meaning. "You wish me to talk to her, as a man would to a dog, and thereby learn my own secrets?"

Shi Po nodded but said nothing. Moments later, she stood and bowed respectfully to him before departing.

Ru Shan remained where he was, staring at his cooling cup of tea. This was a strange religion, he thought to himself, one that turned a woman into a teacher. Though he knew a woman's body naturally predisposed her to enlightenment well before a man, he still believed there were flaws in the method.

Shi Po, he decided, was not a good teacher, for she had that lack of understanding all women shared: she believed inherently that all men spoke the truth. She had been told that the ghost people were no more than large monkeys with an excellent capacity to mimic their betters, and so she believed. As Ru Shan had believed for many, many years.

Until lately. Now, he wondered if perhaps the Chinese had it completely wrong. Perhaps the white barbarians were not as barbarian as the emperor wished his people to believe. And if that were true, then Ru Shan's soul was in grave danger. He had helped in the murder of a man, not an animal. And he had kept enslaved a free woman, not a pet.

There was only one way to learn the truth, and in that his teacher had been correct. He needed to learn more about the ghost people. The only way to do that was with Li Dee.

Resolved, he pushed up from the cushions, slipping quietly out the back of the teahouse. He had much to think upon before tonight's session.

She was surprised to see him; that much Ru Shan could see as he stepped into the apartment. He had decided to spend his afternoon with her—an unusual change. But there was little he could do at the store while his mind was occupied with Li Dee, so he had gone to her residence and found her in deep conversation with Fu De. About fruit.

Dragon fruit. Mango fruit. Banana fruit. Apple fruit.

But what was even more bizarre was that she spoke in Shanghainese, and Fu De responded in English. And between them, in fading water upon the floor, were the Chinese characters for the fruit and English lettering beside it.

Obviously, they were teaching each other. As if to prove the point, Li Dee sprang to her feet and bowed politely to him, speaking slowly and clearly in Shanghainese.

"Welcome, Cheng Ru Shan. I am pleased to see you today."

Beside her, Fu De had already cleaned up their papers and writing instruments. He, too, bowed, his face split by a grin as he spoke in the foreign tongue. "I have learned a great deal of English," he said clearly. "But your skill is still far greater than mine."

Ru Shan felt his yang fires begin to churn. Like hot oil within him, his stomach twisted in fury at the sight of his servant and Li Dee so close together. What else had they been doing when he was away? What secrets had they shared?

He knew his reaction was illogical. He understood jealousy when its burning fire darkened his skin and tightened his jaw. But he had risked everything to buy Li Dee. He had borrowed money his family did not have to rent a home better than his own mother's room. And for what? So Fu De could reap the benefits?

No!

He felt his hands clench in fury and he took a step forward. "Remove yourself," he hissed in Chinese.

Fu De saw the danger. With a quick bow, he scampered out the door. But Li Dee, apparently, did not understand. Her own small fists settled on her hips and she stared at him in horror.

"Why do you send him away?" she asked in Chinese, her accent atrocious.

"He does not belong here," Ru Shan snapped in English, even more irritated that she thought to question him. In a few quick steps he grabbed the two tiny buckets of water, angrily tossing the liquid out the open window without even watching for people below.

"But we were doing nothing wrong," she pressed, switching back to her native language. "It was just a way to pass the time."

Ignoring her, he reached down to grab the parchment. It was of poor quality, meant for little more than a child's first attempts with ink and paper, and yet it infuriated him. Even this kind of paper was expensive. Was this how Fu De spent the money he was given for food? For Li Dee's comfort? On his own education?

"Fu De is my servant," Ru Shan snapped. "He serves me, not himself!"

"He knows that! I know that! Sweet heaven, how can we not know that?"

"Be silent, woman," he growled in Chinese.

"Or what? You'll lock me in a concrete cave with nothing to do, no way to occupy my time or mind?"

He stepped forward, the parchment crumpling in his fist. "Or I will sell you back to the whorehouse where I found you. You are still undamaged." He sniffed, scenting ginger mixed with orange blossom perfuming her skin. "And better scented. I may even make a profit."

She raised her hand to slap him—an obvious gesture and one he easily anticipated. He grabbed her arm, halting her in midswing.

"Think carefully, slave."

She swallowed, and he watched as the dull flush of anger burned through her pale skin. Tears pooled in her eyes, and her arm trembled within his grasp. Still, she would not yield.

Instead, she stood, facing him eye to eye as if she were his equal. A more ridiculous position could not be imagined for a white slave woman to take with her Chinese master. And yet, for some bizarre reason, it pleased him. He liked seeing her flushed with heat, her breasts heaving, the knot in her robe slipping open from her exertions.

"What do you want from me?" she whispered, her voice thick with tears.

"I do not know," he answered truthfully. "Your yin was not as satisfying as I had hoped."

She swallowed, and he saw fear flash through her. "What does that mean?"

He shrugged, tossing her hand away from him with the motion. "It means I have done something wrong. Or you are not yet right. I do not know."

She folded her arms across her chest, her manner defiant even though she still trembled with fear. "Could it be that it is not right to lock a woman in a cage and use her for your pleasure?"

He looked at her, considering her words, unwilling to admit the possibility and yet unable to deny it. "Slaves are a fact of life in China. It is unfortunate for the poor, but they are treated fairly and given tasks suited to their ability."

"I am not a slave. I am a free Englishwoman."

He almost smiled. "You are my white pet, and you will remain with me until I choose to release you."

She stiffened, then softened and looked away, defeated. "Just so long as you do release me."

He frowned, surprised that the thought of releasing her did not please him. Up until now he had looked forward to the time when he would be rid of her expense, rid of the need to draw white yin from her. Yet now he disliked the thought, felt a stirring of unease at the idea that he would not see her each morning and evening.

Perhaps her yin had helped him more than he thought. Perhaps he simply needed more of it. He sighed. He did not know enough about this situation, about what he had begun. He had to learn more about these ghost people.

So thinking, he tossed the parchment aside, then ushered

her firmly back into her bedroom. As always, they sat upon her bed. And though he felt the absence of Fu De most keenly—he still feared that she might escape him in a moment of surprise—she gave no indication that she intended to try.

Until, of course, she glanced at the door. Her expression lightened. "It will be better without Fu De here. More private."

He frowned. "Private? Do you understand the meaning of that word?"

"Of course I do! Why would you think I wish for an audience every time I bathe or dress or . . . or whenever we . . ." Her voice trailed away, but her meaning was clear. She was obviously insulted. In truth, he got the impression that she felt abused by the presence of Fu De in her chambers.

"But the English have great drawing rooms where people gather to view one another as the women dress. They have no desire for privacy." He shifted, completely baffled.

"We most certainly do!" But then she hedged, clearly forced to admit the truth. "I am told that the wealthy women dress themselves in their bedrooms, then come out to another room—a kind of parlor—for their closest friends. They chat there while she finishes her toilette. Her cosmetics and jewelry. But I most certainly do not do . . ." She gestured vaguely toward the bed. "These things with others."

He shook his head, knowing that it was not true. "I have heard of great gatherings of Englishmen and women alike for the purpose of copulation. Indeed, the Chinese talk often of such activities." He straightened. "You are like monkeys, living all together in a colony. The women are most comfortable with such scenes."

"We most certainly are not!" She was clearly agitated,

jumping up from the bed to pace about the room. "How could you think that? It's disgusting!" She spun on her toe, turning to glare directly at him. "I do not know where you get these ideas, but I cannot believe that every Englishman in China has behaved with such . . . such . . . debauchery!"

He did not understand this word. *Debauchery*. But he guessed her meaning. She truly was upset, and her reaction verified one of his fears: that the Chinese has grossly misrepresented the nature of these foreign barbarians.

But before he could believe such a strange thought, he had to find out more. Leaning back against the cushions of her bed, he folded his arms. "I wish to know more about you Englishmen. How do you live?"

She stopped, clearly frustrated by his question. "What do you mean, how do we live? We live as people live. In houses. With our families."

"Families? What kind of families?"

"The normal kind! A mother, a father. Their children."

It was as he feared. His leaders were misinformed. But just to make sure, he leaned forward on his elbow, studying her face carefully for any type of deception. "But you live in colonies. Isn't that the word? A group of English people all living together."

She shook her head. "Not like a monkey colony! The very idea is preposterous!" She stepped forward. "We have separate houses. A colony is merely a group of families living in the same area. Each in their own little house."

He nodded. "Because you learned from the Chinese."

"No!" She was becoming more exasperated, her anger clearly vibrating through her. "I assure you, the English have been living in homes for many, many hundreds of years."

He frowned. "That cannot be possible. Surely some of you live like monkeys."

"We most certainly do not!"

"But the emperor has said—"

"Then he is wrong!" she spat.

"You are barbarians!" he returned, startled to realize his tone had risen along with hers.

"We most certainly are not! You are!"

"Don't be ridiculous." He was angry, but he made no effort to modulate his tone. "You English people came to us—to China—seeking our goods. We want nothing from you, and yet you come, begging for silk, for jade, for all our good things."

"We came seeking trade. To sell our goods to you in return for your things. Trade."

"But all of your things are of inferior quality. You have no silk, no ivory. You do not even posses the ability to lacquer wood. You are uneducated." He wasn't even sure why he was arguing with her. He knew the truth of his words. Perhaps he was merely being kind, giving her the truth.

Except she had no wish to understand. Instead, she turned and glared at him. "Our machinery is infinitely superior to yours. You have no clockworks similar to ours. Your culture is still rife with superstition. And worst of all . . ." She drew out her tone, obviously wishing to make her point excruciatingly clear. "We do not buy and sell people as if they were no better than cattle."

"Then do your poor starve when they have too many children?"

She opened her mouth, no doubt to argue with him, but she shut it with a snap. Eventually she sighed. "Every country has its poor. But we do not sell our children."

"Then you doom them to the same misery and torment the parents suffer. At least in the service of a great family, the child will be well cared for. Some even gain a degree of refinement and education."

She frowned and began to speak, but he had heard enough. "No more of this," he snapped. The English were indeed an inferior species. Though perhaps they were not as barbaric as he had at first supposed. "I wish to begin drawing out some of your yin."

Her expression was mutinous, but she slowly complied. "Do you treat all women this way? Or just your white slaves?"

He didn't think she expected an answer, but he gave her one anyway, his yang fire burning in his tone. "I have done everything I can to make you comfortable. I cannot afford silks and gold. My mother never had those things—why would I lavish them on you? You will have to make do with what a mere shopkeeper can afford."

She gaped at him, her jaw slack with astonishment. But not for long. Indeed, she apparently had more yang than he had previously guessed, because she spit back her answer with an equal amount of venom.

"I have never wished for silks or jewelry, nor do I expect them now. I am talking about something to do, Ru Shan. I have no books to read, no colors to paint with, and now you have taken away my sponge brush and teacher so I cannot even practice Chinese."

He frowned, completely stunned. It was as he'd suggested to Shi Po. "You wish for something to do? Something that occupies your mind?" He could not believe it. Not one of the ghost people he had ever met would want such a thing. Flashy jewelry, costly silks, that was all the foreign devils cared for.

"Of course, I do! Look about you, Ru Shan. Would you be content here?"

Of course not. But he was a well-educated Chinese. He understood the finer aspects of life. How could a ghost person—and a woman at that—ever enjoy such things? Or despair at their lack? And yet, looking at Li Dee, he realized that she did indeed wish for a way to occupy her mind.

He squinted at her; seeing once again her round flat eyes, her golden hair. She appeared to be as English as the most ghostlike of the other barbarians. And yet, she was nothing like he expected. "Do you have Chinese in your lineage?"

"Don't be ridiculous. It is becoming abundantly clear that your race despises mine. Even here in Shanghai, don't you live in entirely separate quarters?"

He nodded. There was indeed strict separation of the races, with large walls meant to keep the foreigners out. It was only because of his shop that he had any exposure to the ghost people at all. And Li Dee, of course.

And his mother, as well. But that was another topic altogether.

"Your mother did not meet a Chinese man somehow? Fall in love with him perhaps?"

"My mother married an English boy she met in the veterans hospital when she was barely eighteen. They married and lived happily together. She has never met a Chinese man nor does she ever wish to. Indeed, I wish I could say the same!"

He listened to her impassioned speech, seeing the flash of yang in her eyes, the anger in her tone. She certainly thought she spoke the truth. But for all that, he still could not believe her. She was too intelligent, too capable. To think that she was even learning Shanghainese from Fu De.

He could not credit that the ghost people could spawn so capable a creature on their own.

"You must be thought a rare genius among your people."

She frowned. "I am considered bright, but no more so than many others."

He shook his head, still confused. Sometimes his countrymen were not ashamed at having sexual relations with barbarian women. Perhaps that was how Li Dee came by her intelligence. Or perhaps she was just one of nature's rarest creatures.

"Was that why you came to China? Because you were not accepted at home?"

She huffed in disgust, dropping onto the edge of her bed in clear annoyance. "I came because Maxwell Slade—"

"Your fiancé. Yes, I remember."

She turned, pinning him with her gaze. "Then why do you not return me to him?"

He smiled then. He did not know what prompted it, but he did not stop himself, because he liked the unaccustomed feeling of pride.

"I keep you, Li Dee, because you are mine." Then he tugged her around to face him, his hands already untying the belt of her robe. "No more talk now. It is time to release your yin."

From the letters of Mei Lan Cheng

2 July, 1873
Dearest Li Hua—

I have met him! I have met the ghost captain, and it is worse than I feared! He is as thin as a snake and has the hungry eyes of a starving mongoose. And he bellows at me! He thinks I do not understand him, and truthfully, I pretend this is so, but that makes him angry. He thinks if he yells louder, then I will suddenly understand his words. All it does is make me angry.

Sheng Fu is angry, too. I try to tell him this ghost person is evil, but he will not listen. He calls me stupid and superstitious and has sent me to a tutor—at my age!—to learn more English. Meanwhile, this terrible captain has gone away, taking only a few bolts of cloth at a very cheap price. Normally, Sheng Fu would not have sold the fabric so cheaply, but I think he is a little afraid of the Starving Mongoose Captain and wished to see him go away happy.

It is very bad, Li Hua, very bad to do business with the ghost people. But my family wants the ghost gold too much now for me to stop them.

Oh, I must go now. I have much work to do now before I go to my lesson!

—Mei Lan

P.S. I forgot to say that there is one good thing about my lessons. I must take Ru Shan with me. Sheng Fu hopes our son will soon be able to translate instead of me, so he lets me take him along. We have a lovely time, Ru Shan and I, walking to the mission and back. That is where we take our lessons, because no one speaks better English than the priests. But I am surprised by how wonderful my son is—attentive and fun as we walk. We laugh often and have the best of times, him and I. For that reason alone, I hope it takes a long, long time for me to learn English.

Sincerely, Mei Lan

You see! That is how the English sign their names. Looks ugly, doesn't it? Going side to side instead of up and down. And the shapes are all wrong. They don't even use a brush to write but little wooden logs with charcoal inside. But Ru Shan likes it, and he can make their writing look pretty. Even the English teacher says Ru Shan is very smart.

Oh! I really must go now. I must give more money to the monks today, in addition to my other tasks.

Li Bai when young did not show well in learning,
and so he decided to give up his studies halfway.
On the way home, he saw an old woman grind-
ing an iron rod. In wonder, Li Bai asked her
what she was doing. "Making a needle," she an-
swered curtly. Feeling ashamed at his own lack
of perseverance, Li Bai went back to learning
and finally acquired great scholarship.
                                    —Qian Que Lei Shu

Chapter Seven

The Chinese were strange creatures, Lydia thought with a
languid stretch. Or perhaps, more accurately, she should
say Ru Shan was a strange creature. On the one hand, he
thought nothing of buying her, locking her up in a ten-by-
ten-foot room and then daily milking her for her yin. On
the other hand, he had shown her unexpected kindness and
respect. He still always bowed when he entered and left her
presence, thanking her for their time together. He spoke
honestly, and had even begun to give her sketching paper
and painting supplies to fill the long hours between his visits. Sometimes she wondered if Maxwell would have done
as much. Plus, Ru Shan had begun closing the door so that
Fu De could not watch. And all because she told him she
did not like the young man staring.

As best as she could understand, Ru Shan thought of
her as a treasured pet—like a monkey or cow that one
cared for, played with, even spoke secrets to, but would by

no means release into the outside world. And, apparently, this was an attitude that was shared by most of his countrymen: that the white man was no more than an advanced monkey.

She wondered briefly what Maxwell would think of such an attitude. Probably he would scorn it as nonsense. Especially as he considered the Chinese were in turn, beneath him. He could no more imagine that they thought of him as a monkey than he could imagine being bested in a competition by a woman. Maxwell, like many of his friends, believed himself superior to all he surveyed.

And perhaps therein lay the problem, she realized as she stood to pace her tiny chamber. Not the difference between the English and the Chinese, but between men and women. Men thought themselves superior—over animals, over women, over other men. It made no difference whether the man was white or yellow or purple or green. Men believed themselves kings, and no amount of reason or logic would sway them.

No, it was not surprising that the Chinese men thought themselves more civilized than the English, or that the Englishmen believed themselves smarter than the Chinese. And both were completely wrong.

Who would have thought that her entire problem would boil down to misguided male ego? Or that she—a woman— was the only one who seemed to see reality? It was a very odd thought, given that she was locked in a tiny concrete cell.

Odd as it was, she still planned to find a way to escape. But how? She had very few leverage points, as her father would call them. She was a woman locked in a room. She had managed to parlay her charm into a working understanding of Shanghainese, thanks to Fu De. She had even convinced Ru Shan that she was heartily sick of her silk robe and wished some real clothing. He had given her soft but serviceable peasant clothes. She had a tunic made of soft brown cotton and matching pants with an unsewn crotch. Apparently, according to Fu De, peasants could not be bothered to leave the fields to visit a water closet. They simply squatted in the field, fertilizing the ground wherever they stood.

And they thought the English barbaric!

No matter. At least now when she finally escaped, she wouldn't be running through the streets of Shanghai in a silk robe.

Which brought her back to the problem of escape. Since Ru Shan's explosion of a few days earlier, Fu De had been extra vigilant during the time they spent together. They only conversed in Chinese (for her) and English (for him), which was wonderful, but never worked on the written languages. Which meant he never had his hands full and always maintained a strict focus on her face. It was hardly an easy escape environment.

At this point, she'd decided her best bet was to develop a relationship with Ru Shan. The more he saw her as a real person, the more likely he would see caging her was wrong.

She knew her chances were slim at best. No man liked admitting that he was wrong, and even fewer men liked giving up a possession that brought them joy. But it was her only plan, and so for the moment she decided to devote herself to becoming friends with her captor.

Strangely, the idea did not upset her. She found herself beginning to forget she was a prisoner. After all, until her father had grown ill, she had lived her entire life in London. True, there were excursions into the city, but only well supervised visits to family and friends. There was little money for entertainments or pleasure. So, for the most part, she had lived within the confines of her home, making her entertainment inside those walls. She had helped her mother with the cleaning, she had read, and she had painted. Indeed, the entire household had revolved around her father's coming and going, his pleasures, his needs.

All in all, life was not so very different here. Except, of course, that Ru Shan's needs were very, very different from her father's. And therein lay the difficulty.

She was beginning to like Ru Shan's needs. She was beginning to like them very much indeed. She truly did not want to think of herself in that manner, but she refused to fall into the same mistake as the men: She would face the truth, no matter how painful.

She knew Ru Shan thought of her as little better than a monkey. She knew he kept her as one would keep a pet, using its assets as one might milk a cow. But when he put his lips on her breasts, the yin flowing hard and fast into him, she truly did not care.

It felt fabulous. More fabulous than anything else in her entire life. The only thing that kept her remotely sane was the vague dissatisfaction that always lingered after Ru Shan left. There was something more. Something beyond what she had already experienced. And when she had mentioned that to Ru Shan this morning, he had smiled and nodded.

"There *is* more," he had said. "And I believe you are ready for that as well. Tonight. A woman's yin is strongest as the moon rises. That will be a good time to begin."

And so he had left, and Lydia had begun to pace. And think. And worry. She already found it difficult to focus on escape. Her mind constantly lingered on Ru Shan. On what they had done last. On when he would come next, and what would be his mood. What would they do together? And for how long?

If that were not bad enough, she still had to do her exercises with the stone dragon. Her muscles were amazingly strong now. Indeed, she had performed so well, he had given her two stone eggs connected together by a long thin chain. Her job was to insert one egg and, using just her muscles, lift and lower the egg. The other stone created a counterweight that would pull the first egg out if she allowed it.

She didn't explore it, of course, but the constant shift and tug of the weight as she stood made for a kind of stimulation that she found vaguely unsettling, but mostly very intriguing. Very, very intriguing.

Would Ru Shan's "next step" involve her muscles down there? Would it involve things that Maxwell would disapprove of? She strongly suspected it would. And she knew without a doubt that she couldn't wait. Her only salvation would be to find a means of escape before Ru Shan arrived. Then she would force herself to run as far and as fast as possible. No matter what she might be missing out on. What she might never know.

But, of course, no opportunity came. And so when Ru Shan walked into her tiny room that evening, she greeted him with a mixture of resignation and secret delight.

And then came dread, because Ru Shan was clearly in a towering rage.

"My goodness," Lydia cried as he stomped into her little room. "What has happened?"

"It is not important," he snapped in the way of all stubborn men.

"Well, of course it is important," she argued smoothly. "You are not the type of man to be upset over nothing."

The compliment seemed to mollify him somewhat, but he was still bullheaded enough to huff out, "You would not understand."

She guided him to a seat on her poor bed, trying to make her manner submissive. She knew just how to do it. Had she not seen her mother do this a thousand times when something upset her father? Indeed, Maxwell too seemed to need such coddling at times. "I probably won't understand," she lied. Indeed, she was beginning to see that she very much needed to learn as much about Ru Shan as she could. "But it may help you to talk to me anyway."

He turned and glared at her. "That is what Shi Po says. Women's nonsense."

She stilled, her chest tightening even as she asked the question. "Who is Shi Po?"

"She is my mentor in the dragon and tigress arts."

He worked with another woman? The same way he worked with her? The very thought sent hot coals whipping through her system, but Lydia tamped down her anger. Right now she only needed him to talk with her. And so she pasted on a smile. "Then perhaps you should tell me. What is it that has upset you so this day?"

"Another shipment of cotton fabric has not arrived. Today I learned it went to Shi Po's husband instead."

"Her husband?"

He glared at the floor. "My competitor."

"Your mentor is also your competitor? Isn't that . . . awkward?"

He straightened, clearly irritated. "Of course not. She is a woman and has nothing to do with her husband's business."

Lydia sincerely doubted that, but she knew better than to argue.

"Besides," Ru Shan continued, "teachers of her ability are rare. If I wish to become an Immortal, Shi Po is the only one who can guide me. It was a great honor to be selected to be her jade dragon, for all that she is a woman."

Lydia nodded, startled to feel a twinge of rancor for this Shi Po. But then she chanced to look up into Ru Shan's eyes. Usually his expression was serene, almost masklike. But not now. And perhaps not nearly as much lately. At this moment, she read worry and anxiety in his face. "You do not believe she is as separate as she appears?"

Ru Shan released a heavy sigh. "I do not know." He shifted on the bed, turning to look more directly at her. "My family buys cloth," he said. "We use that fabric to make beautiful clothing. My mother used to embroider the most stunning designs on them. We were sought throughout China for her embroidery." He gestured to his jacket, which sported a flock of delicate cranes in flight. "My mother stitched this."

"You have the most beautiful clothing. I have always admired it."

He reached out and stroked one of the flying birds. "She is dead now. Two years ago. And the shop has suffered greatly for her lack."

"I am sorry. That must have been a great blow."

He nodded, but did not answer. Then he sighed. "It was difficult, but never before have our shipments gone astray. If it were only one, there would be no fear. But there have been so many mishaps lately." His voice trailed off.

"You do not think they are accidents."

"No."

"You think Shi Po has done something."

He glanced up, his gaze sharp. "Shi Po has done nothing. It is her husband, Kui Yu. But what? And why?"

She shifted to smile more fully at him. "The why is easy. You were never this vulnerable before. Your mother was still alive."

"But Kui Yu has nothing to do with the shipments. How could he convince the weavers to send it to him and not me? We have always been good customers, treated the weavers fairly."

That she couldn't answer, nor did he expect her to. He simply sat, speaking aloud as he worked his way through the problem.

"I have heard there are rumors, but I do not know what. I have heard that someone is speaking lies, but I cannot discover who. Not yet."

"But you will." It wasn't a question. Lydia knew enough about Ru Shan already to be sure he would discover the reason behind his current problems.

He seemed to agree. "Yes, I will. But can I do so in time? If this continues, our shop will be empty, our customers gone."

"You will find out. I am sure of it." Lydia didn't understand why she was working so hard to reassure her captor. For all she knew, his business could go bankrupt tomorrow. But she needed him to see her as a person, an asset with skills and value. Someone who should not be locked away. And if that meant soothing his worries, then she would soothe his worries.

Besides, she liked it when he smiled at her. His eyes crinkled at the edges and his face seemed to lighten, becoming both brighter and less heavy. And then he reached out, cupping her cheek with his hand.

"I am sorry, Li Dee. I had thought to expand your yin

river today, but I do not have the focus. My yang burns too hot."

She suppressed a twinge of regret at his words, which was echoed by an equally strong feeling of relief. Instead, she lifted his hand from her cheek, pressing her lips into his palm. "Is there a way to release your yang? As you do my yin?"

He sighed, rubbing a finger across her mouth. The tingle he created made her purse her lips, as if to kiss him. But before she could, he pulled away. "There is a way," he said slowly. "But I had not thought to teach you such a thing."

She lifted her gaze to his. "Why not?"

"Shi Po tells me things about your people, things that the government has encouraged us to believe. But taken altogether, they contradict one another. You say that you do not live like monkeys—in colonies."

She nodded, pleased that he was beginning to see her more truthfully.

"Is it true that you stop up your passions? You are taught not to enjoy your bodies or another's touch."

She hesitated, doing her best to answer honestly. "That is perhaps stating the extreme case. We are encouraged to enjoy wedded life."

"Have you ever seen a man's jade dragon?"

She frowned, her glance slipping to the carved dragon he had given her. He gently pulled her chin so that she looked at him.

"A man's organ."

It took a moment for her to understand, and then her face heated with embarrassment. But rather than hide from the truth, she confronted it, confessing her shame. "I have seen statues. And pictures. In my father's anatomy books." She shrugged. "I found anatomy most helpful in my art." She rose to her feet, rushing to cover her awkwardness. She grabbed a pile of her sketches, shifting through them quickly to bring up her sketch of a Chinese man in western-style clothing. Or perhaps not completely western, as it incorporated both styles, giving him western trousers and a tie, but changing the jacket to an Asian cut with Chinese frog buttons. "See? My first clothing designs were too tight on men. It wasn't until my father showed me his Gray's Anatomy that I understood why they couldn't have high seams in that area."

Ru Shan frowned, flipping quickly through the pages. "What is this?"

She paused, at first not understanding what he meant. "My sketches? They are nothing."

He shook his head, clearly distracted. "You have drawn people. In strange clothing."

"I have always done so. Sometimes I make the clothing as well, but my stitches are not as even as a modiste's." He looked at her, clearly not understanding the word. "A seamstress. Someone who sews clothing."

"But these dresses . . ." He slowed to look at a picture of a white woman in an Asian gown. She had not seen many Chinese women in her short trip through Shanghai, but she remembered every detail of what she'd seen. Like her previous sketch, she combined both Asian and English styles, using silk fabrics in a relatively narrow English gown. Then she added a tight, short Chinese-style jacket on top. Indeed, of all her sketches, it was her favorite design, and she planned to have it made the moment she escaped.

"Do you like it?" she asked, unable to stop herself. Women dressed to attract their men. If Ru Shan liked it, then she knew she had a good design.

"Yes." He said the word flatly, as if confused. But then

he looked up, straightening to his full height. "I wish to keep these."

She stared at him in surprise. He was clearly asking her permission, though the question was phrased as a statement. "They are just drawings," she said slowly.

"Nevertheless."

She smiled at his stiff phrasing. Clearly, he was unused to asking permission for anything from a woman. So she smiled, nodding regally to him. "Then of course you must have them."

"You must show me any of your other sketches."

She settled back on the bed beside him. "But those are all I have."

"Then draw more."

Her eyes narrowed as she considered him, wondering at his sudden interest. "Your shop. It adds designs to cloth. Do you also make clothing?"

He nodded. "Of course. We employ many seamstresses."

"You want to use my designs to make clothing."

She watched his eyes widen in surprise at her understanding, and she nearly laughed out loud. Many of her friends had asked her to design clothing specifically for them. That he would want to use her talents in his business was not a large leap. And in the end, he confirmed her thought.

"I will allow my customers to see your sketches. If they like the designs, then we will sew them."

"You need more than just the rough sketch. You need directions for the seamstress."

He nodded. "Can you do those as well?"

She smiled. "Of course. I have done it many times." She leaned back, focusing all her attention on his face, making sure she made her next point clearly. Loudly. "Which makes me very similar to your mother, does it not? She created embroidery designs that you sold at great profit. And I have designed clothing that you will sell—"

"No one has purchased anything yet!" he snapped, clearly irritated by her suggestion.

"But my designs have been copied throughout England," she lied. In truth, some people had copied her gown designs. Others had called them ridiculous in the extreme. But she felt no guilt at her claim if it would make her seem more human to him.

"This is not England," he snapped. Then he left her side, roughly pulling open the door and calling Fu De. Lydia could not follow their rapid exchange of Shanghainese, but she guessed what was happening anyway. Especially as Fu De bowed, then carefully took her sketches. After a quick, surprised look in her direction, he rushed out of the flat.

Lydia shifted on the bed to lean back against the wall. "He is taking my pictures to your shop. To show to your customers."

Ru Shan nodded, carefully closing the door before returning to the bed. But he did not sit. Instead, he began stripping off his jacket. "It is time," he said firmly, "for you to learn about yang."

She had been relaxed, feeling a bit smug at her progress. But at his words, a shiver of terror slid down her spine. Exactly what was he going to do? What would she have to do? He didn't make her wait long. Indeed, his motions were brisk, almost as if he, too, felt uncomfortable about what would happen next, but was determined to see it through. It seemed impossible to her, and yet, as he continued to strip off his clothing, she saw the soft blush of embarrassment heating his skin. Then she had few thoughts at all as he continued to disrobe.

Before long, he stood before her completely naked, his hairless body displayed openly before her.

"Look all you want," he said, his voice somewhat constricted. "And then you must touch."

Her gaze flew to his face in shock. She was supposed to touch him? Where? Then, even more shocking, he began to slowly turn, letting her see him from all sides.

At first she could not get past her surprise. But then curiosity took root. She had seen her father's anatomy book. She knew about bones and muscles and what parts of the body went where. But lithographs and charcoal sketches were nothing compared to seeing a man in the living flesh. Especially a man with so little fat upon him. Indeed, as she reached out to trace the contours of his back, she could see the curve of each muscle. A few of them even rippled beneath her fingertips.

His skin was so different, and yet so similar to her own. Maxwell called the Chinese yellow-skinned, but Ru Shan did not seem yellow so much as vellum. A fine, warm paper, mellowed with age, on which was written the power and strength of an entire race of people—if only she had the intelligence to read it. Next to him, her skin seemed pale and insubstantial. Like the ghost he sometimes called her.

He began to turn, and she let her hands slide with his movements. When she had put both her hands upon him, she did not know. But she used them now to measure the breadth of his shoulders—a good eight or nine inches wider than her own—and the circumference of his biceps.

"You are strong," she said softly, startled by the truth of her statement. His clothing did not hide lax, flaccid muscles, but a body rippling with power.

"Fabric is heavy. It builds a strong back."

No wonder she hadn't been able to escape him during

their earlier struggles. He was much more powerful than she had ever guessed.

She let her hands flow over his collarbone, feeling the solidity. She used it as an anchor, pausing there to steady her breath before letting her hands slide lower, over his chest. She didn't wonder why she felt so breathless, attributing it to the excitement of seeing such a beautiful man up close. Still, she needed a moment to calm herself before stepping back a bare inch or so, in order to give herself a better view.

His chest was broad, the skin smooth. He felt warmer than silk, and now that she stood this close, Lydia smelled his scent as well. Musk and sandalwood together. She closed her eyes and inhaled deeply, barely even realizing she was memorizing it.

Her hands slipped lower, over the hard nub of his nipples. She stopped a moment there, seeing how his body puckered as hers had, only smaller. Firmer. Glancing up, she looked into his dark eyes. "Should I suck on them, as you do to me? Will that release your yang?"

His face seemed taut with tension, but his voice was smooth and steady. "It will release some, but not much. The breasts are the centers of yin, and so you will likely drain off the yin I have collected from you."

"Oh," she said softly, and she rubbed her nail back and forth across his nub. It felt surprisingly like the raised portion of the snap fastener so popular with Americans. And yet it was more pliable, and so much more intriguing. Without even thinking about it, she found herself circling his nipples as he'd done hers, and she wondered if he felt the same tug of power within him that she experienced when he touched her.

Then she slowed her fingers, thinking back over what he

had said about the breasts being the center of yin. "I suppose I should not do that."

"No," he agreed, his voice deepening as he spoke.

She nodded, but her attention was already wandering lower. Her hands skimmed over his ribs, narrowing into the hollow of his stomach and the tight muscles of his belly. He must have seen where her gaze took her, because he gently pressed upon her shoulders.

"Sit," he urged, and she complied, dropping somewhat heavily upon the bed.

This, of course, brought her eye level with the most astounding sight she had ever seen. He was hairless here, though she saw a kind of shadow on his skin and wondered if he'd shaved. It must be difficult to wield a razor there, she thought with a frown. He would have to avoid the . . . item that stood hard and long right there in the way.

And such an item it was. Flushed a dark red, it thrust upward like a thick arrow made of flesh. It jiggled slightly as he breathed and even had a tiny bead of moisture on the very tip.

"This is a man's jade dragon," he said. "It is very sensitive, so it must be handled with careful respect."

She tilted her head to one side, even holding out her hand with the fingers spread wide. But she did not touch it yet. She was measuring the length of his dragon, and thinking of the pictures she had seen in her father's anatomy text.

"Are all men so long?" she asked. "If so, I fear I have miscalculated in the design of men's trousers."

"Your designs are fine. I have performed many exercises to straighten my dragon. Unfortunately, that means it has also lengthened."

She glanced up at his face, wondering at the trace of humor in his voice. Or perhaps it was pride, she wasn't sure. Either way, his expression did not hold her attention for long. She was soon looking again at his organ. "You are too long?"

"A dragon's best length is that which matches exactly his woman's cinnabar cave. It is one of the requirements when seeking a tigress with whom to practice." He paused. "I have not found a woman yet who matches me completely."

"What of Shi Po? Isn't she your mentor?"

He sighed and shook his head. "Shi Po and I do not match in this manner, and so we have been unable to perform certain exercises. I believe it has hindered my advancement significantly."

"Perhaps you will find one soon," she responded. "Then you will no longer need me for more yin."

He did not answer, and she did not press him. The thought of him with a suitable tigress was not one she wished to dwell upon. Instead, she hunched herself lower, looking at the sac beneath his dragon. She recalled such from her studies in her father's book, but she did not know its purpose. Fortunately, he answered her questions before she could even phrase them.

"That is the base of the dragon, sometimes called his house. It is the center of yang essence and where my yang fire begins."

"Then it must be released from there?"

"No. It is where the fire begins." Then she felt him extend his hand, lifting her chin to look directly at him. "A man is built differently than a woman. A woman's fire builds, lifting naturally to her breasts and to her mind. But nature directs a man's fire outward, spending it uselessly outside his body. It is the work of the tigress to build a man's fire, then stop it from flowing outward. This takes much focus and control on the man's part, but with practice, it can be directed upward, to the mind. If enough yang and yin combine, that energy will flow upward launching him into immortality."

She merely stared at him, trying to understand his words.

"Do not worry," he soothed. "You do not need to understand this to help me."

"But I do understand," she finally said. "You wish me to build your yang fire so that it can heat your mind. And when that happens—"

"It cannot be done alone. It must combine with yin."

She nodded. "When it has combined—"

"And the fire is hot enough."

"Then you will become immortal?"

He nodded, a surprised smile on his face. "Yes. The exact manner in which the combination takes place is unknown. Many have ideas, and there are mental images we use to encourage the process. But you understand the essentials."

"So a tigress would build your fire but prevent its expulsion from your body." She frowned. "How is this done?"

"When a tigress knows that the fire is about to erupt, she presses on two places. The first is the dragon's mouth." He reached down and demonstrated, using his thumb and forefinger to squeeze closed the tiny hole at the tip of his dragon. "She also presses upon the *jen-mo* point. It is here, behind the dragon's home. It is exactly where the cinnabar cave is located on a woman." So saying, he lifted up his dragon home to give her a better view.

She tried to see, but it was in shadow, and no matter how much she twisted her head, she could not understand where he meant. At her sigh of exasperation, he reached out with his free hand for hers.

"You must press it now, Li Dee. I will tell you when you find it exactly."

"Touch it?" she practically squeaked. "Now?"

He smiled encouragingly. "Yes, now. Otherwise, how will you know what you are to do?"

"Of course," she said, mostly to herself. "How else will I know?"

And so, with his hand to guide her, she reached forward, between his legs. But her aim was not accurate, and her hand touched the side of his thigh. She had no more than brushed against him, but he jumped back as if burned.

"Your hand is very cold, Li Dee," he said by way of explanation.

She looked down at her hands, sympathy rising inside her. "Oh. Sorry."

"Rub your hands together."

She did, but her skin remained ice cold. "I cannot get them to warm up."

"Let me." And so he pressed her hands between his two larger ones. His heat was like a blast furnace, surrounding her and sending a shiver of appreciation all the way down her spine.

"Your hands are smaller than I expected. For some reason I thought all English were larger."

She smiled, her entire body warming under his attention. "Some of us are. But some of us aren't. The English like long fingers, and I am afraid I never quite grew enough."

He shifted his grip, adjusting his hands so that he cradled hers. "Your hands have an excellent shape. Usually water people have doughy hands that look plump like a water-filled sack. But your hands are narrower, without the plumpness of water. This means you have gold in your body and that your art may make a great deal of money."

He raised her hands to his mouth, blowing gently upon them as he spoke. "That is why I have hope for your designs and will allow my customers to see them."

"Because my hands aren't fat?"

"Because your destiny is shown in your body." He gently released her hand. "Try to find the jen-mo point now."

She nodded, looking stupidly at her hands. They weren't cold now. Indeed, she felt as if his breath had scorched them into a hypersensitivity. And he was already gently guiding her to that spot between his legs.

"Curl your fingers, but don't use your nails. Many tigresses use their middle finger, but any solid pressure will serve."

She didn't respond. What would she say? Instead, her entire focus seemed to be on her hand. The edge of her thumb brushed his thigh, and she started. He, too, jerked a bit, his dragon bobbing its head in a most interesting manner. But he did not release her hand. He guided her higher, while a kind of power seemed to envelop her hand. It was warm and tingling, coming from all sides of his body.

"I . . . I think I feel your yang fire."

"It is most strong there," he concurred. Then he began to release her hand. "Feel around. Gently. I will tell you when you have found it."

She did as she was bid, nervously brushing her fingers across the back of his dragon home. The flesh moved slightly with her, and she marveled at the wrinkled texture.

"You are doing well, Li Dee. Explore. It is good to understand the dragon's environment if you wish to draw him out."

"Your dragon is already well out," she said, stunned by her own brazenness. But when he rewarded her with a low chuckle, she felt emboldened even further.

Without further hesitation, she began to stroke his sac, noting the two solid ball-like things beneath the skin. She tested them very carefully, lifting them to feel their weight. She even squeezed—very gently—to see his reaction. She looked up at his face, seeing that his skin had indeed flushed rosy, and that his breath was harsher and louder as he breathed.

"Are you in pain?" she asked, abruptly pulling her hand away. But he guided her back.

"You are merely stoking the yang fire. It is just like when I prepare you to release your yin. You are bringing the yang to life."

And so she continued, cupping his dragon home again before sliding her finger further back.

"There."

She froze. "Here?"

"Yes. Push one finger in. Excellent. That will hold back the yang release and allow me to channel it correctly."

She slowly removed her hand, wondering at what she was supposed to do now. She had a guess, and all too soon Ru Shan began guiding her hand to its next location.

"It is time for you to meet the dragon, Li Dee. First you must touch it with your hands, stroking it from its home all the way to its head."

"Touch it?" she echoed softly, her voice thankfully more normal than before.

"With your fingers first. Then your mouth."

She jerked backward. "My mouth?"

He smiled. "Of course. Just as I sucked upon your breasts, you must also suck upon my dragon."

She looked at his huge dragon, feeling anxiety knot her stomach. She didn't know what to say. She wasn't sure she could put it in her mouth.

Then once again, he was lifting her chin to look directly at her. "You said you wished to help me."

"Yes, but . . ." She didn't know what to say.

"Have you ever put your finger in your mouth? Have you ever sucked on it after eating, or perhaps after pricking your finger?"

She nodded. "Yes. Of course."

"I tell you now that my dragon is cleaner than your fingers, for I am extremely careful with it. I keep it protected from the outside dirt and bathe it more often than most people wash their hands."

She nodded, torn somewhere between nervousness and excitement. But before she could resolve herself one way or another, she heard him sigh.

"I have pushed you too fast again. You English are difficult to manage."

"We most certainly are not!" she exclaimed, unsure why she reacted so strongly to his statement. "It is simply very new to me."

"You do not need to do this if—"

"No," she interrupted. "I want to learn." And she did. Very much.

And so with that thought in mind, she took hold of his dragon.

From the letters of Mei Lan Cheng

21 December, 1873
Dearest Li Hua—

  The Starving Mongoose Captain is back! Oh, he makes my stomach sick, but he wants more cloth and Sheng Fu wants to sell it to him. Sheng Fu has had the stitchers embroidering day and night now on long bolts, just so we can sell it to him. The work is very shoddy, very ugly, but Sheng Fu says the ghost people will not notice. He is wrong in that, but he would not listen to me. That is the first thing the Mongoose Captain said—that our work is worth very little.

I had hoped that the Mongoose Captain's words would anger Cheng Fu, but my husband simply smiled stupidly at the man. He is so greedy for the English gold that he has lost all sense! I pretended to be hurt by the captain's words. I began to sob loudly, then ran away as if I was too upset to continue. Cheng Fu was left to stare helplessly at the captain, unable to do any business at all that day.

But I paid for my deception last night. Cheng Fu was very angry, and now I must hide my face until it heals. I did not mind so long as it kept me away from the Starving Mongoose, but this morning Cheng Fu took our son away from his studies. He said that if I was too ill to translate, he would take Ru Shan.

There was nothing I could do, Li Hua. I had to go back to the store. I could not allow Ru Shan to be distracted. He is too unsettled a student for me to allow him a full day's escape. So I went to the store, limping on my bruised legs, my face painted and hidden behind a fan. I even brought Cheng Fu his favorite lunch of pork dumplings and prostrated myself before him in shame. I thought that with my contrition, he would send Ru Shan home.

He did not. He kept the boy at his side as a threat to me. To show me that I would have to cooperate or he would keep Ru Shan from his future as a scholar.

And that was not the only surprise, either! When the Starving Mongoose appeared, he brought someone *else with him. I do not remember the man's name. I call him Mr. Lost Cat because he had a beard like whiskers pointing in all directions—some even straight out from the side of his face! He seemed to look at everything, his beard quivering like cats' do when they are sniffing. He seemed to me like he was lost, looking all over for something familiar. Perhaps the pathway home. And so that is how I named him.*

The captain said Mr. Lost Cat knew Chinese and would interpret for us. Truthfully, he speaks very badly, and only in the way of the Cantonese First Boys—the servants of the other English. But I think he is less lost than I first believed. I think perhaps, like me, he understands more than he shows, and so now I must be very careful when I translate for Cheng Fu. I cannot lie anymore about what is being said.

—Mei Lan

Zen has nothing to grab on to.
When people who study Zen don't see it,
that is because they approach it too eagerly.
—Ying An

Chapter Eight

This should have been easy. But then, Ru Shan was beginning to understand that nothing with Li Dee was easy.

Over the years, he had been with many tigresses, from the most inexperienced all the way to Shi Po, who had developed techniques that strained the lengths of any man's control. Especially with the cubs—the novice tigresses—Ru Shan had learned to stand still, to focus on channeling his yang fire almost to the exclusion of all else. The woman, whether novice or experienced, became almost incidental. Irrelevant.

But not Li Dee. How an inexperienced white woman could so disrupt his concentration, he couldn't understand. But that, he supposed, was what he needed to learn. Or to overcome. He wasn't sure which.

Her hands were tentative, but not afraid. They were simply careful as she explored the length and girth and texture of his jade dragon. But then she became bolder, pulling slightly at his foreskin, moving the dragon left and right. She even sniffed it, unaware that her gentle exhalation against his dragon mouth had his entire body tightening with greedy anticipation.

He reached down, guiding her hands as he showed her how to slide his foreskin up and down.

"Like pumping the bellows in a smithy," he explained, "that will help the yang fire burn hot."

"But I thought you wanted me to . . . I mean, you said I should use my tongue."

He shook his head. "If you are not ready—"

"No," she interrupted. "I want to. I want to learn."

Of course she did. Li Dee was very bright and very curious.

"Do what you choose, but be very gentle. I will not react. I am going to begin the work of diverting the yang fire." At her confused look, he did his best to explain. "Nature makes a man expend his yang because that is how a child is planted in a woman's womb. But if I have no wish to create a child, all that qi—that *energy*—is wasted. What a jade dragon does is rechannel that energy, directing it not outside the body, but into the creation of an Immortal."

"You?"

"Yes. If I succeed."

"And so you wish me to heat your yang fire so that you can use that energy to become immortal." She tilted her head, looking at him with a mixture of awe and confusion. "This is possible? People have done this?"

"Oh yes."

"They live forever?"

Clearly she wanted to learn, so he crouched down before

her, deciding to help her understand. "Their bodies eventually die, though their physical life is much prolonged. It is the spirit—"

"Your soul?"

He shifted onto his knees. "I do not understand this word 'soul.' "

"It's our spirit. The part of us that lives forever. Everyone has one. After our bodies die, the soul continues forever with God."

He frowned. "But does your consciousness—your mind—walk with the Eternals now? With your God in the Heavenly Realm while you still breathe here on Earth?"

She shook her head. "No. Of course not."

"Then how do you know this spirit embryo—this soul—exists within you?"

She bit her lip, obviously thrown. "I don't know," she finally said. "It is what we are taught."

He sighed. "Then I believe you have an inkling of the truth, but do not possess full understanding. Your 'soul' does not exist until it has been created by mixing male yang and female yin. When the two are sufficiently stirred together with enough energy and fire, then an Immortal is created."

"But what does that mean? I mean, how do you know when you have stirred enough?"

"Because our minds go to the Heavenly Realm, and then we walk with the Immortals."

She gasped, wonder lighting her beautiful face. "Truly? Always?"

He smiled, remembering that he had asked the exact same questions so many years ago. "Truly," he answered. "But not always. Our bodies do need sustenance, so we return here. But a true Immortal can visit the Heavenly Realm often."

She glanced down, looking at his chest, his still hungry dragon, at his entire naked body. "Are you close?"

He sighed. "I was. I have entered the Chamber of Swinging Lanterns three times now. But I have not progressed further. And I have not even gotten that far for the last two years."

"But you want to try again. Because you have so much yang?"

"Yes. And because you have given me so much yin." He straightened. "Do you wish to help me?" He wasn't sure why he asked. She was his slave. He could order her to assist him. But he had no intention of angering the woman holding his genitals. And besides, Li Dee had a good heart. She seemed genuinely interested in helping him.

True to his expectations, Li Dee straightened her shoulders. "What should I do?"

He smiled in appreciation, then began his instructions. "Continue to stroke the yang fire but do not seek my advice or help. It will disrupt my focus. I will appear as if in a trance and can stay that way for many hours." He felt his lips curve into a smile. "The creation of an Immortal takes much time."

She nodded and gently reached out for his jade dragon. "I will be gentle."

"I know you will." And then, in a supreme act of trust, he closed his eyes and began the process of redirecting his yang.

As before, she learned quickly. With little more than an occasional murmur from him, she understood how much pressure was required, how fast a stroke, how firm a grip. Soon, he was able to enjoy the sensation of his yang building, the exquisite feel of a woman's tongue on his dragon, the warmth of being surrounded by Li Dee's yin.

She was an extraordinary woman, he thought, even as his mind began to stir his yang into the eternal circle of creation. Both his major river of yang and the minor river of yin began to flow, and all was kept in wondrous agitation by Li Dee.

She had a beautiful laugh. Low and throaty, and so different from the Chinese women he knew. They had high-pitched giggles, like very young girls. Even his mother had tittered rather than laughed, and he was startled to realize that he preferred Li Dee's more open sound.

She didn't laugh in his presence. No, she made soft low moans of enjoyment when he suckled her yin, but she had never actually laughed. But he had heard her. Nearly a week ago with Fu De. She and the servant had been studying each other's languages, practicing the written words with sponge brushes. Ru Shan had come to the apartment early and ended up standing out in the hallway, wondering at the joyful sound from within. Just hearing that sound— so happy and carefree—had churned the yang within him into hot lava.

Her strokes on his dragon were getting longer now. Full and practiced. But it was when she used her tongue that his yang surged. She didn't do it often, still nervous. But every tentative touch had his body soaring with power.

It was during one of those bursts that he at last understood his anger at Fu De that day so long ago. It did not really bother him that the boy had been learning English. His fury was because Li Dee had shared such happiness with a servant rather than with him.

The yang fire was burning hotter now. He could hear his breath becoming more ragged, less controlled. But he redoubled his focus, visualizing his breath as a large mixing spoon, stirring his yang with Li Dee's yin, bringing the two together to create a great new creature—an Immortal.

And as the image stirred his dual rivers, it also brought to mind the memory of his mother standing in her courtyard stirring the dye she sometimes used to color the cotton they sold. It was a great, laborious task, and though she had helpers, she rarely trusted them. Servant girls were small and frightened of the hot cauldron—with good reason. The dye was heated to a boil and the cloth was heavy and bulky, especially when wet. Many people had suffered terrible burns from similar tasks. Her servants did all they could to be incompetent at the dangerous task so they would be excused from assisting.

As a boy, Ru Shan had helped her, but as an adult he was often too busy selling their wares to assist in their construction. So it had been with considerable surprise one afternoon when he had returned home to hear a man not his father in his mother's courtyard.

Ru Shan was not supposed to look. He knew to respect a woman's private garden. But just then his mother released a peal of laughter, quickly stifled, but true laughter nonetheless. It had been a long time since he had heard such a thing. Not since he was a child performing antics for her amusement. And so, without thought, he walked to the wall and peered over.

He recognized the man with his mother. A sea captain from England with a bushy beard and an infectious laugh. The man wished to buy bales of cotton, but they had not been dyed yet. Obviously, he had come to help with the work.

Still, Ru Shan had been stunned. True, Mei Lan his mother knew the ship captain from before. She was often called to help as a translator. She had learned English from a missionary and it had been a great boon to the Chang family business. The English liked to converse in their own language, even if that meant speaking through a woman. And so the two obviously knew each other, but that did not mean the captain should come to their home. Should burden his delicate mother with his white smells and his thick hands.

Ru Shan had been on the verge of bodily throwing the man from his home until his mother laughed again. At a silly antic of the captain's. Again the sound had been quickly stifled against his mother's tiny hand, but Ru Shan had heard it nonetheless. And so he had backed away.

What son would take joy from his mother? The woman worked tirelessly for the benefit of the Cheng family. If the captain eased the burden of the arduous dyeing task, he would not interfere.

But he had never forgotten the moment either.

His body was tightening now, readying for release. Similarly, his mind was ready as well, the yin and yang mixing freely. He was prepared to step into a Heavenly Courtyard, prepared to see the images the Immortals chose to reveal to him.

Except, he could not seem to remain focused. Li Dee had slicked his dragon's mouth with her tongue. She had even ventured to put her entire mouth around him, sucking in the same manner in which he had done to her. Great Heaven, she learned quickly. His legs were shaking, and his breath rasped in and out of his throat. Surely he would reach immortality today.

And yet, his mind would not settle enough to allow the transformation. Memories, images, began flashing through his mind. He heard once again Li Dee's laugh. Then it was not Li Dee but his mother who giggled. He saw the white captain as the man danced around carrying dripping red cotton that splashed his face. But it was not dye. It was blood.

He saw himself as a boy, stirring the dye pot, the heat beating at his face, his arms aching with the strain. His blood pounded in his ears as the dye churned and boiled, splashing red over his arms, his face. The taste was rank, the pain real.

His mother screamed.

The stir stick was heavy in his hand as he fell to his knees.

The captain was dead.

A bellow roared up from his throat, erupting like a volcano of sound. His body spasmed as his control shredded like paper. He tore himself away from Li Dee and fell to his knees. His body convulsed, over and over, as his seed and the qi energy that went with it spilled onto the floor. Over and over it spewed from him, and there was nothing he could do to prevent it.

In the distance, he heard Li Dee cry out, shocked and afraid. Her words came in anxious English that his mind had no way to translate.

"Are you hurt? Did I hurt you?"

He didn't know what she said or what she intended, but he reached for her hand, clutching it to his chest as his ragged breathing steadied. Her fingers were small but powerful, and he took comfort from the strength in her delicate bones.

And eventually, his sanity returned.

She was kneeling beside him, one hand tucked against his chest, the other supporting his back. And she was saying something.

"Do you need a doctor?"

He shook his head, a sigh releasing the last of his

strength into the air. "I was almost there, Li Dee. I was almost an Immortal. It felt so close."

"What happened?" Her breath was a warm balm across his shoulder.

"Memories. Distractions." He looked down at his spent energy that dirtied the floor. "And now I have to begin it all again." He pushed slowly up to his knees.

"You want to start again now?" she whispered, clearly doubtful.

So was he. "I cannot try that again just now," he answered. It took great effort to climb onto the bed, bringing her with him, but he would not release her. He liked the feel of her hand in his too much. "We believe that every time a man expends his qi like that, he shortens his life by as much as a year." He settled onto his side, gently tucking her against him.

"You are staying here?" She moved easily, but her voice was high and anxious.

"Fu De cannot serve you tonight," he said firmly. "I will tend to you." Then he pushed her forward slightly so he could drape his leg around hers. With his head tucked into the sweet perfume of her hair, he closed his eyes knowing they would sleep easily in the Cleaving Cicadas position.

But rest did not come to him. Despite his exhaustion, his mind would not let him sleep. All too soon, he found himself speaking to Li Dee what he knew she could not possibly understand. His story came from nowhere, having no relevance to their situation. And yet, he found he wanted to tell her, wanted her to know how his journey had begun.

"I first learned of the dragon and tigress practice when I was a young man, already growing angry in my heart. My cousin came to stay with us from Peking. He had taken the Imperial examination a few years earlier, but had not done well. He was given a low government position and everyone called him a failure, even his wife."

He smiled to himself, remembering his cousin's wide face. "Zhao Gao was also a water person like you, Li Dee. But his was mixed with earth, which hindered and stopped his flow. Everything he did seemed to be hard for him, and his life was filled with obstacles. Even his body was awkward, with wide-spaced eyes and a mouth full of gaps."

He sighed, pulling her body tighter against him, his yang naturally seeking to be linked to her yin. But even with her tucked so intimately against him, he could not quiet his thoughts or still his mouth.

"I did not want him to visit us. I was very afraid of his fortune—his life path. No greater shame can befall a Chinese man than to spend years in study, a fortune on tutors, the enormous expense of traveling for the exam, only to perform badly. I did not want to be associated with such a man because I was very afraid of that future myself." He sighed at his own stupidity. "Of course, I didn't take the exam. My father had already decided that I would spend my life with him in the store."

"Is that why you were angry?" Li Dee asked. "Because you were not going to take the exam?"

He shook his head, rubbing his chin across her shoulder as he answered. "I was angry because I had to study. Locked in a tiny room with an old man to learn about men long since dead. I found it stupid and difficult, but I wanted to make my mother proud. She was the one who wished me to become a great scholar."

"Caught between a mother and a father. It must have been difficult."

"Everything about the Imperial exam is difficult. Truthfully, I was secretly overjoyed when my father liberated me to work in the store. My mother was the only one who grieved." He shifted slightly, raising up on one arm. "But I did not know that then, and I greatly feared my cousin's fortune would somehow contaminate me."

He leaned forward, letting his cheek feel the smoothness of Li Dee's shoulder. Except, of course, she was still clothed, and he frowned at the stiff peasant fabric. "Remove your shirt," he ordered. "I will perform your breast exercises from this position tonight."

She did as he bade, sitting up to remove her coolie tunic. He was pleased to see that there was no hesitation in her movements, only a slight confusion as he shifted her to the Goat Hugging-Tree pose. Though not the full position, it was still one of his favorites. It allowed him to remain seated, his back relaxed against the wall while still able to perform his tasks. At his direction, she settled between his legs, her back toward his chest.

At first she remained rigidly upright, but as he reached around her to begin stroking her breasts, she gradually settled back, lying against him, her naked chest open to his view.

"It pleases me that you are comfortable like this." He spoke without thought, not even realizing the truth of his statement until he had said the words aloud. "I have never wished to harm you," he added.

"I know," she answered. He heard resignation and unhappiness in her tone.

He sighed. "I know you wish to be free, Li Dee, but surely you must see that I cannot release you yet. I need your yin. And even more than that, I need to understand."

She turned, looking at him over her shoulder. "Understand what?"

"How I have lost the middle path."

"But I can't help you—"

He pressed his finger to her mouth, stopping her words. "Not now, Li Dee. Let us do your exercises." He felt her nod in acknowledgment, then she returned to her position facing away from him. Once again, he began circling her breasts. He hoped that this activity would quiet his mind, but he had done it so many times with her that his hands performed as if by rote, leaving his thoughts to wander where they would.

They returned to his cousin Zhao Gao.

"I didn't know why Zhao Gao was coming to Shanghai, merely that he wished to visit."

He pulled Li Dee close to his chest, letting his cheek rest upon her hair as he stroked circles around her breasts and tugged gently at her nipples. She was well used to this by now, and no longer gasped or moaned when he stirred her yin. But pressed this closely together, he could hear the increase in her breath and feel the added heat from her skin. Indeed, by now, he knew the early stages of her arousal almost as well as his own.

"He came to our home early in the afternoon on a day so hot even the flies did not move. I had been watching for him instead of studying." He felt a chuckle rumble through his body. "I will never forget my first sight of Zhao Gao. I expected him to be small and wretched as befit a family disgrace. Instead, he was a large man, wreathed in smiles and large gestures. His voice boomed through the courtyard, announcing his presence the way a mountain river gushes in spring. Except it was summer and we were all weak from the heat."

"One of my father's friends is like that," Li Dee murmured. "Large and happy. There is no other way to describe him, except that everyone wishes to be near him."

He dropped a gentle kiss upon Li Dee's forehead, mentally sending her some of his yang with the gesture. "That is exactly how it was with Zhao Gao. Everyone liked him. He even made my mother happy enough to sing while she worked. Joy ran through our home like a river and everyone rejoiced. Everyone, that is, except me." He shifted uncomfortably, wishing he had been brighter as a child. He had wasted so much time hating what he did not understand.

Li Dee shifted, trying to look at him, but he did not allow her to turn. "You didn't like him?"

"I didn't understand him. I thought he should feel ashamed because everyone called him an *a dou*—a useless one—and so when he didn't, I reminded everyone what a failure he was." He sighed, feeling guilt weigh down his spirit. "I was cruel, Li Dee."

"You were young."

"Not that young. I knew better."

He had begun the next set of circles, the ones that stimulated yin flow rather than quieted it. And so he was not surprised when she began to stir slightly in his arms, her breath coming in deeper rhythms as she pushed for more information. "What happened? To Zhao Gao?"

"He invited me to serve as Shi Po's green dragon. That is how I met her."

He could feel her confusion. "I thought you were a jade dragon. Or is that the name of . . ." Her voice trailed away.

"Yes, that is the name of my yang center. But it is also my status. Not then, of course. I was just a green dragon— a man Shi Po used for her training, the training of a tigress." He smiled in memory. "I had no idea. I thought Zhao Gao was trying to make friends with me by taking me to a prostitute. Later he told me it was because I obviously had too much yang, and Shi Po needed more."

"What did she do to you?"

He paused, drawing out Li Dee's nipples as he remembered. "She did almost exactly what you did earlier. Only many more times, drawing out my seed over and over." He shifted so that he could look into her eyes. "That is what a tigress does. She takes a man's yang, mixes it—"

"With her own yin to become a female Immortal," she finished for him.

He smiled, pleased that she understood. And then she startled him even more.

"Teach me how to do that," she ordered, though she phrased it more as a plea. "I wish to become an Immortal as well."

His hands stilled. "But you cannot."

"Why not? Because I am English? A ghost person who is only a pet?"

He did not want to confirm her words, because he could see that would make her angry, but that was indeed the truth.

She shook her head, obviously reading the truth from his expression. "You are wrong," she said firmly. "I am a person, not an animal. And I can learn."

He nodded slowly, wondering if what she said might be true.

"What must I do?" she asked.

It took him a while to answer. He did not want her to try and fail, then fall into despair. But perhaps he underestimated her. Perhaps some of the ghost people like Li Dee were more substantial than anyone in China believed.

"You have taken my yang," he said. "I will stimulate your yin to its fullest extent, if you wish. When the yin river is upon you, you must mix it with my yang, letting it carry you to Heaven."

She nodded. "I can do that."

He smiled. "I said much the same thing when Zhao Gao explained the truth to me." He sighed. "That was Zhao Gao's secret, you see. He could not be a great scholar or even a great official. But he could become immortal, and it was that journey that brought him—and everyone else—such joy."

"So he was not such a failure after all," murmured Li Dee.

"No, he was not." He redirected his energies to raising Li Dee's yin, but something in his voice must have given him away, because she stopped his movements. With her two tiny hands, she held his in place as she turned to look at him.

"You think you are a failure like Zhao Gao, don't you?" It was more a statement than a question, and when he did not respond, she continued, narrowing her eyes as she studied his face. "You did not pass the Imperial exam."

"I did not take the exam."

She nodded. "Very true, but that means you did not get a chance to shine. To take a high government position. Right?"

He hesitated. Instinct warned him to stop her thoughts now, to use his power over her to silence this line of questions. But Shi Po had told him to reveal his secrets to Li Dee. She had said he would never find his way back to the middle path unless he did. And so he remained silent, letting Li Dee find him.

"Would you have done well on the test?"

He could not look at her when he spoke, let his gaze slide away. "I was an indifferent scholar at best. I would have done as badly as Zhao Gao."

"So you didn't take the test, and now the shop isn't doing well?"

He shook his head, unable to answer.

"Is that under your control? Or your father's?"

"My father injured his back . . . some time ago. It still pains him to walk. I have been in exclusive charge of the shop now for two years."

He was unable to keep his gaze from hers as she nodded, her expression thoughtful. "Your control then. Except it isn't doing so well." Her gaze slid to the floor where he had so recently released his seed. "And even this Taoist middle path of yours isn't working out so great."

Spoken so baldly like that—especially in English, the language of the barbarians—made Ru Shan's temper rise. He could not even blame it on his yang. It was his pride that was pricked, and it made him push her forward, away from him.

"I grow tired of this," he snapped. But she would not stop.

"And I grow tired of waiting for you to realize that I am as smart, as capable as any Chinese woman."

"Moreso," he admitted before he had the chance to stop himself.

"And do your countrymen keep Chinese women as pets? Locked in their rooms, never able to leave?"

"You are fed, you have clothing. It is more than many of my countrymen."

"I do not have my freedom."

"Neither do Chinese women." And with that he pushed her aside, stepping to the floor to tower over her, his voice curt. "I am done with this conversation. If you wish me to stimulate your yin, I will do that now."

She glared at him, her lips pursed into a tight circle. "Would you keep an Immortal locked in?"

"Of course not."

She abruptly squared her shoulders. "Then I will become one, and you will be forced to release me."

He sighed, the wind coming from the farthest reaches of his body. "Li Dee, why do you strive for something you cannot attain?"

She pushed to her feet, her movement quick and abrupt. Standing before him, she did not reach much farther than his chin, and yet she faced him as if she were three times his size. "My name is Lydia! Lih-dee-ah. You always drop the A."

He bowed slightly, giving her this tiny measure of control. "Very well, Lih Dee Ah."

She stood there, her emotions warring upon her face. He saw fury, hatred, desperation, and an odd kind of hope slip through her mobile features. "I hate you!" she spat as her fists bunched uselessly at her sides.

"I know," he answered softly. How different she was from the Chinese women he knew who went about covered in white makeup and a bland expression. Without the Confucian discipline the Chinese imposed from birth, Lydia had never learned to control the tides—the passions—that could so dominate a water person. And yet, he found he liked her this way. Happy or furious, she seemed more substantial than any woman he had yet met. Even Shi Po.

And that thought shook his world.

"You are not what I expected," he finally acknowledged. "And yet, I find myself most pleased with you."

He reached out, touching her face in a tender caress. "Become an Immortal, Lydiah," he challenged. "Because I will never release you otherwise."

NAME:_____

ADDRESS:_____

_____

_____

TELEPHONE:_____

E-MAIL:_____

_____ I want to pay by credit card.

__ Visa   __ MasterCard   __ Discover

Account Number:_____

Expiration date:_____

SIGNATURE:_____

Send this form, along with $2.00 shipping and handling for your FREE books, to:

Historical Romance Book Club
20 Academy Street
Norwalk, CT 06850-4032

Or fax (must include credit card information!) to: 610.995.9274.
You can also sign up on the Web at <u>www.dorchesterpub.com</u>.

Offer open to residents of the U.S. and Canada only. Canadian residents, please call 1.800.481.9191 for pricing information.

The tigress first learns from her mother how to survive. She then has three paths on which to begin her hunt. No matter which path she walks, the Green Dragon is her prey. She gathers the essences of the Dragon and Tiger. When the essences fuse, the spirit embryo manifests and carries her to the Heavenly Abode, where Hsi Wang Hu happily bestows the Peach of Immortality upon her new daughter.

— White tigress Manual

Chapter Nine

Lydia trembled as Ru Shan's caress sent a trail of fire across her cheek, but she did not let it frighten her. She was becoming used to his touch. Indeed, she greatly feared she was beginning to crave it. Especially now, when the breast circles were finished and he readied himself to leave. Except, of course, this time he wasn't leaving.

She straightened, steeling herself for the challenge. "What should I do to become an Immortal?"

He smiled and she couldn't decide if he was mocking her or pleased with her determination. A little of both, she guessed. He clearly didn't think she could do it.

"I will raise your yin to a great river—"

"Which I direct into your yang, mixing them together," she finished for him. "I know that. But how exactly do I do that?"

He paused, tilting his head slightly and staring. She hated when he did that. All the men she knew looked through her, as if they already knew what they would see and couldn't be bothered with actually looking. But not Ru Shan. He looked at her. He *studied* her. He tried to understand exactly what she was thinking and doing.

She knew that was good. After all, the more he saw her as a person, the more likely she would be to gain her freedom. And yet, whenever he looked at her with such focused intensity, she felt as if he were stripping away not only the layers of her clothing—after all, she stood barebreasted before him even now—but her skin as well.

Did the Chinese have the ability to read minds? She didn't think so, and yet Ru Shan looked as if he were trying. Then he sighed, lifting his shoulders in a shrug.

"I don't know how to mix the yin and yang properly, Lydiah. If I did, I would already have achieved my goal."

"But you have an idea."

He shook his head. "I know what I do. I think what I wish to happen, and sometimes my body reflects my thoughts. And sometimes—"

"It doesn't work at all." She took a deep breath. "Very well. I will direct my thoughts."

He nodded, acknowledging her desire even though he thought it ridiculous. Better yet, he was willing to help her achieve it even though he thought it impossible. She couldn't help but compare such openness to Maxwell. Had her fiancé ever helped her do something he thought silly? She suspected not. And though she knew she was being disloyal, she had to acknowledge that in this respect, Ru Shan was the superior man.

She was still gripped in the shock of that realization when Ru Shan spoke, effectively cutting off all other thoughts.

"You must remove your pants."

"What?"

He raised a single eyebrow in irritation. "The yin source is at your breasts. But the river flows through your cinnabar cave. I must have access to that."

"But . . . ," she stammered. He couldn't possibly mean . . . "You said I would remain a virgin." Indeed, she had clung to that promise from the very beginning: that she might escape from Ru Shan with her purity intact. If he had lied . . . She swallowed. He was still larger than she; he could force the issue if he chose.

"You will remain a virgin. I have no intention of placing my jade dragon inside you." He almost sounded repulsed at the thought, and she stiffened at the insult. Then his expression softened into an understanding smile. "I have expended enough yang tonight, Lydiah. I will not risk losing my seed again."

She nodded, mollified. "But then . . ."

He folded his arms across his chest, clearly impatient. "Do you wish to question, or do you wish to act? I can obtain all the yin I need from you simply from your breasts. But if you wish to pursue the path of the Immortals, then you must undress completely. It is your choice."

She swallowed. They both already knew her choice, so without another word she began to slowly untie the cording that held up her peasant pants. But her hands were shaking, her fingers clumsy. He did not help her this time, as he usually did. He was making sure she chose this option, with no coercion from him. But still, it took all her will to untie the knot.

This was the only way. The only way to escape. To gain her freedom. And so she released the cord and let the peasant pants slip to the floor. Then she stood before him, completely naked. She didn't even have the covering of her body hair as Fu De had instructed her to keep herself completely shaved.

Ru Shan looked at her, his almond eyes darkening as he began to walk, stepping to her side to view her from all angles. She shifted uncomfortably, feeling awkward with his inspection, but startled to see his jade dragon rise even as he continued to stare.

"What are you looking at?"

He was eyeing her legs, his expression thoughtful. "Would you like me to tell you what I see in your body? As I've said, we Chinese believe that a person's body reveals his or her fortune. Would you like to know yours?"

She didn't speak, her embarrassment making her throat tight. But she was able to nod, and he began to speak.

"The body has three stations: the head, the torso, and the legs, starting from the waist. Yours are evenly proportioned, suggesting that you are flexible, able to achieve in both the physical and mental aspects of life. Your neck and your legs are long, but not too long, indicating you are a swan—meaning you could have great success but only if you make the right choices." He paused, lifting his gaze to look directly at her. "Your water encourages you to wash one way or another, but it is your intellect that must direct the flow. Never forget that."

"I am a prisoner, Ru Shan. My intellect does not choose at all."

His expression darkened as he glared at her. "Your intellect chooses a great deal, Lydiah. Or do you claim now to be simply an ignorant beast?"

She felt her face heat with shame, and she looked away. "No. Of course not."

He nodded. Returning his gaze to her lower body, he

said, "Your waist is short and thin. Much better than when you first arrived into my care. This also indicates good balance and flexibility in all things." He sighed, stepping forward to touch her lower back. "It is your buttocks that show your downfall, Lydiah."

He flattened his hand, letting it drift slowly over the curve of her bottom. She felt her muscles clench there, stronger after all her work with the stone dragon, and yet such intimacy did not frighten her as she expected. Instead, his caress felt admiring even as he criticized her shape.

"Rounded, Lydiah. Rounded hips, rounded bottom mean you are both strong-minded and idealistic." He shook his head, even as he stepped behind her, bringing his other hand around to stroke and lift her bottom. "You do not want to see the world as it is, Lydiah, but as you wish it to be."

Then to her shock, he pressed himself forward, his jade dragon a hard, hot ridge between her buttocks. He was still naked, seemingly at ease with his body in a way no Englishman was—to her knowledge, at least. And she actually jumped when she felt it pulse against her backside.

"Soft, Lydiah," he whispered. "Soft and giving. Very pleasing to the jade dragon, but you cannot let your bottom rule your head." He sighed. "I do not think your mind will overcome the yin rush," he warned.

"We'll see," she returned. But despite her bravado, she was well aware of her rapid pulse and the roaring of blood through her body. She had not meant to react to his jade dragon; it was merely an organ, nothing more. And yet, as it heated the crevice between her legs, she could not stop herself from pressing against it, from feeling the textures and pulse of his living flesh.

It was like nothing she'd ever experienced before, and she wasn't sure she should enjoy it so much. And yet there it was—hot, hard, and so alive. Not more than an hour ago, she had touched it, stroked it, sucked on it! Indeed, she had done things to it she could never imagine doing to anyone else. Not even Maxwell. And yet this feeling, this presence between her buttocks, was so different. So intriguing.

Perhaps he was right. Perhaps her bottom was stronger than her mind. And then, before she could pull away, Ru Shan reached around her, effectively trapping her with his arms. He began to circle her breasts again, pulling her upper body back against him while simultaneously pushing his jade dragon forward. Not piercing between her legs, thank God, but longwise against her, as if he too enjoyed just feeling her.

"I will begin with your breasts, Lydiah. Imagine the yin flow swelling, growing behind your nipples."

She did. Indeed, that was what always happened when he rubbed her breasts; and he had been priming them for a while now, so that when he began tugging on her nipples, the tingling cord was already there, pulling from his fingertips, through her body, all the way to deep within her belly. Then he was speaking again, his voice a low murmur behind her right ear, a deep sound that echoed in the yin flow throughout her.

"Give yourself up to these sensations. We are merely beginning, Lydiah. You do not need to control the flow yet."

She nodded her assent and did as he bade, relaxing as never before into the sensations of his hands upon her breasts, the swelling crest of each breast turning molten, as if she were melting inside into a bright liquid line straight to her womb.

"Your yin water is beginning to flow. Do you not feel it?"

She frowned, unsure what he meant. He demonstrated as if she had voiced her confusion aloud. Instead of upward from her belly to her nipples, this time his hands flowed downward. From the peak of her tightened nipples, he opened his hands, pulling down until he cupped each breast. Then his fingers continued to flow down, over her ribs, tucking close to her waist before flaring again over the jut of each hip bone. He had done as much many times before, only in the opposite direction, but this time his fingers continued questing lower, into the valley above each leg. That naturally pulled each of his hands closer together and he extended deeper, his fingers fluttering over her shaven mound and then deeper still.

She squeaked in alarm, but he did not release her. Indeed, as she began to struggle, he held her tighter.

"Trust me, Lydiah," he whispered. And then the fingers of his right hand pushed deep between her legs.

She had no name for what he touched, but she felt his long finger in a kind of superawareness. The movements were excruciatingly slow, and she held her breath as she felt him wiggle slightly, slipping deeper into the places no one had ever touched.

His hold slackened, his attention clearly diverted to what he was touching. She knew she could surprise him now and break his restraining grip. But she didn't want to. As alien as his finger felt, it also felt hot and silky. And when he touched a certain point, a special point, her body shivered in the most amazing way. It began right where he was and expanded swiftly outward, simultaneously moving down to her toes and up past her breasts, all the way up into her mind. But oddly enough, the shiver did not leave her feeling more relaxed, just more tense. More curious. More . . . Just *more*.

It made no sense, but such were her thoughts as his finger continued to delve deeper.

"Do you feel the wetness here? That is your yin rain as it begins to flow."

Yes, she felt the wetness. But more she felt his fingers, still there, still probing. He was still touching, and so she relaxed her legs, letting them slip farther apart. Letting him touch more.

But he didn't. Instead, he withdrew his hands, stepping away from behind her. She shifted, shocked and confused. "Is that all there is?" she asked. It couldn't be possible. There had to be more.

"There is much more," he answered, his voice a deep rumble. "But we cannot do this standing. All your concentration will be on what you must do and all my concentration will be on stimulating your yin flow. You must lie down. On your back."

She did as he directed, feeling the heat fading slightly even as the anticipation built. But Ru Shan did not seem concerned. He took his time, gently placing a pillow behind her back lengthwise so it slid between her shoulder blades.

"You will want your head to tilt lower than your buttocks to encourage the yin flow to your head," he explained.

She nodded, lying carefully backward only to lift back up when he did not sit beside her as before. This time he crossed to the bottom of her bed, gently raising and stroking her calves as he separated her legs.

She wanted to ask him what he was doing, but she could not. Her throat was too closed, her embarrassment high as her captor knelt between her legs. She was completely exposed to him, her—what had he called it?—her *cinnabar cave* open as never before.

And then, to her shock, he continued lifting her right leg higher and higher to rest upon his shoulder. "This is called the Horse Shaking his Hoof position. I will be able to judge the flow of your yin by the movements of your left leg. But this one," he added as he once again stroked her right leg, "can rest upon my shoulder or back." He suddenly smiled, his face brightening with a rare mischievousness. "You will probably hit my back with your heel. Do not worry that you will hurt me. I am very strong."

She didn't know how to respond. She had never seen him look so boyish before.

"Many dragons don't enjoy this part as much. They prefer to work on their own immortality. But I take great pleasure in a woman's yin river." He tilted his head, a moment of uncertainty flashing in his eyes. "Many people say the ghost women do not enjoy their yin flow. I hope they are wrong."

Lydia nodded because he expected her to. In truth, she didn't know how to react. This was all so strange. And yet, even though the tingling had faded the moment Ru Shan pulled away from her, she felt a burgeoning sense of daring. Whatever would come now, Lydia actively sought it, could not wait for it to begin, even as her skin flushed a hot red of lingering embarrassment.

"I will begin gently," he said, "with soft strokes and massage to heat the water." And then he fitted action to his words.

His hands stroked the inside of her thighs, flowing smoothly upward toward the opening of her cinnabar cave. The yin heat returned in a rush, and she discovered she was impatient with his slow strokes, anxious for him to approach closer as he had before. Would he never touch her cinnabar cave?

But then he did. Just as with her breasts, he traced the outside of her cave with each thumb, moving slowly from back to front. Without thinking, she arched into his hands, pushing for him to go deeper or closer or something. In truth, she didn't know what she wanted, only that she did.

But he would not be rushed. His thumbs connected, but too high, above the spot she wanted. And then he reversed direction, moving back the way he had come.

"Ru Shan," she murmured, not even knowing why.

"Patience, Lydiah. You must do this slowly. Focus on moving your breath. It helps the yin flow."

She nodded, trusting him. And so she closed her eyes, relaxing her body, doing her best to keep her heartbeat steady and her breath even. But there was no controlling this. There was only his touch and the fire it produced. And still he continued to circle her cinnabar cave, flowing up— too high—and flowing down—too shallow.

"It is not enough," she gasped, only now realizing that she had arched again, seeking his fingers. She used her legs as well, drawing him closer with her upraised leg and wrapping the lower one about his waist.

"The river is stronger now. It will rush upon you soon, Lydiah. Be ready to direct it."

She nodded, trying to hold her focus, not even sure for what. And then he began pushing into her cave. Not deeply. Just in and out, in and out, with both thumbs. And she felt each press, each slide of his fingers like the breath of a great bellows stoking the heat inside her. The yin river was strong now, like hot lava flooding her body, invading her blood. Perhaps it was her blood as it rushed about inside her, seeking an outlet.

"Your rain is most sweet, Lydiah. And it flows so easily."
She heard awe in his voice, even a kind of reverence, but it
wasn't enough. She squirmed beneath him, barely register-
ing that he had shifted positions. Where before he had
knelt between her legs, now he lay down, placing his face
closer to her cave.

"What . . ." She meant to ask what he was doing, what
would come next, but she had no breath, and so she simply
closed her eyes, giving herself up to the yin.

"Now, Lydiah. Control the yin now."

She barely heard him, so loud was the rush of blood in
her ears. But when his meaning at last penetrated her consciousness, she made one last-ditch effort to corral her
thoughts.

And then he touched her. One thumb pressed into the
spot above the cave. It wasn't a hard push, but it felt like a
bolt of lightning, destroying her control. Then he began to
circle his thumb slowly, clockwise, while the yin lava took
over. Her body convulsed, surging upward from just that
spot. It was as if her entire body were controlled from
there. One circle of his thumb, and she became a whipcord
of power, flying out of control.

She cried out in shock as power and joy warred for full
expression. It was uncontainable—this immense feeling—
and her mind went numb from the power of it all.

But it did not end there. Ru Shan's hand slipped forward,
holding down her bucking hips. She clung to him, her only
bulwark in this tumultuous sea. And as her legs gripped his
back, he bent his head.

She could not see what he did, but she felt it. Hot and
wet, stroking once then twice in the same first pattern as his
thumbs had. She fought to move away from him, needing
less, not more. But he would not release her. Instead, he

pressed into her, extending inside, then withdrawing. She barely felt it, though some part of her registered his thrusts. Ten of them, in and out.

The stormy yin sea was just beginning to calm when he changed the pattern. This time he pushed not inside her, but above, on that one spot. Ten pulses, each one finished with a tiny circle.

Again the power crashed down upon her, tossing her body about. Her mind floundered, trying to find sanity in this explosion, but there was no safe haven, no place to regroup. These feelings would not be contained, and so she gave up, allowing herself to be carried along into the bliss that awaited.

Over and over the pattern repeated. Ru Shan would return to thrusting into her cinnabar cave, and she would gain breath and strength . . . but only for a moment. And then his tongue—for that's what he used—would press back to that spot. Ten tiny circles that shattered what little control she'd established. Ten tiny circles that spiraled through her body, convulsing her muscles however they willed while her mind reveled in the wondrous power of it all.

She had no control. Only joy.

On and on and on it went. In fabulous rhythm, in glorious abandon.

No control.

Only circles of bliss.

More!

She came back to herself slowly, by inches, and with a languid contentment that would have made her smile if she'd had the energy. The most she could do was catalogue her own body and her surroundings with a slow laziness.

She was lying flat on her back, her coarse blanket tucked

over her naked body. Beside her lay a person—Ru Shan—his face and body beautiful in sleep. Odd that she had never thought him beautiful before now. Awake, he had too much vitality for her to think about beauty. He was strong. Powerful. Dominant. And oddly gentle. But never anything so passive as pretty.

But asleep, his entire being settled into a most pleasing aspect. His skin turned a kind of golden yellow and his jawline softened to handsome rather than stern. Like her, he was naked, and so she could see the definition of muscles in his upper back and arm. And though the hard cording of his neck did not stand out, she knew it was there, as well as the impressive girth of his shoulders.

She stretched out her hand, wanting to touch him, to feel the pulse of the sleeping Ru Shan. Did it beat gentler now? Or was his heart as thunderous as when he was awake?

She froze, her awareness spinning back to her. Not just of her surroundings, but also of her situation. She was a prisoner. Not just a prisoner, but Ru Shan's prisoner. It made no difference that he was a kind master or that his culture accepted everything he did as perfectly normal. She was still a prisoner.

She had no business touching her master with any kind of tenderness at all. In fact . . .

And that was the moment she remembered. She remembered just how much she'd touched Ru Shan. And how much he'd touched her. And that she'd wanted him to. That she'd wanted . . .

So much. Too much.

Why had she allowed it? Because she thought she could become an Immortal? If such a thing existed, it would not happen for her. She would never be able to direct that incredible yin tide. That Ru Shan had come close was a testament to his incredible force of will. That she had even conceived she could do something that he had not attained in years of study was patently ridiculous.

But now she knew the truth. She would never become an Immortal. Not anytime soon, at least. Which meant it would be forever until she could regain her freedom.

It took less than a moment to make the last leap of logic. That last step was to realize her jailor was asleep. Heavily asleep, by the looks of him. And Fu De was still gone. She had become so used to accepting their complete power over her, she had nearly forgotten to look for opportunities.

Her heart began hammering triple-time, urging her to move quickly. After all, the outside sky was gray, not black. It was probably an hour or so before dawn. Fu De could return at any moment. Or Ru Shan might wake. Either way, she had to leave now if she had any hope of escape.

Still, she forced herself to move slowly, easing out of bed. There was little to choose from by way of clothing. Her peasant garb was better than her silk robe, so she quickly pulled that on. The key to both doors—her inner room and the exterior door—was in Ru Shan's clothing, so she quickly searched there, finding the hard metal soon enough.

She was in the act of pulling it from an in-sewn pocket when Ru Shan stirred. He murmured slightly in his sleep and his hand extended, as if searching for her. She quickly dropped his clothing, tucking the key into her palm. She had an excuse ready if he were to wake. She was simply going to the necessary, she would tell him.

But there was no way she could explain having the key to her room. So she waited in tense silence while Ru Shan quieted again, his breath coming in gentle snores.

She had no shoes, but that couldn't be helped. So with

silent steps, she crossed the room and slipped the key into the lock. Moments later, she unlocked the front door, moving with increasing speed as she flew down the stairs and out of the tenement building.

From the letters of Mei Lan Cheng

23 December, 1873
Dearest Li Hua—

Do you remember Mr. Lost Cat? The man the captain brought with him to translate? He IS smarter than I thought, and he has caught me in a lie! I told Sheng Fu that the Mongoose Captain was not interested in our better designs. I did not want my beautiful stitching on the bodies of those smelly apes! But I lied. The Mongoose does want my best work and will pay very well for it.

If Cheng Fu finds out, then he will have me working day and night for the Starving Mongoose! I will never be able to do anything else ever again!

I can already guess what you are thinking. If Mr. Lost Cat caught me in the lie, then Cheng Fu must know. But that is the strange thing. Mr. Lost Cat did not say a thing! Not to his captain or to my husband. But he knows, Li Hua. I could tell by the way his eyes narrowed and he looked hard, straight at me. I turned my head away, hiding behind my fan, I was so flustered. And then everything went on just as if nothing had happened.

Cheng Fu and the captain made their trade—all those bolts of badly embroidered cotton for some English gold and enough opium to last my mother-in-law nearly all year. To be fair, it is not a bad trade, but I still do not like the ghost people at all. I warned Cheng Fu not to give him anything until we were paid. In advance. He called me a stupid woman and would have hit me, but he could not with the ghost people right there.

And that is when Mr. Lost Cat proved he understood. He suggested—in his ugly, halting Chinese—that he and I meet to finish the details. He even suggested such tasks were beneath my husband's attention, and Cheng Fu—the fool—agreed!

Now I am to meet with Mr. Lost Cat alone. Li Hua, I am afraid he will murder me! I know that Cheng Fu will be in the room. I am to see Mr. Lost Cat in the store. It would not be seemly otherwise. But we will be in the back at the old table while Cheng Fu talks with customers. A world can change between the space of two heartbeats. How much more can happen before my husband notices anything that has happened to me?

—Mei Lan

*A man's career here is in his own hands, and he
makes or mars his fortunes unaided and unrestrained by those petty restrictions of class and
caste and the jealous rivalries which are so rife
in convention-ridden, sham-loving, Mammon-
worshipping England. . . . Here are prizes waiting to be won. . . . All is for the quick eye, the
stout heart, the strong will.*
—Edward Bowra, a young junior clerk writing
of his hopes in Shanghai

Chapter Ten

Lydia ran, her heart pounding in her throat. There was
garbage everywhere in the tight, narrow streets, but she
didn't dare think about what she was stepping through. She
moved quickly, barely even stopping to catch her breath.
There were signs all around, but they were in Chinese.
Thanks to Fu De, she could read some of them—GOOD
FISH, HAPPINESS GARDEN, LUCKY FORTUNES TOLD—but
they didn't help her find her way.

At last she found a few sharp-eyed boys playing in the
street. They were startled by her looks, and two even ran
away when she spoke to them. But one stayed, and he
pointed the way to the international settlements.

It wasn't far, and soon Lydia merged with the line of do-
mestic servants crossing into the French concession. From
there it was a couple of miles to the English district of the
foreign settlement, but with her understanding of French,

English, and now some Shanghainese, she found her way easily enough.

Not so easy was enduring the frightened stares of the Chinese or the outright laughter of the Caucasians, but she lowered her head and kept quietly repeating Maxwell's address. She had no money for a rickshaw, even if she dared risk one again after her last experience, so she continued doggedly on, wincing with every step on her bruised and cut feet.

She tried to hold Maxwell foremost in her thoughts. She would finally see him. They could at last get married and this whole strange nightmare would finally be over. But even as she kept repeating that to herself, she found her thoughts drifting back to Ru Shan. What would he do when he woke and found her gone? Would he be hurt, or just angry? Would he send Fu De after her? Was she about to be caught again? Or did he understand that keeping her imprisoned was wrong?

She didn't know. She didn't know if she imagined his tender side, the part of him that was learning to accept her as a person and not a pet. Maybe he was just a monster, but she didn't believe it possible. And yet . . .

Always at this point, she discovered her thoughts were centering around Ru Shan again, not her fiancé, and so she ruthlessly redirected her thoughts. Maxwell was her future. Ru Shan was in the past. Gone forever. If only she could get to her fiancé.

Then she was there, right in front of Maxwell's building.

The door was locked, of course, but she pounded and called and wrenched at the door until a woman came to open it. She was a young Chinese woman with tangled hair and blotched lipstick, and as she released the latch, Lydia pushed through, nearly toppling the tiny woman over.

"Maxwell? Maxwell Slade," Lydia gasped.

The woman gestured upstairs. "Third door. Right side." Then she turned sleepily back to her flat while Lydia scrambled up the stairs screaming her fiancé's name.

He met her at his door, his eyes bleary and bloodshot from sleep. He wore pajamas and a silk robe, but his face was still indisputably Maxwell. Lydia took one look at his rough jaw and his pale blue eyes, then threw herself into his arms, at last releasing the torrent of sobs she had been suppressing from the moment things had begun to go bad that very first morning in Shanghai.

"Lydia? Lydia!" He pushed away from her, wincing as he held her at arm's length. "What are you doing here?" His gaze took in her attire. "And what are you wearing?"

Lydia couldn't speak. It wasn't her tears, which were still flowing without stop. It was simply that too much had happened for her to explain. She simply wanted to be safe in Maxwell's arms. *Safe.*

The mere thought had her knees collapsing, and she crumpled, reaching out to him to support her. He didn't. Or his reactions were too slow. Either way, she wound up on the floor of his hallway, still sobbing.

"Good God, Lydia. Pull yourself together! And come inside. People are staring."

Lydia tried to do it. Indeed, she hadn't even realized that the other renters were standing in their doorways watching her display. But Maxwell was obviously keenly aware of it as he half carried, half dragged her inside his room.

She clung, not releasing him even as he tried to shut his door.

"For God's sake, Lydia, let me close the door!"

She came more to herself then. This was Maxwell. This was his voice, his attitude, his very English propriety. Oddly enough, she found that reassuring, though she would have found his arms around her more so. In any event, he was forcibly removing her from his body, and so she released him, wrapping her arms around herself as he quickly closed the door behind him.

Then he turned to stare at her while she hiccupped and did her best to control her sobs. She managed eventually, but she could not stop from shaking. Just shaking. The best she could do was wrap her arms around herself and focus on breathing.

In. Out. Just as Ru Shan taught.

But that thought brought on a fresh bout of tears. Why, she couldn't fathom. But they just kept coming while Maxwell stood and stared at her, obviously feeling awkward. In the end, he dropped a blanket about her and patted her shoulders. Twice.

"There, there," he said, in time with each pat. Then he straightened. "Come now, Lydia. Buck up and tell me what is going on." He frowned at her. "Your letter said you weren't coming until today."

She swallowed back her tears, doing her best to calm her ragged nerves. "I took an earlier boat. It was cheaper. I thought I would surprise you."

"Well," he drawled, "you've certainly done that. Oh my, your feet are bleeding. Did you walk through the whole of Shanghai like that?"

She nodded, then watched him pour water into his wash-basin. Setting it on the floor beside her, he grabbed a towel and handed it to her. Then with a sigh that came from his bones, he dropped down onto the settee across from her. He watched, his chin in his hand, as she released her hold on the blanket and awkwardly tried to look at her feet. The only way to do it, of course, was to bend her knee, but as soon as she did so, Maxwell shot up from his seat.

"Good God, Lydia! Those pants! They . . . they . . . cover yourself, woman!"

It took some moments for her to understand what he was saying. Fortunately, Maxwell's extended finger was there to explain, pointing at the juncture of her thighs. Even then it startled her to realize what he meant. She had been wearing these coolie pants for nearly a week now and had forgotten that pants without a crotch were unusual.

Embarrassed, she quickly pulled the blanket from her shoulders, dropping it into her lap. And yet, Maxwell remained nearly purple from head to toe. "You cannot say you have been wearing those pants throughout Shanghai? Without . . . they are . . . they are indecent!"

Lydia stared at her fiancé, tears filling her eyes. After all that had happened to her, could he not just let her explain? "They were all that were available," she finally said.

"Where are your clothes? Your dresses? Your mother!" he practically squeaked.

She sighed, weariness overcoming her. "Mother is home with Aunt Esther. My clothes and luggage have all been stolen." She looked up, wishing he would just look at her. But he had collapsed backward again, holding his head in both hands. Well, she would just have to say it out loud and get the worst over with. "Maxwell, I was sold to a brothel. I have only just now escaped."

His head snapped up, his face ashen. "Good God," was all he could say. And then his gaze dropped to her lap. "Is that why . . . ?" He swallowed. "I mean, I should get you a doctor." He stood, but did not move for the door.

"No, no!" she gasped, not wanting anyone to see her, not even a doctor. "I am fine."

He looked again at her lap and she drew her knees together, wrapping her arms around the blanket that swathed her lower body.

"I am fine, Maxwell. I'm not hurt at all. Except my feet, that is. And I expect they will heal in time."

"But the brothel . . ." He practically choked out the word. "Were you . . . ? I mean, what . . . ?" He snapped his mouth shut, then opened it again, only to gape at her like a fish. Then, once again, he sank down on the settee. "Bloody Chinese."

"It's over now," she said, as much to herself as to him. "I'm here with you now. And we can get married. And everything can be how it's supposed to be." Then she looked up at him, another bout of tears threatening. "But I'm tired, Maxwell. So very tired. Can I please just go lie down?"

He straightened. "Of course, Lydia, of course. But where . . . ?" Then he blinked. "My bedroom, of course. Can't send you out looking for a room like that, can we? Well, don't you worry about that. I'll just . . . just head out to work. Bloody early, but then I'm awake now anyway, right?" He swallowed again, then pushed to his feet. He stood there, rubbing his face with one hand as he looked down at her. "Are you sure . . . about the doctor, I mean."

"I ran away, Maxwell. I'm still a virgin." She winced as she spoke, hating to say it aloud even though that was the entire reason she'd cooperated with Ru Shan—because he'd promised to keep her pure. Of course, she now realized that 'pure' and 'virginal' were not necessarily the same things. In fact . . .

She shook off the thought. It was over. Whatever had happened was done now, and she was back with Maxwell and everything would be fine.

"Just help me to your bed, please," she whispered.

He leapt to his feet, gingerly helping her rise. "Of course," he murmured as the blanket slipped from her hips. She was standing now, so everything was covered appropriately. But still he stared at her hips and legs so much that she wished for the blanket again. Indeed, Maxwell must have been thinking the same thing, because he knelt down and handed it to her, helping her wrap it about her entire body.

"Bedroom's there," he said, gesturing deeper in. "I'll just grab my clothes and be off."

She nodded, though in her heart, she wanted him with her, his arms wrapped around her, his body pressed intimately against hers. Just like last night. Except, of course, it would not be like last night because that had been with Ru Shan.

She climbed into his bed, clothes and all, tucking her knees up close to her chin. But she still looked at Maxwell, wondering if she could say something—anything—to make him stay.

"Max. Let's get married today. This afternoon."

He jumped—actually jumped—in surprise, his feet taking him farther away from her. "Today?" he squeaked.

She sat up, pulling the covers up to her hips. "Surely there's a priest somewhere in Shanghai."

"Loads of them. Can't cross a corner without tripping over one of them. But Lydia, you said you were tired."

"No, I—"

"You rest," he interrupted. "I'll . . . I'll just get my clothes and go to work." And with that, he grabbed items willy-nilly, moving faster than she'd ever seen, escaping from the bedroom almost at a dead run.

It was not an auspicious beginning to their marriage, she thought as she stared morosely at the shut door. She could hear him changing his attire on the other side. At home, in England, Maxwell took over an hour to prepare himself for public. But not today. Today, he accomplished everything in less than fifteen minutes.

And then he was gone from the flat and she was left alone to stare at a new set of four walls. She closed her eyes to shut out the view and buried her face in the sheets. Except that brought a strange scent to her nostrils, and she frowned, sniffing tentatively.

Back in England, she would not have been able to identify the scent. But she had spent the last month learning the exact smells of passion, and so could now recognize both a woman's musky odor and a man's yang release. It was subtle, of course, but definitely there.

But Maxwell wouldn't have been able to bring a woman into his rooms, she thought with a frown. Then she remembered that this was not an English establishment, but a Chinese one. And a Chinese woman had opened the door to Max's bachelor home. Which meant that women did frequent these rooms. And beds.

She sighed, finding tears threatening all over again. She made all sorts of excuses for Max's behavior, of course. A man alone in a foreign country. Mother had told her that men had needs. She had even reminded Lydia that Max had been in China a long time, now, and that Lydia and Max were an arranged marriage, an agreement of sorts between their families so that meant Lydia would need to excuse all sorts of behavior. Just so long as it was clear that such nonsense ended the moment they got married.

Lydia, of course, had agreed. She knew that "boys would be boys," as her mother often said. But she'd been in England at the time. And she had never truly believed Max capable of such inconstant behavior.

Well, she had been wrong. But after her last month's experiences with Ru Shan, Lydia could hardly be one to cast stones, could she?

So she curled the linen specifically away from her nose and tried to rest. But her mind would not let her be. She couldn't help but contrast Ru Shan's tender caresses to Max's distant behavior. Her fiancé could hardly wait to escape her presence. Whereas many times, Ru Shan had been loath to leave her side, clearly anxious for the time when he could return to her.

She tried to excuse Max, of course. She had caught him unawares, and he had never liked surprises. It was a bit much for anyone to take, she supposed, being told that one's fiancée had been abducted into a brothel. And yet, as she curled into a tight ball, her knees clutched to her chest, she felt the weight of disappointment grind at her excuses.

At the very heart of it all, she knew only one fact: that Maxwell wasn't with her. She wanted him beside her, holding her, and he wasn't there.

"But he will be," she whispered to herself. "As soon as we're married."

With that happy thought firmly in mind, she finally fell asleep.

Lydia woke a few hours later to a gentle tapping on her door. She opened her eyes and saw a large, curvy redhead saunter into the room, her clothing all the height of English fashion.

"You awake, ducks?"

Lydia blinked, then pushed herself upright in bed. It took a moment. She had been wrapped so tightly around herself that it took some time to uncoil her muscles. Meanwhile, the redhead plopped down on the mattress, her eyes widening at the sight of Lydia's peasant clothing.

"My goodness, I thought Max exaggerated, but I see it's all true." She leaned forward, her light green eyes round with interest. "Did you really just escape from a brothel?"

Lydia frowned at the strange woman. "He told you that?"

The woman stiffened. "Course he did. Had to, didn't he, when he asked me to loan you some dresses."

"I suppose so," Lydia murmured, though truly she didn't think he should have. Everyone would naturally jump to the worst conclusion about her experiences there. Especially if they ever found out she had been with Ru Shan for nearly a month. No one would ever credit that she was still a virgin. Which meant her reputation was completely ruined.

She lifted her chin to stare fully at this new woman. "Has he made arrangements for our wedding this afternoon?"

The redhead pulled back abruptly, her eyes narrowing slightly. "He didn't say anything about that," she answered somewhat tartly. "He merely asked me to bring you some clothing. Which I have. Expensive clothing," she added as she stood up from the bed. "*My* clothing."

Lydia nodded, seeing that she had somehow insulted the woman, and she hurried to make amends. "I apologize. I thank you for your assistance." She slipped out of bed, still wearing her peasant clothing. "As you can see, I can hardly go about dressed like this."

"No," the woman sniffed. "You can't." Then she frowned at Lydia. "Though I don't know that my dresses will do you any good. You're much smaller than I am."

Lydia couldn't disagree with that. Even before leaving England, she'd never been well endowed. Certainly not as much as this woman. And since coming to Shanghai, she guessed she'd lost about a stone.

"Well," she said soothingly, "I'm sure Maxwell will reimburse you for the cost of the dress." Then she straightened to her full height—still a good two inches below the redhead—and extended her hand. "I'm Lydia, by the way. Maxwell's fiancé."

The woman nodded, deigning to extend her fingertips to brush fleetingly against Lydia's palm. "My name's Esmerelda White. Max's personal assistant."

Lydia nodded slowly. "Personal assistant?"

"I help him with his private things—his laundry, his meals, sometimes even his cleaning. Though not often, as you can tell." She released a soft trill of laughter as she waved at Maxwell's unswept and dusty rooms.

Lydia pushed past the woman, making sure to keep her voice firm as she tried for a light tone. "Yes, Max is rather fussy about his things," she answered. "Fortunately, though, you won't be plagued with him any longer." She turned to look over her shoulder, her eyes slightly narrowed. "We are to be married today," she stated firmly. "And as his wife, I shall of course take care of those things for him."

She smiled as warmly as she could manage. "But I thank you for your help while I was still in England," she lied. She already had a good idea exactly what part of Max's personal business this Esmerelda had attended to, and she would be damned if she let any of that continue.

And how could Max send this creature to her anyway? The very thought of wearing this woman's gowns revolted her. But then, beggars couldn't be choosers, so Lydia turned back to the settee, seeing a plain, misshapen brown gown lying there.

It was a travel dress, stained and oversized. But it had ties in the back and would at least cover her decently. Esmerelda had also thought to bring underclothing, stockings, and shoes that were too large, not to mention a bonnet more suited to a different season. All the necessities were there, and Lydia smiled as graciously as she could manage.

"Thank you for your help."

"Ooh, but we ain't done yet. Maxie said I was to take you to buy things. All the clothing that a woman would need. Not too much, mind you, but enough to get you by for a while. Told me to take all day," she added with a bit of a sneer. "That he won't be back until late today. So I guess that means there won't be no wedding today."

Lydia clenched her jaw, keeping her thoughts inside. Whatever was Maxwell thinking, asking her to gad about town with this creature? And no wedding? Where was she supposed to sleep tonight if not here? They had to be married today.

"Well," she finally managed. "Let us go shopping, then, shall we? And then we can meet Maxwell for luncheon and discuss the rest of the day."

"Ooh, he won't like that, ducks. He's working."

"Well, he'll have to adjust. After all, a man can't be expected to work on his wedding day, can he?" She knew the address of his office. She would storm the building, if need be, and drag him out by his ear. They would be wed by the end of the day.

But first she needed appropriate attire. With a tart nod to her companion, Lydia gathered up the clothing and stepped into the bedroom, firmly closing it in Esmerelda's face. The woman had meant to follow, but she would get dressed on her own, by God. The last thing Lydia needed was for that woman to realize she had shaved in places that no Englishwoman ever had.

Finally, the shopping excursion began. Lydia could bargain, and knowing some Shanghainese helped enormously. Not at first, of course, since all of the shops' owners Esmerelda chose were Caucasian. It was Lydia who spotted the cheaper goods in the side streets with Chinese vendors. And it was Lydia who insisted that she need not have French lace when Chinese cotton would do. Lydia also kept strict track of every penny spent, despite her companion's belief that it wasn't necessary. She intended to give a full accounting to Max so that he could not accuse her of being a wastrel no matter what his personal assistant might say.

She was completely outfitted by two in the afternoon. And though she had not found a gown appropriate to a wedding, she had at least found one of serviceable blue cotton that was both respectable and flattering. She was, in fact, wearing it now, as well as new underthings, allowing her to remove Esmerelda's clothing at the earliest opportunity.

She absolutely refused to be married in anything that woman owned.

And after meeting and discussing an appropriate service with a missionary at a nearby chapel, all that remained was to collect the groom.

Except, knowing where Maxwell's offices were and actually finding Max were two entirely different matters. Upon entering the hallowed halls of Fortnum & Mason—Suppliers of English Foodstuffs—she was flatly informed by a red-faced clerk that her fiancé was not there. He was at the docks, checking on a shipment of wine. And then, before the young man disappeared, he bowed slightly to her and mumbled something about being sorry for her "unfortunate accident."

Lydia's eyes widened at that, horror only beginning to slip through her polite smile. If a junior clerk knew of her "unfortunate accident," that meant every foreigner in Shanghai knew, and soon everyone in England as well. She had no doubt news of her misfortune was even now going out in the day's post. Soon all of London would know as well.

Which meant she and Maxwell had best get married with all speed or she was completely without options.

She rushed outside, taking a rickshaw to the docks, for Maxwell had neglected to leave her and Esmerelda use of his phaeton. Except that rickshaws were rather slow-moving vehicles compared to horse-drawn carriages, and that gave Lydia much too much time to sit and stew.

Whatever could Maxwell be thinking, telling the world what had happened to her? He must know that his friends could never keep silent when the gossip was so good. He might as well have posted the news on broadsides.

Esmerelda, of course, enjoyed every moment of Lydia's discomfort, and was gleefully chatting on about how difficult it must be to have everyone know that she had appeared at Max's door without pants. Lydia didn't bother correcting her, but sat staring out at the shops along the street.

Which is when she saw Fu De.

At least she thought it was Fu De. It had to be. And he was ducking into a clothier's. A Chinese clothier's with the family character *Cheng* carved boldly in the wood near the door.

It had to be Ru Shan's family shop. It had to.

Lydia was climbing out of her seat before she even knew she'd stopped the rickshaw. And as Esmerelda squealed in alarm, demanding to know exactly what was going on, Lydia was already pushing into the rather large, two-story shop.

Some part of her mind trembled with fear. Some part of her worried that Ru Shan would lock her away again and she'd never be free. But the rest of her was in English clothing again with an Englishwoman at her side, giving her confidence as she boldly walked through the shop.

And then she saw him, in a gray silk tunic with embroidered cliffs rising from the bottom hem all the way through the shoulders. It gave him the subtle appearance of a mountain—solid, imposing, and amazingly stoic as she confronted him.

She felt no fear. In truth, she had never felt physically threatened around Ru Shan. But she did feel the weight of his stare, of his every movement, as if the mountains on his clothing pressed down upon him as well as her.

Neither of them spoke. Lydia felt too much emotion—too much anger and pain and confusion—to give voice to any one thought. And into this silence broke Esmerelda's grating tones.

"Lydia! What are we doing in here?" The woman came to her side. "This is a terrible shop," she whispered in an undertone.

"A terrible shop?" Lydia echoed, her attention finally diverted away from Ru Shan. "Why?"

"Well, can't you see? Look, even his own people won't supply him."

And at Esmerelda's gesture, Lydia did see. For a clothier's, Ru Shan definitely had very little fabric. Indeed, he appeared to be down to only a few bolts of coarse cotton.

"Why do you suppose that is?" Lydia asked, her voice purposely loud, purposely casual.

As expected, Esmerelda wasted no time in reporting the gossip. "They say he is evil," she answered in a low whisper that could nonetheless be heard. "That he worships some heathen god with strange, lascivious rites."

Lydia frowned. "But surely that would not keep the Chinese people away. It is, after all, their religion—isn't it?"

Esmerelda smiled, her expression practically gleeful. "That's just it. His religion is bizarre for even them! And there's something worse. . . ." She let her voice drop for dramatic effect.

Lydia did not disappoint her. "What?" she asked eagerly.

"They say he has a white lover!" Then she giggled. "Personally, I think that's perfectly natural—we are much more attractive—but his own people won't go near him because of it."

"But what if that lover wasn't a lover at all, but a purchased slave? A white slave that he bought for the sole purpose of using?" She couldn't keep the edge from her voice, the anger from infusing her words. Unfortunately, Esmerelda was completely oblivious to any undercurrents as her raucous laughter filled the room.

"Oh ducks, you are so provincial, aren't you? They wouldn't dare do such a thing. The government would be upon him in a moment for threatening a white woman. He would be locked in chains in moments. No dear, the sad fact is that there are plenty of white women around who will consent to that sort of depravity. After all, Chinese gold spends just as well as English, and a girl must eat."

Lydia felt her heart sink at those words, for right here was the answer to why she hadn't exposed Ru Shan the moment she escaped. No one would believe she had been kept a prisoner against her will for an entire month. They would all assume she was a different sort of woman altogether. And if she had any hope of marrying Maxwell—respectably—then she had to keep the last month quiet.

Of course, she thought with a secret smile, that didn't mean she couldn't have her own measure of revenge. After all, it looked as if the Cheng dressmakers were on their last legs. And though Lydia found Esmerelda's presence a burden at best, the woman did appear to have a fine eye for clothing. Which made her the perfect person for the next question. Assuming she found what she was looking for.

Lydia began wandering about the shop, noting various things. Though the shelves were bare, the wood furniture was sturdy and of the best quality. The dust only emphasized the emptiness of the place; and the building was in the best area of town. Technically inside the foreign concession, it was actually part of Old Shanghai. Therefore it was in the very rare few blocks frequented by both whites and Chinese.

Then she spotted it: her sketchbook, dropped casually among the tables.

"Why, look at this," she called to her companion as she opened the book. "What do you think of these designs?"

In truth, she had often toyed with the idea of setting up a dressmaking shop. She had been designing clothing all her life. Except, her set did not go into trade—and besides, she was going to be a wife and mother; there would be no time for a business. So she had contented herself with making her own clothing, helping her friends, and creating a trousseau.

Except, everything was different here in Shanghai, and the idea of becoming a dressmaker—in this exact location—definitely appealed. What a sweet revenge it would be on Ru Shan as well. The man who had bought her as a pet would be forced to sell his family business to her.

She was already smiling at the thought. Except that all depended upon whether anyone would buy her designs. And by all appearances, Esmerelda was an excellent judge of such things.

The woman sauntered over, peered curiously at the sketches, and Lydia felt her belly tighten with anticipation. To one side, Ru Shan also edged forward, his interest evident in the tense set to his shoulders. Lydia tried to glare him away, but he refused to be intimidated. He did, however, remain silent, apparently as interested in Esmerelda's opinion as Lydia.

Except Esmerelda wasn't saying anything. Indeed, for the first time all day, the woman was maddeningly silent.

"Well?" Lydia finally asked when her patience was exhausted. "What do you think?"

Esmerelda didn't answer at first, her frown expanding as she lifted her gaze to view Ru Shan's bare walls. "Interesting designs," she finally said. "Apparently the Chinese have learned something of dressmaking from us." But then she shook her head. "Except I don't believe they actually sew such outfits. Pretty pictures are one thing. Sewing is something else entirely."

Lydia stepped forward, her eagerness barely restrained. "But you like the *designs*?"

Her companion nodded. "Most intriguing. Yes, I like them." Then she sighed. "But they haven't any fabric."

Which is when Ru Shan stepped in, his bow deep and respectful. "Fabric can always be purchased," he said. "If madame is interested—"

"No," interrupted Lydia, "I agree with you, Esmerelda. They haven't the ability to sew such excellent designs." She was speaking more to Ru Shan than to Esmerelda, her anger at last turning into a kind of glee at his comeuppance.

He bowed, but she could see the stormy anger in his eyes. "Our seamstresses are the very best."

"Truly?" she challenged. "Please, let me see the specifications for this." She flipped through the book until she came to a complicated ballgown.

Again Ru Shan bowed, though Lydia detected a stiffness in the movement. "My apologies, madam, but the notations are in Chinese."

"I read Chinese," she said firmly. Because she did.

"They are not here at the shop."

"They are not here at all, I wager." Then she straightened, buoyed by the knowledge that Esmerelda liked her work. "Do you know what I wish to do, Esmerelda?" she mused loudly, her gaze becoming contemptuous as she surveyed her surroundings. "I believe I will wait until this poor man becomes truly desperate."

"Well, that can't take long," laughed her companion.

"No," Lydia agreed with a smile. "It probably won't." Then she turned to Ru Shan, making sure he understood exactly what her intentions were. "Then, I believe I shall come here and buy this shop at an amazingly cheap price, turn these incompetents out on their ear, and make a go of dressmaking myself."

Esmerelda's jaw went slack with astonishment. "Surely you don't mean to go into commerce yourself."

Lydia grinned, pleased because Ru Shan had gone sickly pale at her words. "I certainly do," she said firmly. "And I believe I could negotiate a very low price indeed. This is, after all, in the foreign concession. All we need do is expose this man's depravities to the authorities, and the French magistrates will be all too happy to evict him. His only option would be to sell the business to me. For a song."

Then she turned on her heel and left, her laughter ringing sweetly through Ru Shan's empty shop.

From the letters of Mei Lan Cheng

9 February, 1874
Dearest Li Hua—
I must apologize for not writing in so long. You must have thought I was murdered by that ghost man, Mr.

Lost Cat. I cannot tell you how silly that seems to me now. Mr. Lost Cat is very much like a cat—large, furry, but actually very sweet.

Are you surprised? That I would call a ghost person sweet? I am. But he is. Polite and kind. And he has taken to bathing before he comes to our store, so he does not smell like the other Englishmen. He likes our tea and made me laugh when he tried to use chopsticks to eat a bowl of rice. He had come during lunch, you see, and so out of politeness Cheng Fu offered to share. Mr. Lost Cat even seemed upset when he realized I would not eat with them. In fact, he refused to share until I was given a bowl as well. Cheng Fu was shocked, of course, but he wants the English money so much that he will tolerate any strangeness so long as the gold comes.

There was not enough rice, of course, and so I refused. But Mr. Lost Cat even understood that. He gave Ru Shan some money and told him—in Shanghainese—to buy my favorite food. If any Chinese man had done such a thing, Cheng Fu would have flown into a rage. But he wants the English gold so much he told me—me!—not to be offended. That the English are simply very strange, he said, and I was to do as Mr. Lost Cat wanted.

As if I was the one who did not understand kindness, even from a ghost person!

Do you remember that lie I told Cheng Fu? When I said the English were not interested in my good stitching? I was right that Mr. Lost Cat knew what I had done. That very first meeting with him, when I was so afraid he would murder me, he was very polite. He paid for our badly embroidered fabric and *arranged for its delivery to his ship. And then, before he left, he spoke to me in English so Cheng Fu would not understand.*

He said he knew I did not want to sell our good fabric to him, and that he did not blame me. That I did not know him at all and how could we do business with a stranger? It was too dangerous to risk our best goods on someone we did not trust.

He said that to me, Li Hua, and I knew right then that this ghost person knew more about business than my husband. But are you wondering the same thing I am? How could that be? How could a barbarian know more than my husband, who has been raised in the clothing business since he was a small boy?

I tell you, Li Hua, I do not know. But it is true. And I do not know if that makes me more afraid of Mr. Lost Cat or less.

There is more, Li Hua. Mr. Lost Cat has been coming to the shop every three days now. Yes, every three days! At exactly the times when I will be in the shop either checking the work of the embroiderers or giving them my new designs. He is there sometimes when I bring Cheng Fu his lunch. And lately, I think he has begun waiting on the corner to walk with me as I travel.

It is not seemly for me to allow this to happen. It is not good for my reputation or that of our shop. You know how the Chinese will avoid any place that does great business with the foreigners.

But Li Hua, I have not ended it. And worse, Cheng Fu does not wish me to. He sees only the English gold. What I see is a kind man, even if he is a barbarian. And he makes me laugh. Yes, a ghost person makes me laugh.

Have I been infected too? Am I now as sick as all those other Chinese who are desperate for foreign attention—doing anything for the gold and the opium that they bring?

Mr. Lost Cat sails tomorrow, and his ship will carry some of my best designs to England. I cannot say if I am happy or sad at that. I cannot even think beyond the knowledge that I will not see him again for many months.

Oh, I must go, Li Hua. There is so much more that I wish to write, but Ru Shan is angry again. He does not like his studies and will sometimes throw his books in a fit of temper. Perhaps I should visit the monks today. Perhaps if I give them more money, Heaven will end these troubles and I can sleep peacefully again.

—Mei Lan

Effort and stress are our unhappiest compan-
ions. They seem to follow us wherever we go and
to inhibit our need to be still. Indeed, with them
as companions, what room is left for Tao?
    —Lao Tzu interpreted by Priya Hemenway

Chapter Eleven

True fear dropped Ru Shan to his knees. It was an instinc-
tive motion, one all children learned in China—a prayerful
position. But he did not feel as if he were praying. Instead,
he felt a mind-numbing anguish.

Lydia plotted revenge.

It had been bad enough to wake this morning alone, Lydia gone from his side. Her absence had rocked him to his
foundations, for he truly hadn't thought her capable of
such deception. No white person could hide their passions
from him—or so he'd believed. The ghost people were
tossed about by their emotions, completely unable to think
of or carry out long-term plans. That's what he had been
told. That's what everyone in China believed.

Except, it obviously wasn't true. At least not for Lydia.
Not only had she waited patiently for her opportunity to es-
cape, but she had carefully hidden her plans from him and
Fu De. To all appearances, she had accepted her lot. Now

she had escaped and was capable of doing even more. That alone left him stunned as he sat on her empty bed.

Then, because no raindrop falls alone, her disappearance was only one of the calamities to strike him today. When he'd finally arrived at the shop, he'd learned that his latest shipments of silk had inexplicably disappeared. He wasn't truly surprised. When the Chinese turned their backs, they did so without reservation. His fellow countrymen believed he consorted with white women, which naturally meant he was untrustworthy, irresponsible, and even unclean. It didn't matter that he and his family had paid their bills for decades. Suddenly, everything was cash only—assuming supplies happened to exist.

This, naturally, had all come just after he spent all his cash on the purchase of Lydia. And now that his family was at its most vulnerable in three generations, the rumors had begun. His name was inexplicably besmirched, and no respectable Chinese would deal with him.

He did not think Lydia had created his current problems, but she was certainly profiting from them. There had been a great deal of notice taken of her sketches yesterday and all through today. Many white customers expressed interest. But Lydia's statement was correct—he did not have seamstresses who could convert her designs into workable gowns. He had sewers who were trying, but the fabric didn't fall right, the look was not quite like Lydia's pictures. And no customer would buy—certainly not pay gold in advance for—a gown that was not even on display.

In short, he had the designs but no cloth to make them and no seamstress to sew them. He had the means of his family's success right in his hands, and no way to succeed. Because Lydia had escaped. And with her had gone the yin water he needed to turn his yang fire to gold. Not only had he lost the golden embryo that creates an Immortal, but also the gold that would bring his family comfort throughout generations.

Worst of all, he could not be sorry that she had escaped. Indeed, that was the cause of his greatest agony. He had been wrong. Lydia was not a Chinese woman to be kept behind walls and used at a man's leisure. She was also not a pet or an inferior species. She was indeed the match of any man he knew: smart, resourceful, and absolutely determined to destroy him.

But why would she? Because he had unlawfully stolen her and kept her his prisoner.

He knew that now. Which meant his current calamities were his own fault—Heaven's just retribution for violating one of Its greatest creatures. That mistake would be his downfall. He could not regain Lydia's help or trust. Worse, if he pressed the matter, he could very well find himself in jail. Lydia had apparently spent the day reestablishing herself among white society. And though the ghost people cared little for the lost women who washed up on the Shanghai shores, they would be very angry with any Chinese merchant who'd chosen to harm their elite.

In short, he had no escape. All he could do was sit and wait for the knife blade to descend. Would she be content to merely force him to sell his shop to her, thereby destroying his family income forever? Or would she go even further, have him arrested? Would she expose his jade dragon practices to one and all?

Lydia's friend was correct. His religion was not one openly spoken of. Most Chinese considered it unsavory at best, perverse at worst. That this was simple ignorance would not help him. People chose their own opinions, regardless of the truth.

It would be bad enough to ruin the family commerce, but exposing his unusual Taoist practices would shame him and his family forever. He would be stricken from the Cheng records, disowned by his father and relatives, and cast aside without family connections or recourse.

In China, a disowned man was nothing.

The weight of shame pressed Ru Shan down, making his body sink even farther to the wood floor, his shoulders dropping down to a traditional kowtow.

He would be ruined. By a white woman. And he could not even be angry, for it was his own fault. What he had done to her was wrong.

But how to make amends? How to appease her and Heaven?

He could not think except to know that he needed her. Only she could craft her gown designs into reality. Only she could bring life and gold back to the family store. And only she had ever given him yin power like water flowing from a fountain. His family needed her, and he wanted her.

Which meant he would have to marry her. It was his only option.

Still, the shock of that thought echoed like a crack of thunder through his body. He shook in terror, his forehead still touching the ground. His friends and family would be appalled. If others shunned him because they believed he kept a white woman as a lover, how would they feel about a white wife?

And yet, try as he might, he could think of no other possibility. As his wife, Lydia would continue to create her clothing designs. He already knew they were spectacular enough that someone would pay in advance for such gowns. And with gold to pay for fabric—in advance—his suppliers would return. Gold forced a blind eye to many evils—even that of having a white wife.

Eventually, the Cheng store would flourish again. Meanwhile, he would have access to Lydia's yin power, which could only aid in achieving his financial and religious goals. And lastly, as his wife, Lydia's honor would be restored. Which meant Heaven would be appeased. Once again, Ru Shan's path would be assured.

There was no other option. He had to marry Lydia.

But how to begin? The obstacles were numerous and seemingly insurmountable. He had no influence with these foreigners. And she had a fiancé.

He would find a way. His life and his family's survival depended on it.

Lydia was shriveling inside. The docks were a teeming mass of noise and confusion. Once that would have thrilled her, but right now it was keeping her from her future husband. And even though there were perhaps a dozen white women watching the noise and bustle, she felt as if everyone's eyes were on her. They all stared and whispered behind their hands, their words obvious. *"That's the woman who was in a brothel. And you know what happens there."*

It was silly. Even if Maxwell had been spreading the tale far and wide, no one would know what his fiancée looked like. But try as she might to convince herself she was merely being hysterical, she couldn't shake the feeling of being watched. And judged.

She had never expected to become one of *those* women. "A poor, misguided trollop," as her mother used to say.

And yet, suddenly, she felt as if everyone cast her in that role whether or not it was true.

And maybe it was true, she thought with a crushing panic. Because she missed it. She missed her morning routine with Ru Shan, the flow of yin that made her feel full and lush. She ached to touch herself as Ru Shan had done, but knew she could not. Certainly not in public. Thankfully, she would be married soon. She knew that husbands often enjoyed touching their wives' breasts, and so, hopefully, would Maxwell.

If only the man would appear! Then everything would be set to rights.

Except when Lydia and Esmerelda at last found his company's dockside office, the young man inside was unsure of her fiancé's whereabouts. He had left some twenty minutes ago in search of Maxwell, leaving her and Esmerelda to wait with increasing impatience in the stifling little room. And as her companion passed the time by recalling every party and entertainment she and Maxwell had enjoyed together, Lydia felt herself grow smaller and tighter and more frightened.

Where was Max? Wasn't he supposed to protect her from experiences like this? Wasn't a husband supposed to make sure his wife was treated with respect and honor? Not force her into the company of his own mistress!

Thankfully, the young clerk chose that moment to return. Unfortunately, he came into the tiny building alone, his face beet red with embarrassment.

"I . . . I . . . um, I'm sorry, m-miss," he stammered. "I can't find him."

"I told you," Esmerelda chortled. "Max don't like to be bothered at work. He wouldn't come if you was on fire, he's that particular."

"But I'm his wife," Lydia said to the clerk.

"Not yet, you ain't," crowed her companion.

The young clerk wouldn't look her in the eye. She waited a moment while Esmerelda became positively gleeful at her discomfort.

"Look ducks—," the woman began, but Lydia didn't let her finish.

"Thank you, Esmerelda, for your help today. I believe I can handle things from here." Then she held out her hand. "Max's purse, if you please."

It took a moment for Esmerelda to understand Lydia's meaning. Then, when she finally did, she puffed herself up to her full, impressive height. "Why, of all the cheek!" she sputtered haughtily. "Is this the thanks I get fer helping out a poor woman in need?"

"You helped because Maxwell ordered you to. So it seems we are both dancing to his tune, and you have no cause to act superior." Feeling childish, Lydia abruptly snatched the purse from the woman's wrist, breaking the ribbons and no doubt bruising the woman's skin. She hardly cared. Esmerelda had been picking at her from the very moment she'd let herself into Max's flat.

Esmerelda's eyes went stone cold. "Wrong, ducks," she hissed. "I'm the only one dancing, 'cause you ain't never going to be his wife. Yer damaged goods. Think on that when yer tossed out." And with that, she sailed out of the room, the ribbons of her overly large hat waving a jaunty good-bye.

Lydia simply stood, her insides tightening even more while the young clerk shuffled in embarrassment beside her. She knew he was about to disappear, finding some pretense or other to escape her presence, so she abruptly turned, grabbing hold of his arm when she saw he had begun to sidle away.

"Please, sir," she began as he squeaked in alarm. She took a deep breath, trying to find an impassioned way to express what she wanted to know. One that wasn't completely humiliating. "Is it true?" she finally asked. "Is Maxwell simply avoiding me?" *Is he going to break our engagement?*

The clerk's face flushed to a bright tomato color. "It ain't seemly, miss," he managed in a high squeak. "To visit the men while they're working."

She nodded, her heart a cold knot in her throat. "Very well," she said, with as much dignity as possible as she released the man's coat sleeve. "Please tell Maxwell that I shall wait for him at dinner." Then she paused, needing to feel gracious if only to salve her own pride. "I apologize for subjecting you to such a scene. It was most unkind of me."

He looked up, obviously startled by her words. "I'll . . . I'll make sure Mister Slade knows."

She smiled as best she could. "Then you have my thanks." And with that, she ducked out of the building.

It was a sad walk back to the flat. She could have taken a rickshaw, of course, but she wanted to walk, even on her bruised feet. In truth, back in England she had always been on her feet, running errands, assisting her mother with chores, sometimes even helping her father organize his medical instruments and potions.

That had been perhaps the hardest thing about her incarceration—that she was no longer able to do much of anything. She knew that both Ru Shan and Fu De had been confused by that. Obviously in Chinese culture, the women longed to be locked away and cared for. Indeed, looking about her, she saw only the men. True, she was still in the foreign concession, but there were Chinese about—coolies, merchants, even high-class servants in livery. But every one of them was a man.

What would become of her if she didn't marry Maxwell? she wondered. Truthfully, she didn't want to acknowledge such a possibility. Of course Max would marry her. He loved her. They were engaged. He *had* to marry her.

And yet, Lydia could not dismiss Esmerelda's words. *Yer damaged goods.* But I'm not! she wanted to shout. She was still a virgin. Indeed, she had clung to that knowledge during her imprisonment. She was still a virgin. She could still marry Maxwell.

But what if he refused? What if he did think her damaged? What would she do then? She had no money to return to England. She had no means of support at all. She would absolutely not become a woman like Esmerelda, a mistress living off the dubious attentions of a philandering man.

She thought briefly of Ru Shan—though in no context whatsoever. She would not go back to being his slave. The very idea was repulsive. Indeed, she was very much looking forward to her revenge on him. To see his face when she bought his store. To know that she—a ghost woman— could find success where he could not.

Lydia actually found herself smiling at the thought, her spirits buoyed as never before. She had a plan now, knew what she would do.

First and foremost, she would make dinner for Maxwell. She knew his favorites. She'd made a special point of learning his tastes and making sure she could cook them. The house he rented must have a kitchen.

She had only the one gown she wore, so there would be little primping in that area. However, she had purchased a few cosmetics earlier in the day. She would use what she had to best effect.

Then, tonight, she would convince Maxwell to marry her. She wasn't entirely sure how. Excellent food. Wonder-

ful company. Seduction? Could she do that? Could she
have him touch her and kiss her . . . and . . . and merge his
yang with her yin? He would know then, wouldn't he, that
she was a virgin? That he was the one who had taken her?
And then he would have to marry her.

It seemed so drastic, and yet the thought was appealing
on a purely physical level. She longed to be touched again,
stroked again, to feel that wondrous thing that Ru Shan had
shown her . . . had it only been last night? Oh, how amazing to do that with Maxwell. To feel that within the bonds
of marriage.

She nodded to herself, feeling her resolve harden. It was
drastic, indeed. "Rushing her fences" as her father would
say. And she would only resort to it if she couldn't convince Max of the need to marry immediately. If only to
prove her virginity to him.

She swallowed, her feet picking up speed as she headed
for the nearest market. She had seen it on the way down to
the docks and knew exactly where it was. She had a plan
now for tonight. For Maxwell and her future.

And if that failed, she had a secondary, backup plan. If
worst came to worst and Maxwell threw her off, then she
knew exactly what she would do. Somehow, some way, she
would convince Maxwell to give her money. Enough
money to buy Ru Shan's shop. Enough money to set her up
in a business she knew she could do.

She would be a dressmaker. In Shanghai. And she would
rub Ru Shan's nose in the fact.

Of course, either way it all depended on Maxwell. He
would have to come through for her. Either as her husband
or her business partner, they were going to be together.
Even if she had to seduce him to accomplish it.

* * *

Her fiancé burped indelicately as he leaned back from the table, then flushed as he murmured politely, "I do beg your pardon." Lydia smiled in forgiveness as she studied him across the table.

She had never seen him looking so content. Indeed, his blond good looks were startling in the candlelight. And yet she still felt the need to press him, if only to reassure herself.

"Did you like it, Max? I'm sorry if it was too heavy. Especially the sauce. But—"

"No, no," he responded congenially. "It was perfect. Can't see why you didn't eat up as well."

Neither could Lydia. Indeed, this had once been her favorite meal, too. But now the meat felt too heavy, the sauce too thick. It had to be the nervousness she felt, the anxiety over what she was about to do. So she made up a convenient lie.

"I suppose I just wanted our first night together to be perfect."

His smile faded somewhat. "Hardly our first meal, Lydia. We've known each other since we were in leading strings."

Or near enough, Lydia amended. Which was one of the reasons they had become betrothed. They both felt so comfortable together, and both their parents wanted the union. And yet, she felt anything but comfortable now. She stood, mostly because she didn't know what else to do, and walked around their makeshift table. Gently brushing her hand up his arm, Lydia tugged him toward the settee.

"I'd like to talk to you, Max. About our future."

He grimaced. His nose wrinkled and he actually groaned out his first words. "Aw Lyd, why must you spoil a good meal?"

She felt her stomach clench tighter, but none of that anxiety came through in her voice. "I hope we will only be adding to the wonderful meal, Max." She tugged even harder, and he at last stood from his chair.

"I know you want to rest after your ordeal, Lyd," he said, rushing his words. "You can sleep here. I'll be at . . . at a friend's."

"At Esmerelda's, you mean?" She hadn't meant to sound so tart, but the words came out caustically nonetheless.

"Of course not!" he exclaimed, but from the guilty flush to his cheeks, she suspected he lied.

It didn't matter. Esmerelda was going to be a thing of the past. She sidled close to him, leaning against him when he would not join her on the settee. "We need to talk about our wedding, Max," she said in a tone as seductive as she could manage.

"Wedding!" he sputtered. "But your ordeal—"

"My ordeal is over," she snapped. "And not so much of an ordeal," she lied. "I wasn't even conscious most of the time."

He paled. Even in the dim candlelight, she could see that he'd gone ghostly white.

"Max?" she asked, suddenly alarmed.

"Gods, Lydia, do you know what happens when you're unconscious? In one of those places?"

"They steal all your money and clothing, chain you to a bed, and sell you to the highest bidder? Yes, Max, I know." She was handling this all wrong. She knew it. But she was becoming annoyed. With Max for wanting to go to another woman after all the trouble she'd been through. With the food, for not tasting the way it ought. For herself, for getting annoyed with Max when she needed his cooperation.

And for all of life that was simply not moving according to plan.

Nevertheless, she was still determined to see things through. She took a deep breath and re-pasted on her most beguiling smile. Clearly the man was nervous about marriage. Well, he had never been loath to talk about money. So, skipping ahead in her plans for the evening, Lydia jumped straight to her other idea.

"Max, I have had the most wonderful thought." She leaned forward to make sure she got his attention. "About a way to make lots of money."

She succeeded. He allowed her to pull him down to the settee. "Lyds, there are a million scoundrels in Shanghai. Please don't be foolish."

"See, darling?" She grinned. "That's why I need you. A husband always keeps his wife away from scoundrels."

He flinched at that, but no more than she did. She knew better than to prick him about not protecting her. After all, it had been her choice to come to Shanghai early. Of course, it had been his job, once she escaped, to keep her reputation pure, and he had failed miserably in that. Odd, really, given how desperately important image was to him. But then, he had damaged *her* reputation, not his own. Which meant it was up to her to fix the situation.

"Do you recall how I was always designing dresses back home?" she asked.

He nodded, though his expression remained wary.

"Well, I could never become a dressmaker in England. Both our families would have objected. I'm a doctor's daughter, and you are practically aristocracy."

"You can't go into trade, Lydia."

"Exactly what they would have said," she agreed, knowing that was not what he meant at all. "And besides, all the best dressmakers were already established in London." She scooted closer to him. "But Max, things are different in Shanghai. You said so yourself. You wrote me that all it takes to make a fortune here is determination and work." In truth, he had said a *man*'s determination and work, but she was adjusting it. "I have determination, Max. And I can work hard—you know that."

He opened his mouth to speak, but she rushed on, needing to get everything out before he disagreed. Because once he said no, not even Queen Victoria could make Max Slade change his mind.

"You said in your letter that you were looking for an investment, that you had the money. Well, there is this shop. Right on Joffre Avenue—"

"That's the French settlement!"

"Actually, it's on the old Chinese side," she corrected. "But either way, it's in an excellent location. It brings in both Chinese and European customers."

"It'll cost the earth," he countered.

"No, it won't. It's struggling. Some problem with suppliers." She smiled sweetly at him. "Didn't you write me that these Chinese can't manage anything?" She hardly believed he was correct in that, but Max always liked it when she echoed his own words. "Well, I'm sure that's the problem there. They just don't know how to manage it." She straightened. "The Cheng millinery has fallen on hard times."

"Just because they don't know how to manage it doesn't mean you do, Lydia."

"Ah, but I do! And my dress designs have already sparked interest. Esmerelda would have bought a dozen of them."

Max was shaking his head. "She was just being polite."

"No, Max, she wasn't. That woman is anything but polite. And besides, she didn't know they were my designs."

Max straightened. "What do you mean she wasn't polite?"

Lydia sighed. Why could he not stick to the topic at hand? The last thing she wanted to talk about was Esmerelda. "Max, please listen. I want to buy the Cheng shop. I'm sure my dress designs could make a lot of money. I could work hard, establish myself, and then later, when the children come, I could hire sewers and the like. But I would still be the designer." She scooted closer to him. "I can do it, Max. I know I can."

Now was the time for her fiancé to lean into her, declaring loudly that he knew she would be a fabulous dressmaker, before kissing her soundly on the lips. They would set their wedding date and go on to a fabulous future.

Max did not do any of those things. He practically threw her off him as he shoved to his feet. "You're not thinking clearly, Lydia. You don't know anything about running a business."

"You're right, Max, I don't. But you do. You've always wanted to run your own. You've said so yourself."

"I am not a dressmaker!"

"Of course not," she countered. "I'm that. But the product doesn't matter. I mean, it matters because that's the product I can do. It would be your business. Your name on the door. You could direct everything. I would merely be the designer. That's all." She stood up—not sidling up to him as she had all evening, but facing him square on as she had done so long ago in England. Back when they were children. "Max, we can do this. And we can make a fortune." She smiled slyly up at him. "Do you know what women spend on dresses these days? Especially for an elite designer? Max, we could be rich!"

He was softening. She could see it in his eyes. It was greed, pure and simple, but sometimes, greed was the fastest way to a man's heart. Especially when that man was Max. Why else would a man leave everything he knew to come to Shanghai?

"Cheng's, huh? On Avenue Joffre?"

She nodded. "We can make a fortune. Enough to go back to England like kings, maybe even buy a title. Just like you wanted from the beginning. Before you left for Shanghai." Before things had changed between them.

"Very well," he said grudgingly. "I will look into it."

She leaped up, planting a kiss of delight on his lips. "Oh, thank you, Max! Thank you so much!"

He grabbed her elbows, setting her back on her heels. "I haven't said yes, yet. There are still a great many details to work out."

"Of course there are." She grinned happily up at him. "But you are a master of that type of detail. You will bargain wonderfully, I'm sure."

He nodded, obviously pleased with her compliments. "Now, Lydia, I've got to go, and you've had a trying day, I'm sure. So I'll leave you to clean up and rest."

Lydia blinked stupidly at her fiancé, her throat impossibly dry. After the elation of a moment before, this felt like a crushing blow. "You're leaving?" she finally whispered.

His color darkened, along with his expression. "Well, I can hardly stay here. It wouldn't be proper."

"Proper?" she practically squeaked. "My reputation is already ruined, Max. You saw to that this morning when you blabbed what had happened all over town."

"I most certainly did not!" he countered, his tone rising along with his volume. "Dammit, Lydia, people saw you! They saw you arrive barefoot and naked."

"Naked! Max, I had clothes on."

"Coolie clothing! Without . . . without . . ." He gestured mutely at her cinnabar cave. He sighed, glaring darkly at her. "I had to say something. I had to tell them the truth."

She slowly dipped her chin in acquiescence, even though she completely disagreed. "Fine. You had to say something. But now I'm ruined." She stepped forward, leaping to her last resort—seduction. She pressed her body close to him. "You're my fiancé," she whispered as seductively as she could manage. "You have promised to marry me. It's time, Max. Time to be a gentleman. Time to save me from my own folly, just like we were kids." In her boldest move yet, she reached up and pulled his mouth to hers. "Marry me, Max."

Then she stretched up on her toes, kissing him with all the passion and desperation inside her. She pressed her mouth to his, her lips closed. It was the way they had kissed before—back in England—and she knew no other way. Ru Shan had never touched her lips.

She felt him soften toward her. His mouth opened and she shivered as his tongue stroked the seam between her lips. She gasped slightly at the sensation—the wet tickle across her lips. And as she did so, his tongue ventured farther, deeper into her mouth.

It was an odd feeling, this widening of her mouth. Then his tongue pressed inward, invading her mouth, pushing roughly in. At first she was appalled—such a big thing thrust inside her—but then she got a flash of memory. She recalled Ru Shan's hands upon her. Lower. Opening her legs and pressing his thumbs inside her. In and out. Just as Max was doing to her mouth.

And that memory excited her.

She felt her yin begin to flow. Her breasts seemed to

plump and her yin dew softened her stance. She melted into Max's arms, though he staggered some with her weight.

Laughing slightly in embarrassment, she tugged him back to the settee. But he moved awkwardly, as if he was unsure of himself. So, her face flushed with heat and yin and hunger, she smiled at him, urging him closer.

"Kiss me again, Max. Please?"

He did and she eagerly opened her mouth this time, wanting the reminder of what Ru Shan had done. She even echoed the movement, imitating what both Ru Shan and Max had taught her. She swirled her tongue around and with Max's, then boldly thrust into Max's mouth.

He reared back, clearly appalled.

"Max?"

"You've never done that before!" he exclaimed, his voice accusing.

"I've never done any of this before," she returned hotly.

He frowned at her. "Very well," he finally said. "But don't do that again."

She nodded, briefly wondering what Ru Shan would say. Would he object to a woman thrusting her tongue into his mouth? She doubted it. But she wasn't with Ru Shan. She was with Max, her husband-to-be, and it was up to her to learn his preferences. Or risk losing him to the likes of Esmerelda.

"I won't do it again," she murmured. "I promise. I was just imitating you."

He nodded, slowly, then leaned forward. "A man likes a woman to be demure," he instructed formally. "To accept his attentions shyly."

"I promise," she murmured as she lifted her mouth to his. In truth, she would have promised almost anything to get him to return to what he was doing. Her yin felt like it was bursting through her, and she needed to feel his hands on her. On her breasts. And perhaps—if she handled things properly—lower down. At her cinnabar cave.

So she remained cool as he kissed her again. She kept her lips pressed together until he coaxed them open again. And when he did, she allowed him to plunge his tongue inside her, tasting her as he wanted. She returned his movements, dueling as much as she dared, and all the while her mind was on Ru Shan and what he had done before. How he had pushed his thumbs inside her cave.

Then Max's hands began to wander. He stroked up her sides, and finally, mercifully, he touched her breasts. Or rather, he grasped them—hard and without seeming purpose. There was no gentleness in his touch. Merely the grasping of a hand without Ru Shan's stimulating circles.

And yet, so desperate had she been for stimulation, that she let her head drop back in appreciation. "Yes," she whispered even as she silently prayed that he would go more gently, in the circles she knew.

His hands slowed their attack, and she smiled.

When he seemed as if he would stop, she pressed her hands against his, urging him to move in a circular pattern such as she was used to. But he didn't do it. Instead, his hands grew more lax until he finally stood up.

Only then did she open her eyes. "Max?"

"What happened to you in the brothel, Lydia?" His face was dark and strained.

She frowned, straightened slightly on the settee. "What?"

"You said nothing happened. That you managed to escape. But you know they chain girls. You know they sell them."

Lydia didn't speak. She couldn't, because her yin, which had been flowing so hotly a moment before, was slowing, growing sluggish and cold.

"How do *you* know these things, Max?" she countered, trying to avoid his question.

He sat back with a huff. "Because I'm a man, that's how," he snapped. "But you're a gently reared girl. Your father would never have told you these things. Nor anyone else."

She bit her lip, wondering what to say that would make him understand.

"What happened, Lydia? Tell me the truth." He straightened. "If I am to be your husband, I deserve the truth."

She nodded, knowing he was right. So she sighed and sat fully upright on the settee, folding her hands before her. In truth, it would be good to talk to someone about this. It would be good to start her marriage without a lie thickening the air between them.

"I arrived in Shanghai nearly a month ago," she said, and he groaned, dropping his head into his hands. "But I'm still a virgin, Max. I swear it! You can bring in a doctor if you like. I wasn't . . . In that place, no one . . ." She straightened her shoulders. "I know what happens between a man and a woman. My father was a doctor. And no one did that to me."

He lifted his head, confusion warring with disbelief on his features. Finally he spoke, his voice heavy with emotion. "Tell me exactly what happened, Lydia. All of it."

She nodded. "I don't remember a lot of the brothel." She winced as she said the word. Gently reared females were not supposed to even know what one was. "I was looking for you, but the captain brought me to that place. Gave me tea."

"Drugged?" His voice was heavy with despair.

"I suppose so. I woke up later in a back room. I was chained to the bed. My head was pounding and I felt so sick, but I fought them, Maxwell. Truly I did." She didn't know why it was important that he understand that, but it was. She looked into his face, hoping to see some understanding there. But all she saw was horror, and so she looked away, her words slipping out despite the turmoil of her emotions. "They brought men in. To buy me. To . . ." She shook her head. "I don't know. I don't really remember. I was just so afraid. . . ."

Her voice trailed away, and she longed to be touched again. To be held as Ru Shan had held her: his arms and chest supporting her back. But she knew Max would not do that. Not now. And so she had little choice but to continue.

"A man bought me. A Chinese man, and the next thing I knew I was in a sparse flat."

"He took you to his home." It wasn't a question, merely the voice of dread. Still, she had to correct him.

"It wasn't his home. Just a place for his practice." She sighed. "His religion, I suppose."

Maxwell snorted, clearly thinking what she and Ru Shan had done was depraved.

"It wasn't like that!" she exclaimed. But of course, she didn't know what normal relations between a man and a woman were like. Not really. So how would she know unusual appetites? She sighed. "We made a deal of sorts. If I cooperated—gave him my yin—then he would not take my virginity, and he would not send me back to the brothel."

"Is that what the Chinese call it? Yin?" Maxwell pushed to his feet to pace in tight circles beside their dinner table.

She shook her head. "Yin is the female essence. Yang is the male." She said the words, but she could tell Maxwell wasn't listening. "I did nothing wrong! No one knew I was here. There was a guard at the door. I had to cooperate or risk going back to that . . . other place." She looked at his closed features, seeing the way his pacing kept taking him farther and farther from her. "I escaped as soon as I could."

Finally he stopped, rubbing a hand over his face. He turned to stare at her hands where she held them tightly in her lap. "So you've been here a month now. Learning deviant Chinese sex." He shuddered as he spoke.

"What horrifies you, Max? That I was captured, sold into slavery and escaped? Or that I learned something no good Englishwoman is ever taught?"

He didn't answer. Instead he just stared at her, his shoulders dropping more and more with every breath. He looked like a man defeated, and her heart went out to him. She was on the verge of going to him when he abruptly rejoined her on the settee.

"Lydia," he began, but he didn't finish. Instead, he stood back up and grabbed his glass. He poured himself the last of their bottle, swallowing it in one gulp. Then he grimaced. "Damn frogs. Can't even make a good wine."

Lydia remained silent. She knew he wasn't truly cursing the French wine. He hated something else entirely. She just prayed that it wasn't her.

Then Max was finished drinking and he returned to his seat beside her. He reached out, grabbing her hands, holding them like he had when he'd proposed so many months ago. Only then, he'd been looking into her eyes. Right now, he seemed to be looking everywhere but at her.

"Listen, Lyds. I know you won't believe this, but I've been meaning to write you. I just couldn't do it after your father died. And then, well, you showed up. The thing is . . ." He lifted his chin, but still did not meet her gaze. "It isn't time for me to take a wife yet. I didn't want you to come to Shanghai because I knew I couldn't marry you yet." He bit his lip, then stood, his hands slipping from hers to push deep into his pockets. "I can't marry you at all."

She gaped at him, her mind reeling. He couldn't possibly be serious. "But a few moments ago, you said . . . You told me that you deserved the truth. *As my husband*, you said. As my husband, you deserved the truth."

He spun around, anger and guilt flashing in his eyes. "I had to know, Lydia. You wouldn't have told me otherwise. This way, I could tell if you need . . . you know, a doctor or something."

She wanted to push to her feet. She wanted to confront him eye to eye, but her legs wouldn't support her. Instead, she simply sat like a stone, her insides collapsing in on themselves as she imagined she shrank into almost nothing. "*I* know," she whispered. "I know if I need a doctor or not."

Abruptly, he dropped to his knees before her, looking so loverlike that she had to close her eyes. "But you couldn't, Lydia. It's just like you said. Good English girls aren't taught these things."

"And the men are?"

He shrugged, and she understood. Suddenly she saw it with a clarity that made nausea roil in her stomach. "You've been there, Max. Haven't you? To the brothels. Maybe not the one that bought me, but to ones like it. You've done it, haven't you? You've had sex with a chained woman whether she wanted to or not."

She saw him swallow, his dull flush becoming bright red as he shoved away from her. This time he didn't pace, merely turned his back on her, his shoulders hunched defensively, his words sounding childish and stubborn. "Every man wants to try a virgin. It's what men do, Lydia."

"You hypocrite," she spat, bile burning in her throat. "You bloody hypocrite!"

"See here now!" he returned, shifting to face the wall just to her right. "There's no reason to start calling names. It's unfortunate what happened, Lydia, but I wasn't going to marry you anyway."

"Marry you!" she screeched, at last finding the strength to stand. "I wouldn't marry you if you got down on your knees and begged." Except she would. She knew she would. Because what else could she do? If she didn't marry Max, she would be destitute. No money. No connections. No respectability at all. The very idea froze her blood.

"Look, I'm sorry it turned out this way," he said, frustration putting an edge to his words. "But we never really loved each other. Our mums wanted our marriage, and we went along. You know that's true."

She did. But she didn't want to admit it. Not when the horror of being ruined still clamored in her brain. She knew what happened to ruined women. Women without the protection of a man, women who for one reason or another found themselves unwed and alone.

They ended up in brothels. Sold to the highest bidder.

She couldn't risk that again. She couldn't! Which meant she had to marry Max. By whatever means necessary. She would do anything rather than risk that other, hideous fate.

Max seemed oblivious to her thoughts. Instead, he pushed his hands in his pockets, hunching his shoulders as he spoke. "I'm an honorable man. I'll pay your passage home." Then he shifted nervously on his feet, his tone softening as he tried to persuade her. "You'll prefer it there anyway, with your family all around you. Shanghai's no place for a woman."

"You asked me to marry you," she said, more to herself than to him. "I was going to be your wife." Mrs. Maxwell Slade. She'd even bought stationery, not that she had it anymore. That had disappeared with all the rest of her belongings.

"I won't say a word about this, Lyds. You have my word on that."

She almost laughed. He'd already said too much. The tale was surely already winging its way back to England. Her reputation was destroyed. On two continents.

He reached into his coat pocket, pulling out a ticket and dropping it on the table. She looked out of reflex, not intention, but what she saw there crushed the last of her hopes, her pretend dreams that she was still in her bed in England and that none of this had ever happened.

"Esme said it'll take a few days until your dresses are finished. You can stay here until then. I've booked you on a ship that leaves next week."

She didn't answer. She was too dried up to say anything. She didn't even have the strength to shift her gaze away from the damned ticket—the one that he'd purchased before dinner. Before she'd told him the true story of what had happened. Before everything.

"What about my shop?" she whispered. She didn't even know where the words came from, but she didn't stop them once they started. Instead, she lifted her chin and glared directly into his eyes. "I want to become a dressmaker, Maxwell. I want to buy Ru Shan Cheng's shop and sell expensive dresses to whorish Englishwomen like Esmerelda."

He shook his head. "You can't do it without me, Lydia. You haven't the head for business."

She shifted, her eyes narrowing. Hatred joined the fear in her brain. Together, they gave her an icy determination the likes of which she'd never felt. "Don't I, Max? Well, let me think. How's this for business? What do you think your employers would think of a man who proposed to a woman then abandoned her in her hour of need? Who brought that young, innocent girl to Shanghai, then dumped her without a farthing to her name? And that was *after* spreading ridiculous lies about how she was abducted into a brothel, hmm?"

He straightened, his eyes widening in shock. "I did no such thing!"

She felt her spine straighten, as if abruptly reinforced by steel. "Of course you did, Max. Who would ever believe that a good English girl could get stolen and sold—sold!— into slavery? No one wants to believe it possible, Max. They'll much prefer to think of you as a scoundrel. The worst kind of cad: one who would tarnish a good woman's name rather than be a man and end the engagement honorably. I think it would be enough to get you sacked."

"You can't do that! Image is crucial in Shanghai. It's the only thing that separates us from the heathens. Lies like that would hurt me badly."

"Really?" Coldness seeped into her, filling the empty space where her heart had been. "Try me. After all, half a dozen of your friends and fellows saw me yesterday. I even lined up a priest. But where were you? Hiding, Max. And spreading your own lies."

"But they weren't lies!" he gasped.

She smiled, though the expression felt distorted. "All I have to do is make a scene in the front lobby of your firm. I'll have tears streaming down my face, mud stains on my gown as I beg for help. 'Please, please,' I'll sob. 'Help me!'" She grinned. "There's nothing an Englishman likes more than rescuing a damsel in distress. Especially when it's easy to help her." She snatched up the ticket from the table. "You see, I won't need money or a passage home. I'll just need to hurt you in your employer's eyes. How long do you think it'll take before you're sacked? A day? An hour? Shall we make a wager on it?"

She was bluffing. She doubted he would be fired. As far as she could tell, he did his job well, and good English employees were hard to find in Shanghai. But it was the only card she had, and with Max, it was a good one.

He cared about his image, about appearances. He always had. But it was only now, when faced with the stark reality of a man who didn't love her, that she realized the truth. Appearances were exactly why they had become engaged. Because everyone said they were a good match. Because their mothers wanted the alliance. And she had been stupid enough to believe it was love.

Well, then, appearances were going to be what kept her at his side. If not as his wife, then as his partner. Because even if they weren't married, she would not be penniless and alone. She would not risk ending up in a brothel again.

Watching his tortured expression, Lydia turned the screws one more time. "I know you won't believe this," she said in a rude imitation of his earlier words, "but I had no intention of harming you until you acted like such an idiot. But take heart. You'll be happier back in England anyway, with your friends and family around you."

He swallowed. Twice. "I can't go home like this," he whispered. "Penniless. Dishonored."

She folded her arms, pleased that he had at last seen the light.

"What do you want?" he whispered, though his gaze was filled with loathing.

"Ru Shan Cheng's shop." And with that, she opened his door and pointed out into the hallway. "Buy it for me. Now."

From the letters of Mei Lan Chang

22 April, 1876
Dearest Li Hua—

Mr. Lost Cat is gone and I am despondent. I cannot believe that I would miss a barbarian, but I do. I miss him terribly. No one else notices the difference. No one, except perhaps Ru Shan. He has been extra good lately, studying very hard not for himself, but because he knows it makes me happy.

Dearest Li Hua, what am I to do? I cannot even bring myself to end my studies in English. In fact, I am applying myself even harder than before. Ru Shan, too. We are studying English like fiends, all because of one whiskered barbarian.

I should take opium. Let it kill me as it has begun to kill my mother-in-law. Do not ever touch that evil substance, Li Hua. It will kill you, and you will not even realize what it is doing. My mother-in-law is never happy unless the pipe is in her hand. And yet, bit by bit, she is dying. It is ugly and brutal, but only to those who watch. She is in bliss, she says. And, corrupt woman that I am, I enjoy the peace the opium brings.

At least the children know now not to touch it. Even

my daughter sees its devastation and has stopped asking for it.

Aii, Li Hua, I am so lonely. I wish you could come for a visit.

—Mei Lan

The Master said: To bless means to help.
Heaven helps the man who is devoted; men help
the man who is true. He who walks in truth and
is devoted in his thinking, and furthermore
reveres the worthy, is blessed by Heaven. He has
good fortune.

—Ta Chuan

Chapter Twelve

Ru Shan spent an entire day learning what he could about Lydia's fiancé, so the next morning he was not at all surprised to see Maxwell Slade walk into his shop. The Tao often worked that way.

The Englishman tried to be subtle, casting a disdainful eye here and there. Ru Shan was not fooled. He had much more experience in prevarication than the ghost people. After all, not only did he study the dragon/tigress way, but he lived in occupied China. Though the Mongolians had been ruling poorly for hundreds of years now, his family and all true Chinese remembered their heritage. No, the ghost people did not have even the first understanding of subtlety.

And that, apparently, included Lydia's fiancé.

The man looked about the shop, his lip curling in distaste. At what, Ru Shan didn't know, but he allowed the man to sneer.

Bowing politely, Ru Shan smiled. "How may I serve you, honorable gentleman?"

"Your shop is dirty, its stock poor."

"Yes, your honor, it is. But it is all we have, and so I count it a castle."

The man nodded, clearly annoyed. Then he abruptly smiled, as if he had just thought of an amazing idea. "Perhaps you would be better suited for another line of work. Have you considered anything else you might enjoy doing? A restaurant, perhaps. In the Chinese section."

Again Ru Shan bowed. Not because courtesy required he do so, but because it annoyed this ape. "You make a worthy suggestion," he lied. "But alas, my family has owned this shop for generation upon generation. We know nothing else. Every dirty shelf, every lost grain of rice has its story rooted deep in my family history. Surely, as a man of breeding, you understand." Lydia had once told him that the ghost people put great stock in their heritage. It was one thing their two peoples had in common.

"Well," the man drawled, taking another too-dainty stroll around the shop. "I may just have an idea of how to help you, old chum."

Ru Shan did not know this English word, *chum*, but he did not like the sound of it. It was too familiar, in that apelike way of the ghost people. As if merely smiling at a man could make him your friend. But Ru Shan had a plan, so he bowed again to annoy the ghost man and smiled as if in great relief.

"Assistance from so worthy a gentleman is always welcome."

The man's lip curled. "I'm sure it is," he said. "Look here, I've got a friend looking for a shop. He's most particular, you understand, but he fancies this general area. Now, there's a place down the street he might prefer, and the man there's willing to sell. But seeing as how you've touched my heart, how about we talk about a price for this shop, hmm?"

Was the man a baboon? Did he think that Ru Shan could have grown up here, learned this business at his father's knee, and *not* learned every boy on the street? Every child—now a man—who would stand in his shop now just as Ru Shan did? No one on this street would sell. And certainly not to an ape like this.

But this man's stupidity was Ru Shan's gain. Perhaps he could create his solution. The Tao often smoothed the way if a man took the first steps and trusted that the rest would be made clear.

"Oh," Ru Shan groaned in a most un-Chinese-like fashion. "My heart is full of cares today. First, my dearest friend has need of a wife—immediately—and he cannot find one. And now, you come and offer me a wonderful opportunity that I cannot accept. Oh, my pain is deep." Then he moaned and bowed to his knees. In truth, he was hiding his grin. He could not believe the look of surprise and shock on the ghost man's face. Could the man really think he would sell his inheritance to the first person to walk in and offer?

"Your friend needs a wife?" Lydia's fiancé asked.

"Oh, most desperately. But he has odd tastes. He wishes for a white woman." Ru Shan shook his head in despair. "No one understands it. He is a dressmaker, you know, but with such strange tastes. He wishes this white woman to help him in his shop. To work with him making clothes. None of us has ever heard of such a thing, but he says he must have one immediately."

"Or what will happen?"

Ru Shan let his shoulders droop and bowed again, as if a great weight pulled him over. "Oh, it is most evil. A curse, honorable gentleman. A curse that will not be satisfied by a Chinese girl. He must do these things or die." Ru Shan winced at the lie. No Chinese would speak lightly of curses. And yet, he felt the situation dire enough. "He would treat the woman most honorably, great sir, or the curse will strike him dead. But where would he find such a person? A white woman? To make dresses as his wife? It is inconceivable."

"*Reeeeeeally,*" the fiancé said. His thick mind was obviously churning.

Ru Shan smiled. It was indeed as he had suspected. Maxwell Slade was too thickheaded to appreciate Lydia. Indeed, Ru Shan suspected that Lydia had somehow asked the man to buy the Cheng family shop. But Slade clearly had no head for this business at all.

"An honorable marriage, you say?" the fiancé continued. "To a dressmaker." Then he frowned. "But the man is Chinese."

Again, Ru Shan bowed to hide his smiles. "Yes, most honorable gentleman. Do you have a woman who would serve? If so, we could meet at the Siccawei mission at four o'clock this afternoon."

The ghost ape smiled. It was a cold expression, filled with malice. He nodded. "I," he said with a jaunty wave, "shall provide the bride." Then he was gone, taking his foul scent and his stupidity with him.

Which left Ru Shan to make his own preparations.

Lydia was speechless. She did not for one second believe that Maxwell had seen the error of his ways, had suddenly realized he was deeply and devotedly in love with her, and abruptly wanted to marry her at an out-of-the-way Jesuit mission on the outskirts of Shanghai. He had shown up carrying flowers and falling over himself trying to please her.

In truth, she was a little sickened by the sight. Had he always been this stupid? Had she been so in love with the idea of love that she'd ignored what was right in front of her? Possibly. Of course, it was also true that she hadn't seen much of Maxwell for many years. Perhaps he had been kinder before. He'd been younger, certainly. And never so cruel.

Truly, foreign travel did change a person. Now he was here pretending to a love he obviously didn't feel. And that, perhaps, hurt even more than yesterday's dismissal. Yesterday, he simply hadn't wanted her and was looking for the easiest way to extricate himself. Today, he was scheming.

But what was the scheme? And why?

The only way to find out was to go along. And so it was that at precisely four o'clock in the afternoon, she found herself carrying a bridal bouquet into a Jesuit mission, feeling more unbridelike than she'd ever thought possible.

It was a spare building, quiet and not at all filled with the pomp of the churches back home. The altar was simple, lighted by a pair of plain candelabra, and the air was dusty in the way of large rooms that cannot remain clean no matter how many times they are swept.

Lydia moved slowly, afraid of what was coming. Two months ago she would have been appalled by the thoughts running through her mind. Would Maxwell try to kill her? Surely not in a church. Neither would he sell her back into slavery—would he? He wouldn't, she reassured herself over and over—and yet he certainly had not brought her here to marry her. One look at his face and she knew all his earlier friendliness had been a lie.

His gaze flew everywhere but her, scanning the shadows, the pews, the altar. More telling still, when a priest joined them from a side room, he grew more nervous, not less. Then another person stepped into the light, and all of Lydia's thoughts disappeared.

Ru Shan.

Her steps faltered, but having seen Ru Shan, Maxwell sped up, dragging Lydia along with him. "Stop," she whispered, but he wasn't listening, and all too soon they stood before the priest and her former captor.

Ru Shan was dressed handsomely, in what was possibly the most beautiful clothing she'd seen him wear yet. It was black silk with bright yellow embroidery. The stitched character was his family name—a kind of family crest, she supposed—bright and bold in the center of his back, while smaller characters seemed to float upon the lapels. Very simple, very elegant. And in his hands he carried a package folded in coarse brown paper.

Lydia felt the air closing in about her, her breath thickening until she nearly choked on it. Maxwell had a firm hand on her arm, and he snapped at Ru Shan, "So? Where's the groom?"

Groom?

Ru Shan bowed deeply—to her, though, not to Max—and when he spoke, his eyes were on her. "He is here."

"Here?" Max said. "Where?"

Lydia began speaking, her voice rising from a hoarse whisper to a near squeak of hysteria. "You're selling me. You're selling me back to him." She shook her head. "No. I won't go back!" She abruptly jerked her arm out of Max's grip, then she fled, running in the opposite direction.

There were voices behind her—Max's, the priest's—but she couldn't make sense of what they were saying. She didn't even try. She was heading for the door with all speed.

Except that Ru Shan stood before her, blocking the way. She had not realized how large he was. How solid. Like the mountain that formed part of his name. And he would not let her pass.

She skidded to a stop, abruptly reversing direction, but he extended his arm, moving swiftly as he followed. Soon she was blocked in, a column at her back, a pew at her side, and Ru Shan before her, preventing movement in any other direction.

"No!" she said on a sob. "I won't be sold again! I won't!"

"Sold?" snapped Maxwell. "No one's talking about selling. This is a church, for God's sake. You're getting married."

She shook her head, tears blurring her vision as she searched for a way to escape.

Maxwell was continuing to spout words, but they made no sense. The priest was also babbling, his high voice intermingling with Max's, garbling both of their messages. And all the time Ru Shan stood before her, blocking her escape.

"Breathe easily, Lydia. No one will force you today. You have all the choice here."

Why she believed him, she wasn't sure. Perhaps it was because he had never lied to her before, even when she'd been in his power. Max, on the other hand, had shown himself unfaithful on so many levels. Ru Shan's words at last penetrated her panic, and she began to calm down. Though her heart still raced, her mind cleared and her body relaxed some. She was still poised to run, but for the moment she would stand and listen.

While she stood there, trapped between Ru Shan and the furniture, he extended his hand, gently lifting a tear off her cheek. "Stolen yin can be powerful," he said in Chinese, "but it twists and poisons." He threw her tear away. "I did not understand that before, but I do now."

She blinked, wondering if she had heard his words correctly. Then Max and the priest were confusing things again. They were there beside her, the priest asking if she was well, saying soothing words that made no sense. Max was bellowing at Ru Shan, demanding to know the meaning of all this.

And then Ru Shan spoke, his tones low and hard. "What lie did you tell her to bring her here?"

Max stiffened, drawing himself upright. "Now see here—" he began, but Ru Shan interrupted.

"What lie did you tell her?"

"I did not—"

"Of course you did," Lydia interrupted. She was still finding it hard to breathe, and yet her voice came out clipped and angry. "You said we were to be married."

Max grimaced. "I said *you* were going to get married." His voice turned high and wheedling. "It's what you want, Lydia. Marriage. Dress-making. Everything. He'll treat you well. Some curse or something."

The priest began to exclaim, but all Lydia heard was noise. She knew he was chastising Max, loudly defending her honor and expressing outrage at Max's perfidy. At one time, she would have relished the moment. Indeed, after last night, she'd dreamed of such a moment when someone punished Max for hurting her.

And yet, right now, she barely heard. Her eyes, her ears,

indeed her entire body, seemed tuned to Ru Shan. To his dark eyes and tightened lips.

"Do you understand how unworthy he is?" he asked in Chinese. "That your intended has . . ." His words faltered as he obviously struggled for the right words.

"The morals of a monkey?" she finished for him in English.

Ru Shan nodded, bowing slightly.

"Yes," she said sadly, because she *was* sad. "I understand Max's unworthiness." And so too did she understand that all the hopes and dreams she'd had leaving England were equally absent. They'd been lost the moment she stepped off the boat.

Her former fiancé was beginning to sputter angry words of denial, self-defense, and outrage. Lydia waved him off in weary dismissal.

"Go away, Max. We are hurting each other, and I can't bear any more." Except part of her was still a young, idealistic English girl who wanted him to fall to his knees begging forgiveness. He didn't, of course. He sighed, the sound coming from deep inside.

"I know it hurts, Lydia. We've been friends all our lives." He shook his head. "Shanghai changes a person, you know. I'm not that stupid boy from before, happy to have his mum pick his bride. You've changed even more than I." He glanced as Ru Shan. "You're getting married, Lydia. And you get to be a dressmaker. That's what you want, isn't it?"

Lydia blinked away tears, wondering what would become of her. Could this really and truly be happening?

Then he said one last thing, one parting shot that crushed the last of her silly, romantic dreams.

"It would never really work between us, Lyds. You're just not English enough anymore."

Lydia gaped, her mind reeling, her body going merci-fully numb. What did he mean, not English? Of course she was English! But she didn't have a chance to ask him; he was already leaving, his footsteps a heavy echoing sound, and she would be damned if she ran after him. If nothing else, at least she had her pride.

But what did he mean? Not English enough?

"Why do you worry about a monkey's howl?" asked Ru Shan, his gentle tones interrupting her thoughts.

Her gaze was still on the door that slipped closed behind Max, but her thoughts went to Ru Shan. Eventually, her gaze found him as well. Why *did* she worry about what Max said?

"Because he represents England," she said, only just under-standing the truth of her words. "What he believes is what everyone at home will believe. And what they will say." She swallowed, her eyes tearing. "And because he's right. I'm not a demure English girl anymore, am I?" Her eyes shifted to the priest, a sandy-haired man in his fifties with gentle green eyes. Her knees were threatening to buckle, and she must have swayed because both men grabbed hold of her, one on each arm. They slowly led her to sit in a pew.

"You are still English," said the priest, his high voice sounding melodic. "But you are in Shanghai now, and that has changed you."

"I can't go back to being her, can I? The girl I was before I arrived."

"Of course not," said the priest, but it was Ru Shan who asked the right question.

"Do you want to? Do you want to be her again?"

She remained silent a moment, her thoughts slipping gently from one memory to the next, one image to another without rhyme or reason: her childhood with her family, her father's funeral, Maxwell as a boy, Maxwell as a man. Maxwell in Shanghai. The boat. The brothel. Ru Shan.

In the end, that was the memory that remained. Ru Shan's calm presence as he began to instruct her in the ways of his religion.

"No," she said without realizing she was speaking. "No, I do not want to go backward." Then she glanced up at the altar, at the very solid mission, built in a simple, European design. It was dusty and dark; enclosed and very, very Caucasian; nothing like the Chinese buildings with carvings and colors everywhere you looked. Their swooping lines and quiet elegance fit Shanghai, whereas the European designs did not.

"I am like this building—an English design in a foreign place." She shook her head. "I'm impractical and ugly."

"Not ugly," Ru Shan countered. "Merely different. And you can adapt." Then he stood, bowing at the waist before her. "As can I," he said as he straightened. "Lydia, I wish to marry you."

She was so startled by his statement that she laughed. A nervous giggle bubbled out of her, then was quickly silenced. Ru Shan did not comment. He merely gazed at her with dark, fathomless eyes. Then he took a breath, preparing to speak, but she stopped him. She held up her hand and shook her head.

"No, Ru Shan. Don't. Not yet." And then, while the two men watched her, she walked slowly off. She had no idea where she was going, but was not surprised when she ended up before the altar. She looked at it. At the cross and the candles. At the wood beams and the square building they supported. Finally she turned to Ru Shan. "Yes, I am like this building," she said loudly. "I am solid. Sturdy. I was raised to be a good wife to an Englishman, with room for love and beauty, children, and a future. I am Christian"—she gestured to the cross—"and I am serviceable."

And empty? she wondered. Was she empty, too? Built only for someone else to fill?

She stepped forward, silencing those thoughts as she moved back to Ru Shan. "I do not know how to cook Chinese foods or be a Chinese wife. I do not know your Taoist ways, though," she added slowly, "I am interested in learning." She gestured to the room about her. "But you do not want this."

Ru Shan had not moved except for his eyes. He had watched her wander and now watched her face with the steady focus she had always found so appealing. He tilted his head, frowning in the way of a man who cannot understand why his broken clock will not tell time.

"The first thing we Taoists learn is not to tell others what to believe, what to do, or how to act. So long as your journey does not impede my own, why would I tell you not to pursue your heart?"

Her eyes welled with tears at his words. "Ru Shan, my heart is lost. It does not know what it wants or where it will go." She looked about, her eyes landing on the priest, then skittering beyond him to the door and, in her mind, all the way to England. But then she turned away. She could not even decide which part of the world she wished to live in.

Ru Shan stepped closer. "Then perhaps I shall tell you what I guess of your heart." She had not realized he was so close until she felt his hands gently lift hers. "You wish to design clothing, yes? It was the first thing you asked of me—"

"No, it wasn't," she interrupted. "The first thing I asked for was my freedom."

He nodded, and through their joined hands, she felt his body tighten. Why? Did he feel ashamed? Angry?

"I was wrong, Lydia," he said slowly. Deeply. Then he lifted her hands, drawing them up to his lips, kissing them each. "I bought a pet only to discover a soul. I drew out her yin, only to find it tainted. I believed she was at fault, only to find the defect in me." He looked into her eyes. "If this building is you, then what am I? A shack in the mountains? My store within Shanghai? If you are lost, then I am equally misplaced. Can we not find our way home together?"

She swallowed, moved by his words. "But what if our home is not in the same place?"

He hesitated, then shrugged. "China is a large, large country. Surely there will be someplace here for you."

She felt her lips curve into a slight smile. "And what of you?"

"My happiness will be in the bed you make for me, with the food you cook for me." His eyes began to glimmer with humor as well. "With the clothes you design for me."

"You want me to work in your shop?"

He nodded. "Isn't that your wish as well?"

She echoed the movement, though more slowly. "Of all the things we have talked about, that is the one thing I understand the most."

"You will marry me, then?"

She hesitated, unsure if she could make the leap as easily as he did. Then he spoke, showing that he understood her fear.

"In China, you will have more respect as a wife who designs clothing for her husband's business than as a woman alone who works as a designer." He reached out, cupped her face. "And I thought you were built for children as well. Did you not wish for that?"

She nodded, finding another thing of which she was certain.

"As a designer alone, you will not find a respectable man. Not in China."

"And not in England either," she concurred.

Ru Shan leaned forward, nearly touching her lips. "I wish you to be respectable, Lydia." Then, for the first time ever, he pressed his mouth to hers. His touch was gentle, his lips amazingly warm. They heated her chilled body. He did not push his attentions, merely let her accustom herself to them. And in time, she molded to him; she brushed her lips across his.

In a most calm and seductive manner, he extended his tongue, using it to trace the curve of her lips, the ever-widening seam between them, and then finally, the opening within. She tried to remain detached, to analyze the feelings within her. Did she want this man as her husband? After everything he had done? After all they had done together? Could she make a home with this man and honor him as she would a husband?

She tried to think of these things as they kissed, but all too soon her thoughts slipped away. Her mind—or as much intellect as remained—could only understand that Ru Shan was kissing her. Ru Shan was holding her. Ru Shan's tongue was touching her—deeply, intimately, and completely. And now that she was no longer forced into these acts, she found she did enjoy them. With him.

So much so, she was the one who pushed for closer contact. She pressed her body to his, let her hands slip around his neck, pressed her pelvis against him, seeking his jade dragon. It was he who pulled back, remaining controlled when she had lost all sense of propriety. He remained solidly himself while she seemed to melt, trying to form herself around him.

And was that not the essence of being a wife? To form

yourself around your man, to support his efforts, to bear his children, to be his helpmeet?

Yes, of course it was. And so, at that moment, she decided she would marry him. Provided . . .

She straightened, looking about her at the very Christian building that surrounded them. "Ru Shan," she began softly, her voice gaining strength as she found the words to shape her thought. "I want to learn more about your religion, but I was raised Christian. I cannot simply abandon it for you." She gestured to the cross upon the altar. "That means something to me. Something important."

He bowed, his head dropping low, almost to the level of her waist. When he straightened, he smiled. "Lydia, do you not understand that there are many Christian Taoists? To walk the middle path does not mean you must leave behind your Jesus." He frowned, obviously searching for the English words. In the end, it was the priest who spoke.

"Taoism," said the priest, "is a philosophy, Lydia. Not a religion. It is simply a way of searching for God."

Beside her, Ru Shan nodded. "We seek the Immortals. If you find Jesus there, then I shall be in awe of you for attaining what I have not."

She frowned, trying to understand his words. "I can still worship? I can go to church on Sunday, pray to Christ, and observe my holidays?"

"Of course," answered Ru Shan.

"And perhaps," added the priest, "you could teach him of Jesus. Of our beliefs, and he will come pray with you."

She looked to the priest for confirmation. "And there is no conflict between Christianity and Taoism?"

"Perhaps that is something you can assure me," he added with a smile. "But as far as I have seen, the middle path, as they call it, is what we would call a temperate, chaste way of life."

"Chaste?" she almost squeaked out the word. There was nothing chaste in what she and Ru Shan had done.

"The Taoists I know are very solid and moral people. They only lack a name for their Immortal. They only need the education to call him Jesus."

Lydia hesitated, wondering if she could trust this priest. Surely he knew more about such matters than she did. And, in general, Ru Shan did seem to be an upstanding citizen. Except in the purchase of a woman pet. Except that he practiced yin harvesting. Except that what they had done . . .

Was wonderful. And intriguing. And more alive than any Christian prayer or act or holy day she had ever experienced. So, she asked herself honestly, if Ru Shan's Taoism conflicted with Christianity, which would she pick? Which direction did she want to explore?

Taoism, she answered herself, horrified by her thought. Horrified and intrigued. But mostly, she was being honest. She wanted to learn more about Taoism. Then Ru Shan spoke, his mellow tones warming her long before she understood his meaning.

"Do you not understand why I have brought you to a church to marry you? It is so you understand that I support your choices. I do not wish to change you, Lydia. I wish to add you to my home, my life. Not as a pet," he said before she could ask, "but as it should have been in the beginning. As my wife."

She smiled, suddenly finding forgiveness in her heart for his one evil act. "We would not have met otherwise. I would have come to Shanghai, been thrown off by Maxwell, and returned home unchanged." She took a deep breath, finding her body and heart expanded as she at last embraced the truth of her experience. "We have a saying in England. That God works in mysterious ways. Perhaps, hard as it may seem, God wished for things to happen exactly this way. So that we could meet in the only way possible."

Abruptly Lydia straightened, feeling both taller and softer than she had in a very long time. "I will marry you, Ru Shan. Indeed, it will be my greatest honor to become your wife."

Once again, he bowed deeply before her—three times, as he acknowledged her gift to him. Then, hand in hand, they walked with the priest to the altar.

Within moments, it was accomplished. The words were said, the papers signed, and she became Mrs. Ru Shan Cheng. Their first kiss as man and wife was tender. Sweet. And had none of the passion she hoped would come later.

Now that she had agreed, had become his wife, his attention seemed focused on accomplishing the deed, on making it legal in the English court and in securing her promise to remain faithful to him always.

She might have worried if it had not all happened so quickly. By the time it was done, she had no time to question. Especially as he lifted her into the English closed carriage he had rented for the occasion, and as he at last bent his considerable focus back to her.

"Tomorrow we will perform the ceremony that will make our union official in China. We will do this in my home, before my family."

She nodded, a knot of fear already tightening her throat. She knew nothing of Chinese ceremonies. She had no idea what to do. Once again, he seemed to read her thoughts, soothed her fears before she could even frame them in words.

"Do not worry yourself about this formality. I have the clothing you should wear." At this, he handed her the package wrapped in brown paper that he had been carrying when he first walked into the mission. "I will teach you what to say and what to do." He smiled as he took hold of her hand. "It is a simple ritual, Lydia. You will have no difficulties."

She smiled, squeezing his hand as she tried to calm the butterflies that were churning frantically in her stomach. She succeeded in a small way, her breath evening out and her heart steadying at a slightly slower tempo.

At least, it did until his next words penetrated her consciousness.

"Tonight, we will celebrate our honeymoon. Now that we are man and wife, I have so much more that I can teach you."

From the letters of Mei Lan Cheng

10 October, 1883
Dearest Li Hua—

When I said I wished I could see you, Li Hua, I did not mean for it to be that way. The death of your daughter was terrible, and I grieve constantly for you. I will not write what I think of that hideous Imperial soldier. The corruption in our beautiful country is growing more and more hateful. And yet, how can I not also be thankful—that I could at last see you for a while, even under these wretched conditions? I was thankful. And you know I hold you with all tenderness in my heart.

Perhaps now you have suffered enough, and Heaven will grant you a son.

My own son has deserted me. While I was gone for

the funeral, Sheng Fu dismissed our son's tutors. Ru Shan is to work in the shop every day now, learning what to do from his father. He tells me I always knew this day would come and to quit my weeping. But I cannot, Li Hua. How much must we suffer before Heaven smiles upon us once again?

After all the money I scrimped and saved, after all the things I have done for the monks so that Ru Shan would become a great scholar. All destroyed. All useless. He is to be a shopkeeper like his father. Like all the Chengs, and I am to stand aside with bowed head and accept my husband's pronouncements.

But what if I do not like them? What if I wish to be heard in this house of opium and foreign gold? I cannot. That is not my place, and so I am silent and miserable and alone except for you. I thank Heaven daily for you and the comfort your letters bring. I pray that mine bring joy to your heart.

Please forgive me. I cannot write more. My tears are destroying the paper.

—Mei Lan

Those who adapt themselves
will be preserved until the end.
That which bends can be straightened.
That which is empty can be filled.
That which is worn away can be renewed.
—Lao Tzu, founder of Taoism

Chapter Thirteen

Lydia did not know what to expect from her first night of married life, but the last thing she wanted was to return to the same apartment, the same room where she had first met Ru Shan. The bare walls of the flat and the depressing, kept-woman atmosphere had her hesitating on the doorstep, unwilling to enter.

"If I had the means, Lydia," Ru Shan said softly from inside, "I would take you to a palace and love you in perfumed gardens with the pearl moon overhead. But I am only a poor shopkeeper, and this is all I can afford. I cannot take you to my home yet. I would have to introduce you to my entire family, and I have no wish to share you just now. Please, Lydia, you must understand. I am your husband now, not your owner. You are my wife, not a pet. Please forgive me the pain I caused you in the beginning, but do not damage our future by remembering too much of the past."

She didn't answer, thinking instead that she had married

a man with a beautiful voice and a persuasive manner. She had not thought so at first. He kept too much hidden, told more often than he asked. But he was asking now, even when he did not have to. He was her husband, and it was her moral and legal obligation to obey him. And yet he asked her to please come in, to return to the place where she had first been his.

She smiled at him, took his extended hand and walked into her new life. She was his wife, and she was going to enjoy her honeymoon. So what if she was not carried over the threshold. So what if Ru Shan was not an English aristocrat. He was her husband and her choice.

"This is a wonderful place for our first night together, Ru Shan," she said as happily as she could manage. "It is only bridal nerves that have me hesitating."

He nodded as if he understood, then pulled her closer to him, drawing her in by tugging on her hand. She moved slowly, unsure what he wanted, then flushed a hot red of embarrassment and pleasure as he pulled her hand to his lips. She wore no gloves and so he had easy access to her bare skin. And as she stood there, just inside the door, he took his time kissing her hand, gently stroking each finger before following it with soft kisses and long, erotic strokes of his tongue. By the time he had reached her palm, her yin dew had begun to flow.

He was a master at what he did, and her nerves shifted from anxiety to anticipation. But before she could do more than stand frozen in embarrassment, Ru Shan looked up, a pleased smile on his face.

"Our dinner has arrived." And indeed, as he spoke, Fu De entered, carrying great stacks of food in bamboo containers. "The full bridal feast will be tomorrow," her husband continued. "This is for us tonight. As is this," he said, as he carefully took a large artist's brush from his servant. It rested, handle side down, in a pot of clear liquid. Naturally curious, Lydia stepped forward, offering to take the container from him so that she could discover what was in it. But he shook his head, quietly moving into the bedroom to set it on the floor near the bed.

She was left behind with Fu De, and together he and she quickly set up a picnic meal on a bamboo mat. Though Lydia couldn't help but wonder what her husband was doing in the other room, her stomach was exceptionally pleased with the scents wafting up from the bowls.

One month ago she never would have believed she could relish Fu De's strange Chinese concoctions. But apparently, her stomach knew better. As Fu De carefully set down one dish after another while saying things like, "for cleansing," "for youthful skin and hair," and "for great stamina," Lydia's stomach loudly seconded his words. Apparently, her body preferred these strange foods to the heavy English fare she'd grown up on.

Ru Shan returned, a true smile of joy on his face. He spoke with Fu De, thanking the young man for his services and giving instructions for the morning. All the while, Lydia sat on her knees staring at her husband. He was smiling. Not a small, polite smile. Not even the half grimace, half grin of ecstasy she had also seen. This was a true joy that welled up from deep within him and filled his entire being with cheer. Her husband was *happy*.

The change in him was so shocking that Lydia could barely take it in. It was as if his entire body lightened, his day-to-day mask of polite Chinese stoicism tossed aside, revealing this wonderful being beneath. And he was her husband! She would get to share her life with his wonderful person!

She couldn't believe her luck. So when Fu De at last bowed himself out, Lydia found herself totally content and surprisingly giddy. Indeed, in a moment of girlish enthusiasm, she abruptly leaned forward and kissed Ru Shan soundly on the lips.

Naturally, he was shocked. She had never acted so uninhibited around him before. But after a moment of surprise, he relaxed into her enthusiastic expression. He supported her with his arms while he kissed her back. Then he shifted and deposited another loud smack on her lips. When he was done, he pulled away, looked into her eyes.

"Is that an English custom?"

She shrugged. "Perhaps I will make it one." At his confused look, she laughed. "I am happy, Ru Shan. I am a wife *and* a dressmaker now. Except for children, it is everything I have ever wanted, and I am very, very happy."

He smiled at her, but his expression was not as full as she hoped. When she hesitated, he explained. "I am pleased, my wife, that you are so happy. I hope this state continues." Then he paused, and Lydia found herself bracing herself. She could already tell his next words would not be pleasant ones. "Lydia, you understand that every time a man finds release, he loses much youthfulness. That energy goes into his seed. Indeed, we believe that we lose a year of our lives every time."

She nodded slowly, remembering that he had indeed told her that.

"Lydia, I do not wish for children now. It takes much seed—many emissions from the jade dragon—to create a child. I have no wish for that right now."

"Because you want to become an Immortal," she

guessed. "Because you wish to take all of that energy to . . ." She didn't know the rest. Thankfully, he answered her unspoken question.

"That energy will launch me to Heaven, where I will commune with the Immortals. After such an event, I will return to Earth. A man cannot live with the Immortals. We can only visit."

She nodded, wondering where he was leading.

"After such a time, when I am an Immortal," he continued, "we may discuss children again, but not before."

"But don't you wish for an heir?" She didn't know why she was arguing, why she so wished to change his mind. She was only just now beginning to imagine Chinese society. She had a whole new role to learn as Ru Shan's wife. The last thing she needed was a child to complicate matters. And yet, the thought of not even trying to get pregnant left her with a deep, abiding sadness.

Ru Shan shook his head. "My heir is already taken care of." He paused, looking closely at her eyes. "Do you understand? I already have an heir."

She nodded, assuming he referred to a cousin or nephew who would inherit the shop upon his death. He was telling her she might not have a position as a dressmaker if he suffered an untimely death. "Well," she said with an attempt at a laugh, "your heir is a matter for the far-off future. We have many, many years to discuss children."

He smiled, though his expression was still wary. His touch was too, as he grasped her hand, bringing it once again to his lips. The kiss was quick and perfunctory. "I would enjoy watching our children grow, Lydia. But they will have a difficult place in China, and we must think very carefully before we do such a thing."

She nodded, her ebullient mood fading. Ru Shan was right. A half-white, half-Chinese child would face a hostile world. Neither race would embrace him. She sighed. "With luck, our shop will make enough money that our children will never suffer want."

He nodded, clearly agreeing. But that did not stop him from repeating himself. "So you understand, my Lydia? We will not try for children just now."

She nodded, feeling a rush of warmth at his address. She had always wanted to be someone's "my Lydia," and now she was. In the best and most wonderful way—as a wife and a lover. What more perfect world could exist? Except, of course, for the lack of children. "We will face the issue together later. When we are sure we can make a place for a child."

And with that, they both had to be content. Indeed, she was grateful for his foresight. She would not want to harm her children unduly simply because she had not thought through conceiving them in the first place.

"Come," Ru Shan said, gesturing to the feast before them. "Let us fill our stomachs before we fill our hearts." He looked at her, a wealth of hunger and anticipation sparking in his gaze. She felt her own face heat in response, and in a strange moment of shyness, she ducked her head, looking down at her food rather than at the promise of secret delights that seemed to burn in every fiber of her husband's body.

She looked away, but she did not forget. And soon, the delights of the table faded in the anticipation of the night to come.

Either because he was a master in those arts or because he knew her so well, he drew out the meal, extending her anticipation until she was at a fever pitch. Ru Shan leaned back in his cushions, taking time with his food, picking up tiny morsels and single grains of rice with his chopsticks. Yet all the while, his eyes were on her, watching her every movement, seeing her every expression and God alone knew what else. Still, his attention warmed her from the tips of her toes all the way up through her blushing cheeks.

He began to ask her questions. He wanted to know everything about her. Even more than before, he encouraged her to talk about England, her family, and her childhood. She warmed to the topic of her father, dead now nearly three months. In truth, she confessed, he was an average doctor, but he'd had a great heart and large, gentle hands. As a child, she had brought him wounded dogs, hurt birds, and once even an angry ferret. He had been a loving father, and she missed him terribly.

Ru Shan did not comment when she spoke of him, except to encourage her to talk more. His eyes betrayed a great hunger. Eventually, she slowed in her reminiscences to look at him.

"Your father is not a gentle man, is he?"

Ru Shan shook his head. "My father is a man of goals. He creates challenges for me and expects them to be met."

"And if they are not?" she asked, almost afraid to hear the answer.

Ru Shan shrugged. "The Chinese beat disobedient children, but not often. Parents have other ways of enforcing discipline."

She leaned forward, anxious to hear more. Eventually, he answered her unspoken question.

"Entire families live as one, Lydia. Parents, grandparents, aunts and uncles, cousins—all live in the same compound together. If a child disobeys, the anger of the entire family falls upon him. All, from the youngest child to the oldest great-grandparent, can discipline a child however they see fit. It is our culture's greatest strength."

"That the entire family holds together?"

He nodded, but his expression was sad. "It is also our greatest weakness. For the family can decide as a unit what a child must do." He sighed. "The weight of that responsibility is terrible."

Moved by the sadness in his voice, Lydia reached out and stroked her husband's cheek. His gaze immediately lifted to her face, but she was not looking at his eyes. Instead, she was watching his mouth, the way it pinched tighter, suppressing great pain.

"You find it hard, don't you? That you must make your family shop profitable. You would much rather study philosophy."

He shook his head, but slowly, as if feeling out his answer. "I enjoy selling things." He flashed a grin. "And I am good at it." Then he shrugged. "Well, perhaps not at actually selling items. In truth, my father was much better with customers. But I am the one who made sure we had the best supplies, the best things to sell. I made contacts and arranged deliveries. I made sure we were always well stocked, even in the worst of times. . . ."

"Until now," she said when he did not. She remembered the empty shelves, the bleakness of his store. "What happened?"

He sighed, his shoulders drooping. His gaze slipped away and he toyed with his food. "This is not the time to talk of such things."

She frowned, feeling his stubbornness like a thickness in the air. "Do not put a wedge between us, Ru Shan. Not so early in our marriage." Again she reached out, lifting his chin. This time she put more force into her movement because he resisted. In the end, he gave in, lifting his gaze to hers. His eyes were stormy.

She leaned forward, putting weight behind her words. "This preys upon you, Ru Shan. If a wife cannot help her husband when he is dismayed, then what good is she?" She paused while he thought. Then she pressed further. "I need to know what has happened if you wish my help."

He gave in. She watched it happen. It was as if something gave way within him, the stone that locked his feelings inside abruptly cracked. His body even flinched. He closed his eyes. She didn't think about her next movement. She simply shifted on the cushions until he could rest his head in her lap. And while he lay there, her hand idly stroking his side, he began to explain.

"Shi Po allowed my secret to escape. She told certain people that I kept a white pet. To my people, that alone is enough to make me untrustworthy as a businessman."

Lydia frowned. "Having a . . ." She could not even say the words.

"What do the English think of a man who consorts with animals?" he asked, an apology in his tone.

Lydia flinched. Even as a protected daughter, she had heard whispers of such things. "We think him unnatural. Unclean, perhaps, is a better word."

"And would you do business with him?"

Lydia sighed. "Many doctors would not even treat such a man."

Ru Shan sighed. "So it is in China as well. Only in China . . ."

"White people are considered animals."

He nodded. His gaze lifted to hers. "We are wrong, Lydia. I didn't know how wrong until I met you."

Lydia nodded, knowing he spoke the truth. An ugly truth, but true nonetheless. She smiled, quietly telling him that she forgave him his mistake even as she redirected their thoughts.

"Tell me of Shi Po. She was your teacher in the one thing that you chose for yourself—these Taoist secrets—and she betrayed you in the one way that means the most to your family." Lydia paused. It hurt her to even say the next words. "This woman has used her position to destroy you."

Ru Shan didn't speak, but the tension in his body answered her.

"Was it an accident?" Lydia asked. "Did she mean to hurt you?"

Ru Shan's eyes slipped closed, but his body remained like stone. "Shi Po does nothing by accident." Then he breathed—with obvious thought and intention. Lydia felt his chest raise in stuttering inhalation, but then his exhalation flowed fully out in a great gust of frustration. "Her husband is my greatest competitor. They profit much by my loss."

Lydia shook her head. How could he have put himself in such a position? "Why did you choose to study with her?"

"She is the greatest tigress in Shanghai. Many travel from all over China to study with her." He shifted, pushing out of her lap and rising to look directly at her. "There are few who study these arts. Many consider them immoral. As I said to you before . . . if my father knew the full extent of my study, he would disown me."

She stared at Ru Shan, seeing his fixed gaze, the taut cast to his features and raised shoulders. She could tell he had just told her something significant, but she was not sure she understood.

He explained. "For a Chinese son to be disowned means he would be cast out—not only from the family but from all of Chinese society. And from life after death as well. A disowned son is worse than nothing in China. He is evil incarnate. It is more than shameful, it makes you unclean and . . ." His words faltered as he searched for some way to express the horror he described. "To be unfilial is the worst thing a man can ever do."

"Unfilial? Meaning to . . ."

"To disobey, to dishonor a parent." He took a deep breath, and Lydia could see that he was making a decision. She waited in silence, wondering what he would say next. But he didn't speak. Instead, he stood, abruptly pulling her to her feet. She went easily, studying his face for clues to his thoughts.

Then suddenly he was kissing her. His mouth was on hers, his tongue thrusting harshly into her mouth, taking whatever it touched, as if he were branding her. She did not understand his actions, only the feelings that went with them. She felt his desperation and pain, his need to know she was his, completely and without reservation.

She opened her mouth and allowed herself to melt into him. Her body rested flush against his and her head fell back, giving him complete access to her body—and to her mind and spirit as well. He took greedily from her, first plundering her mouth, then feasting on the skin of her neck, even the swell of her breasts where she was still covered by her English-style gown.

Eventually he slowed, his frenzy diminishing. Slowly, he pulled himself away, tucking her close to his heart with arms that slowly tightened, not to hurt her but to keep her so close as to be one with him. Only then did he speak, his cheek pressed to the side of her head. His words flowed straight from him into her.

"My father learned of my interest from my cousin, Zhao

Gao—the one who long ago I thought ought to be ashamed, but instead was filled with life."

She nodded, remembering the man he had called "a dou," meaning one of great potential who turned out worthless.

"My father is not a foolish man. He knew who Shi Po was, knew her to be the only teacher available to me and also the wife of Kui Yu. He forbade me to study, Lydia. He told me that following this course would destroy the shop, destroy our family."

"But you disobeyed him?"

He nodded, and she could feel his body tighten. "I wanted to study, Lydia. I wanted to know what Shi Po knows. To feel what Zhao Gao felt. To be—"

"To be happy." She sighed. Ru Shan had been happy in his studies. She had known it from the first moment they began to practice together. There was great concentration, yes, but also an inherent joy in what they did.

"The holy men of China have great honor. They are great scholars and moral men."

"You thought Shi Po was like them?"

He nodded. "I did not think she would betray me." He released a laugh then, a silent explosion of air that had no humor. "I still do not understand why. They have enough. More, even, than we do. Why would she do this?"

"Because she is greedy." Lydia spoke without thought. "Because she is not as holy as you believed."

Ru Shan remained silent, his body growing increasingly heavy as he held her. And though it took some time, she at last understood that he was holding himself back. There was more to the problem than he had let on.

"What aren't you telling me, Ru Shan? What more is there?"

He didn't answer at first, but eventually his arms slipped free and he moved backward. His focus was low at first, as he stared at the floor. Eventually his gaze moved up until it came to rest on her face. "I borrowed money, Lydia. To buy you. I borrowed it from Kui Yu, Shi Po's husband."

Lydia felt her throat tighten, but she somehow found the breath to speak. "How much do you owe? And how much time do you have to repay it?"

He shook his head. "A few more months."

"How much?" she pressed. "Do you have any?"

He shrugged. "I think I can still do it. I think . . . if your designs sell well." He took her arms, his grip strong but not bruising. "I even have orders, Lydia. I can get fabric because of the orders. But only if you help. You must show our sewers what to do."

She smiled. "Of course I will help. I can do it first thing in the morning."

He shook his head. "No, Lydia. Not tomorrow. Tomorrow I will introduce you to my family as my wife."

She frowned. "But if the pressure . . ."

He put his finger to her lips, cutting off her words. "You are my wife, Lydia. I have made it so before your God today, and tomorrow before my family. I will not release you from your vows. I wish to make everything legal between us. Man and wife."

She nodded, unaccountably pleased with his determination. He wanted her, legally and morally. "So no man can tear us apart," she murmured, echoing the words of their wedding ceremony.

He grinned. "No man. Nor even Shi Po and all her conniving."

She smiled, lifting up on her toes to kiss him lightly on

the lips. "I will work very hard, my husband, to make our shop very, very, very successful."

"That would bring me great joy, my wife."

Lydia let her expression grow more coy, her smile more sensual. "Is there anything else that would bring you great joy, my husband?" she asked.

He paused, as if considering, but she could see the yang heat building in his eyes. Even if she had not, she felt it where their bodies still pressed tightly together. Slowly, with excruciating care and a great deal of rising yang fire, he began to unbutton her dress. He started at the top, in the center of her neck where the buttons seemed to choke off her breath. Bit by bit, he slipped the fasteners free. And as he released her clothing, she released her yin, letting it flow fully between them.

She didn't know how it happened, only that it did. Before, he had needed to stroke her breasts to bring her blood to a simmer before the yin power began to flow. None of that was required this time. She felt the power already moving, the yin energy slipping easily between them.

He must have felt it too, because he let his hands slip to her hips. Holding her there, he prevented her from pressing against his jade dragon, stimulating him even further.

"I want to become an Immortal tonight, Lydia. The yin and the yang flow freely today between us."

She smiled. "Yes, I know."

"You can feel my yang?" He seemed surprised, and she laughed at his puzzlement.

"Of course I can. It's like a flame licking at my skin." She gave him a quick kiss. "I have felt it from the very first moment, you know."

He nodded slowly. "They say that women learn much faster than men. It was many months before I could feel yin flow." He smiled, though the movement seemed thoughtful. "With such sensitivity, you will be a wonderful partner for me. Do you object?"

This time she laughed, her joy bubbling out of her. "Of course I don't. I am your wife."

He shook his head. "Many women in China—even many wives—consider this sinful."

She hesitated, thoroughly confused. "But you are . . . intimate with your wives, right?"

He nodded. "Yes. But many times such an arrangement is purely for the parents' convenience, not for the happiness of the wife or the groom. Intimacy is required for an heir, but not pleasure."

She smiled. "For us, it will be our pleasure."

He grinned, and again she was startled by how young his unrestrained smile made him appear. "Then, you will be my partner? My tigress?"

"Of course."

He caressed her face. It wasn't a simple stroke, but a reverent feathering of his fingertips, as if he could not resist touching her. "You are a wonder, Lydia." Then he sobered. "It will require much yin from you. Much . . ." He frowned, searching for the English word. "Many times of . . ." Again he faltered.

"That moment, that . . ." She too struggled for the right words. "That tide of power that you said could launch me to immortality."

He nodded. "Yes. You will have to ride those waters many times." He hesitated, as if fearing to confess all. "You may become very, very tired."

"Or I may, too, become an Immortal." She straightened, once again reaching up to kiss him. This time she lingered, slipping her tongue across his lips. Then she acted on impulse, sucking his lower lip into her mouth, and she felt an answering blaze of his yang. She drew back, unable to hide her grin. "Perhaps we should get started."

He nodded, already leading her to the bedroom. It was the same room as before, same bed, same linen. But somehow, she saw it differently. She had chosen this life and this man, which made this room a haven rather than a prison. It was a lover's bower rather than something ugly.

He saw her looking around, and she felt him tense. "I should have made this prettier for you. Or perhaps taken you to a different place." He sighed. "But the money—"

"No," she interrupted. "I was just thinking that it is our minds that create prisons, not our location. This is just fine, Ru Shan."

He searched her face, no doubt looking for a lie, but she had been honest and so she let him search, knowing he would find only happiness. Eventually, she felt him relax, reaching behind him for the large artist's brush and pot. "I wish to paint you, Lydia. And when your yin flows freely, you may paint me."

She did not understand, but she trusted he would explain, even as she stretched to see the liquid in the clay pot.

"It is scented water." He brought the pot closer and she smelled an exotic scent with a hint of something floral. She identified ginger and lavender, jasmine and something else. Something dark and sensual. Something that seemed to haze her thoughts.

She abruptly jerked away, flashing on the drugged tea she had drunk in that evil place. She would not—

"There is no opium in this. I would not poison you with that, Lydia. I swear it."

Slowly, she brought her heartbeat and her panic under control. "I do not want any drug. Not like that."

"There is no drug. Only spice." He paused. "And us. Remember though, hours and hours of study such as this will cause the mind to crumble, our restraints to give way. It can feel like the haze of a drug, but it is much healthier." He paused, clearly wondering if she understood. "It is necessary to break down the restraints of our thinking minds to become immortal. We do it through a kind of exhaustion."

"But not through a drug?"

"Not me," he said firmly. "I do not trust such methods."

She smiled, pleased. "Then tell me what I should do."

Gently dipping the brush into the water, he nodded. She watched as the fine bristles spread slightly as they absorbed the perfumed water. And then she gasped as he brought it to her face.

"I will paint you, Lydia. As a way to begin the yin flow."

She giggled, embarrassed at how girlish she sounded. "The yin—"

"Already flows," he said. "Yes, I know. But this will make it even sweeter." And so saying, he began to paint.

From the letters of Mei Lan Cheng

17 June, 1885
Dearest Li Hua—

Mr. Lost Cat is back! But he is Captain Lost Cat now, sailing his own boat.

I knew he was due back soon. I knew it. But I didn't think . . . And then there he was! Right before me, offering me a gift. It wasn't really for me, he said, but for Ru Shan. An English book on boat making. I did not understand it at all, but Ru Shan adores it. He has been studying it over and over. When I ask him why, he says it is because the ghost people know things—se-

cret things, that we do not. Perhaps it is because they are so much closer to the dead. Either way, he likes studying how they think.

Sheng Fu is thrilled, of course. He says one must always know more about the customer. He calls Ru Shan industrious for learning these things. Sheng Fu won't sully himself with such, but he praises his son for it. I think, perhaps, he is trying his best to hurt me. He knows that Ru Shan loves working in the shop so much more than he ever did studying. And Sheng Fu must always have something to boast about.

My dear friend, I am so tired, and yet I cannot sleep. I hear Sheng Fu next door with Ru Shan's wife, and their noises anger me. But not as before. Before I wanted to scratch her eyes out. Now, I am merely angry at my father. How could he marry me into this family? To be their slave, to work my hands to the bone for their gold, their opium? And without even a son to shine in the way of my family—in scholarship.

But I should not complain. You have your own share of sadness. At least your husband has a son now. I know he gives his attention to the boy's mother, but that is the way of things, and she is his wife as well. We must both learn to be content. Me with my designs, and you with your remaining daughter. Eventually, we will both attain favor from Heaven for our submissiveness.

And so I will go to sleep now. I know I will dream of Mr. Lost Cat, but I cannot stop myself. Such is the way with women. We must find our joy wherever we can, even if it is with a ghost barbarian.

—Mei Lan

The image of Difficulty at the Beginning.
Horse and wagon part.
He is not a robber;
He wants to woo when the time comes.
The maiden is chaste,
She does not pledge herself.
Ten years—then she pledges herself.
                                    — I Ching

Chapter Fourteen

What an exquisite sensation—a paintbrush on the skin. Lydia was nearly purring with delight as she felt Ru Shan stroke perfumed water across her face. Because Chinese characters were written with a bamboo brush, Ru Shan had years of study with the delicate writing instrument. His technique with the larger artist's brush showed that he was a master.

Lydia had expected simple thick strokes, but Ru Shan varied them, sometimes stroking large, cool trails across her skin, other times feathering light whispers. And other times, she felt strokes as thin and precise as her father's scalpel, but not cutting. They were arousing. Intriguing. And wonderfully detailed.

The sensuality of it all was amazing, but it was nothing to having a man's focused attention on her. He spent long moments on defining, outlining, highlighting, and simply admiring her face. Then, as her skin seemed to tingle with every breath of air across her brow, she felt his brush stroke lower: across her jaw and spiraling downward.

He had already unbuttoned her dress halfway between her breasts, and so he took his time, brushing the exposed skin around her collarbone.

"Are you tired?" he asked, his low tones mesmerizing. They felt like just another brush stroke, just another caress, this time of vibration rather than texture.

"Lydia?"

She blinked, opening her eyes in surprise. "Oh," she said. "I'm sorry. No, I'm not in the least tired."

"Do you think you can stand for a while?"

She nodded, her skin on fire. There came more whispered caresses of Ru Shan's brush. It was as if only his strokes could waken her skin, and there was so much more of her that wanted to be awake.

He smiled, as if understanding her thoughts. Then he gently shifted her position so that she faced the edge of the bed, but he did not sit as she expected. Instead, he slipped behind her, reaching around to unbutton the front of her gown. She tried to lean back against him. Indeed, she felt almost weak as her head dropped to rest against his shoulder. But he did not allow her to fall into his arms. Instead, he pushed her forward again, back into balance as he dropped tiny kisses along her neck and shoulder.

"Remain standing please," he whispered. It was not a command, but a gentle request, and she smiled at the warmth in his tone. "You will enjoy it more if I do not have to support you."

"Yes," she murmured, unable to voice anything more. *Yes*.

Gently, he eased her gown down, carefully pulling her arms out of the sleeves. She felt the whisper of air across her skin, even more so on the drying water, and the different temperatures only heightened her awareness. Bit by bit, he slid her gown down, letting it settle heavily upon her hips. Then she felt the ties of her corset slacken, breath filling her lungs as the bindings were released.

Once again, she felt the heat of Ru Shan's arms around her, though he didn't actually touch her, and the soft pops as he released each hook that bound her in front. One by one they were released, and her breath deepened, her heat rose, and the yin energy flowed.

She felt him tug at the corset, trying to lift it out from under her clothing. But the garment was attached to her stockings. "You have to unhook it. Below my skirt," she explained.

"Truly?" he asked. The surprise in his voice made her open her eyes. "English clothing is very strange. So many hooks and ties."

She smiled and nearly answered, but her words fled as he knelt at her feet. She watched him lift her right leg, setting her foot on his thigh. Then he untied the ribbons of her footwear. She had not thought the sight would be so moving, but it was: her husband, kneeling before her as he performed the services of a maid. She could not imagine any man she knew doing such a thing, including Ru Shan. He had such an aura of power and control that this act seemed much too servile for him.

Yet, here he was, gently removing one slipper after the other, and she was amazed to the point of tears. This was an act of devotion. An expression of feeling that she truly had never thought to experience, much less feel from her husband.

And all the while he continued to work, gently returning her unshod foot to the floor before sliding his hands up underneath her skirt.

"Ru Shan?" she whispered, suddenly nervous as his fingers trailed up her right calf, then knee, then spread wider as he explored her thigh.

"Shhh," he soothed, while his fingers continued to move higher and higher.

Her entire body shuddered with too much feeling, but Ru Shan smiled, his fingers still high on her leg.

"Do not be afraid, Lydia," he said. "That was your body throwing off the English contamination of the last few days. It is letting you know that you are mine now, a Chinese wife."

She swallowed, unsure what he meant, her focus completely trained upon his fingers. They still rested much too far from her throbbing cinnabar cave. "Ru Shan, the yin river flows very strongly," she gasped.

His smile widened. "It is but a fast-flowing stream, Lydia. Before I am done, it shall be a gushing waterfall."

She did not know what to think of that. She stared down at him, seeing his pleasure—his satisfaction—at her confusion.

"Do not be concerned, my wife. I will show all to you."

She nodded. Then, at his urging, she slowly widened her stance, spreading her legs to allow him more room.

"Close your eyes, my wife. Encourage the yin stream to expand."

She didn't need his prompting because his fingers were once again moving. But not to her cave. She felt his hands on the tops of her stockings, gently untying the bindings there, before slipping the material free all the way down her leg.

Her leg felt suddenly cold, abandoned. But there was little time to mourn as he began to repeat his actions on the other leg. She knew what to expect this time, and so she closed her eyes, wanting to enjoy the sensations of his solid thigh beneath her foot, the gentle tug of his fingers on the ties, then his hand cupping her ankle and heel as he slipped her footwear away.

He had such large hands, warm and gentle. He seemed to envelop her foot and ankle with his power. That was very much as her entire body felt now—totally surrounded by his command. And, much to her surprise, she enjoyed it. Indeed, she reveled in it, wanting his possession, wanting his amazing yang force within and around her. Completely.

Once again, his fingers began their quest up her leg. From calf to knee to thigh he went, his touch playful as her breathing increased, her simmering yin becoming more frenzied in her bloodstream.

His hands were so close, nearly there, almost touching her cinnabar cave. But they did not go there. When his single knuckle accidentally brushed the inside of her other leg, she felt her entire body shudder.

But she did not say anything, and slowly, he pulled her stocking down and away. And when he stood, she felt him take hold of her loose corset, lifting it away. Her dress remained a heavy weight upon her hips.

She was naked from the waist up, her breasts full and peaked, anxious for his touch, her very skin begging for his attention.

"Keep your eyes closed," he whispered next to her ear. "You will feel each stroke all the more powerfully."

She had not needed his suggestion. Her body felt too languid to open her eyes. But she could still smell, and once again the scents of the perfumed water slipped into her senses. He was wetting his brush again, and then— wonderful!—he was stroking her skin, using the brush to paint designs. Not on her chest, as she wanted, but on her back. And yet, it felt incredible, and she found herself bowing forward to give him better access.

Then he stopped, and she felt her body tighten in surprise.

"Your hair should be down," he said. Before she could react, she felt his hands high upon her head, carefully discarding pins. Locks of hair began to tumble down. He gathered it all together, lifting it off her back and shoulders, only to slip it forward, so that as he painted her back, she felt her own hair tickle and torment her breasts.

"Do all Englishwomen have hair that curls as yours does?" His voice interrupted her reverie, granting her the focus to answer.

"There is great variety in hair, Ru Shan. Mine barely curls compared to many. It is more wavy than curly."

She had opened her eyes, twisting as she answered, and so she could see him nod, his gaze still on her rather unremarkable hair.

"I like it," he stated firmly as he lifted a lock, rubbing the blond strands gently between his fingers. Then he brought it to his nose, inhaling deeply before letting it slip across his cheek and face. "The scent is strange. . . ."

"Rose water."

He nodded. "Yes, that is it. And the texture is soft. Lighter and silkier than Chinese hair." He grinned. "I most definitely like it."

She couldn't help but grin back. "I am glad you are pleased."

He sobered into a mock frown. "But I will not be pleased if you move more, my wife. Please remain still with your eyes closed."

She nodded, obediently turning her face away from him as she bent slightly forward, allowing him her back. But he did not go there. Instead, he delicately opened the fingers of her left hand, stroking the brush in and around her fingers. He spent some time playing around the plain gold band on her finger, the symbol of their union.

Before she could comment, he expanded his strokes, slipping the brush underneath her forearm, around her elbow, and up to her armpit. He was not as thorough as before on her face. And his strokes became more hurried, as if he was becoming as hungry as she.

He still went much slower than she wanted, painting both hands, both arms, and the rest of her back before at last shifting to sit before her on the bed. He paused there, and she was about to open her eyes, but he stopped her.

"Remain still," he whispered. Then he lifted her hair from her front—slowly, excruciatingly slowly—and pulled it upward, allowing the tendrils to tug at her breasts. They tweaked her nipples too lightly, brushed her skin too gently.

"Ru Shan," she said, her voice hoarse. "The yin—"

"Is growing stronger, the river wider." He leaned in close. She could feel his heat on her cheek, the touch of his breath across her ear. "Let it grow, Lydia. We have only just begun."

So saying, he began to paint her breasts. Here, he used a pattern she recognized, though with its own variations. He began by stroking lines beginning from her nipples moving straight outward. He made her breasts like a radiating sun, her tight nipples the very center as they twitched every time the brush stroke began. And when he was done, he began to circle again, drawing the brush in a tightening spiral until he wet her nipples over and over.

Her knees were weak, her body swaying with throbbing desire, and she had to brace herself against him, placing her hands on his shoulders. She could feel the tension in him as well, but he seemed to keep it contained. Indeed, he seemed to be unaffected.

Except he wasn't. He was halfway through the circles on her other breast when she heard the clatter of the brush hitting the floor.

"I cannot wait," he rasped. "Lydia, I must have some of your yin now."

And so, with her eyes still closed, she felt both his hands gather her breasts, lifting one in each of his large palms. She cried out in joy as, finally, she felt the strong grip she so desired. His hands were wide, as wide as they could spread, but then they began to narrow, pulling the yin toward the point of each breast.

He began to suck. First on her left breast, pulling long and hard on her nipple. She felt it distend into his mouth, aching to be released, while on the other side, he continued to squeeze in a rhythmic pull.

Her flow began, the river larger than ever before. The yin energy drew from her womanly core, up through her chest, becoming a fiery strand as it concentrated into her nipple and poured into his mouth. There was no fluid release, but a high vibration of heat and power and ecstasy.

She cried out in joy, her knees buckling only to find them supported against his thighs. Indeed, she was pushing him open even as he suckled on her yin. Her mind was reeling and she felt the tide begin. Too fast, too much for him to draw off of her. Too much, especially when he abruptly stopped.

"No!" she gasped, and then was rewarded with his lips on her other breast. Sucking. Drawing. The river expanding to engulf them both. Below, her cinnabar cave contracted, creating more yin, more power, more energy to pour into him. Her body convulsed again and again, and still he held her, drinking it all in.

She could no longer control her body, no longer keep on her feet. He abruptly shifted her weight, allowing her to tumble onto the mattress. Then, without warning, he stripped off her gown, leaving her wondrously naked. Still the yin river flowed, but without the continual tug on her nipples, her contractions were easing, the power slowing.

"You will not stop!" he practically growled. And with strong hands, he spread her thighs. She opened willingly, wanting it to continue, needing whatever he wished.

He kissed her below, at her cinnabar cave. His kiss was rough and hungry—just as she wanted. He thrust his tongue once, twice, then three times into her cave, but it was not enough. She writhed in frustration, and somehow he knew what she needed. Soon his thumbs replaced his tongue, pressing hard, opening her up. She stretched to meet him, but he did not allow her hips to lift no matter how much she tried.

Instead, he shifted his grip, pushing one thumb deep inside her, stroking in circles until he found a place that felt like it was the inside of her belly. But lower. Better. Harder. *Yes!*

She did not know what that place was, but his hard pressure right there was glorious. And yet, her contractions had nearly stopped, the power of them feeble compared to before.

"Give me more, Lydia. Give it now."

So saying, he put his lips around her higher-up place. Once he had called it her little dragon. He stroked it with his tongue and she felt an explosion in her mind, like lightning bursting across her senses, obliterating all her restraint, nearly all her consciousness. Then he began to suck, drawing the yin river down there as it had once flowed through her nipples.

But it was more powerful here, the current overwhelming, pulsing like an ocean tide. This time the contraction felt like eighty-foot waves, almost brutal in their intensity as they crashed again and again against her little dragon, fighting to be released, fighting to flow into his mouth.

And he continued to suck, continued to draw the ever-widening, ever-increasing ocean of yin out of her. She had long since lost breath for screaming. Instead, her body was like a conduit for a power that burned through her, obliterating everything she was. Making her into something new. Something incredible.

Something that was irrevocably his.

Yes!

Lydia floated in a swirling ocean of colors, contentment slipping in, through, and around her body. She had no thought beyond joy, no existence beyond what was eternally now; and right now there was nothing but perfection.

Until she heard a distant murmur of disgust.

She could have ignored it. She could have stayed here a little while longer, but that sound called to her. Or more specifically, his pain—whose pain?—pleaded for her attention.

Ru Shan. Her husband.

Lydia opened her eyes.

Her first sight was of his knees, slightly bent, the circle of his knee cap clearly outlined by tendon and skin. She frowned, once again startled that he was so very muscular. His typical clothing hid much physical strength.

Strength—or perhaps she should call it frustration—that was even now vibrating through him even though he appeared to be completely relaxed. She frowned, looking down toward his head. Why was she lying upside down?

She flushed, abruptly remembering everything they had been doing. Things she had not thought possible! Physical sensations she couldn't possibly have imagined, had she not been with Ru Shan. Had he not shown her, and with such patience and . . . thoroughness. It brought a smile to her entire body just remembering.

But as she pushed up on one elbow, she could see that Ru Shan was not pleased, not nearly as content as she. Indeed, he had rolled onto his back, his dark eyes staring angrily up at heaven.

"It did not work, did it?" she asked, already knowing the answer.

He did not speak, but simply shook his head.

"It is my fault," she said as she slowly shifted to lie beside him. "I am not experienced in these things. But I will try harder next time. I will learn—"

"You are not to blame, Lydia." His voice was curt. She knew the harshness was not aimed at her; still, it hurt for him to be so angry and not talk to her. She wanted to help.

So she did what she could, snuggling closer, curling into his side. Eventually, his arm fell from his eyes and draped around her, his hand idly caressed her cheek. She sighed happily at his touch, knowing that if she could remain silent, he would eventually tell her what was wrong.

Or so she hoped.

Indeed, seventy-three breaths later, he finally spoke. "Your yin flowed like a neverending fountain, Lydia. I have never seen or felt such a thing before." He turned, dropping a light kiss upon her forehead. "You are a miracle to me, my wife."

She smiled at his words, warmed through and through.

But she could not let him stop there. "What happened?" She pushed up onto her elbow so she could look directly into his eyes. "If I have enough yin, and I know you have enough yang, what stops you from becoming an Immortal?"

His hand dropped to the small of her back, and she felt it tighten into a fist. His anger was a palpable field, emanating from him like pulses of biting electricity. She even flinched from its power. Yet she could not run from this. If she did, he would never open up to her again.

"Please tell me, Ru Shan. I want to understand."

He didn't answer at first, but she felt his fist begin to relax. Not in the way of a man at last finding peace, but as an act of will. His hand opened in jerks, and then he flattened it against her hip, a hot, wide presence that was hard to ignore. Then Ru Shan spoke, his voice filled with a forced casualness that did not fool either of them.

"I suppose I am not worthy of immortality," he said.

"Don't be silly," she snapped. "Everyone is worthy of immortality, including you. Especially you." She pulled tighter to his side out of loyalty, but even as she moved she wondered if the Chinese gods worked that way. Just because her Christian God taught that all souls were worthy of salvation didn't meant that the Chinese ones did too. But she didn't voice her worry aloud. Instead, she tried to focus on Ru Shan, on saying what he most needed to hear. Assuming she could figure that out.

"Tell me what happened," she pressed again. "My yin was flowing." She couldn't help but heat at the memory of how very much her yin had flowed. "I thought I stirred your yang." His dragon had been thick and hard in her hand, his yang a blazing flame of leashed power. She had felt it—not just with her body, but in her mind and soul.

"Yes," he finally said. "All the ingredients were there."

"So?"

He sighed. "I felt the alchemical process beginning. I felt your yin and my yang combine. I was climbing the stairs to Heaven. I know I was." His voice was tight, but no more so than his body that was growing rigid against her. It was obvious, even now, that he still strained toward Heaven. But what had gone wrong?

His eyes clouded, and she knew he fought tears. "I was almost there," he rasped. "And then . . ." He was struggling, trying to find the words. Or perhaps an answer. "I fell off."

"Fell off?"

"My focus. My intent. I saw images. Memories. And then . . ." He waved his hand in disgust, gesturing toward the floor beside the bed.

She raised up higher, seeing their blanket crumpled and tossed to the floor. She looked closer and at last understood what he meant. He had released his yang seed. She had been so caught up in her own ecstasy that she hadn't even noticed. And while she floated in her joy, he had quietly cleaned up his disgrace and tossed it aside.

She bit her lip, wondering what she could say. Then, before she could frame a thought, he shifted, turning toward her as he asked his question. "What did you feel?"

She blushed red hot and was rewarded by his grin.

"So you experienced joy?"

"And much more," she whispered.

He had been correct when he said that he would require much of her tonight. He had kept her yin flowing for hours and hours. Never would she have thought such a thing possible. But he had done it. And her mind had fought and struggled to contain the experience. Wave after wave of turbulent yin had wracked her body. With pleasure yes, but such pleasure as could not be held by the mortal mind.

In the end she'd had to release herself completely to the experience, giving up total control of her mind, her ego, her individuality or risk going mad.

That was when the experience had changed. She'd become almost separate from her body, which continued to pulse and contract. She'd felt . . . not launched. Never anything so explosive. Lifted. She'd been lifted into a sea of beauty, merging seamlessly into that amazing wonder.

"You went to the first portal." Ru Shan's words startled her, not with their meaning but his total amazement.

She looked at him, feeling confused and a bit guilty. She could not have accomplished so quickly what he had worked years for.

He shook his head, still stunned. "I can see it in your face. You are glowing with peace such as I have rarely seen." He nodded, apparently sure of what she barely understood. "You made it to the first portal." Then he fell back. "And I have fallen in disgrace beneath your feet."

"No!" she exclaimed, leaning forward in her earnestness. "I do not know where I went. . . ."

Behind her back, she felt his hand begin a gentle caress. "Do not be ashamed, Lydia. You are very gifted in this. I knew this from the first moment I saw you. Indeed, it is why I consented to . . ."

"To buy me."

He sighed, guilt bringing a ruddy color to his cheeks. "Yes. Because you were made for this kind of practice." He looked back into her eyes. "I am very pleased, my wife." Then he shrugged. "And very jealous."

"But you have gone to the first portal before, haven't you?" She prayed it was true.

"Yes," he answered. "Many times. But . . ."

"But you want to go beyond," she finished for him.

He released a bitter laugh. "Right now, I would be happy with such a thing. I cannot even make it there now, much less push further."

She sighed, slipping lower as she rested on his shoulder. Then she closed her eyes, silently praying to any Heavenly spirit who understood to give her the words to help her lost husband.

"Please tell me about the memories, the images you see." She didn't even realize she'd spoken until the sounds came to her ears. Then, once she'd heard her request, she doubted that Ru Shan would answer. She had pressed him so many times before.

But, to her surprise, he began to speak, his words slow and thick, as if each carried a great weight beyond their surface meaning. "I see blood, Lydia. And my parents. First my mother, then my father. I see them as they were many years ago, then as they are now. I see . . ." He paused as he swallowed. "I see death, Lydia. And such an explosion of hatred and anger that it boils past my restraints. I cannot contain it."

"And so you cannot contain your seed either, much less the power to send you to Heaven."

He nodded, but not just with his head. The movement seemed to curl in on itself. His chin dipped lower and even the arm behind her back pulled her into him. His other arm came around her, and suddenly she was being enfolded in his pain. A misery that had her crying the tears he would not.

She held him as tightly as she could. She allowed him to squeeze the breath from her lungs, and still she made no protest. Instead, she gave him all her strength and breath and power, wishing with all her heart that it was enough.

And eventually, it was. Or perhaps eventually he learned

to be content with his pain, for he slowly released her, rolling onto his back with a silent whisper of sound. Not a sigh. More of a sob, except that no tears wet his face and no anguish showed beneath the placid mask he wore.

"Don't hide from me, Ru Shan," she whispered. "I can't bear it."

He glanced at her, surprise widening his dark, almond eyes. Finally he spoke. "I am unaccustomed to sharing such things with anyone."

"Even with Shi Po?"

He nodded. "Especially with Shi Po. As much as she was a great teacher, her first goal is always her own immortality." He shrugged. "I cannot fault her for that. We all wish to be great."

"You are great," she snapped. "And I certainly do fault any teacher who thinks of herself first and her pupils second."

Ru Shan smiled, his features softening for the first time since she awoke. "You are fiercely loyal, my wife." Then he dropped a kiss on her lips. "That pleases me greatly."

"Good," she answered, returning his kiss. But she did not let their play deepen. Instead, she pulled back, unwilling to let their conversation shift. "You said you saw your mother as she is now. But . . ."

"She is dead, yes. I see her as she was just before she died. And I see her again as we buried her."

"Oh, how awful!"

He merely nodded, his mouth pulled tightly shut.

"How . . . how did she die?"

His jaw worked. She could see the muscles flex, but he did not speak.

"Was she killed?"

He closed his eyes. "She fell down. Her neck broke."

Lydia didn't answer at first. She had heard those words

before. Her father was a doctor, after all. He had used those words too many times to cover what she knew was the truth. She'd probably been beaten to death, likely by her own husband. "It would appear that there is ugliness in China as well as in London."

Lydia didn't know what triggered it, didn't understand what she had said, but at her words, the dam finally broke. Ru Shan pulled her tight to him as he began to sob. They were not soft sobs as she was accustomed to, the gentle misery of wives and mothers. This was a man's grief, and it tore at them both. It ripped from his chest with heaving gasps and clawed at his throat as it passed. His cries were guttural and frightening, but she knew better than to stop them. The sound, the pain, the aching horror of it all had to be released.

So she held on to him, cradling him as best she could while he sobbed and fought with his pain. It won, of course. He had been holding it inside too long, allowing it to grow into this huge thing that wracked them both as it escaped.

Finally it was gone, and Ru Shan slept in her arms.

From the letters of Mei Lan Cheng

1 January, 1895
Dearest Li Hua—

My friend, I cannot tell you what I have done. It was wrong. Evil. I know it, and yet . . . Li Hua, the barbarians are beautiful. Handsome and strong and beautiful. I cannot say how I know, and yet I do. Perhaps I am like my mother-in-law, trapped in another drug like their opium. I do not know. I do not care.

Oh, Li Hua, I am happy. I know it is wrong. I am wrong. Evil. Wrong. Terrible.

I write those words to chastize myself. But I am still smiling. I am still so filled with joy, I cannot speak of it.

Pray to Heaven that Sheng Fu never finds out. But perhaps the beating would be worth it. Yes, I am sure I would brave a thousand beatings for one more day— one night!—like this.

I cannot say more. But I had to tell someone! Please, dear friend, keep my secret.

—Mei Lan

Knowing the truth is not difficult; it's knowing how to react appropriately thereafter which is really difficult.

—Han Zei Zi

Chapter Fifteen

Ru Shan woke first, but not by much. The moment he stirred, Lydia opened her eyes. Her mind did not engage though, and she frowned in confusion. Why was Ru Shan . . . ? She remembered. Her escape, Max's betrayal, and finally, her wedding and wedding night.

A smile curled through her entire soul as she pressed a slow, languid kiss to her husband's lips. He returned it, of course, but there was a reserve in his movements, a tension in his body that had nothing to do with her embrace. She pulled back, a question on her face, but he did not even let her ask.

"I must go now. I must help my family prepare for your arrival." He swallowed as he gently shifted her off him. "Fu De will be here soon with cosmetics and a palanquin. Truly, there is little ritual to the event beyond that, but I must prepare my family."

She nodded, absorbing the information. Yet something

didn't add up. Ru Shan seemed too nervous for a simple feast, and so she pulled herself to her knees, wrapping the blanket around her body. Then she watched warily as her husband donned clothing and shoes. He even combed out his long queue and rebraided it with deft fingers. All the while, her certainty grew: her husband was troubled to the point of twitchiness.

"What's the matter, Ru Shan?" she finally asked. "What aren't you telling me?"

He turned, an obvious denial on his lips. But then he stopped and sighed, his hands dropping to his lap. He shrugged. "You are too clever, my wife. It will be very hard for me to keep any secrets from you."

She raised a single eyebrow, doing her best to look insulted. "Is it a Chinese custom to keep secrets from wives?"

He nodded, obviously surprised. "Of course it is, Lydia. Chinese women are not educated in much beyond beauty and art. They have little knowledge of the world and little interest in gaining it."

"So you men believe. So men have thought for eons. But we women are not so stupid as you imagine."

He sighed. "Yes, I am learning that." Before she could do more than smile, he was abruptly before her, dropping to his knees in earnestness. "But this I swear to you, Lydia. I shall not keep secrets from you. Whatever you wish to know, I will answer. You have only to ask." He raised her hands to his lips, his expression as ardent as she could ever have wished. "You are my heart, Lydia. I shall not release you."

She stared at his bowed head and felt his lips pressed against the backs of her hands. He quickly flipped her hands over to drop kisses onto her palm. She meant to ask more of him, to find out exactly what was going on behind his impassive expression. But his lips tickled, and his tongue sent shivers through her body. When he began sucking on her fingers, she had to pull away, giggling.

"Ru Shan, you make my head spin."

He gave her a smug smile, which made her laugh even harder.

"Very well," she said, deciding to guess his thoughts. "Your family will not be happy with an English wife." She shrugged. "I don't suppose my family will be thrilled with you either. They were absolutely set on Max, you know."

"And what about you, Lydia? Are you happy with your choice?" His tone was so sober, so serious that her gaze sharpened in surprise. Surely he understood how she felt? Surely he knew . . .

Apparently he did not, because she saw doubt in his eyes, worry in the lines that creased his forehead. She stood, moved before him, and as she did, she let the blanket slip from her shoulders so that she stood before him completely naked in body and soul. She made no attempt at seduction. In fact, it was a completely asexual gesture. It was a simple presentation of herself for whatever he willed.

"I am your wife, Ru Shan Chang. And I am greatly content in my choice."

He stepped forward, mesmerized, and she saw that his jade dragon had come alive. His hands lifted slowly, reverently, before he smoothed his palms across, around, and beneath her breasts. She closed her eyes, loving the feel of his hands on her body. She heard him smell her skin as he pressed his lips to her forehead, her cheeks, then to her neck and shoulder.

"You cannot know how precious you are to me, Lydia.

You are a pearl of great price, and I am a man most blessed."

He was speaking to her shoulder, so she reached out, needing to kiss his lips, to feel his mouth merge with hers.

There was a knock at the door.

They groaned in unison, and then Ru Shan leaned forward, quickly grabbing the blanket and wrapping it gently around her. Then he turned, speaking in rapid Chinese too fast for Lydia to understand. She gathered he was giving instructions to Fu De, because no more knocking sounded. In the meantime, he began smoothing out his clothing, preparing to leave.

When he turned to her, his words were formal and he spoke in slow Shanghainese. "We will rest our heads on the same pillow and tune our zithers clear and pure. Our music is always harmonious."

She smiled at him, flushed with love and joy and an overwhelming peace at his words. She wanted to respond in kind, but her Chinese was not that fluent. Before she even began, he was already bowing out, closing the door behind him. A moment later, she heard the front door open and close, and she knew he was gone.

Fu De appeared, knocking on her door, politely offering her clothing for the morning event. Paints for her face. Flowers for her hair. All the details of beauty that had to be relearned in the Chinese style.

Thankfully, Fu De seemed well versed. She had little time for thoughts beyond not wanting to appear like an unkept idiot before her new in-laws. Well, that and the memory of Ru Shan's face as she'd stood naked before him. That memory alone could last her through any number of trials.

Or so she prayed.

* * *

She felt starched and primped and ridiculous by the time she was done, in her high wooden shoes and strange Chinese dress. The decorative ivory sticks lifted her hair high, but her veil kept tickling her nose and making her sneeze, which naturally dispersed the extensive amount of white paint on her face. Silly that—painting her already white face white. But Fu De assured her it was traditional, and so she did as he said.

Now she sat in a covered litter carried by four big Chinese men, on her way to meet her new in-laws. She kept thinking she ought to feel like a princess. Instead, she felt like a total fool. What had she been thinking? Marrying into a culture she truly knew next to nothing about. And why had Fu De said her feet were too large? He had bragged that it was impossible to buy special bride shoes for a woman with feet her size, but that he had somehow managed.

And what was wrong with her feet? The same thing that was apparently wrong with all of her. According to Fu De, she was too big. Bridal attire could not easily be found in her size. Her feet were huge, her body too tall, her face too large, her waist too thick, and her breasts too plump. Apparently, she was perfectly acceptable as a pet, but not as a wife.

She knew it was simply her nerves, but instead of being delighted with her new Chinese finery, Lydia found herself hating everything about it, her body, and her new family. Before she'd met any of them.

"Oh, for Heaven's sake," she snapped at herself. "Quit being such a ninny." Except she was a ninny. A newly married ninny whose palanquin had just stopped somewhere outside of the Shanghai foreign territories.

Fu De's head appeared as he lifted the bright fabric

away. Since she had no one to present her to the family, he had been given the honors. Indeed, since Ru Shan didn't want his family to know that he had purchased her at a brothel, Fu De was apparently going to claim her as a daughter of a friend of a distant relative, or some such thing. Lydia had already forgotten the story.

Whatever the case, it meant that Fu De handed her a ball of red ribbon even as the litter was set on the ground and she stepped out. She teetered on her high wooden shoes. He steered her through a gateway in a high wooden fence without gaps. Beside the archway fluttered red paper with black ink characters, but she had no time to read them, especially as the wind and her veil obscured much of what could be seen.

"Watch your footing," Fu De whispered, but his words were lost as she struggled to both stand and hold a fan and his large ball of red ribbon. Especially as he was pulling it away from her by one end. She held the other end, watching as he stepped backwards, allowing the long, long piece of corded fabric to dip and sway between them, revealing the elaborate coil that decorated the center. It was a beautiful piece, and she was momentarily distracted by it. But then she looked up at Fu De, only to see that someone else held the end of her ribbon.

Ru Shan. Wonderful Ru Shan, dressed in a red silk tunic, covered in elaborate embroidery too varied for her to follow.

The ribbon jumped in her hand, tugged by Ru Shan. She held fast, her eyes trained on her love. But he continued to tug, pulling her step by tottering step into his home.

She made it through the courtyard, unable to see much of anything because she remained focused on her husband. He would see her through this.

Except, of course, he was walking away. Backing up as he tugged her into a recessed chamber. She knew what it was. Fu De had already told her.

She was going into the Cheng family ancestral place. That was where she would be formally introduced to all of Ru Shan's family. Before the ancestral altar. So she followed Ru Shan's tugging ribbon, walking calmly, pleased that she was getting the hang of these ridiculous wooden shoes.

Until she saw the other obstacle. The large slat of wood at the base of the doorway. It was there by custom because the Chinese believed ghosts could not climb over obstacles. Therefore, traditional doorways had a long slat of wood before the entrance. If forced the humans to step over the board to enter. Ghosts, of course, were blocked.

Whatever the reason, it made it excruciatingly difficult for her to maneuver in her high shoes and tight gown. She ended up gripping Fu De's arm and trying to half jump, half stumble across the threshold. Not the most auspicious way to enter the ancestral temple.

She thought she made it. She was hauling herself up by sheer will, no doubt nearly yanking poor Fu De's arm off as she went. But her gown got caught behind and beneath her. In English shoes, she might have made it. Without grace, certainly, but not bodily harm. In high Chinese formal shoes and a foreign gown, she hadn't a prayer. Her feet went out from under her, and she released a puppyish yip of alarm as she began to fall.

Her fan and the ribbon went flying, her free arm started flailing, and she couldn't even get a knee under herself to catch her fall. Her gown was still half a step behind her, preventing her from finding any purchase beyond flat-out on her face.

It was horrible, especially as it seemed to happen in excruciatingly slow motion.

Just before she was about to land face-first in a smear of oily water, she felt her body stop. It took a moment before she realized she had not hit the floor, but that strong arms had caught her.

Another breath, and she knew who had saved her. It was Ru Shan, of course. And what an entrance she'd made, falling flat out at her husband's feet.

Or rather almost flat out. Instead, he was holding her, gently supporting her while Fu De apparently released her gown from whatever demon nail had grabbed hold. It was another long moment before he could gently, carefully, set her on her feet. Especially as her knees were weak and she had to find the strength and balance to stand again on those damned shoes.

But that didn't matter now, she reminded herself. Because Ru Shan had caught her. Ru Shan was here. In fact, he was smiling warmly at her as he slowly lifted her veil off her face.

"Well met, my wife," he said formally in Shanghainese.

She was supposed to say something in response. Something Fu De had coached her in, but for the life of her she couldn't remember. Indeed, Lydia couldn't think at all except to see his wonderful face smiling at her.

Except, he wasn't smiling at her. He was turning, leading her into the ancestral building. She looked quickly around. At the center of the building stood a table supporting long wood tablets with etched Chinese characters. She didn't have time to read them, but she knew from Fu De that they were the names of all the male Chengs. The surrounding pillars also had colorful decorations—dragons, phoenixes, and ancient proverbs—all painted with loving care.

But none of that held her attention. Instead, she was looking at the people standing in a line along the side wall. Ru Shan's relatives. And she was to serve them tea by way of introduction.

But first she had to greet the ancestors. Ru Shan led her to the altar, then assisted her to her knees. That, too, was exceedingly difficult in her tight dress, but fortunately, she had long slits up the sides of the gown, allowing her to move. The air hit her bare legs, and she tried not to be embarrassed. After all, the Chinese considered a low neckline scandalous, but a leg was nothing exciting to them. Only she, a Victorian Englishwoman, would feel embarrassed by it.

And she was a Chinese wife now, she reminded herself. So she knelt down and kowtowed three times to the ancestors, touching her forehead to the hardwood floor.

"This is Cheng Lydia, my ancestors," Ru Shan intoned. "She will bring great prosperity to your descendants."

Then he helped her stand, holding her up as she tottered on her shoes. She had barely straightened to her full height when Fu De appeared beside her, offering a chalice of sorts. It was small and made of fine porcelain, and was obviously the ceremonial teacup, already filled with tea. It was time to greet her new relatives.

With Ru Shan's help, she tottered to the head of the line, Ru Shan's father. He was a stern-looking man with fleshy cheeks and a scowl. He leaned heavily on a cane and barely deigned look at her, even as he raised a bored hand to take the tea.

"The Cheng father," said Ru Shan, an extra measure of flatness in his tone.

Ru Shan's father drank from the cup, but he did so slowly, his eyes trained not on Lydia, but on Ru Shan. Was the man angry that she was white? Lydia couldn't tell. But there was clearly something unspoken between father and son.

Then it was Ru Shan's grandmother's turn. She had white hair, red eyes, and a sweaty, beady, sullen expression. Her clothes seemed to hang on her, and there was an emptiness in her expression that quickly filled with maliciousness the moment Lydia offered her the cup.

"The Cheng grandmother."

She took the cup, but Lydia didn't think the woman would drink. From her expression, she was more likely to spit in it. But eventually the old woman raised the cup, barely wetting her lips with the brew while her eyes burned with bitter hatred.

Lydia swallowed. She would not cry. She would *not* cry. She had already been warned that these people would not appreciate a white daughter-in-law. Thankfully, the worst of the introductions were already over. There was only a small boy of about eight years old left, standing before a woman who looked to be at least ten years older than Ru Shan. His sister no doubt, though Lydia could detect no family resemblance.

"And this," Ru Shan intoned, "is my wife number one and our son."

Once a statue is finished
It is too late to change the arms.
Only with a virgin block
Are there possibilities.
                                    —Deng Ming-Dao

Chapter Sixteen

Lydia blinked, sure she had misheard. This woman—this haughty-looking, angry woman—couldn't possibly be Ru Shan's *wife*. Lydia was his wife. She remembered quite clearly going to the mission and getting married. Getting legally and ecclesiastically married. To Ru Shan. Which meant he couldn't possibly have another wife. That would be impossible.

More than that, it would be just plain wrong.

"I'm sorry," she said, hating that her voice came out in a trembling whisper. Then, in order to strengthen herself, she switched over to English. "I apologize, my love, but I must have misheard you. Who exactly is this woman? Your sister?"

Ru Shan turned, clearly confused by her tone of voice, but he obediently switched into English, his words unmistakable. "My sister and her husband will not be joining us today." He sounded angry at that, but Lydia barely cared. Her attention was completely focused on his next words.

"This is Tai Mei, my first wife. And our son, Zun Ran."

Lydia tried to swallow, but her throat felt too tight for such a movement. All she could do was close her eyes, hating the tears that prickled beneath her lashes. "You are divorced then?" she whispered.

"Divorce? I do not know this English word."

She opened her eyes, searching his face, looking at the man she loved, desperately hoping to find some answer in his expression. All she saw was confusion. "Divorce," she said clearly, "means you were once married, but then are not anymore. Both husband and wife go their separate ways and can marry someone else."

He reared back as if slapped. "How can someone be married and then not married? Only a true barbarian would do that."

She stiffened, her shoulders squaring as anger began to rise within her. "It is very rare," she snapped, "but it happens. So is this woman your former wife?"

"Of course not," he responded, his tone equally curt. "When the Chinese marry, it is for life. We do not take and abandon women like toys!"

She nodded, though why she was doing so, she couldn't possibly fathom. At the moment, it was all she could do not to scratch out his eyes. But she would not act in such a fashion over a simple misunderstanding. And so she tried again. "If this woman is your wife, Ru Shan, then what am I?"

He stared at her, his expression slowly clearing. "You are my second wife, Lydia. The first wife of my choosing."

"Second wife?"

He nodded. "Of course."

"We don't have second wives in England, Ru Shan. We have only first wives."

He smiled at her, then, though the expression remained

tentative at best. "Ah," he said. "Now I understand." Though clearly he did not. "I am a man of wealth, Lydia. Our family is a great family. Of course I have a first wife. We were wed when I was eight." He smiled and patted his son's head. "There was much pressure for me to choose more wives earlier, but I resisted." He turned his attention back to her. "Lydia, you are the first wife of my choosing."

She didn't know what to say. How did one respond when face-to-face with your husband's other wife? A wife you didn't know existed before now? "We don't have second wives in England," she repeated.

"You don't need to. You toss aside your wives in this divorce. Then you pick another."

She shook her head. "That doesn't happen."

"But you just said—"

"It doesn't happen often." She straightened. "What never, ever, *ever* happens is for a man to have two wives at the same time!" She hadn't intended to screech, but by the end of her sentence, her voice had risen to near hysteria. All Ru Shan could do was stare at her in stunned shock. He and all his bizarre relatives.

"But Lydia, you are in China now," he said, his very calm tone only adding fuel to her fury. "In China," he continued, "a man of means has many wives."

She squared her shoulders, lifting herself up to her full height on her ridiculous shoes. "Not my husband, Ru Shan."

He frowned, his expression becoming darker. "Lydia," he said in a warning tone. "Do not shame me before my relatives."

"Do not shame you?" she asked, her tone becoming mocking. "Did it ever occur to you that I might feel a bit of shame being introduced to my husband's wife?"

He lifted his hands, clearly at a loss. "I told you, I am a

man of means. How could you think I did not have a wife?"

"I am English," she shot back. "How could you think I would marry a man who was already married?"

Lydia began to tremble, fury lending strength to her movements. The beautiful teacup she held flew from her hand to shatter on the floor at his feet. Then she reached up into her hair, dragging the ivory sticks out and whipping them onto the floor in front of her husband's feet. Ru Shan stared at her in shock, flinching as the second hit the tile with a clatter. Behind him, his grandmother began to laugh—a cold, dark titter that grew in volume. Lydia barely heard. She was too intent on unstrapping and kicking off her stupid shoes, using as much violence in her motions as she dared. If she could have, she would have ripped the gown off her body as well, but she had nothing else to wear. She had to be content with wiping off the makeup onto her sleeve. It was a terrible thing to do to such beautiful silk, but the ugly smear of white, black, and red gave her some measure of satisfaction.

And all the while, Ru Shan's grandmother continued to laugh, now joined by Ru Shan's wife. His father, too, began to chuckle, while Ru Shan's face turned dark red, similar somehow to the stain upon her gown.

Only the boy seemed unaffected, his almond eyes larger than normal, their dark centers seeming to encompass not only his face, but his whole body as well. The child, it seemed, was simply a witness, absorbing everything in silence. Lydia spared a moment to wonder if he understood anything of what was happening. Probably more than she did, she thought with a near hysterical laugh.

All the while, Ru Shan's family continued to guffaw, their mockery echoing in the small room.

"God, I was such a fool," Lydia said to no one in particular. "Love. Marriage. Children. I knew you were Chinese—"

"Yes, I am—" Ru Shan began, but she didn't let him continue. She spoke without thought, not caring that she was saying things she hadn't even acknowledged to herself.

"I loved you, Ru Shan." She didn't say the words. She spat them. Right at his face. "That's right. I. Loved. You." Then she straightened, glaring disdainfully at everyone around her. "I am such a fool!"

Her stocking feet were quickly soaked with spilled tea, but she barely noticed as she spun on her heel. She headed straight for the door and freedom. She cared little for what she was doing, only that she left Ru Shan far, far behind.

He stepped forward, easily cutting her off. "Don't be a fool, Lydia. Where will you go?"

His tone couldn't be less loverlike, but that only steeled her resolve as she stomped past.

"Lydia!" he snapped again, this time grabbing her arm. "We were wed in an English church. By both our laws, you are my wife!"

This time she could not restrain it; a caustic, bitter sound welled up from some painful center within her. It burned as it went, eventually coming out as a half sob, half scream. She had no ability to shape it into words. It was merely sound and pain and anger all merged together as she tore away from him and ran for the door.

This time she had no trouble leaping over the door frame and then out of his home. Her only difficulty was in keeping her gown out from under her stocking feet—but even the English knew how to hold up skirts. Part of her mind demanded to know what she was thinking. Where was she going? Indeed, it was possible those were the very words that Ru Shan was bellowing after her. But she gave him no more heed than she had before.

She wanted escape. Distance. Silence. And so she ran. As fast and as far as she could, her attention focused completely and totally on keeping her steps out of the street garbage. She allowed no other thought, no other emotion. Simply keeping her feet out of the garbage as she ran.

Until she could not run anymore. Until her feet ached from the pounding and her side screamed from the stitch that felt more like a knife. She slowed then, knowing as she did that she would soon be forced to think. She would soon realize she was sobbing. She was in the middle of Chinese Shanghai. Dressed as a second wife. Without shoes, in the middle of the street.

She did not want to understand that, but of course she did. She knew. And pain brought her to her knees.

Noises surrounded her. Sounds not much farther than her own gasping breath. They were foreign sounds. Chinese sounds. But she wanted nothing to do with anything Chinese ever again. Nothing! So she blocked them out, covering her ears when they would not go away.

Another sound penetrated her consciousness. English words, muffled, but clear enough. She straightened slowly, allowing her hands to slip from her ears.

Definitely good, solid, English words. Spoken in a foreign accent.

Fu De.

She wanted to slap her hands over her ears again but knew it would be childish. Besides, she had now actually lifted her gaze from the pavement to see a mass of babbling Chinese people on a strange street. She was completely lost, dressed bizarrely, and without the heart right now to find the Shanghainese she needed to sort it all out.

She needed help. And right now, that help was Fu De.

Slowly, she pushed to her feet. A thousand tiny hands helped her up, though the result was that people crowded ever closer to her.

"Fu De?" she croaked, the sound barely above a whisper. She swallowed. "Fu De?" she called, her voice gaining strength and clarity.

"Mistress Lydia!" Fu De answered as he pushed through the crowd. "Mistress Lydia!"

She winced at his words, even though he surely didn't understand the other meaning of the word *mistress*. He simply knew it as a form of address, and likely intended it as such.

But she knew the truth now, didn't she? She knew that she was something worse than a mistress. After all, in London, some courtesans were actually lauded as intelligent, amazing women desired by all. A mistress was simply one step below that.

Not so a concubine. That was a foreign word, indicating a woman trapped in slavery to some foreign devil.

"Mistress Lydia, please wait!"

She did, though she doubted he could see her. And then the young man finally appeared at her side, his long queue in disarray beneath his sweat-stained cap.

"Mistress Lydia! Please, I beg you . . ."

"Take a breath, Fu De," she said with as much calm as she could muster. "I am not running anymore." She didn't know what made her say that, but once the words were out, they felt correct. And they strengthened her. She wiped off her face with her stained gown and tried to take stock of her surroundings. "Back away, please," she said in Shanghainese.

All around her, people gasped in shock and stepped back. Apparently a white woman in concubine clothing was not nearly as remarkable as hearing her speak their language. Whatever the reason, Lydia and Fu De abruptly had more breathing room.

"Mistress Lydia," Fu De began in English. "You cannot run about Shanghai like this. It is unseemly."

"More unseemly than marrying a married man?" she shot back. She instantly regretted her words, because Fu De simply blinked in confusion. She waved her hand in his direction, intending to tell him to "never mind," but he was too quick for her.

Bowing, he spoke with great ponderous formality. In English. "I do not understand your surprise, but it is clear Master Cheng has offered you a grave insult." Once again she opened her mouth to speak, but was forestalled. "I do not seek to reconcile you with your husband, Mistress Lydia. I offer a location for you to rest until such matters can be resolved."

She nodded, fussing stupidly at her gown as if she had an alternative. "That is very kind, Fu De," she said slowly. "Where is this location?"

"It is a place near . . ." He paused, clearly trying to explain. "It is a location near to where you spent last evening, mistress. Please . . ." He gestured imperiously at a nearby rickshaw driver. "Please, will you accompany me?"

She bit her lip, automatically wary of going anywhere again with a strange man offering her a ride. Except Fu De was not a strange man. And she was not nearly as naive as she had been those weeks ago. With a nod, she smiled at him as warmly as possible.

"Thank you, Fu De. You are most kind."

But as she climbed into the carriage, she could not prevent her thoughts from returning to a different ride in a different vehicle yesterday with an entirely different man.

How had she gone from being engaged to Max, to the ecstatically happy new bride of Ru Shan, to a runaway concubine, all in the space of twenty-four hours?

Another thought struck her, one so funny she began laughing in painful gasps until the tears once again ran down her face: She was still a virgin.

After everything that had happened, she was still a virgin. Which meant, according to her mother's teaching, Lydia was still pure as the driven snow.

Ru Shan stood staring at the broken ivory sticks in his hand. They were intricately carved—a tigress on one, a dragon on the other. In his mind, they represented himself and his Lydia, together forever, holding up the beautiful tendrils of her hair just as together they would support the entire Cheng family. He had spent much time selecting the gift for her and been overwhelmed with pleasure the moment he had first seen them in her golden locks.

Now they were in his hand, the tigress broken in half, the dragon stained with dirt.

He could not bear to think beyond that. Beside him, his family still made their mocking noises, but he had no room in his thoughts for them. Neither could he think of Lydia, her face half-smeared with bridal paint, her clothing torn, stained, and all in disarray as she pulled off her shoes.

Only her words echoed in his head. "I. Loved. You." Spit out with such venom as to burn straight through him. "I. Loved. You." And then she had run.

He had meant to go after her, was already at the door behind her, but Fu De had stopped him. He had spoken quickly, and in a low undertone that the Cheng family had not heard. Fu De promised to retrieve her. He promised to explain everything. And he promised to take Lydia to a place where Ru Shan could see her alone, without the disdain of his short-sighted family.

Ru Shan had not wanted to stay. Well beyond the driving need to return Lydia to his side, he had desperately wanted to escape his family. To leave now, and to forget that they were firmly planted on his shoulders: his responsibility and his burden.

Only one thing kept him rooted where he was. One person, rather. His son, Zun Ran. The boy had come to his side just after Fu De disappeared, nervously slipping his hand into Ru Shan's. They'd stood together, right by the open door, Ru Shan searching the streets while the boy lifted his somber face to his father. And in time, Ru Shan's gaze slowly slipped from looking outward to looking down.

"A confusing time to be alive, my son," he said gently.

The boy nodded, not because he understood, but because it probably seemed like the best response.

He waited a moment, looking one last time out at the gates. Fu De had disappeared after Lydia. Though he prayed for the sight of his white wife soberly—no, *joyfully*—returning to him, he knew it was a vain hope. She would not come back. He would have to seek her out. Meanwhile, he had things to say to his still-laughing family.

He straightened, barely caring to glance at his elders or first wife. Let them hear if they chose; he had no time for them if they did not. Instead, he looked at his son, speaking in a normal tone, simple enough for a child and soft enough that the others would have to cease their humor if they wished to hear.

"They think I am insane. They think I do not know this, but I do. I suppose you knew of their opinion?"

The boy glanced nervously at his mother, then at Ru Shan. "Yes, father," was all he said.

"Their stupidity did not bother me before. I knew what I was doing and why. But it infuriates me now," he said. "Because it may have destroyed your future."

His son's eyes widened and his jaw slackened in shock. The boy had never heard such an unfilial comment before. No good Chinese man ever spoke ill of his family, most especially his elders. Even within the family circle, where all was considered private.

He saw doubt in the child's eyes, so Ru Shan confirmed what he had said. "Yes, my son. Only you have shown your worth this day, and your trust in me gives me great pride. The others have displayed only ignorance." He lifted his gaze to his stunned family. As expected, they had quieted enough to hear his words, and his father was already mottled with rage. Ru Shan waited calmly for the tirade to come, startled to realize how much he relished the idea. Just how long had he been aching for the chance to offend the man?

"You rat-grubbing cur," his father spat. "You bring a barbarian woman here and dare call us fools?" He hobbled forward, his movements still powerful despite the awkwardness of his cane. "I have ears to hear and eyes to see. I know you have destroyed us with your white pet. I know that our store shelves stand empty because of her. And yet you dare bring her here. As a wife!" He reached forward, abruptly grabbing Zun Ran's other arm and yanking him away from Ru Shan. "You disgrace all of us!"

Ru Shan barely even blinked. His father enjoyed making others lose their calm, but it had been some time since he had been able to crack Ru Shan.

"Release my son," he said.

"You are not fit—"

"The boy is old enough to decide his own fate. Release him now." Ru Shan straightened. "Unless you are ready to claim him as your own son and no flesh of mine."

His father's body jerked backward as if slapped. As did Ru Shan's first wife. Once again, the boy remained a quiet center of confusion standing amidst an adult maelstrom.

"Of-of course you are Zun Ran's father," stammered the old man, releasing his hold on the child. "It is a measure of your depravity that you could suggest differently."

Ru Shan did not respond. The Chinese were often hypocritical beyond reason, his father more so than most. Everyone here with the exception of his son knew the truth: that Zun Ran was Ru Shan's half brother. Still, that did not lessen Ru Shan's responsibilities to the boy. He turned his attention to the child, extending his hand.

"Come, my son," he said, "let me explain to you what they do not know."

The boy obediently walked forward, but he did not offer up his hand. Instead, he stood like a great scholar, waiting for instruction before making up his mind. Ru Shan paused a moment, hand still extended, but still the boy refused, his expression dark and intense.

Behind them, the boy's great-grandmother released a nervous giggle, but Ru Shan found himself smiling even as his hand slipped to his side.

"Your grandmother would be pleased with you, my son. A great man always listens before choosing his course." Then Ru Shan did a most unusual thing. He dropped to one knee so that he was eye to eye with the child. How odd that in doing this, he imitated his a-dou cousin, the failed scholar whom everyone loved. And yet the gesture seemed right, even if he appeared to be kneeling before his own son.

"This family loves the white barbarians. Your grandfather loves their gold, and your great-grandmother their powder. Even your mother disdains jade, wanting their diamonds and emeralds upon her body. But foreign gold is hard to come by now that your grandmother is gone. It was her talents with brush and dye that the barbarians wanted. Her skills that the rest of us sold and prospered from."

He spared a moment to look at his father. From Ru Shan's grandfather down the generations and now to Zun Ran, the truth would be spoken aloud.

"It was your grandmother who supported the Cheng family, my son. We were merely the fleas upon her back," Ru Shan said. He straightened, turning to face his father's purple rage, knowing that he was merely adding oil to the fire. But these words would be spoken. "So now that Mei Lan is gone, who will support the Chengs? A dead woman makes no product to sell, and this wife"—he gestured disdainfully at the woman who had joined his bed when he was eight years old—"has no skill in such things." He turned back to his father. "So, how is it that the Cheng family will stand?"

"That is your responsibility, my son." Though the words sounded polite, his father spat on the ground at Ru Shan's feet to show his disgust. "I am crippled now. It is a filial son's task to uphold the family honor and see to the pleasure of my old age."

Ru Shan nodded, unable to deny the weight of his responsibilities. "And so I did. I found a woman Heaven-blessed in the ways of making the foreign gold this family loves so much. Did you not wonder, my father, who made the dress designs that spark so much interest in our shop? Did you not look into my wife's face and see that gold runs like water through her veins?"

"The foreign devils bring nothing but pain," his father half growled. "I will not have them in my home."

"Then you should not have killed the woman who supported us."

And there it was. Spoken aloud for the first time ever in this courtyard. Spoken in the light of day from son to father and with such a cold certainty that even Sheng Fu could not deny it. Except, of course, that he would. He went into such a rage as Ru Shan had never seen.

But Ru Shan did nothing. He didn't need to. His wife had already seen the tantrum coming and taken Grandmother inside to hide. She would hide inside her opium pipe and Wife One inside her bower with her dresses and jewelry. There was only Ru Shan and his father. And little Zun Ran watching from the side, half hidden behind the table laid out with a wedding feast.

The rage lasted less than fifteen minutes. Sheng Fu had lost much in physical stamina and could not sustain his emotions for long. Still, he tried, roaring and stumbling about like a mad boar. Fortunately, Zun Ran was too fast to be hit by his grandfather's cane, and Ru Shan was still strong, easily blocking whatever violence came his way. In the end, all his father had left were curses to release upon the air, wounding barbs that Ru Shan expected. They hurt nonetheless.

He was called all manner of ugly things; his character, body, and mind all attacked. Everything was damned as worthless, but in the end, his father retained some sense. He did not disown Ru Shan. He did not break the tablet on the family altar that bore Ru Shan's name. He spit on it. He gripped it and raised it high over his head as if he were going to shatter it into a thousand pieces. But in the end, he let it drop unharmed back into its place. He knew that the Cheng family would starve if Ru Shan left. He knew, too, that Ru Shan was his only hope for redemption.

And that was the insight that Heaven visited upon Ru Shan as he stood there watching his father. The venom in his sire's words, the black qi of hatred flowing from Sheng Fu's body and soul, was directed at the one person who still damned him for murdering his wife.

Ru Shan.

Which meant Ru Shan was also the one person who could help his father find peace. For until he forgave his father's crime, Sheng Fu would remain bitter and dried up and wounded in body and soul. Until he found forgiveness.

From Ru Shan.

That realization vibrated in the air between the two men just before Sheng Fu collapsed in a sobbing heap at the base of the family altar. His hair was askew, his body filthy with sweat and grime, but his eyes were crystal clear. He looked at Ru Shan, the question clear despite the fact that it went unspoken.

Could Ru Shan forgive his father? Would he?

The pull was unmistakable. The need and pain in his father's eyes tugged at Ru Shan the way a dying man pulled at all who cared for him. Added to that was the weight of Ru Shan's entire culture; like the mountain he was named for, it pressed upon him, telling him to go to his father, for that was what a son did. *Forgive your father,* it said in powerful words that all heard but none spoke. *Forgive him, and support him in his old age. That is what good sons do.*

Ru Shan took a step forward, a single step, as if pushed from behind. But that was all he could do before dropping to his knees. He wasn't even sure how he landed there, his feet behind him, his knees in a puddle of oily water. Then the motion continued, the weight pulling his head down, exposing the back of his neck while his hands remained tucked in his lap.

He was laying himself bare, not before his father but before his mother's ghost. Before the sword he imagined she held in her hand. And in that moment, he longed for death.

He was Ru Shan, faithful as a mountain. And yet he had failed his mother and abandoned his father. He could not forgive the man who had sired him. He could not release his mother's spirit to the afterlife. He could not even hold on to a white wife who could save the Cheng family.

He could do none of those things until he accomplished one single task. He even knew what the task was. Shi Po had told him. She had seen it in a dream and knew it to be a true divination. So she had told him, and so he had done it—or so he thought.

He had bought a white pet and milked her for her yin water to cool his yang fire.

He had done this thing, risking what was left of the Cheng fortune on the task. And yet, he now understood that he had done nothing at all. Nothing at all, for Shi Po had neglected to tell him the last piece of her divination. It was a small thing, no doubt ignored by the tigress as a natural extension of the work they did. After all, who could spend hours milking a woman—even a white one—and not feel affection for the pet?

It was such a simple thing, she had forgotten to tell him. But he saw it now. Saw it in the oily water before him as clearly as he had seen it in his father's tirade and his son's wide, somber eyes.

He had to buy a white pet and milk her for her yin. During this process, he had to love her.

In the last, he had failed completely.

*Which is the nearer to you, your name or your
person?*
*Which is the more precious, your person or your
wealth?*
Which is the greater evil, to gain or to lose?
Great devotion requires great sacrifice.
Great wealth implies great loss.
—Tao Te Ching

Chapter Seventeen

Ru Shan walked into his bedroom. He did not stumble, he did not crawl. But it felt that way nonetheless. He felt as if his entire spirit were broken as he inched his way to the sanctuary of his room. Indeed, he waited a moment outside the step up into his chamber, like a cursed ghost, before forcing up his legs to enter.

Once he arrived, he felt the darkness enfold him. Though the sun continued to shine through the dull covering of clouds, its weak rays could not touch him. If any dared try, he quickly closed the interior shutters to ensure his utter bleakness.

Why could he not love Lydia?

He closed his eyes, understanding the question for a stupidity. Of course he could not love Lydia. She was white, a barbarian and a pet. A smart one, to be sure, but still beneath any true child of China, the blessed kingdom of Heaven.

And yet the question still plagued him. Why could he not love Lydia?

He shouldn't love her. She was a tool. A second wife, of little importance except that she could make the designs that would bring gold to the Cheng family. And, of course, that she supply the yin he needed to attain immortality.

Except it wasn't her yin he needed. It was her love.

He sighed. No, it was *not* her love; he already had that. Indeed, he had seen and felt her love last night. It had been a pure thing of joy that had humbled him with its power. Indeed, last night, Lydia his barbarian pet had humbled him.

It was not her love he needed. It was his own for her. And yet, he could not.

Why?

His legs weakened beneath him and he dropped onto his prayer mat. There had been no conscious will in the movement, only the touch of Heaven's hand. He collapsed into an attitude of prayer, his forehead pressed forward onto the cured reeds, his legs bent and folded beneath him. And in this pose, he poured out his anguish.

To no avail.

He had no understanding of how long he stayed in that position. He roused himself only once, when a messenger from Fu De arrived. Ru Shan listened without comment as he learned that Fu De had taken Lydia to a safe hotel—a place most understanding of tigress/dragon practices. Ru Shan could meet her there if he wished.

But of course he could not. Without clearer understanding of his path, he could go nowhere. He had nothing to offer Lydia. Certainly as his Chinese wife, he could legally drag her back to his home—in chains if necessary. But he knew that would only deepen the evil that beset the Cheng family. She had to come willingly or any work she did would be cursed.

He paused, his brows drawing together into a frown that frightened the young messenger. Ru Shan had not even realized how angry he appeared until the boy dashed off in terror, without even a coin as payment for his service. But his thoughts had sparked a memory, and that memory would not release him.

And so he returned to his room, the image of paying for Lydia trapped in his mind.

He had paid for Lydia: a free woman who had been enslaved by a madame, forced into a lifetime of prostitution simply because she was young and beautiful and foolish enough to trust someone she should not. Yes, Lydia had been caught, and Ru Shan had bought her.

It did not matter that he had treated her honestly, that he had fed and cared for her better than he had for his own first wife. It did not matter that eventually she came to him freely, marrying him with an open heart and a pure love. He had taken advantage of her then as well, using her circumstances to push her into marriage.

In short, he had begun badly with Lydia, buying her when he should have simply freed her. And that one evil act had tainted his whole life thereafter. He had not attained immortality despite the power in Lydia's yin. He had not saved the Cheng family despite the money her designs would bring. And worse yet, his own emotional well—his yang, and what little yin he possessed—had completely deserted him. He could not forgive his father. He could not even face his son with an open heart. Little by little, the curse of his own evil act—buying a free woman—was destroying him.

He had to reverse this curse. He had to find a way to obtain forgiveness—from Lydia and Heaven—and in so doing, return to the middle path. But how? The answer was simple, for all that it made his body tremble. He had to release Lydia. He had to set her free, legally and morally.

The very thought terrified him. He still believed she contained the yin he required to reach immortality. He also thought her the only possible chance to save his family. How could he release her, cut all the ties that bound them together? Would she not flee in terror, just as she had earlier this day?

She would leave and never return. He and the Chengs would be lost.

There had to be another way. Had to be.

Resolved, he returned to his chamber and his prayer mat. He burned incense, paper money, and even his own clothing as a symbol to Heaven of his earnest pleas. He did not eat at all, not even water as he prostrated himself upon his mat before the tiny altar in his chamber. He begged and moaned and wept in prayer.

Yet as the hours slipped past, he came to one inescapable conclusion.

He was offering prayers to the wrong person. His earnestness, his devotion, and most especially his humiliation were useless before Heaven until he did the same before Lydia. There was no alternative, no other way to evade his fate. He had to release her and pray that she came to him of her own free will.

When the sun slipped beneath the smoky horizon, Ru Shan emerged from his chamber. He called for bathing water and his best clothing, but spoke no more than that. His every action was like a prayer, performed in complete consciousness of intention.

He went to the storage room, taking the best silk embroidery, stitched by his mother's own hand—and expensive oils from his grandmother's collection. From his father he gathered Imperial jade rods, the currency most often used between Chinese men of wealth. And from his first wife, he took diamond earrings. Then, finally, from his own back garden, he harvested his best ornamental plant, tended from a seed by his own hand.

These things he would give to Lydia, hoping that they would weigh down her feet and prevent her escape. Altogether, the price was barely a fraction of what he had already spent to buy her. But these things were owed to Lydia, and he didn't begrudge the expense.

Not so the rest of his family, but they knew better than to complain. His grandmother merely closed her eyes and reached for her opium pipe, finding she had to share the white smoke with Ru Shan's father. His first wife tried a different approach, bringing him sweetmeats and juicy fruits while dressed in her sheerest gown.

Ru Shan was tempted, though not by his wife. His interest in her had died the moment he began learning the ways of a jade dragon. Indeed, she had not graced his bed since he was a boy too young to understand such things. It was the food that tempted him, for he had not eaten since the day before. The steam rising from the dumplings alone nearly brought him to his knees. But he would not appear before Lydia impure. And he would certainly not allow his first wife to steer him from his course. So he passed her by, stepping quickly past the tray of food lest weakness overtake him.

It did not. Not until he had gathered everything together and was heading toward the front door. It was at that moment that he faltered.

His son stood before him, the boy's dark eyes somber

and hands filled with a long velvet pouch. "You have not yet taken my gift, father," Zun Ran said, and he held out his package. Before Ru Shan could speak, the boy quietly opened the pouch, withdrawing a long scroll of finest parchment. "It is a prayer," he said, unrolling the paper to reveal the characters written upon it. "Though a poor example, it is the best I have ever done."

Ru Shan felt his heart twist painfully. "You have an excellent hand, Zun Ran. And . . ." His voice trailed away, at last seeing the characters his child had painted. "That is a prayer of good journeys." He swallowed, his throat painfully tight. "Why would you give that to my second wife?" He took a deep breath. For all that his son was still a boy, there were times when Zun Ran understood things that were beyond an adult's comprehension. "Do you believe she is leaving?" The very thought made his blood run cold.

"It is for you as well, honored father," said the child. He bowed again, his small body folding nearly to the ground.

Ru Shan frowned, setting the basket of other gifts aside. "But I am not leaving. I am merely going to make amends. Whatever happens, I shall return here." He said the words, even believed them, but in his heart, he began to wonder. What did his son know that he did not?

Zun Ran did not answer, but his eyes spoke of a sorrow so great, Ru Shan could not believe it came from a boy barely eight years old. And so, twice in one day, he knelt before his son, dropping down to the child's height as he spoke.

"I am a man of honor, my son. I do not abandon my responsibilities." Then he abruptly reached forward, needing to touch the boy. "Come with me," he pressed. "Put your gift in her hands. Show her you wish her to return to our home."

He saw a flash of yearning in his son's eyes, but in the end it was quieted and finally disappeared. "You must go alone, my father. I am needed here."

"Surely you can be spared your chores for one night . . . ," Ru Shan began, but the boy scampered away. Ru Shan continued to stare into the courtyard long after the child escaped. He remained there as the servants lit lanterns in the darkened skywell. He remained there, listening to the sounds of the Cheng family as if Heaven had increased their volume a thousandfold.

He heard his grandmother's deep hacking cough as it rattled through her where she lay on her opium-saturated sheets. He heard his father and his first wife grunting in their exertions, consoling one another in their pain. He heard the servants in the kitchen, the vendors outside as they shuffled to their homes. He even heard the cats and the vermin that scuttled beneath the floorboards.

But in all that, he heard nothing of his son. A memory whispered through his mind, the words as loud as a clanging bell, despite the silent nature of such things.

I am needed here.

Ru Shan shuddered. It was a full-body shaking that rattled his teeth and tormented his joints. It was as if a great tiger grasped him in its jaws and shook him like a toy before dropping him once again in the middle of the skywell, just before the front gate.

I am released.

That was the thought that came through Ru Shan's mind. The great tiger of China, of tradition, of filial piety had released him. As simply as that, it had opened its jaws and released him to escape with his barbarian lover if he so chose. He could leave with Lydia to another home, another world, another life of his own making—with her.

He could, if he so chose.

And with that knowledge came a sure and certain fury. As fierce as any storm, it blew through him, mounting upon a great, hot wind, searing everything in its path.

"I am Ru Shan!" he bellowed. "I am the Cheng mountain, and I will not abandon my duties!"

As his vow exploded out of him, Ru Shan looked to the second floor and his son's room. All around him, the sounds stopped. His grandmother's cough silenced. The kitchen activity ceased and the vermin quit their scampering.

Yet no sound came from his son. Neither did the boy's face appear in the upper hallway. It was as if his words had never been spoken, his vow to remain true to his family duties as insubstantial as the rantings of a madman.

"I am Ru Shan," he repeated, but this time in a whisper. "The mountain of the Cheng family."

Again, there was no response. And so, in the end, Ru Shan had no choice. He had to present his gifts to Lydia before it grew too dark and dangerous to walk the Shanghai streets. With heavy steps and an aching heart, he gathered his basket and went to prostrate himself before his concubine.

Now what?

Lydia truly did not want to think. She didn't really want to cry anymore either, so that left few other options.

Thanks to Fu De's excellent hotel, she was cleaned and fed. Her concubine dress was tossed aside into a corner of her sparse room, and she frequently glared at it whenever she felt the need of more anger. Right now, she wore a loose-fitting shirt and coolie pants. A pair that was closed at the crotch. If she forgot the fact that her attire was scandalous beyond belief, she actually felt comfortable.

Certainly much more comfortable than in her beautiful courtesan gown.

But now that she'd bathed, dressed, and eaten, there was little left to do. Nothing except pace around the large bed and glare at her silk dress. And think. Except, the only thing she could think of was a two-word question.

Now what?

She didn't know. Life as a concubine was out of the question. Even to Ru Shan, the man she loved. Tears blurred her eyes. She loved him, the damned Chinese dog! How had it happened, and why?

She spun around and glared at the dress until her tears dried. Then she took a deep breath before dropping miserably back on the bed.

Now what?

She could go back to England. Assuming, of course, that she could borrow the money from Fu De. If he had it. She was already deep in debt to the man anyway; why not throw in the cost of passage back to England? That was the land of one man and one wife in love.

Tears threatened, but she'd barely looked away from the dress, so it was easy to glare at again. Which, of course, meant the cycle repeated itself until she could manage to think about going home without the distraction of love, or men, or could-have-beens, interfering with her decision.

Could she go back to England? In truth, she'd already asked Fu De to inquire about the various ships leaving port. At the moment, she had wanted to get as far away from Ru Shan and things Chinese as possible. But now . . . She didn't know. Was England where she wanted to be?

She certainly could crawl back into her mother's arms. She could eat a good hot plum pudding and read her favorite book by the fire. But after that, what would she do?

She knew her mother would never understand the things Lydia had experienced. Indeed, no one she knew could possibly comprehend. China had changed her. Ru Shan had changed her. She had fallen desperately in love and discovered many wonderful things. He had been the tenderest of lovers. The most patient of men. The . . .

No, no, no, no, no!

She would not deify the rat either! She ought to burn his dress as an act of defiance. No, no, then she'd have nothing to glare at. She could rip it to shreds. She sighed. She truly hadn't the heart to destroy such a beautiful garment, no matter its significance. Besides, it was the only thing she had in her possession.

She supposed she could sell the dress, use the money to repay Fu De. But it would have to be cleaned first, and she hadn't the heart to start on that now. Besides, she couldn't glare at it if she sold it.

So the garment remained crumpled in the corner, and Lydia remained stuck right back where she'd been hours ago when she'd first finished her bath.

Now what? She did not truly want to go home. She couldn't imagine how she'd explain what had happened to her. Worse, she couldn't see herself calmly taking up the reins of her old life, even if her mother found the money to support them both. After all, that was the reason she'd left for Shanghai in the first place; there was not enough money for both her mother and her. Lydia simply had to find a way to support herself.

At the time, she had expected a glorious life with Max. Then she had leaped joyously into wedded bliss with Ru Shan. And now . . . what?

"No men." That was her first resolution. Perhaps that had been her mistake all along. As bizarre as the thought was, she simply could not face a future with any man in it at all. She was done trusting them. Men simply could not be relied upon to keep her safe. And so they were gleefully tossed out of her future, whatever that was going to be.

Well, with that decided, she would have to find a way to support herself. What exactly did women do when they didn't have a man to support them? The obvious answer was out. No prostitution in any form. In her opinion, there was little difference between walking the streets and being a second wife to the man she loved.

Or so she told herself, glaring at the gown.

Yet, what else could she do? Her only marketable skill was in clothing design. It was something she loved, something she was good at. And since she was a tolerable seamstress, she could find a job doing that.

But with whom? Where?

Ru Shan's closest competitor leapt to mind. She didn't remember the name, but she would wager anything that Fu De knew. Assuming he would tell her. It was Shi Po's husband.

Would she do that? Go work for Ru Shan's enemy? Could she do that?

She looked at the silk gown again, this time actually stopping to look rather than glare. Could she learn something from its pattern? Could she remake it into a gown to use as an example of her abilities? Could she use it to market herself to a different employer?

She bit her lip, slowly moving to the corner. She actually hesitated, somehow fearing to touch the dress. As if picking up the thing would inevitably suck her right back into that evil Chinese rat's clutches. But that was ridiculous. It was just a gown, after all. Fabric and stitches and decorations. A *gown*.

And one that could start her on a new future.

Without another moment's hesitation, she snatched up the gown, rushing before she could stop herself. She quickly called for scissors, needle, and thread. And then, moments later, she sat down to begin carefully picking the damned dress apart.

Ru Shan arrived in good time. The hotelier knew him, so was able to quickly and quietly direct him to Lydia's room. But despite his rights as Lydia's husband, Ru Shan could not bring himself to open the door.

What would she do when she saw him? She claimed she had once loved him, and yet she had done so in fury, storming out of his home seconds after her declaration. With such a woman, how could any man know her next action? A wife was supposed to see to her husband's comforts, not leave him standing before her door in anxiety.

But such complaints were useless at best. He had known from the beginning that Lydia was different. Neither barbarian nor Chinese, she was her own soul. And a higher compliment could not be given to anyone—man or woman, barbarian or son of Heaven.

With sudden resolve, he knocked on her door, knowing he came in supplication to this creature, this woman. His Lydia—or so he hoped.

"Come in. My hands are full, so you'll have to open the door yourself."

Her voice did not sound thick with sobs or tight with anger. She sounded calm. Rational. A good sign, he thought. And so he pushed open her door, his heart in his throat despite his thoughts. But what he saw terrified him even more.

She sat on her large bed, calmly picking apart her wedding gown. She had not torn it into pieces in a fury nor burned it as women often did in the grips of their humors. No, Lydia was methodically disassembling, stitch by stitch, the symbol of their union.

His heart sank like a stone, and his hands grew slack where he held his basket. She did not appear to be a woman in a temper, or one easily swayed by pretty gifts and words of poetry. She would demand logic and cold practicality. Unfortunately, he had little of such persuasions to offer.

"Good evening, Lydia," he said, mostly because he had no idea what else to say.

"I thought you were Fu De," she said, her eyes wide with surprise. "He said he would bring me . . ." Her voice trailed off, and Ru Shan frowned.

"What?" he demanded, stepping into the room. "What can he bring you that your husband cannot?" Fear made his stance firm and authoritative, even though he knew such a tactic would not work on her.

True enough, her chin shot up and she glared at him. "News of the boats leaving China." Then she deliberately turned her focus back to her work. "And I have no husband."

He dropped his basket of gifts on the floor, quickly crossing to her side. He should have dropped to one knee before her, but he was terrified. And so he stood, needing his pride, if nothing else, to keep him from sobbing like a small boy. "You know we are married, Lydia. By both our laws."

She looked up, the bleakness in her eyes cutting at his soul. "Even if English law accepted a marriage to a man who was already married . . ." He watched her eyes shimmer with tears, but she did not allow even one to fall. "I am still a virgin, Ru Shan. I can get the ceremony annulled."

Then she swallowed, using the movement to look away from him. "As for your country, what do I care about your barbaric ways?"

He winced, knowing she chose her words deliberately to wound him. It was her people who were barbaric, discarding wives like old shoes. But such arguments were useless, and they would not get her back where he wanted her—in his home, in his bed.

He abandoned his superior pose. It was vanity in any event, and would not help him here. Instead he knelt beside her, drawing his basket of gifts to his side before displaying them one by one before her feet.

"My family feels most unhappy for the way they have treated you. They have sent gifts with me to you. To show you their shame and to beg your forgiveness." Out came the silk and oils, the jade and diamonds, but Lydia barely glanced at them.

"I did not expect your family to embrace me, and they were not the ones who hurt me," she said, her voice flat and dull.

"And this plant," he continued as if she had not spoken, "is from my own garden, raised by my own hand."

No response.

"This is from my son. He wrote it himself. It is excellent work for a child." He did not tell her the content of the poem. He had not the heart.

Instead of a recognition of his son's goodness, Lydia merely sighed, dropping the fabric to wrap herself in her own arms. "Ru Shan, this is pointless. You have a wife. A son. A family. There is no place for me in that." This time she did not prevent the single tear that trailed down her cheek. "I can't share you, Ru Shan. I . . . I just can't."

He frowned, looking up into her face, seeing the misery

there and desperately trying to understand it. "But you would share me with the shop. And I would have to wait as you worked on your designs as well. We could not live as we did on our wedding night. Not every hour of the day."

She shook her head. "How could you get married at eight?" Then she frowned, as if that was not what she'd intended to say, and yet she still continued. "She must have been more than twice your age."

He had no answer except the truth. "It is the custom, Lydia. Your people have done this as well. Marrying children as young as three or four."

She shook her head. "Not for generations, Ru Shan. And even then, it was a matter of governments, not simple folk such as me."

He almost laughed at the statement. Lydia was anything but simple. Rather than argue, he simply bowed his head. "What must I do to gain your forgiveness?"

She was silent a long time, and he almost gave up hope. But he knew that as stubborn as Lydia was, she was also tenderhearted. If she once loved him as she claimed, then she could remember it. She would forgive him. He needed only to wait.

True to his expectation, she set aside her half-disassembled dress and slid off the mattress to kneel before him. He lifted his head just as she was reaching for his face, drawing his lips to hers in the tenderest of kisses.

His heart soared at the touch. Their mouths and tongues meshed together as man and wife. And yet, she was soon pulling away.

"You are already forgiven, Ru Shan." Her voice was low and trembling, but not with passion or the forgiveness she spoke of. Instead, he sensed an aching sadness that filled her entire body. "I did not realize, but I've already forgiven you. This was merely a confusion of cultures. You did not mean to hurt me."

He smiled at her, choosing to focus on her words and not her demeanor. "Then you will come home with me," he said, greatly fearing that she would not.

"I can't, Ru Shan." She straightened, pulling firmly away. "I just cannot share you."

"She is only a first wife!" he exclaimed, but he knew it was useless. He understood her meaning more than he let on. After all, how would he react if Lydia wished to have another lover, another husband? Indeed, if she wished to continue her quest to become a tigress, she would likely have many green dragons before she settled upon one of jade.

The very thought filled his mouth with bile. He would not share her any more than he could ask her to share him. And that was such a strange thought that he truly wondered if this woman had made him insane.

He tried again. "I would shower you with wealth, Lydia. I would see that my grandmother never abused you, my father never repudiated you. My son would treat you with honor and our children would revere you."

She merely pulled her arms tighter around herself, her thin coolie shirt pressing against her slim back. "That is not what I require, Ru Shan. You know that."

Yes, he did. He was beginning to see that she required more from him than respect and honor. She required his heart. It was as he'd feared.

"You require my love." He spoke as if it were his death sentence. "I have no heart to give love, Lydia. It was lost long before I met you." He looked up at her then, knowing he was begging but needing to try nonetheless. "I should not have bought you, Lydia. That was an evil deed, and for that I am truly humbled and sorry. I would give you your freedom now"—he swallowed, looking at the undone wedding gown discarded on the bed—"but I believe you have taken it whether I give it or not. I will not drag you through the streets back to my home, much as I wish to do so. You are too fine for that." He sighed. "I believe captivity would destroy you. It is not in your nature to remain docile."

She nodded, though the movement was slight. "No, I don't suppose it is."

He shifted, looking at her pale face, revealed in a wash of red by the lantern that hung from a ceiling hook. "But what will you do, Lydia? How will you live?"

"I don't know," she said, moving to sit on the opposite side of the bed from him. "I thought to offer my designs to your competitor. Shi Po's husband."

He flinched, terrified at what such a thing would do. Those two would quickly see Lydia's worth. They would pay her well, use her designs to gain the white people's money. Unquestionably, the Cheng store would fade into obscurity.

"Don't look so pale, Ru Shan," she said, her voice lighter now. "It was only anger." She shrugged. "I find I have little desire for revenge."

"You could establish your own business. You might manage." He didn't know why he was suggesting it. As a white woman, she had no hope of doing such a thing. Neither his people nor hers would support her. But then again, Lydia had already accomplished so much more than he'd ever thought possible. Perhaps she did have a chance.

She shook her head. "I thought of that, but I do not think I could do it alone."

"It would be very, very difficult," he agreed. He stood, coming forward as a supplicant. "You could work for my family. We would pay you well for your designs. Well enough to have a home of your own, to be able to buy whatever you want, to do whatever you will. So long as the English continue to buy your designs, my business will prosper."

She nodded, the movement thoughtful, as if she had also considered this. "But could you do it, Ru Shan? Could you see me every day, work with me every day and not touch me? Not want to hold me and continue as we have been?"

He did his best to remain unmoved by her question, but Lydia knew him too well to be deceived. A moment after she spoke, she turned away.

"Ah," she said with much wisdom in her tone. "I see that you thought we would return to how it was. And then you would once again have it all, wouldn't you? My designs for your coffers and my yin for your studies."

"You would have an income of your own. You could be rich and independent. No Chinese woman can say so much."

"And very few Englishwomen either." She bit her lip, and he waited anxiously as she thought. "I would be a fool to turn down such a thing."

"And yet you intend to do just that," he said, seeing the truth in the slump of her shoulders. How did one deal with such a woman? He had offered her riches to no avail. Independence such as few people—men *or* women—could ever achieve, and she was not happy. "What is it that you want?" he exclaimed, frustration making his voice hard.

She turned to stare at him, her expression surprised. "What I have always wanted, Ru Shan. A husband to love me. A man who will share my life, who will work alongside me, and who will help me raise children." She paused, her head tilted to one side. "Why do you say you cannot love me? Why do you say you have no heart?"

She would have it all then, he realized. His humiliation and his pain. There would be no corner of his life that she did not invade, no part of his soul that was not open to her inspection. He would do it, he realized. He would cut apart his soul, spill it on the floor before her like his entrails. And she would at last understand that he was a broken man, and she would leave him.

But she was leaving him anyway, he thought angrily. She had already made that clear. Why should he add this one last indignity to an already lost cause? He would not. And so he began to turn away, already intent on gathering his gifts. His family would have need of the money the things would bring.

She did not allow him to escape. She was beside him in a moment, grabbing his arms to force him to look at her. She did not have the strength, of course, but he did not have the heart to deny her. And so he allowed her to pull his face close, his gaze to her own, and then, lastly, his lips to hers.

The kiss was tender and sweet, almost like a gift shared between children. And yet, he also felt his body tighten with desire.

"What are you not telling me, Ru Shan? What has happened to you?"

He did not mean to answer. He meant to trap his pain inside him where it had festered for so long. But her yin had begun to flow into him. Her power rose like a sweet river before his parched throat, and as he opened his mouth to drink, he found his words escaped instead.

"My family has a weakness for the ghost people," he began.

Honor and shame are the same as fear.
Fortune and disaster are the same for all.
What is said of honor and shame is this:
Whether absent or present, they are inseparable
from the fear
that they give rise to.
What is said of fortune and disaster is this:
They can befall any person.
—Tao Te Ching

Chapter Eighteen

Lydia didn't dare move. So taut was Ru Shan's body as he spoke that she feared even her breath would break the flow of his words. He appeared like a man caught in a nightmare: his eyes glazed, his body rigid. And yet he continued to speak, the sounds more like a shaped moan that would not stop no matter how he fought.

"My family craves what the English bring," he said. "My father hungers for your gold, my grandmother cannot live without your opium. Even I am here with you instead of at home with my wife and son." His gaze lifted from her lips to her eyes, but only for the briefest of seconds. Then he closed his eyes, shutting her out. His words continued. "I am here with you," he whispered, "just as my mother was there with him."

She frowned, unsure she had heard correctly. "Your mother?"

"And a sea captain. English. With thick, wiry hair, strong hands, and an overpowering laugh." Ru Shan shuddered. "I thought him hideously ugly."

Lydia sighed, already guessing the tale that was coming. "Your mother thought him handsome."

"I don't know," he answered, his words slow as if he still could not fathom his parent's choice. "But I remember that she laughed when she was with him. I had never heard it before. Not like that. Sweet, like a melody. Such joy, I cannot describe it." His eyes opened with a yearning that startled her. "Joy, Lydia. My mother had such joy in her, and I had never known. Not until . . ."

"Not until this sea captain brought it out," she finished for him.

His gaze slipped to the floor, and his head dipped down, allowing his long braided queue to shift, exposing his bare neck. "My mother did not have a happy life."

She leaned back slightly, still holding both his arms, but not pulled in so tight that she could not see him clearly. "Let me guess," she began. "There was an arranged marriage to your father, probably because she was such an artisan. Someone in your family knew she would bring great wealth to the Chengs. So she was married in and was worked as a slave, not only to create beautiful cloth to sell, but as a handmaiden to your grandmother."

He lifted his head, his wide eyes clearly showing his surprise.

"I have thought a great deal about what was in store for me," she said dryly. "Isn't that how it would be for me too? As your wife?"

He did not answer, but the flush on his features told her she had guessed correctly.

She sighed, the sound coming from deep within her. "At least I would be with the man I love. Your mother didn't even have that, did she?"

Ru Shan's back remained firm, his tone stiff. "Such is how it has always been in China."

"I'm sure that was a great comfort to your mother. Frankly, I would have taken a lover as well." Her statement obviously shocked Ru Shan. Indeed, it startled her as well, but she had no interest in giving sympathy to a country that made its women into slaves and married their sons off while the boys were still in leading strings.

Then her attention returned to Ru Shan as he shook his head, his tone musing. "I do not think you would find yourself in such a situation. You do not have the weight of five thousand years of tradition upon your head."

"No, I suppose I don't," she reluctantly agreed. And as she watched his bowed head, she began to see him in a different light. Did Ru Shan struggle beneath such weight? It certainly appeared so. And so she reached out, caressing his cheek before gently lifting his mouth to hers. But she did not kiss him. She wanted to, but he was resistant. He was still fighting the words that continued to flow out of him.

"My father rarely spent time with Mei Lan, my mother, but he was not a fool. Happiness such as she had cannot be hidden, and he knew . . ."

"He wasn't the cause of it." Lydia grimaced, hating that she knew the ending to this terrible tale. Hating that she'd guessed the truth a long time ago. "So one night, he grew so angry that he beat her to death, right? And that's how he got the limp. That's why you're steeped in guilt. Because you didn't interfere. And because your father killed your mother for being happy." She didn't mean to sound so callous, but she already knew these things. Worse, she'd heard a similar tale from some of her father's patients. Too many women in England and China both were brutalized by their husbands, and Lydia had little sympathy for any of the men associated with the crime—father or son.

"No," Ru Shan whispered, his voice thick and hoarse. "That is not what occurred."

She frowned, startled to find herself caught in her own assumptions. "But then . . ."

"My father did not beat her. It was his right as a cuck-olded man, but he did not. I think he had some fondness for her, and so forgave her."

She paused, needing to reorient her thoughts. "But then . . . what happened?"

Ru Shan looked down at his hands. "She was pregnant. With the sea captain's child." He sighed. "We all knew this. Though she tried, she could not hide it forever."

"She died in childbirth?"

Again, he shook his head. "Lydia, you do not understand the Chinese. We knew she had a lover." He took a deep breath. "We all knew because she was so happy. But only I knew the man was English. Only I knew that she took a white man to bed and that the child . . ." He swallowed, clearly unable to continue.

"That the child would be half-English, half-Chinese."

"Yes."

She looked at him, seeing the anguish that permeated his entire body, and at last the pieces began to fall into place. "You told him, didn't you? You told your father the truth."

He nodded, obviously struggling to explain. "In such sit-uations, lovers are not . . . they are not unusual. And if the child is a boy, so much the better. The Chengs have few children. Another son would not have been a burden."

"But a half-white child would be."

"It would proclaim to all a great shame, Lydia. A great and terrible shame." He looked to her then, begging her to understand. "She had no choice, Lydia. She had to kill herself."

Lydia felt a shudder of horror run through her entire body. "She killed herself? But . . ."

"She could not bring herself to kill the child. And she could not face her family or anyone else once her shame was known." He swallowed. "She hung herself."

"She . . ." She could not say the words. "But the child . . ."

"Still died. Yes, I know. But that is how women think in China." He looked up at her, his expression pleading. He wanted her to understand something he obviously struggled with himself. "I believe you English feel it a great shame to kill oneself, but in China it can be thought a great strength. The ultimate honorable act."

She could see that he himself did not believe it, for all that he tried to explain it to her. His body was still rigid, his hands shaking with the strain. And so she did the only thing she could think of. She reached for him, needing to hold him. Needing him to hold her.

He held her away. "You do not understand!" he rasped, his voice harsh enough to make her flinch. "I was not home. I didn't know."

"Of course not," she soothed.

"I know he was trying to help her. He was helping her die with honor, but I cannot forgive him. I have tried, but I cannot!"

She frowned, trying to understand. "The sea captain?"

"You do not understand," he groaned. "She would have had no rope, Lydia. And no knowledge of how to do such a thing. But it is what tradition demanded. To keep the

Cheng family pure." He released a strangled sob. "He thought he was being an honorable man, and yet I hate him for it."

"Who?"

"My father!" He gripped her arms in his anger. "Don't you understand? He gave her the rope. He taught her how to do it. And then he sent me away on a task that lasted all week. Out of kindness, he sent me away, while at home he helped her." He swallowed, his whole body shuddering with the effort. "For the good of the Cheng family."

"Oh, my love," she whispered, but again he pushed her away.

"It is not done, Lydia. You must know it all."

She flinched. There was more?

"He found out. The sea captain. He found out when he returned to port."

She nodded, her thoughts struggling to keep up. "Of course, he would."

"And he came to our home. Drunk. Furious. Screaming obscenities." He paused, and his next words came out softer, more in a whisper. "There was such grief in him. An agony such as I had never seen. Certainly none of my own family felt her death so deeply."

She didn't respond. She was too sick at heart to do more than stare.

"He attacked my father. I was home, Lydia. I was there, and yet, I was still so angry. They were brawling in the courtyard, churning up dirt and oil and filth inside my home. And I stood there and watched." He turned away from her, his hands tightened into angry fists. "My father is old, his bones frail. As his son, I should have helped. I should have defended him." He moaned softly, his shoulders slumping with the sound. "But they both killed her,

Lydia. Her white lover and my honorable father." He seemed to spit out his words. "And so I watched, not caring who won or who might be hurt." He closed his eyes, and again his head dropped forward and exposed his neck. "I did not interfere."

"How did it end?" she whispered.

"The sea captain died," he said, his entire body shuddering. He choked back a sob. "He simply fell down and did not get up. He just fell down."

She reached forward, wrapping her arms around him, holding him, praying she helped.

"He loved her, Lydia. More than any of us. He loved her with such passion. It almost seemed fitting that two people with such love should die together."

He spoke the words, but she could tell he did not believe them. And yet, part of her did. Part of her understood how a man and a woman caught in this terrible place could find death a release, a fitting end to so terribly twisted a life. "But it is so wrong," she whispered. "Everything about it was just so wrong."

He did not deny it, and he continued, his voice filling the small room with sounds of his pain. "It was then my father called upon me. He had been hurt. . . ."

"His leg."

He nodded. "He needed his son to take care of the body. He called upon my duty as his son. He demanded it as a father demands from his only child."

She closed her eyes, not wanting to hear the rest, but unable to keep herself from asking. "What did you do?"

He shifted to see her more fully, his face echoing the blank confusion of that time so long ago. "The Englishman was already dead. And to refuse my father then would have ended everything between us. Besides, what did I care about a barbarian's honor? If it were not for him, my family would still have been whole. My mother would be alive."

She tightened her grip on him. "What did you do?" she pressed.

"I carried the body to the red garden area. Behind . . ." He swallowed, his gaze slipping from hers. "Very near to a place where I first found you," he said, clearly uncomfortable with the knowledge that he had found her in a brothel. "I left him there. The stench of liquor covered him. He was in a violent area of Shanghai. No one ever questioned it." He turned to her then, his body slumping forward into her arms. "Even Shi Po does not know the full truth. She believes I defended my father as any filial son would and so killed a barbarian."

He shuddered, his body curling in his pain. "To everyone else, it is over. A barbarian is dead, an unfaithful wife's honor is kept pure, and a son remained loyal to his father."

"Everyone except you," she whispered. "You know it was all wrong."

He did not answer her, or perhaps he couldn't. Instead, he gripped her tighter, speaking to her heart as if that could redeem him. "They haunt me," he murmured. "My mother and her sea captain. They haunt me in the way true lovers haunt those who harmed them."

She leaned down, pressing a kiss onto his forehead. "There are no ghosts, Ru Shan. Only guilt and pain."

He lifted his head, his mouth curved in a sick smile. "There are ghosts in China, my Lydia. Mistreated parents, doomed lovers, even lost children—they all wander my country to torment those who hurt them. How else can they have their revenge?"

"Then perhaps you should leave China. So they cannot find you anymore."

She could tell he was shocked by her suggestion. After all, he was the Cheng mountain, the one his entire family depended upon to be all that was good and proper in this strange land. And a true son of China did not leave his native land.

But what if the true son was dying here? What if his soul sickened every day that he lived in a family twisted by traditions that were completely unwholesome?

"What will happen, Ru Shan? If you stay here, what will happen to you?"

His body shifted slightly, and she knew he was thinking of her words. "I must find a way to make the store profitable."

"So that your father will have gold and your grandmother will have opium?"

"So my son will have something to honor and a place to grow into adulthood."

She nodded, thinking of his son. All she remembered was a small, quiet boy who had watched everything with a seriousness well beyond his years. "You can make another place for him, Ru Shan. You can create a new home. One that isn't—"

"I cannot leave!"

His anguished cry startled her. She had never heard him so desperate. It was as if he truly knew, deep within himself, that he had wanted this from the very beginning.

"What do you want, Ru Shan?" she asked softly, not understanding where the words came from but knowing they were correct. "Do you wish to uphold the honor of a corrupt family? Of a tradition that married you to your father's lover?" He flinched at that, but did not disagree, and so she knew she had guessed correctly again. "Do you wish to struggle hard just to support a grandmother's habit? And all the while, you pursue your own desires secretly. You hide your dragon practices and take a white woman as your hidden lover. Is this how you want to live?"

He looked at her, his anguish raw. She reached forward, pressing his lips to hers despite his stiffness. And when she pulled back, it was barely enough to allow her room to speak, praying that he understood.

"Do you want me to stay with you? To fashion your designs? To be your second wife?" She didn't know if she could do it. She didn't know if she loved him enough to survive such a path, but she had to ask. She had to know if he wanted to be with her as much as she wanted to be with him. "I love you, Ru Shan." She knew that now, knew that she loved him to the depths of her soul despite the problems between them. "I can try to be your second wife. If you want it."

"You would hate it," he answered, the words rasping. "And I have already hurt you too much. Over and over."

She swallowed, her heart breaking for the words he did not say. Did he love her? Was he denying himself as much as her? "Ru Shan," she tried again. "What do you want?"

He did not want to answer, but she forced him. She lifted his chin, pulling his gaze to her eyes. Only then did she see her answer. Only then could she read the love and pain mixed in his gaze.

"What do you want?" she whispered.

"You," he answered, the one word seeming to come from his entire body. "Only you."

And then there were no more words. Only his lips on hers, his hands on her body.

She went willingly into his embrace, needing his touch, his kiss. But as he quickly pulled her coolie top off her body, she felt a strange difference in him. Gone were the practiced techniques of dragon and tigress. Gone was the steady stroke to raise her yin and control his yang. Instead, his movements were frantic. He touched her breasts, barely pulling them to their peak before his mouth was upon her, sucking her nipple with a hungry desperation.

She began to tense, fearing this new, tumultuous Ru Shan, and yet she was responding as if he had already spent hours preparing her body. As his mouth began to pull at her breast, her yin flowed full and ready, the tingling current already heating her body as it rushed to satisfy Ru Shan. Her nipple actually seemed to crackle with power as his tongue stroked and pulled its peak. Her other breast as well began to pulse with the strokes.

She gasped out in surprise as his other hand began stroking her. It was not the measured circles she was used to, but the caress of a man who could not have enough, who could not touch her enough. His whole hand, spread wide, extended over her full breast, slowly drawing in and up, as if pulling her toward him.

Once, twice, he stroked her in this manner, while on the other side, his tongue teased and twisted and tweaked. And then, abruptly, he switched sides, drawing her yin through the other breast, making her entire torso yearn for him, pulse with the pull of his breath, the nip of his teeth, and the flick of his tongue.

"Oh, yes," she cried, already plunging into the roaring ocean of yin that consumed her. With what little control she had left, she began pulling at Ru Shan's clothing. She wanted to touch his hot body and grasp his hardened muscles. She wanted to feel the stroke of flesh against flesh while his yang fire set her blood to boiling.

Her hands were not gentle as she stripped the clothing from him. Neither were his as he dragged off her coolie pants. Her cinnabar cave was already wet, and it took little prompting for him to spread her legs wide. His tongue stroked long, wet trails up her thighs and to her core.

She moved naturally into the pattern he had taught her. She twisted, bringing her mouth to his jade dragon, stroking its length with hand and lips and tongue. Touching his tightened dragon eggs behind, even pressing into the jen-mo spot. He mimicked her actions as well, opening her cinnabar cave with his thumbs while his tongue circled her yin pearl, her little dragon. With each pass of his tongue, her body tightened, the flow of yin rising higher and higher.

She was familiar with its path now, but never had the tide risen so high or fast. The flood hit with such power, such intensity, that she screamed her ecstasy. She was no longer afraid of drowning. She knew from experience that now was Ru Shan's time to drink. While her body shuddered and convulsed from the flood, Ru Shan would place his mouth at her cave, drawing in her essence before concentrating on his own. When he had enough, he would sit back, breathing heavily as he fought his way toward Heaven and immortality. Then, when Lydia's flood receded enough for her to gain breath, she would shift, turning her focus on maintaining his yang fire. With touch and tongue, she would keep his dragon hot until he stepped into the Heavenly realm. Or—as had happened every time before—until he pulled away from her in frustration and failure.

So it was that even immersed in the tumultuous shuddering of her yin tide, she was already preparing the mental distance she needed to help Ru Shan. She wanted him to reach his goal; she wanted to give him that gift. But as she shifted, reaching for him, he abruptly pulled away.

"No," he practically growled, his breath hot where he

pressed against the inside of her thigh. "No," he repeated more firmly as he shifted his body away from her.

Then, as she frowned, doing her best to focus on him, he began to shift. He kissed her belly and her navel. He pressed his mouth against her skin, using his tongue to stroke in a chaotic, ever-rising pattern.

Below, his thumbs continued to press rhythmically into her, while his long fingers tweaked her yin pearl.

"This is called plucking the yin lute," he murmured, and he began pulling at her breast once again. The sensation was incredible. Her body became his instrument—shuddering, trembling, humming with each pluck of her strings. The yin tide echoed his movements, which were taken up by his mouth as well. Each pluck of his fingers, each stroke of his tongue, each pull of his lips against her nipple had her body singing in higher and higher notes.

Then he shifted again, his jade dragon a hot presence against her thigh. She felt the weight of his hips, pressing her down in the most wonderful way as his hands came to replace his mouth against her breasts.

Still her body continued to thrum, his hands keeping up the tempo of the song on her nipples.

"Ru Shan," she sobbed, amazed and enthralled. "What—"

"I want to give you it all, Lydia. I want to give you everything I am. I want you to use it, go to Heaven, become immortal as no white woman ever has. You can do it. I am sure of it. With all of my training, all of my essence, you can become what I have only dreamed of."

She struggled to comprehend his meaning, but he would not allow the yin tide to recede enough. All she could do was gasp out his name.

"I want this for you, Lydia," he continued. "But it will take your virginity. I cannot decide this for you. Lydia, do you understand?"

His hands slowed, eased their tempo, and slowly stopped. In the same way the waves eased and she was finally able to catch her breath in deep, gasping sobs.

"Lydia, will you let me give you all that I am? Will you let me?"

She blinked, at last understanding his meaning. "Ru Shan," she whispered, no conscious thought or control to her words. "I am your instrument. I am here for your path."

He shook his head. "You are not my pet, Lydia. You are no longer here to serve me." Then he leaned down, pressing soft kisses to her eyes, her nose, her cheek. "I am your servant, my Lydia. I will give you everything I am." He pressed his lips to hers and she opened beneath him. His tongue plunged into her mouth then withdrew, plunged deep again. With every push of his tongue, she felt the fire of a hot brand. It was his yang flowing into her, his power mixing with her own.

Then he pulled back. "Please, my Lydia. Let me give this to you."

She saw the need in his eyes, the yearning in his heart, and could deny him nothing. And yet, when she meant to say, "anything," her mouth asked something else entirely.

"Do you love me?"

"I have always loved you," he answered. Then his eyes widened in shock, as if he too had said something he had not intended. Slowly his expression softened, his lips curving into a joyous smile. "I do love you. I can feel the love in my heart. I know it when I look on you. Oh, Lydia, I can love!" Then he focused upon her. "I love you." There was such awe in his words that she could not doubt it. She stared at his face, mesmerized by the beauty love brought to his features. His eyes shimmered with it, his bones softened because of it, and his mouth curved into a smile that spread to his entire body. She could even feel the change where they were pressed together.

"May I love you?" he asked, and at last she was able to answer as she wished.

"You may take me anywhere you like, so long as we are together."

He grinned, dropping a swift kiss upon her lips. "Not together, my love. Not this time. This is only for you." Then he sobered. "I will go slowly to accustom you, but it still may hurt a little."

That is when she felt him. His jade dragon, breathing the fire of his yang, began to press into her cinnabar cave. He went only a tiny way, slowly pushing in before withdrawing, but she felt the heat of his presence like the lick of serpent fire. On a distant level, she remembered the exercises she'd performed with the carved dragon, pulling it in, holding it inside her. But he was no carved stone and she was no longer a frightened slave.

Again he began to press, pushing against her walls, widening them in the most interesting of sensations. Filling her as his hands never had, opening her as nothing else ever could. And all the while, she felt the heat of his yang, the lick of fire, the press of his power mixing into her.

"You are so strong," she whispered in awe. Never before had she felt his yang in this way. Never before had he focused it on her.

"Only with you," he answered. "I did not know love could make me so strong." Then he lowered his face again, taking her lips with steady, potent control, pressing into her above and below before once again withdrawing. "You have given me more than I ever imagined possible."

Once again he lowered his mouth to hers, once again he pressed his yang into her, deeper, harder, while the mixture of yin and yang in her blood expanded. Her body began to hum again, the yin tide rising, but this time with more power, more heat, more . . . more Ru Shan.

"Come with me," she whispered. "We are stronger together." She did not act consciously. She merely felt herself expand, her heart opening to allow her love to flow. It was like a cleansing river, encompassing them both, releasing the pain of their past, ignoring the confusion of the future. They were merely themselves, together and in love.

He was pushing deeper, against a barrier she had not known existed. And though she felt the hot press of his yang, she also felt his restraint, the trembling in his arms and the shuddering control of his breath.

She couldn't speak. She had no words and no breath to form them. She only knew she wanted nothing between them, no barriers, no restraint. And so she wrapped her legs around him, timing her pull with an arch of her back. And with one swift movement, she joined them together.

She didn't feel any pain. Or if she did, she didn't notice. What she felt instead was Ru Shan's yang fire explode past his control. He gasped out her name, but it was simply a sound and nothing compared to the inferno he released into her blood.

She cried out something as well. Perhaps it was his name, perhaps it was simply a joyous eruption of love and power. But as his jade dragon continued to convulse—fiery explosions of yang with every thrust—her yin tide began to surge. Higher and higher it rose, her body moving with his, her yin fusing with his yang.

On and on they went.

Together.

As one.

Until a beauty of light shimmered, surrounding them. It was both an explosion of magnificence and a quiet unfolding of wonder.

The veil parted, and hand in hand with Ru Shan, Lydia stepped into immortality.

By the accident of good fortune,
one may rule the world for a time.
But by virtue of love
one lives forever.
—Tao Te Ching

Chapter Nineteen

Ru Shan felt the veil lift, stunned amazement filling him even as he walked the familiar path. This walk had been for Lydia, not for him. He had given everything he had—all his yang, all his experience, every moment of study and skill he had within him—to her. So that she would walk here, where she belonged, in Heaven with the Immortals. He had not expected to enter the antechamber instead of her.

But here he was, standing in the Chamber of a Thousand Swinging Lanterns, the antechamber to the Realm of the Immortals. As had happened three times before, he stood lost in awe as pinpoints of light danced before him, filling him with an indescribable joy. This was the farthest he had ever come, the journey a struggle and his greatest achievement. Never had he thought he could come here so easily and with a partner, as well.

He looked to his side, surprised to see Lydia beside him. And not surprised. After all, she had been the reason for this journey. Without her, he would never have found love. Never would have known that it was the true catalyst for immortality.

He turned to her, the thought creating the action since they had neither muscle nor bone here. This was the realm of the spirit, and so the merest thought would take him where he wished to be: beside her, looking at her, in love with her.

He expected to see ecstasy on her face. Instead, he saw peace and was enveloped in her joy, surrounded in her love—just as she was surrounded in his. Never could he have imagined a more perfect moment.

Until it became more.

The second veil lifted and, together, they stepped into Heaven—the realm of the Immortals. A golden palace surrounded him, and yet not of wood or stone. It was merely a shimmering of incredible light that filled his heart with awe. All about him walked the Immortals—male and female angels of such beauty that he could do little more than laugh.

Was he laughing?

He meant no disrespect, and yet he could not stop. And beside him, Lydia bubbled over with her own happiness, giggles of sound, melodic vibrations of gladness that mixed with his own to become a beautiful sound that fit this glorious place.

The music softened and another sound joined with theirs—an angel's music coming from a beautiful goddess. She simply appeared before them, her brow radiant, her robes not cloth but tendrils of light that emanated from within her. She smiled at them, and he heard her music shift, becoming deeper, clearer, and even more resplendent; but no more or less beautiful than Ru Shan's and Lydia's.

"Welcome, Ru Shan. Welcome, Lydia. I am so pleased you have come to join us," she said. Then around her he felt an echoing chord, a single vibration that set the entire palace to shimmering with welcome.

Ru Shan wanted to answer, wanted to speak poetry or song, wanted to find some excellent way to convey his gratitude. But he had no words, and yet as the thought entered his mind, his entire soul fit the emotion to sound. Together, he and Lydia made their own music, a vibration of thanks that fitted perfectly with this place.

The goddess smiled. "I wish you could stay longer, but I am comforted that you will make many more journeys here."

Ru Shan felt and heard Lydia's start of surprise, especially as it exactly mirrored his own. "We have to leave?" she asked.

"Soon," the goddess answered with obvious regret. "But first, I have something to show you." Then, with a wave of her hand, the palace of gold disappeared and Ru Shan felt himself plummet.

It was a curious sensation, not in the least bit frightening even though he knew he—with Lydia and the goddess beside him—was dropping out of Heaven, falling back to China with startling speed. His body felt heavier, the air thicker, and the tones—the beautiful ringing notes of Heaven—became more like the slow beat of a very deep drum.

"Do you wish to see?" the goddess asked him.

He nodded. "Of course."

But the goddess shook her head, and he realized he had misinterpreted her words. She had not asked if he wished to see. She asked if he wanted to understand. But again, his answer was the same. "Of course," he repeated.

"Then you must step outside yourself. You must know what parts of your mind are your own and what has been taught."

He frowned, not truly understanding. He only knew enough to realize he was afraid. He desperately wanted to say yes. Indeed, he kept repeating the word to himself—*yes, yes, yes, yes*—a long litany of acceptance and agreement, but in his heart, he could only feel fear. And the more he feared, the faster and more real his plummet to Earth became. Which made him all the more fearful.

"Ru Shan!"

The words of alarm came from Lydia. He looked up, expecting to see her well above him, waiting at the higher place with the goddess. But she was not up there. She was still beside him, holding on desperately. They were falling together, and she was now as terrified as he.

The goddess spoke, her words a dim echo of notes, barely heard over the pounding of his heart. "Remember what brought you to us."

His mind grappled with the thought. What had made them succeed? How had they made the climb to Heaven?

Love. Their love. It was a simple answer, and one he should have remembered immediately. But there was no time for recriminations. Their surroundings were nearly pitch-black. Soon they would fall back into their bodies and would have to start the entire process over again. He had to think of Lydia, of love. Except, that wasn't working. He was beginning to feel the heavy, oppressive weight of his body again. He had to . . .

Not think. Feel.

Love.

And so he caught Lydia's face. How he did it didn't matter. All that was important is that in his thoughts, in his heart, he held his love. He pulled her close, seeing her frightened eyes, feeling the frantic beat of her heart.

"Shhhh, my love. Do not fear. We are together."

He didn't know if he spoke the words or simply thought them. It didn't matter. What was important is that he felt it. He felt the overwhelming need not just to protect her, but to hold her, to be with her, to surround her with his love. To be inside that love.

To *be* love.

For her. For him. For all.

Their plummet stopped. The sky turned rosy pink, then yellowish white, and then it shimmered again with the beautiful vibration of love—neither black nor white, nor any one color at all, but every color and feeling and presence wrapped together.

Heaven.

The goddess returned. "It is normal to fear change, Ru Shan. But know that you come from love, live in love, and go to love. There is nowhere and no change that can separate you from it. So why then should you fear?"

There was no reason for fear—not with Lydia beside him, a goddess before him, and the love of Heaven around him. And so he did not, or at least he tried not to fear. He stepped up to the goddess and dropped into a deep bow.

"I am ready," he said when he straightened. "What must I do?"

"You must say you release your fears . . ."

"I willingly release my fears."

". . . and wish to see your life in all directions of time."

He answered quickly, not allowing his conscious mind to question. "I wish to see my life in all directions of time."

And so he did. But not with his eyes. He felt his body separate into two pieces, as if he stepped outside of a suit of clothing, except that suit was his entire body, his entire life on Earth as Ru Shan. He was not Ru Shan. He was a being of light and beauty and love, gloriously alive, wonderfully joyous, and so free that his mind could not contain it. Indeed, he did not even try. He merely felt whole for the first time in a long, long time, and the whole was so large, so vast that he could not be contained. He was part of everything—a single, changing note in an infinite symphony and the whole symphony as well.

And in that state, he knew Lydia as well. Not only the Lydia of Earth—the body and the life—but also the being of light. Another note in Heaven's song and the whole song as well.

He began to laugh. He could not contain it. And that too, was added to the music that surrounded them.

"Look now at Ru Shan," the goddess directed.

He had known this part was coming. He had known but not wished to see that creature he was and was not. Because he would see his mistakes and frailties. He would know what a failure he was.

Except that when he looked, he saw something completely unexpected. He saw all of himself—his intentions, his education, his actions—but with the all-encompassing eyes of love. Like a parent viewing a child's growth, he watched his birth and childhood. He saw his shift into adulthood and, stretched ahead into a blurred future, he saw his old age. But not just one old age. Many. Many possible futures, many possible directions.

"What should I see?" he asked, needing direction to sort through the chaos of the infinite future.

But there was no direction, no answer. Merely the gentle

and swift fall into one moment in his life. One night, one place.

One person.

Ru Shan. And Lydia. In the hotel bed. Their bodies still twined together while outside the sky lightened into dawn.

To express your courage outwardly is to concern yourself with death.
To express your courage inwardly is to encounter life.
The celestial Tao does not push, yet it overcomes everything.
It does not speak, yet it acknowledges all.
It does not provoke, yet it cooperates.
It is quiet in its methods, yet always effective.
—Tao Te Ching

Chapter Twenty

"It wasn't what I thought." Lydia swallowed, pulling her knees in tighter to her chest even as she curled closer to Ru Shan. "I thought . . . I don't know what I thought. Angels with wings? A palace with a white throne?" She shook her head. "They were all there, and yet it was nothing like I expected."

"And so much more," Ru Shan whispered. "So much—"

"More," she echoed.

She frowned in frustration. There were no words to express their experience. Everything was inadequate, and yet Ru Shan understood. He knew what she meant.

Beauty. Joy. Love, all encompassing and total. Infinite. Amazing. She and Ru Shan had said all these words, and yet none of them were right. None of them fit. And yet they all did. It all was. And he understood.

"What did you see?" she asked. "What did you do?"

"I separated from my body. I saw me . . . as Ru Shan. And yet, I was not Ru Shan. I was . . ."

"More."

He nodded. "Much, much more." He shifted slightly to look into her eyes. "What did you see?"

"The same as you. Lydia . . . me . . . that I'm not what I thought I am. I'm—"

"More."

She nodded. It wasn't the right word, but it was the only one they had. And so they kept repeating it even as they searched for better.

"Bright," she whispered.

"Fulfilled."

"And not full."

He nodded. "Because we can be more. So much more."

"And yet, we are more." She pressed her ear to his chest, liking the sound of his heart. "We are perfect as we are, and yet . . ."

"Ru Shan can be better," he said.

"And Lydia, too." She shook her head. "But we're not Ru Shan and Lydia. We're . . ."

"So much more."

"Yes."

"Much, much more," he repeated.

Then they looked at each other, and she saw shock in his expression.

"We're immortal," they said together, the word feeling alien and cold compared to what they had just experienced. Compared to what they were.

She turned away. "It's not what I expected," she murmured. "It's not like I thought."

He pressed his lips to her forehead. "Yes. It's so much more."

* * *

"What do we do now?"

Lydia's voice was soft and tentative, but Ru Shan heard her nonetheless. Unfortunately, he had no more answer than she, though they had been sitting on this bed for most of the morning discussing that very thing. Or perhaps they had been avoiding that discussion, focusing more on the night's experiences rather than the day's questions.

But now, as the day wore steadily on, well past lunch and heading toward evening, simple things began to intrude. What to eat. Where to live. What to do.

"I don't know," he answered as he tucked her tighter against him. "I want to try again," he said as he stroked his hand down her arm. "But not now."

"No," she agreed. "Not yet. But I do want to go back. I want to know more."

"I want to understand more."

"Yes," she agreed. And then again, they fell into silence.

Finally, she shifted onto her knees, her lush body—already beautiful—radiant with the memory of what they had shared. Of where they had been. "I will go back with you. I will be your second wife."

He shook his head. "No—"

"I know now who I am," she continued as if he hadn't spoken. "I know that I can be that person wherever I am—concubine or wife, slave or master. I am . . ." She paused. "We both are . . ."

"We all are beings of light, Lydia," he agreed, knowing she understood. "We merely forgot for a while."

She nodded. "But I remember. And you do too, so it doesn't matter where I live. I know now who I am."

"Yes," he said slowly, but he knew that the experience faded. Flush with the glory of their experience, she could not imagine that such feelings, such wonder could fade. But it did. Time and money and Earth life interfered, and soon even the best of the Earth-born Immortals could forget. "My family would destroy you. They would beat down your spirit until there is nothing left." He sighed. "We cannot stay in China, Lydia."

She shifted slightly, her eyes suddenly intense. "We?"

He looked at her, seeing not her luscious body, but the heart and soul of the woman he loved. Her body meant nothing to him. She was what mattered. "I love you, Lydia," he said, knowing now that it was a poor phrase to describe what he felt. "I will not release you. Ever. If you were to leave me, I would follow you. I will abandon everything, do anything if only I can stay with you."

She smiled, and he saw the shimmer of tears in her eyes. "I am not going anywhere, my love."

"Yes," he said slowly. "Yes, we are."

She tilted her head but didn't speak, waiting for him to explain.

"China is a large country, weighted with the traditions of five thousand years. There is much good in my country and our traditions, but they would not treat you as you deserve, Lydia. And I find I am not willing to wait for them to learn."

She laughed at that, the sound mellow and sweet. "Women are not treated well all the world over, Ru Shan." Then she sobered. "But you think it will be very bad for me here."

He would not lie to her. "You will not be happy. We will move to your England."

She shook her head. "Even we barbarians have traditions, Ru Shan, and I have broken many of my people's unwritten laws. Neither of us will be happy in England."

"Very well, then. We will go find another country, another place."

She shifted, chewing on her lip as she thought. "Nowhere I know will treat you kindly, Ru Shan."

He nodded, having expected that much. But it did not matter. "I am the Cheng family mountain and an Immortal." He took hold of her hand, drawing her back into his arms. "I am strong enough to weather anything." He tilted her face toward him. "So long as we remember together who we are."

She smiled, her face lighting with the joy of Heaven. "I loved you before we became Immortal, Ru Shan. I will not forget now." Then she kissed him, her heart and her love easily flowing into him, just as his joy melted into her.

They might then have begun their practice, merging into one another in the way of all lovers, but she pulled away from him, a frown on her features. "What of your family, Ru Shan? What of the Chengs?"

He sighed, hating to bring them into this moment, into their joy. "They will not leave China. And I cannot abandon my son." He lifted his gaze, searching her face. "Will you love him, Lydia? If you—"

She cut off his words with a swift kiss. "I love everything that is from you. Your son will be the easiest of all."

He shifted uncomfortably. "In truth, he is not from me. He is my half-brother."

Her answer came without hesitation. "Then I will love him all the more."

He reached up, stroking her face, feeling the long slide of her body against his. His yang fire had already heated, his dragon was strong and eager, but he did not move. Instead, he simply touched her face and luxuriated in the whisper of her skin against his.

"What are you smiling at?" she asked, her voice playful despite the rosy flush of yin in her cheeks and lips.

"How strange that a ghost woman has taught me the one thing of substance that I have needed all my life." He brushed his lips across hers. "Loving you has given me Heaven." He pulled back, looking directly into her eyes. "You are everything, my love."

She grinned, nipping at his mouth. "And how strange that the man who bought me as a slave has shown me how much I am truly worth. Together, my love, we are worthy of Heaven."

He sobered. "The future will not be easy for us, no matter where we go."

"Wrong, my husband," she said. "Heaven and all its glories lie ahead for us." Then her eyes sparkled with mischief as she began to slip lower on his body. "That is, as long as we get busy practicing."

The fundamental delusion of humanity
is to suppose that I am here
and you are out there.
—Yasutani Roshi

Epilogue

Shi Po sank behind the curtain of her sedan chair, tapping her long nails in irritation. Ru Shan's ship had just sailed, taking him and his white pet to America. It was rumored that he took his son with him as well, but that the rest of the Cheng family had refused to sully themselves by living among the barbarians.

They had not disowned him, though, in the hope that he would send barbarian gold from across the sea back to support his family. In the meantime, the servant Fu De had charge of the Cheng family store. Worse, he was running it well. The English people flocked to buy the clothing patterns the white pet had left behind.

The Chengs would be able to repay their debt to her husband after all.

That, of course, was not what caused the steady *tap, tap, tap* of her long nails against her seat. She cared little for matters of business. Her husband did not need to add the

Cheng store to his ever-growing interests. Neither did they require the money repayment would bring. Either way, Shi Po had enough wealth to live in comfort while she pursued her studies.

What truly incensed her was that Ru Shan and his ghost pet had both achieved immortality. Ru Shan had come to see her before his departure, the tendrils of Heaven radiant as they swirled around his serene face. Even her unenlightened husband had noticed his calm, his joy. But she with her tutored eye had seen more than joy. She had seen glory and beauty and immortality.

And then the white pet entered the room.

Cheng Lydia was her name, Ru Shan's second wife. But Shi Po was required to call her Immortal. Worse, Shi Po had been required to write that barbarian name in the tigress book.

How could a barbarian woman achieve what she had not? How could an English pet succeed where years of dedicated study had brought precious little to Shi Po?

A full day's meditation had not brought her closer to an answer. Neither had a night's fasting nor another two nights' practice. It was maddening. And now, Ru Shan and his ghost bride had sailed to America where Shi Po could not even learn from their achievements.

She grimaced, lifting the curtain to stare again at the retreating ship. She wished Ru Shan well with his barbarian bride in a land wilder than Mongolia. She supposed the Enlightened had no need for culture or refinement.

She ought to feel grateful. She should be pleased, because Ru Shan's departure assured her own success. Normally the Immortal Ru Shan would now be China's foremost teacher in the dragon/tigress practices. But in his absence, Shi Po remained the preeminent one. All knew that he had been her pupil. If they could not learn from him, she was the one they would turn to now.

But how would she lead where she had not gone? How could she teach where she was but a pupil herself? She had no answers, no guidance, and more students knocking upon her door every day.

She stewed upon the problem all the ride home. But when her chair was at last deposited before her front door, Shi Po was no nearer an answer. And her frustration became fury the moment she learned that another young pupil waited for an audience.

"I have nothing to tell him," she snapped at no one in particular. "Not yet," she suddenly added. She had been a serious tigress practitioner before, but now she felt the strength of zeal flood her body. It was like yang fire, only more potent. And with it driving her, she knew nothing would prevent her from her goal now.

She would become an Immortal if it took everything she had.

MIDNIGHT SILK
LAURIE GRANT

During their childhood, one girl devotedly followed Bowie Beckett everywhere; in turn, he teased the plantation owner's daughter unmercifully and loved her from afar. But now she is a beautiful woman and his boyhood feelings are a man's passion—a forbidden passion he fears can only lead to ruin for them both.

Maria adored one man all her life, a man society dictated she could never have. She will survive bandits, outrun Yankees, flaunt her well-turned ankle—anything to capture Bowie. For though his words are harsh, she sees desire in his eyes. And Maria chooses to herald Bowie's taunts as a challenge—one to be overcome by a woman's love.

WHITE SHADOWS
SUSAN EDWARDS

For years after his family was massacred, the half-breed Night Shadow harbored black dreams of vengeance—and the hope of someday finding his kidnapped younger sister. Now is the chance. His enemy shows himself and is to be wed. It should be a simple maneuver to steal the man's bride-to-be, to ride off with the beautiful Winona and reveal the monster she is supposed to marry.

But it is *not* simple. Winona is not convinced. Even the burgeoning desire Night Shadow sees in her eyes has not convinced the Sioux beauty of her betrothed's evil. Can love be born of revenge? There seems but one way to find out: Take Winona into the darkness and pray that, somehow, he and she can find their way to the light.

The Temptation
CLAUDIA DAIN

In England of 1156, a gently bred lady is taught to obey, first her father, next her bridegroom. But ever since Eve it has been in every woman to defy any lord. And Elsbeth of Sunnandune is determined to trade the submission of the marriage bed for the serenity of the convent. Yet never did she suppose the difficulty of her task, for the husband given her is a golden knight of godly beauty and grace. His every word and look is a seduction, his every caress cause for capitulation. In this war of wills, she discovers, blood, honor, even the thrill of victory, can take on new meaning, and no matter how much time a wife spends on her knees in prayer, every path can lead into temptation.

TEXAS STAR
ELAINE BARBIERI

Buck Star is a handsome cad with a love-'em-and-leave-'em attitude that broke more than one heart. But when he walks out on a beautiful New Orleans socialite, he sets into motion a chain of treachery and deceit that threatens to destroy the ranching empire he'd built and even the children he'd once hoped would inherit it. . . .

A mysterious message compells Caldwell Star to return to Lowell, Texas, after a nine-year absence. Back in Lowell, he meets a stubborn young widow who refuses his help, but needs it more than she can know. Her gentle touch and proud spirit give Cal strength to face the demons of the past, to reach out for a love that would heal his wounded soul.
